The

Claire McGlasson is a journalis   News and enjoys the variety of life on the r   a TV camera. She lives in Cambridgeshire. *The Rapture* is her debut novel.

Claire McGlasson

The Rapture

ff

FABER & FABER

First published in the UK in 2019
by Faber & Faber Ltd,
Bloomsbury House,
74–77 Great Russell Street,
London WC1B 3DA

This export edition published in 2019

Typeset by Typo•glyphix
Printed and bound in the UK by CPI Group Ltd, Croydon CR0 4YY

Jackdaw illustration by Gallinago Media/Shutterstock

A CIP record for this book
is available from the British Library

ISBN 978–0–571–34518–2

FSC
www.fsc.org
MIX
Paper from
responsible sources
FSC® C020471

2 4 6 8 10 9 7 5 3 1

For all who believed.
And K and F: Here endeth the lesson.

Bedford, England, 1926

A vicar's widow called Mabel believes herself to be Octavia, the Daughter of God – a messiah with the power to bring an end to suffering in the world. For six years she has been gathering followers, who flock to live with her in Bedford. They call themselves the Panacea Society.

The Great War has claimed their husbands, brothers and sons; but God has told them that women will bring salvation – a panacea for all disease and despair. The answer lies in a mysterious box sealed by prophetess Joanna Southcott more than a century earlier. But to open it they must persuade the church of men to recognise the rule of women.

The following is a work of fiction based on real events. All sections printed in bold are quoted from correspondence or published works held in the Panacea Society archive, which spans almost a hundred years. Passages of scripture are taken from various Bible versions used during this time, some of which were paraphrased or reinterpreted by members.

Wouldn't a hostel – a 'Land of Goshen' – be lovely!
Really devoted believers could take up nice homes in
Bedford, which is a most lovely place and is going up
by leaps and bounds. Selfridges is coming and has
taken a huge block in High Street.

Octavia, 1919

THE PRAYER OF ST IGNATIUS

Make what is true the truth to me,
Let fuller light appear,
All that is evil take from me,
All that is doubtful clear.
Let not false confidence betray,
No foolish fears mislead,
But in the straight and narrow way
Be Thou my guide indeed.

WINTER

Were it required of me to emblazon a legend over the gates and doors of these buildings, one which set forth fact and not fiction, it might run thus: 'Leave Self behind, all who enter here. This is the House of Correction, this is the Era of Reproof.'

Octavia, *The Cleansing of the Sanctuary*

Winged Messenger

A devil had flown in through Her bedroom window. That was Her first thought. His eyes were black glass: as dark and deep as Lucifer's soul.

'It was very surprising, I can assure you, to see his little head parting the lace curtains and looking into the room,' Octavia tells us over breakfast. But now She thinks of it, She remembers seeing him yesterday, sitting atop the high wall that keeps us safe inside the Garden. He had stayed for nigh on half an hour, watching as we took tea and waited patiently for Jesus.

Octavia looks flustered. The string of pearls which always decorates Her neck is absent; Her hairstyle has fallen a little short of perfection; and She is late, a very unusual occurrence. Octavia is never late. If a chiming clock dares to accuse Her, She is quick to enter a counter-charge: it is running fast or the congregation has gathered too early. *Have you no more pressing purpose than to sit here gossiping?* But this morning I sat in silence with Emily and Peter for a full twenty minutes before She joined us at the table. That is, I was silent and they compared notes: listing the transgressions they had witnessed in others, each sin recorded neatly in their pocketbooks, ready to be shared with Octavia when they are called to give evidence every fortnight.

We must all keep an inventory of each other's failings, and our own. How else will we improve ourselves in time to receive the Lord?

I'm certain my name is on their charge sheet. Dilys Barltrop, underlined, above a long list of inadequacies and oversights. But I didn't get the opportunity to find out. Octavia interrupted without apology, and began her story without delay. She had been dressing when She saw a large bird sitting on her windowsill. Her first impulse was to cover Herself: perhaps it had come to spy on Her nakedness.

'Devils can disguise themselves in many forms, and of course its black plumage made me suspect it at once,' She says, Her teacup trembling as She lifts it from the saucer. I think of feathers, beak and claws. I think of Octavia's exposed skin.

'Oh! How terrible!' Peter gasps. 'You should have called out. I would have come to Your aid.' But the very idea is topsy turvy. Octavia doesn't need to be saved. She is the one saving us.

'Thank you, Peter,' She says, with an indulgent smile. 'But it should be obvious that this was a creature of God. In the next second I could see very clearly what it meant.'

'A messenger . . .' Emily says theatrically, bringing a hand to the faded lace collar on her throat. 'A winged messenger of Heaven . . .'

It's a line from *Romeo and Juliet* if I'm not mistaken. Octavia loves it when Emily quotes the Bard. It's proof She has succeeded in moulding her, improving her. *God made man in His own image.* And Octavia is doing the same with Emily; she knew nothing of Shakespeare before she came to us, found God and joined the middle classes.

'Emily, I knew you would be the one to see it,' She says, stroking back a strand of grey that has fallen from her chignon. She repositions a hairpin with sufficient force to punish its laxity. 'When I looked into its eyes, God's purpose was obvious. I sprinkled some crumbs of biscuit just below the window and suddenly he jumped into the room!' She is becoming agitated, excited, eager for us to see the significance of what has happened. And Emily, as usual, is keen to oblige. 'No mortal bird would be so tame. He sat quite happily in-doors?' she asks.

Octavia laughs. 'I should say so. He took a bath in my basin, did his business on the top of my looking glass, and after a contented squawk to tell me that the rooms would suit, he went to sleep on one leg.'

Octavia names him Sir Jack Daw and tells us something strange and significant has happened. 'It is proof,' She says, 'a sign that Christ shall soon fly down to us, just as the Lord has promised.'

She is convinced that a message has arrived in the Garden; that God Himself has posted it through Her window.

I must believe it too.

Pondskater

They are watching. I must concentrate on walking, one foot in front of the other, down the length of Albany Road. Head up, back straight, like I'm wearing a corset. Though Octavia doesn't believe we should wear them: we should have the faith and discipline to contain ourselves. Using whalebones would be cheating.

It is not as if I am doing anything I shouldn't. Walks are permitted in Octavia's list of *Wholesome Exercises for Body and Soul*, but my thoughts might betray me. The Devil plants doubts in my head and guilty looks on my face, and that is what they will be looking out for. Fifty-eight believers live around the Garden now, all chasing the same prize: the glittering treasure of a sin or scandal they can unearth and present to Octavia. Today is the Sabbath, so all work is suspended, except the most important job of all, which is to keep an eye on each other's souls and report back where we find them lacking. Behind those net curtains there will be pocketbooks open, pencils poised:

Sunday. 1.38 p.m.
Dilys seen leaving 12 Albany Road. Looking furtive.

Octavia calls it Overcoming. She tells us Jesus will not return unless we are colourless, faultless, zero. So we must evaluate one another. *It is for our own good.* She says secrets are like splinters, they need to be wheedled out before they start to fester. But it is not that simple. Some are far too deep, they burrow into flesh, the skin heals over, the stab of pain is gone and in time you wonder whether they were ever there at all. Those are the secrets that I keep. Secrets from before the others came. Secrets in the box at the back of my wardrobe.

I walk past their windows. Past Mary Massey on this side of the street, and Mary Beedell on the other. Past Florence, Hilda and Agnes at Number 19: three sisters who plainly cannot stand the sight of one another, and spend their days picking over old squabbles like vultures over bones. Then on past Ethel and Mildred Keeley whom I find almost impossible to tell apart, and their lodger whose name I can't remember. I lose track of who they are or how they came to be here. At twenty-five years old I am the youngest by at least two decades; a peculiarity among the band of increasingly indistinguishable middle-aged ladies, the colour receding from their hair and the definition from their waists.

Even the houses look the same, terraced, like their occupants; joined together. One may have a little stained glass in the front door, another fretwork like lace along the eaves, or a chequerboard of black and white tiles leading callers up the path. But these are just details. Stand back and they become a single row. They rely on each other to stay standing: if one brick came loose, everything could come crashing down. But they stand firm. Stand guard. And so must we.

We're almost all women here. Only a handful of men have been allowed to join. Edgar Peissart, whom God sent as an emissary from America. And Peter, who came to us from Australia, though whether he really is a man is questionable: a tiny, frail creature, careful never to have an opinion in case it is the wrong one, non-committal even on the question of his own sex. Anything to please Octavia.

But I must not have these thoughts, they are not good, not of God.

The Devil is whispering again. Doubts and suspicions. Octavia says he pours them down our throats like poison. *And a trickle can turn into a torrent. Then sooner or later you drown in his lies.*

No, Peter is good and kind. But I was surprised She let him move into Number 12 with us. Four of the bedrooms were already taken and the fifth in use for nightly meetings. But Peter said he would make a room up in the attic. I think he imagines himself as a guardian angel suspended above Octavia as She sleeps. And as he stands at little more than five feet tall, the sloping ceilings haven't proved to be much of a problem.

Emily came to Number 12 as a maid, two years ago, but the Lord revealed that He had bigger plans for her than making meals and washing sheets, so Octavia advertised for domestic help, and Betty moved into the box room last year. She is not a member but she understands the need to follow Octavia's commands without question or complaint. If she wants to keep her job.

The others live in neighbouring properties. Those with the means to take their pick of houses made offers too generous to be refused. Ellen Oliver bought the four-bedroomed house to the left of us; Rachel Fox the one on the right. On it went until Octavia had followers on all sides. She called the first of them Apostles, but soon they numbered more than twelve. Word spread, women came to hear Her speak and once they heard Her voice they knew the Truth. And so they stayed and took their place in the society, as landladies or as lodgers; house after house along Albany Road, Castle Street, Newnham Road and the Embankment; four roads that meet to form a square like soldiers in formation. Where they do break ranks there's a high wall that runs between them. So we are completely enclosed. Safe. Contained. And inside the boundary lies Paradise. We thought Octavia was speaking figuratively when She told us that. But She wasn't. *This is the Garden of Eden. Hidden in plain sight. It was here in Bedford all along.*

Those who came later had to make do with houses several streets away. Messengers rush between them to share Her Word; typists, like me, put it down on paper; those in the Printing Room make copies to be sent all over the world. Some of the ladies scour the papers for signs that the End Times are upon us: hurricanes in the Tropics or earthquakes in Italy. Then there are letters to be written and healing to be administered. *And the tea and cake is not going to serve itself.* I see their relief when they hurry past with an envelope in their hand, raising it as proof that they cannot possibly stop and chat to me. 'I must catch the last post,' they call back over their shoulder. 'No rest for the wicked!' If they asked me how I am there's a risk I might answer truthfully. Besides, there are rules about what we are allowed to say out loud. *Limit all dialogue to pleasantries and practicalities. Do not question. Only obey.*

I have left the house in too light a coat: the mouse-grey velvet that was hanging in the hallway. I hadn't planned to walk, but I had to get out; away from the whispered judgements and scribbled accusations. But even here I am not free of them. On the other side of the street I see a familiar figure. It is the top hat that gives him away, as much a part of his silhouette as the gold-topped cane he carries. Edgar Peissart touches a gloved hand to the brim to acknowledge that he has seen me. But he does not slow his pace, perhaps as much in need of solitude as I.

At the bottom of Albany Road the grey sky opens and meets its own reflection on the River Great Ouse: a ribbon of water as wide as the road that runs beside it. A crew of schoolboys rows by, gliding in a mist of frozen breath, their blades moving together like the legs of a giant insect. A pond skater: that's what they look like. Edgar says that in America they call them Jesus Bugs because they walk on water, unaware that they are performing a miracle. The river is so close I could touch it, dip my toe in first, then wade in after. There are no walls or sloping banks to stop me; there is nothing to stop me except the cold. When spring comes I shall sit at the water's edge and watch the twigs and blossoms that it carries to the distant sea. Then in summer the spectacle of day-trippers out on punts, a splash, a shot of laughter, another young man boasting, cock-sure and trying to impress. I will see him panicking as the punt pole gets stuck in the mud.

Sometimes we cling to the very thing that is pulling us under.

There's a couple on the path ahead. From the way she turns her head to his I suppose they must be sweethearts. He is walking on crutches, an empty trouser leg hanging limply as he moves. I cross the street and turn up Newnham Road away from them. I don't want him to meet my eyes and see what I am thinking: imagining how he looks beneath his clothes, pale skin puckered like fingertips that have been too long in the bathwater. I picture him lying in No Man's Land, his torn flesh, the smell of earth and iron as he bled into the wool of his uniform. When we got the news that the war was over, I half expected that the lost limbs would grow back; that the fallen would rise. But seven years have passed and none of my brothers has returned home. Ivan moved to Canada, Adrian went to India and Eric is in France. Well, his body is, but not his soul. That has gone to Heaven.

Pilgrim's Progress

Perhaps it was the thought of my brothers that brought me here. We used to play in the gardens of the Bunyan Meeting Church: the boys took turns with a spinning top and I would make do with a single pebble, tossing it onto the path, playing hopscotch on the paving stones that carve a walkway between the sparsely filled flowerbeds. It is one of those January days where the air hangs perfectly still, where no breeze shakes the bones of the trees; a day when it feels that time itself is frozen. I can hear the hymns we used to sing when I was young. We'd walk into church together: my brothers first, me following behind. I was the youngest and the only girl: two frailties that induced their affectionate contempt. Would it be wrong to go inside and sit with my memories of them for a while, to remember the days when we'd sit and listen to Father preach to his flock?

The church is made of red brick. It is sturdy, practical, unremarkable – like most men, that's what Octavia would say. But inside it opens into a palace of pale light, coloured glass scattering rainbows onto the canvas of muted walls. Everything is made of wood, every surface painted in pastel shades of contemplation: warming from the purest white of snowdrops to the butter-yellow of daffodils. I take a seat at the back. When I get home I can tell Octavia I wandered into church to witness the folly of men; to hear them spill the Lord's words carelessly, like drunks. I can say I came to spy on their ignorance and remember how lucky I am to know the Truth.

'Let us pray.' The minister begins to speak and I bow my head, opening one eye just a little to study the embroidery on the kneeling cushion: hundreds of little crosses standing in line like the sufferings of men. How quickly they blur once I open the other eye, a white dove and the word 'Faith' coming sharply into view.

'Another hymn. Please join me in singing number 402: "He Who Would Valiant Be".' The minister's voice brings the congregation to its feet. No one bows their head to read their hymnbooks, every word is committed to memory. This is their battle cry: John Bunyan's words sung in the very church he established. He is Bedford's most famous son, a bronze statue standing on St Peter's Green. But all that will be forgotten. When God reveals that He has sent His own daughter to live among us here, Octavia's glory will outshine them all. Sometimes I imagine Her as a statue carved from white marble; She'd never stand for anything less, and She would have to be standing. I see Her high on a plinth, Her sturdy shoulders hewn from rock, a long skirt falling like a curtain to the floor; disembodied from the waist down, standing perfectly still with Her eyes raised to Heaven. Unshakeable. Immovable.

I am silent. My lips are moving but forming no sounds. I study the congregation, an anthropologist recording their primitive beliefs: childish, reassuring and familiar. They sing on without me, voices rising to meet the stained glass windows that turn their words to pictures; Bunyan's allegories painted in sunlight. I study the depiction of his hero Christian, dressed in knight's armour, slaying the fiend Apollyon. How I envy the violent simplicity of his task, the chance to prove his devotion, to step into battle with the promise of salvation. Win or lose. It is the privilege of man, but I am a woman: no Great War or great coat; no glory. My test is endurance. Patience. Constancy. All I can do is wait for a sign that God has a purpose for me too. A chance to prove myself to Him. And to Octavia.

After the final verse, the minister concludes the service, sending the congregation on its way with a blessing. They stand and button up their coats, fix their hats and gloves. But I am in no rush to get home. 'It has always been my favourite,' says a voice beside me. There's a woman sitting a little further along the pew. Octavia would say she is barely more than a girl, but she is probably only a year or two younger than I am, in her early twenties perhaps. On her lips she wears a smile: of apology or perhaps amusement.

'The window.' She gestures with her head. 'I saw you studying it. St George slaying the dragon. It's always been my favourite. I think it's the drama of it.'

'It's not a dragon,' I say, surprised at how blunt and distant my words sound. I'm not used to strangers, but I mustn't be rude. She is only making polite conversation. That is what people do. Other people.

'I'm sorry,' I say, 'what I mean is . . . It looks like a dragon but . . . look closely and you can just see . . .'

Small lines appear on her forehead as she exaggerates her expression, narrowing her eyes and lifting her hand above her brows; an impression of a sailor looking out to sea. She is trying to make me smile. And it works.

'The scales of a fish,' I say, 'the wings of a dragon and the mouth of a lion. It is a demon.' I stop there. I don't tell her the difference is that dragons are mythical creatures and demons are real. I don't say that Octavia has seen Apollyon from Her window, or that he waits for Her to leave the safety of the Garden so he can devour

Her. If She ventures more than seventy-seven steps outside She will be taken. God was very clear when He told Her that, so She has not crossed the front doorstep in eight years.

I don't say any of this out loud to the woman beside me. It would be too much for a non-believer to understand, so I say nothing at all. Instead we sit together in the companionship of silence and I watch her at the edge of my vision: a blur on the corner of a page, the margins of a watercolour hidden beneath the frame. Pale skin, auburn hair pulled back loosely from her face.

'I haven't seen you here before,' she says.

'No, I haven't been. Not for a long time. But I was walking by, I heard the hymn and it brought back memories.'

'Good ones, I hope?'

I answer her question with a smile but I don't move my eyes from the window. I wonder why she is talking to me, whether she knows who I am and where I live. Is there something about me that makes it obvious I don't belong here?

'I haven't been for a while either,' she says.

'Oh?'

'I don't have a *church* as such. One week I go to chapel, the next I might be at Catholic mass . . .'

She pauses and I know I am expected to fill the silence. She wants me to ask her why. I should make my excuses and leave. I mustn't ask questions because then she will ask them of me. But I can't help myself.

'Why? Why do you go from one church to the next?'

'I don't know. I'm something of a seeker. Still searching.'

'For God?'

'I suppose so, yes.' She laughs and shakes her head. 'Here we are discussing theology and I haven't even introduced myself. I'm

Grace Hardwick. Do you live nearby?'

Here they come: the questions. I have brought this on myself. But I can do this. I can spread the Word just like the others do.

'I'm Dilys Barltrop, pleased to meet you. Yes, very close, one street away, Albany Road.'

'Albany, isn't that where . . .' I hear words swallowed down; a moment's pause before she speaks again. 'The religious group. Of women . . .'

'The Panacea Society.'

'Yes, that's it. Are you? I mean to say, is that where you live?'

'It is.' I prepare myself for her insults. Or perhaps she will simply stand and walk away in silence. But she does neither. Instead she shifts along the pew to sit right beside me.

'How exciting!' she says, which is the last thing I expected. 'I have always wondered . . . A society of women. How many of you are there?'

I look down at the cuffs of my sleeves, stroking down the nap of the felt. 'We have almost sixty resident members,' I say. 'And half as many again who live in other parts of Bedford. Mostly women, but we do have a small number of men.' Now I am wishing I had brought one of our pamphlets with everything written down. If it is left to me I'll probably get it wrong.

She makes a noise, somewhere between a laugh and a sigh. Octavia always says that non-believers only want to mock and humiliate us, but Miss Hardwick seems fascinated. I am a source of fascination. 'You must tell me everything,' she says.

But I could never do that. There are things that I must never say out loud. Even in the society. Especially in the society.

'There is a lot to tell. I'm not sure what you have heard about our work – the Lord's work. Great change is coming and it is us – us women – who will usher it in.'

'Given the chance, I would tear this world up entirely and start afresh,' she says.

'The time is near. Our time.' I risk a glance up to her face. 'Perhaps you should come and pay us a visit. I could show you the stained glass window in *our* chapel . . . if you'd like to see it.'

'I would,' she replies, 'very much. But, oh, we'd better go. The rest of the congregation have left.'

There's a lively rhythm to her voice. Her vowels unfurl like stretching limbs but there's a tension, as if she is trying to fold them back into sharper angles. As if she can't quite be contained.

We step outside and she retreats into her coat, dark blue wool, the colour of the night where it meets the horizon. A button is hanging loose on her cuff, small and dark to match the fabric. It is one of a line of ten, each paired with a loop, but this one is break-ing free.

'You look terribly cold,' she says, reaching out to touch my arm. Some people are like that, so comfortable in their own skin that they think nothing of sharing themselves; unaware of the pow-er or threat of their bodies. I shrink back and she hides her hand in her pocket, the loose button swinging as her arm grows still. Then, very slowly, her eyes find mine.

She is holding me with her gaze. I am being held.

'So I should come?' she asks, softly.

'Of course,' I say, a little too brightly. 'You *must* come. Next Sunday, at three?'

'I'll see you then. Which house?'

'Oh yes – it's Number 12.'

Grace turns and walks into the last of the afternoon. Her button is lying near my feet, and I pick it up and put it in my pocket. Next Sunday at three. How will I explain this to Octavia? What have I done?

Ugly Ways

'You look much brighter in the eyes. Your little outing yesterday did you good, Dilys.' With Emily it is always a statement, never a question. 'But next time I think it would be prudent to wear a more suitable coat.'

I don't respond. It is the only power I have. She wants me to know that she saw me leaving the house, that nothing is beyond her reach. We both understand she would prefer it if I was out of the way, out of the picture, so she could paint herself at the centre of the scene; at Octavia's right hand. She is becoming more like Her every day, or trying to. Both wear their hair piled high in styles that were fashionable twenty years ago: pompadours that make their heads resemble cottage loaves. Both wear the same high-necked dresses. Octavia's hemlines have retreated to no more than an inch above Her ankles, stubbornly refusing to accept that Queen Victoria is no longer on the throne, or that values have changed outside the walls of the Garden. That's why good manners are so important in here. That's why Octavia insists we call a napkin a napkin, never a serviette. That's why our elevenses have been served on a mahogany stand: a rich fruit cake cut to fill three tiers with identical slices. Though we know without being told that we must not take a piece; that we must choose a teacake from the plate instead. The fruit loaf will return to the kitchen to be brought out as decoration again tomorrow.

'Well, it is lovely to see you looking so well.' Emily's words are like a trail of breadcrumbs and Octavia follows.

'You went out yesterday, Dilys?' She asks.

'Yes, Octavia. Just for a walk along the river.' I should tell Her I went to church. I reach for a teacake. I need time to calm my breathing, gain control.

'Was it pleasant?' She asks.

'I'm sorry?'

She looks to Emily with an eyebrow raised, then turns back to address me. 'Your *walk*, Dilys.' She sighs. 'Was it pleasant?'

'Yes. Thank You, Octavia.' I should tell Her that I went to church. I should tell Her in case anyone saw me.

She turns her attention to a copy of the *Telegraph*, while Emily refills Her cup, and in the interval of silence it is already too late to confess.

'Dreadful,' She says, without lifting Her eyes from the newspaper. 'News of another earthquake in Italy.' She turns the page, scouring the columns for more evidence of disaster, plague or pestilence: signs that the End Times are upon us.

I didn't actually tell a lie. If She had asked me outright, I would have admitted I went to church. I'm almost certain of it.

'I saw Edgar while I was walking,' I say, filling my mouth with other words so the truth won't come spilling out. 'He was out for a stroll too.'

'No,' says Emily, relishing the chance to take control of the conversation. 'He was on his way to the station to meet Donald from the train. That young man seems to be spending more time here than he does in Cambridge. I'm not quite sure how these students get away with so little work.' She pauses to see if Octavia is listening, but Her attention is still focused on the headlines. 'I shouldn't wonder that he'll ask to move here permanently once the summer comes. It is heartening to see youngsters coming into the fold, isn't it?'

'As it happens, I met someone yesterday,' I say. 'A Miss Hardwick . . .'

'Who?' says Octavia, folding Her newspaper and tossing it aside, as if satisfied that the reality of life has lived up to Her worst fears.

'A young lady called Miss Hardwick. She wishes to know about us . . . about the society. I thought we might invite her to pay us a visit.' I don't tell Octavia that I have invited her already. 'What do you think?'

'I think we had better ask the Lord,' She says. 'Let us pray.'

I bow my head and shut my eyes tight. My heartbeat starts to slow, a feeling of calm climbing up my legs and into my stomach, turning like a cat about to settle for a nap. I know that Octavia will say yes. But not because I have asked Her. Because God has. For the first time in a long time I feel He is listening to my prayer. Octavia clears Her throat and I look up.

'Very well,' She says. 'Do you have her address?'

I don't. But I nod.

'Then send word. Invite her to come.'

I try not to show my relief but I drop my guard, become slovenly, and within minutes Octavia clatters out of the room with the wild look that makes me think of doctors and locked doors. I was eating my teacake too loudly. The scraping of the knife as I spread the butter, the crunch as I took my first bite. Perhaps it is the carnality that offends Her: the sounds of the body taking pleasure, the jaw, the teeth, the throat. Perhaps it reminds Her that we are flesh and blood after all.

Octavia leaves in such a hurry She almost knocks into Peter who has just arrived to join us at the table. 'I'm sorry. Please excuse me. My fault entirely. I should not have been late.' He'll be stewing on this all afternoon now. In his eyes he is always the one to blame and, deep down, I think he is always sorry for the same offence. As an Australian citizen, he could have signed up to face death with our boys in France, but to his eternal shame, he chose to live instead.

'Octavia, are You all right?' he calls after Her but She doesn't answer. She is already in the hallway, already climbing the stairs to Her bedroom. Peter looks to Emily for explanation.

'What happened?' he asks, patting the crown of his head as though taming his unruly hair will calm his nerves. The natural curls fall into ridges across his scalp, the ends so frizzy they look as though they have been waved with irons left too long in the fire.

'It was me,' I say. 'It was my fault. A teacake . . .'

I am selfish and I am thoughtless; too big, too loud, too irritating. I forgot the rules and I nearly spoiled it. If I had taken that bite when I asked Octavia about Miss Hardwick, She might have said she couldn't come. I must make myself smaller. Quieter.

The things that make it difficult to live peaceably with a person are the things that must be altered. They are worse than sin because they make other people sin.

I know God will admonish me tonight.

I know just how it will go.

At 5 p.m., Octavia will sit at the desk in Her bedroom, lifting the pen to receive His word, Her body stiffening as His Spirit enters Her.

At 5.30 p.m., She will be holding a piece of paper written in a hand that is not Her own. Heavy splashes of ink beside the scratch of a nib too faint to read, where the words have poured out too quickly.

At 6 p.m., we shall gather in the chapel to hear His daily message. Octavia will begin as She always does, reminding us that we are the chosen ones. Eve ate from the tree. *We, her daughters, must be the ones to heal the rift with God.* Motherly encouragement, which in the next breath turns to discipline.

All ugly noises and ugly ways of eating tend to make people unpopular, however good they are. It may be very pleasant to exercise good teeth in this way but it will not be tolerated here.

She will not say my name, but I will know She is talking about me. And so will Emily, who will take out her pencil and pocketbook and add it to the ledger of my faults.

Disciples

My father came to visit me again last night, while I was sleeping. I was eight years old when he died. It's difficult to know whether my memories really are my own, or planted by someone else, like a cuckoo's eggs. Now they have hatched and my dreams of him are so vivid they've become the truth. An idea starts like a spiral of smoke, but if it is persuasive enough it takes shape, forms sharp edges, becomes solid. When I see him he is always standing behind a lectern: an eagle made of gold. He is looking out at his congregation, his eyes moving across the rows of faces trying to find just one. Lifting his arms, he starts to speak, but the words won't come out. He drops to the floor and all I can see are the bottoms of his legs, twitching, jerking, jumping. One of his turns. We never knew when they would happen or when he would wake up. Then one day he didn't.

I wonder what he would have made of the Panacea Society, whether he would have been a believer, or have covered his ears before the Truth could persuade him. What would he have made of the chapel I sit in now, in the Garden? It is everything the Bunyan Meeting Church is not: small, dark, domestic. God's drawing room. Octavia calls it cosy. You can see her influence in every detail, the ladder-backed chairs, the Persian rugs, the arrangements of artificial flowers: silk roses blushing beneath a layer of dust, velvet leaves faded to carmine by the passing of years.

Wood panels line the walls of the chancel, which is furnished entirely from Liberty's homeware department. A fluted console table serves as an altar, framed by twisted brass candlesticks that stand on narrow shelves at either side. The lectern is a tall plant stand, its legs cut into cusped arches like church windows. From behind it Octavia delivers the Eucharist. She has a handkerchief draped over Her head, embroidered with a dove and an olive branch. She wears a red priest's stole, vestments only ever meant to house a man's form, pulling tightly across Her bosom. And there's a scarf around Her neck: a paisley of dark blues and greens, tassels printed around the edges to make it look like a shawl.

Octavia does not approve of calling out or speaking in tongues, not if it interrupts Her sermons. But I can hear someone whispering, the same words over and over again like the hiss of a train's pistons, picking up speed, pushing on towards Heaven. Others raise a hand above their heads, eyes closed in rapture, like children reaching up to catch drops of summer rain. And occasionally someone will swoon or fall to their knees. All these are signs that they are receiving the Holy Spirit.

I am never one of those people.

The chapel is too small for us to take communion at the altar. We sit in pairs either side of a narrow aisle, passing a tray of bread between us. Octavia insists the sacramental loaves are baked each morning. She doesn't hold with the idea of wafers, which means we have to be careful of crumbs. We recite the liturgy: 'May I drink deep into the spirit of Christ and may his blood cleanse me from all sin.' But we don't drink wine, not when we have a true miracle on tap. A communion chalice is passed between us and we take a sip of the Water, infused with the healing power of Octavia's breath.

'Christ's death on the cross, His atoning for sin, has saved our

souls. But still we suffer such terrible trials in this life. Another re-
deemer is required for the body.' Octavia is reading aloud the words
She has received from God through Her pen this evening. 'There
was a second Adam – Jesus – to reverse the sin of man. Now I come
as the second Eve. I must suffer for the sins of women.'

'Amen.' The cries are loudest from the front rows where Octavia's favourites sit. I am never invited to take a seat there, but at
least from the back I have a view of the entire congregation; from
here I can watch them and collect their faults. If I am lucky someone might yawn when Octavia is speaking, or whisper to their
neighbour when they should be bowing their head to pray. I will
jot down these transgressions in my pocketbook after chapel, ready
to present to Octavia when I am called to Her sitting room to make
my report. But I already know I will be found lacking, that She will
say I am not committed to the Overcoming, to cleansing the society of sin. I suspect some of the others make things up, but I can
never quite bring myself to do it. Perhaps I lack imagination. Besides, you have to think carefully before shining a light on other
people's lives because the glare can reflect back on you, illuminate
your faults for all to see.

Today the only person yawning is Ellen Oliver and I could never
write *her* name in my book. She is the oldest among us. She turned
sixty a few years ago, though we didn't celebrate – we don't have
time for such worldly concerns. I've noticed, lately, that she is
looking frail, fainter, as if the lines of her face and body have been
smudged, a poorly sketched portrait of the fearless woman I have
always admired. It was Ellen who realised that the messiah she had
been looking for was sitting beside her in prayer group; who realised that her friend Mabel was elevated, augmented, divine. When
the others came to see the Truth, they called Her Octavia: the

eighth in a line of prophets. But it was Ellen who deciphered the signs. She can see what others can't; she always sees the best in people. Even in me.

Octavia steps behind the curtain into the small room to the side of the altar and returns with a bowl of water, the corner of a towel tucked into a loop of Her belt. 'Be kind enough to open that for me,' She says, passing a block of soap to Emily, who is sitting on the front row. It must be Sunlight, or Lux. God has told Her that those are the only brands to trust, so She insists that no one buys or uses any other.

'I had intended to have everything ready but the Lord had so much to say this evening,' She says. 'When I woke from my trance I was amazed to see how many pages I had written.' She holds out Her hand for the soap but Emily is still struggling with the wrapping. 'Just as Christ washed the feet of His Disciples so the Lord has bade me do the same . . . Oh give it to me, Emily. I'll do it myself.' With a jerk of Her head She directs Emily to go behind the curtain and prepare herself.

'Since God is fourfold – Father, Son, Holy Spirit and Daughter – so the four of you are the Chosen.' We all know who She is talking about: the front-rowers, the ones She meets with in private after chapel. Peter, Edgar, Kate Firth – and Emily, who emerges now from behind the curtain. She looks uneasy, her shoulders hunched. One hand is curled around a ball of rolled-up viscose stockings, which she has dusted with talcum powder to dull their cheap shine. The fingers of her other hand are hooked inside the backs of her shoes. She is exposed, presenting the worn soles to the congregation, revealing the metal tacks and offcuts of leather hammered in to patch the holes. Even her naked legs look threadbare, greyish with chalky patches of dry skin and flecks of dark hair.

'Please sit.' Octavia directs her to the small pew to the left of the altar, and kneels slowly. Peter jumps to his feet to slip a cushion underneath Octavia's knee before it reaches the ground; attentive as always, terrified that he might miss an opportunity to serve. Emily stifles a shudder as Octavia submerges her feet into the water. 'You came to us with least to give, but most to offer,' Octavia says. 'You didn't have the advantages the rest of us have enjoyed. But you have faith, Emily, and you are obedient. Those are the things the Lord values above all.' She continues with a good lather and scrub, apparently unperturbed by Emily's numerous corns and bunions. But then She could hardly baulk at a little dry skin when Jesus washed a leper.

With her feet patted dry, Emily nods her head in thanks and gives up her seat to Kate Firth, who appears from behind the curtain holding a pair of burgundy shoes, and silk stockings.

'Yes, it's a lesson you have had to learn, isn't it, Kate?' Octavia says. 'Our very own Doubting Thomas.' Kate sits down and arranges the fine pleats on the gathered lapel that runs down her front. Her dress, drop-waisted crepe in the exact shade of her shoes, is yet another that I haven't seen her wear before.

'You doubted the Lord's calling,' Octavia says. 'You doubted *me*. You wanted to be sure that we were not deceived – which was admirable. But *men* are blinded by reason, and look where it has got them. Women should follow their hearts, which is where the Lord dwells. That's why He has chosen *us* to do His bidding. We must *all* remember that.'

Kate was here at the beginning, before the beginning, when Octavia was Mabel, and, of the two of them, Kate was considered the more extraordinary: a fine-looking widow who moved to Bedford from York, bringing her northern accent and two servants with her. She and Mabel would chat over the wall between their gardens, or take turns to have the other round for tea, sharing cake and letters from the front line, sharing each other's despair when the telegrams arrived, with no idea that one of them would soon be revealed as the Daughter of God to restore the hope that war had stolen away.

'I forgive you,' Octavia says. 'The Lord forgives you. You were always generous in spirit and since you came to see the Truth you have been generous in deed too, opening The Haven – your own home – to the believers who have flocked to Bedford.'

I am becoming restless. I wonder what Grace Hardwick is doing right now and what she would think of our service. If she comes, Octavia will see that I have been working for the glory of the Lord. Sometimes I daydream that Grace will stand up and tell the congregation that as soon as we met she felt God's calling; that she felt His power in me. That would surprise them.

It is Peter's turn. Octavia takes the first of his feet in her hands without a word, creating a void of silence for his gratitude to fill. 'Octavia, I cannot let You do it,' he says. But his grave expression is undermined by the airy Australian accent which makes even the most resolute statement sound like a tentative apology.

'Octavia,' his tone is almost pleading now, 'let me be the one to bathe *You*.' Octavia is gratified by his humble attitude but I suspect, by the way he holds on to the sides of his seat, that it is motivated by ticklish feet more than deference on this occasion.

'Hush now,' She says firmly.

In him She has found the son She always wanted. Obedient. Adoring. Present. Though there are very few years that separate them – Peter in his early fifties and Octavia in Her late – he has finally found purpose in his life and plays the part of devoted child with utter conviction. He is juvenile even in appearance. There is always too much tie hanging beneath the knot at his neck, or too little, and his trousers bunch above his shoes as though he might one day grow into them. His neck looks barely able to hold up a head so heavy with curly hair, a protuberant Adam's apple quivering and bobbing beneath a face that seems to be perpetually cast down towards the floor.

Octavia rubs soap onto his feet, lather foaming on the clumps of hairs that sprout from his toes. I find the sight of his pale skin distasteful. Feet are always covered, shrouded in socks, or shoes or slippers. And though I can't see there's anything about Peter's feet that would lead anyone to sin, just the act of looking feels improper. I see his relief when the washing is over and he no longer has to fight the impulse to laugh or the reflex to kick Her away. Neither would help to create the impression that he is taking this ceremony seriously.

'Peter, you are an example to us all.' Octavia looks up to the congregation to make Her meaning clear: an example to those who think *they* should be chosen, those who were here before Peter came along. And long before Edgar Peissart arrived. It is his turn now.

'Edgar,' Octavia says, taking a moment to line up the pair of two-tone Oxfords that he was wearing, black toes side-by-side, white bars perfectly aligned. She takes each hem of his trousers and rolls it up to just below the knee, exposing scarlet socks held up by garters.

'Really, Edgar,' She says, averting Her eyes as though finding the sight of them painful, 'what a garish colour.'

'They are considered rather fashionable in America,' he says without apology.

'They may be considered fashionable in America but here in

England they are considered vulgar.'

He says nothing more and leans down to take them off, bending forward and revealing a thin patch in his white hair. He is a dandy, an old man dressed as a young one. He always wears an air of youthful detachment, but his face betrays his age: eyes so deep-set that they are in perpetual shadow and lips that turn down at the corners even when he smiles. When Kate Firth first saw him she said he looked like the Devil himself, but I've always imagined Satan would be handsome and charming and young. After all, he can take any shape he pleases, and beautiful people always get away with more.

'We women have been instructed not to listen to the opinions of any man, lest we should be led astray,' Octavia says, nodding for him to put his feet into the water. 'But let no one be in any doubt that you are here as a follower, not as a teacher. You bow to the rule of woman. You serve faithfully. Let that not be questioned by anyone in the Garden.' Has She heard the whispered conversations? There are those who think Edgar should not be favoured. *He's a man and an American. What is She thinking?* But Edgar is nothing if not persistent. He started writing to Her last year, asking for Her blessing to move to England and join the society. He wouldn't give up until She gave in, but we were all surprised when She relented. Octavia is not a person who concedes. She doesn't have to, She has the certainty of God's blessing in everything.

'Indeed, Octavia,' he says. 'I am Your servant. Sent by God to represent man's place in the New World.' He turns his head to the congregation. 'For God has a role for all of us.'

'And that role,' says Octavia, jerking his feet out of the water, 'is to serve. Not to seek your own glories. Pride leads to a fall, Edgar.' She does not dry him but stands instead, wiping Her hands on the damp towel with a look of distaste before addressing the room.

'I, then, have washed the feet of my disciples, just as Christ did. And I ask you to remember the words He said: *Verily, verily, I say unto you, The servant is not greater than his lord.*'

Garden of Eden

Eight taps on the front door. Eight. I must remember to tell Octavia. She will know it is a sign.

'Miss Hardwick,' I say, opening the door wide in welcome. 'I knew you'd come.' But that is not the truth. This morning I went over and over our conversation in my head and by lunchtime I was convinced she had accepted my invitation only to be polite. It's what the English do best. But here she is, standing on the doorstep.

'Of course I came,' she says, and there's that smile again, is it amusement? I will ask her not to mention that we met in church. Time turns the truth into a lie: if Octavia found out now She would think I had been up to something. She might stop me going out for walks. She might stop the others too, and then I'd have to suffer their resentment, as well as Her disappointment.

Grace steps into the hall and I am ready this time. I hold out my hand. She is wearing gloves, dark blue like her coat. Which is just as well; perhaps the touch of skin would be too much.

'Welcome to our little society. Are you ready for the grand tour?'

Today this is my place, my story to tell. Today I am someone with something to say. I lead her down the hallway, past the closed door of the sitting room. I'm not ready to take her in there yet. Everything is too heavy: the oversized sideboards, the shelves crammed with rules and proclamations, even the mantelpiece clock labours to tick each step in time. The net curtains and drapes make the light so dim you can barely make out the photographs on the wall: faces that look happier than I remember them. Take a picture and in that flash of light, reality is transformed, a moment becomes a memory.

'Shall we start in the Garden?' I lead her out through the narrow yard which runs between our kitchen and that of Rachel Fox next door, thankful that I invited her to come on a Sunday when the washing line is mercifully free of our weekday offerings. At the end of the wall I usher her left, and see her surprise as the Garden opens up in front of us.

'I had no idea it would be so . . .'

'Big?' I ask. 'This is the main lawn. Not quite a cricket pitch but big enough for croquet. We knocked down the garden walls between the houses, so we can be together all the time. We live, we worship . . .' I stop before I say any more. We watch, but I don't need to tell her that.

Borders line the edges of the lawn, paths leading off through trellis archways to the back doors of the houses around the outside of the Garden.

'And a tennis court!' she says. 'I'd never have believed all this was here.'

'We have some wealthy members.'

The war stole their brothers and husbands and they were left with great piles of money in their place. They inherited freedom. Perhaps they didn't know what to do with it; perhaps that's why they came here. But I don't tell her that either.

'It's a lovely garden,' she says. And as I watch her stand and take it in, I realise she is right. Once the weather turns I rarely linger out here, dashing to outrun the chill before it climbs inside my bones. Octavia would say that I am too sensitive, but I cannot bear to look at the skeletons that summer has left behind. Life shrinks back from winter's bared teeth, the earth exposed like the soil of fresh graves. Lavender is stripped to a stack of silvery needles, the leaves of the rhododendrons left downcast and defeated.

'It doesn't look its best this time of year,' I say. But today it looks more beautiful than I have ever seen it. Last night's frost has retreated to the darkest corners of the garden, hiding in the shelter of the two stone lions that guard the entrance to the chapel, catching the last of the weakening light with a defiant glint. It is not cold enough for snow but the viburnum hedges bend instead with the burden of white blossoms. Today I can feel spring slumbering in the beds that line the path beneath our feet. The sun is getting sleepy too, already slouching behind the chimneypots of Castleside and The Haven that cast long shadows across the lawn. I think of them as generals that guard the west entrance of the Garden, dwarfing the houses on every other side.

'That's Castleside,' I say, pointing out the three-storey villa on the left. 'We only bought it last year. There was a wall running right along here,' I explain, halting our steps in the very centre of the Garden. 'Everything this side was ours, everything that side was theirs.'

'Theirs?'

'It used to belong to Bedford School. It was where the boarders stayed, but Octavia arranged for the society to buy it.'

'And that one, beside it? It looks even bigger!'

'That's The Haven. Kate Firth lives there. She takes in new members while they find something more permanent.'

'So she has boarders of her own?' she laughs.

'Yes, I suppose she has.'

'I envy them,' she says, looking up at the bedroom windows. 'Friends together, sharing all this. That feeling of belonging to something.'

I envy them too.

'She lets us use the rooms at the back for society business,' I say, pointing to the outhouses built onto the back of The Haven. 'We've got our own printing press now to produce books and pamphlets, and next door is where we keep the archive.'

'There's so much to take in,' she says. 'I'd love to see it all.'

'Perhaps another day you shall.' But that's not up to me; that will be a decision for Octavia.

Miss Hardwick turns slowly to survey the Garden. 'That must be the chapel you told me about,' she says, walking towards it. On the outside its design is unremarkable: more walls of red brick to match those built on every side of the Garden, a pitched roof of russet tiles. One could almost mistake it for a low barn or work-shop. But at one end a clock tower rises, clad in lead, with four white faces framed in gold.

'That's where we'll find the stained glass window you prom-ised?' she asks.

'Yes.' Of course. The window. That's the reason she came. I hold the door open and let her walk ahead. She is a bird, a dark blue bird, slim and slight; her head moving this way and that to take in every detail, as if she might take flight at any moment. Beside her I feel plain, oversized and clumsy.

'We meet here every evening,' I say. 'When Octavia tells us what the Lord has said.'

'And Octavia is . . . your leader?'

'Yes. She is the reason all this is here.' Outside the society we don't advertise Her name or who She truly is. It might be danger-ous. The church of men is not ready to hear the truth, but I'm starting to wonder if Miss Hardwick is.

'And there's our window,' I say.

She walks slowly to it, eyes fixed on the woman in the glass who stares straight back, ignoring the little girl depicted at her feet.

'Emily designed it,' I say. 'Emily Goodwin. She lives with us at Number 12.' I'm not sure Grace is listening any more. She doesn't move her eyes from the window, she doesn't speak. It is so quiet. The chapel is usually filled with the chatter of two dozen ladies, Octavia's voice rising above them all.

'She wanted a sort of Queen Mother,' I say. 'A combination of royalty and domesticity. Octavia chose the scripture. *Jerusalem, the Mother of us all* (Galatians 4:26).'

I am talking, still talking. Because silence would be too loud.

Finally, Grace turns towards me. 'Beautiful,' she says, faint smudges of orange and blue staining her pale face. Emily chose vivid colours to make the most of the south-facing window but today the light is weak, kindling them to a soft glow.

'I feel . . .' Grace says. 'I don't know what I feel . . . Strange, I suppose.'

'Do you need to sit down?'

'No. I'm not unwell. I'm just . . .' She turns to me so quickly that I don't have time to avoid her eyes. 'I feel something here I can't explain, as if there is a thinning, a thinning of the space between our world and the next.' She studies my face, waiting for me to fill the silence that has fallen between us. 'Gosh, now I have said it out loud, it sounds like madness.'

But it doesn't. I feel it too. In this chapel God gives the gift of the Holy Spirit to Octavia's followers. But not to me. Never to me. Not until now. Light is flooding my body and washing away the doubts and darkness that the Devil has been planting there. And for a fleeting moment I feel the Lord is standing with us, in the chapel. So real I feel I could reach out and touch Him. Then just as quickly He is gone.

'You think me foolish, don't you?' she says.

No, Grace. You don't understand. I am the fool. The truth was right here all along but I didn't see it. I want to reassure her but I can't find the words. Instead I say, 'Let's walk again, warm up a bit. I think the cold has got to me.' I am shaking. I lead her outside towards the ash tree that stands in the centre of the Garden. Its thick branches curve against a stockinged sky, wearing the gauze of dusk like silk.

'We call this tree Yggdrasil,' I say. 'In Norse mythology it was the tree that connected the worlds. Its branches reaching up to the heavens and its roots down to the underworld. Just as you describe, a thinning of the boundary.'

I won't tell her that this is the Tree of Life: the very spot where Eve sat with Adam. A taste, that's all I'll give her for now. A single bite of the Truth. Enough to keep her coming back for more; enough to keep her coming back to stroll around the Garden. If she wants to. If Octavia allows it.

'This *is* a special place,' I say. 'God has made us a promise. That we shall have eternal life.'

'He has,' she says. 'And we shall join Him in Heaven.'

'No, you don't understand. Those of us who follow Octavia will never die. God has given Her His word. We will stay in the Garden until Jesus returns here. To us.'

Eternal life, here in Bedford. Days without end.

It is a thought we are supposed to find comforting.

'So *that's* what you believe?' she says, as if she has been told the answer to a riddle. 'Truly?'

I nod. I wonder what she is thinking, and whether I have said too much, too soon. In time I will tell her about the box. That we have the means to make everything right: the answer, the promise, the end and the beginning. I will tell her about Joanna Southcott, who placed her prophecies inside and sealed it tight a hundred years ago, and how the bishops will come and open it and bring an end to suffering in the world. But not today. Today I shall stroll around the Garden beside her and enjoy the last of the weakening light.

We sit on the bench that wraps itself around Yggdrasil's trunk, a crowd of snowdrops by our feet. Octavia says they are an example to us all: pious and pretty because they bow their heads gently to the Lord. But today they are a regiment of fighters: Wordsworth's lone warriors, Mary's tapers. They spear the frozen earth and announce that spring is waging war on winter. And soon the Garden will be full of life again.

'This place,' she says, at last. 'There is a lot to take in.'

'There is.'

'But I like it very much.'

'I am glad.' I pause to choose my words. 'Miss Hardwick—'

'Please, call me Grace.'

'Grace then – in here we are protected. Outside, the world is unravelling.'

'The war . . .?'

'Yes, but much more than that. Man has slipped too far from God, from truth, from hope. It is up to woman now.'

We fall back into silence.

'Did you lose anyone?' she asks.

'My brother Eric. His plane was shot down.'

'I'm sorry.' She drops her head and starts to fiddle with the loop on her cuff, the one that has lost its button. I should tell her that I picked it up. She could sew it back on. But I don't.

'I have two other brothers,' I say. 'They survived but they moved abroad. One to Canada, one to India. What about you? A brother . . .?' I can't help myself: 'A sweetheart?'

She pauses as if deciding how to answer. 'There was someone,' she says. 'He said he was in love with me. He asked me to wait for him . . .' She finds my eyes again. 'He asked me to marry him. I didn't feel the same but I went along with it.'

Sometimes it is difficult to see a way out.

'So what happened, did you break it off?'

'No, he never came home. He was killed in the trenches. I wonder how far I would have let it go, whether I would have ended up his wife. I'm ashamed to say a part of me was relieved he didn't make it . . . I'm . . . It was wicked.'

I should be shocked by her confession, but instead I am delighted that she has chosen to confide in me. I feel giddy again, light-headed then full of anger at the young man, that he tried to claim her, tried to force her hand, and did he force his body on her too? Did he come to her door in his uniform and beg to know her as his wife before he faced death? I wonder if she let him. The thought appals and excites me. I will admit these sinful thoughts next time I am called to give my confession to Octavia. I will tell Her that the Devil tempted me with visions of a young man in uniform. It doesn't pay to go in empty-handed.

'What about your parents? Did they want you to marry?' I ask.

'Yes. I mean, they would have done. But it's just me now, they both died some years ago. I have no one to answer to.'

'Except God.'

'Except God.' She smiles: a smile of warmth and sadness. 'I never wanted all that,' she says. 'The things you are supposed to want, to be married, to be someone's wife. Here you are free.'

Free. Is that what she thinks I am?

'What about you?' she says. 'Are your parents still alive?'

'My father died seventeen years ago.'

'I'm sorry.' It's one of those things you are supposed to say, like 'it is God's will'. Nobody stops to think whether they really believe the words, they just speak them automatically. But Grace is different: when she says 'I'm sorry', I believe her.

'What about your mother?' she asks.

'I lost her too.' I pull the collar of my coat around my chin. 'Shall we walk again? It's getting cold.'

We take the path that runs along the wall. 'So Albany Road is on the other side of this?' she asks.

'Yes. You're getting your bearings now.'

'I have to admit, I was curious,' she says. 'The schoolboys sit on the top deck of the bus to try to get a glimpse over this wall. You're quite the mystery. There is a lot of talk.'

'There is a lot to understand,' I say. 'God has revealed many things.'

Some of them wonderful, some terrible. Sometimes it is difficult to know the difference.

The chapel clock begins to chime. 'It must be four o'clock,' I say. 'Octavia wants to meet you. We mustn't keep Her waiting.'

———

Stepping into the warmth of Number 12 makes me shiver more; the cold air of the Garden lingers on my breath. I arrange my face into a smile. 'Ready?' I ask her. Grace nods but I don't suppose she is: you can never really be ready for Octavia.

'I told Her we met by the river,' I whisper as we cross the hall. 'Best not to mention that we were in church.'

'Why not?'

'She has rather strong opinions about the church of men.'

I knock on the sitting room door and hear a 'please come in'. Octavia is writing at Her bureau in the bay window. She doesn't look up or acknowledge that we are behind Her.

One, two, three, four, five . . .

I start to count. Grace looks to me for reassurance: no doubt wondering whether Octavia has realised we're here. Just wait, I tell her in my head, don't cough or try to attract Her attention. She won't like that. There is so much I should have told her before we came in, so much that could go wrong. Octavia is sensitive, it is not Her fault. She carries a heavy burden.

Six, seven, eight, nine . . .

I see Grace's eyes dart around the room. The walls are arsenic green. Beneath a black picture rail runs a painted paper border: a William Morris vine of leaves and fruit. Bookcases hold Octavia's volumes, gold lettering on their spines. And in the centre of the room stands a clothed table surrounded by mismatched chairs, every one carefully chosen and deliberately placed. If anything is moved by even an inch – the black marble clock on the hearth, the brass lion on the sideboard – Octavia knows about it, and then the pain in Her head starts to come on again.

Ten . . . Eleven . . .

Very slowly Octavia screws the top onto Her pen, folds the letter She has been writing and places both into a drawer.

'You must be Miss Hardwick.' She still has not turned around.

'That's right. It is a pleasure to meet you,' Grace says.

Octavia stands and walks across to take the wing-backed chair at

Her side of the table. She used to hold séances here and entertain departed relatives but she knows from bitter experience that demons can pose as loved ones to work their mischief.

'Miss Barltrop has been kind enough to tell me a little about the society,' Grace says.

'Has she indeed? And what are your impressions of what you have heard?'

'It has made me want to learn more.'

Octavia smiles politely. 'Please sit down. We must have some refreshment while we talk. Every good discussion deserves a good cup of tea.'

Grace chooses a leather armchair and I take the embroidered pouffe next to her. I realise my mistake when Betty brings in the tea tray. I am going to be sitting too low at the table; Octavia is towering over me. I can't face the thought of eating anyway and I don't trust myself to lift a teacup to my lips without spilling it, or clattering it down too loudly on the saucer. But Grace stirs her tea (carefully), and sips it (quietly), takes a slice of cake (but not two), and glances at me (but only when Octavia isn't looking). She is reverent but not fawning and answers all Her questions: Where do you work? You live by yourself in lodgings? One of the greatest threats to our great empire is Bolshevism, Miss Hardwick, don't you agree? Oh, I can see that you have a bright mind. And what a pretty shade of blue you wear, the shade is most becoming on you.

I'm not sure either of them would notice if I were not in the room. I have seen this happen so many times before. Now She can no longer step outside the Garden, Octavia craves new company to keep, new conversation to dominate, new minds to impress Herself upon. Faced with the challenge of an unsaved soul She is radiant, shining with the light of God, and when it comes to visitors She always gives them full beam. Grace is not the first to be dazzled.

I memorise her answers to pore over later. She works as a secretary at a legal firm. She rents a room from a widow in Tavistock Street, not the nicest area but she appreciates the short stroll into work. She is twenty-three years old. Only two years younger than me. And I notice that when she talks she runs the tip of one thumb around the knuckle of the other.

Tap, tap. What's that? It's a sound that could agitate Octavia, and that could spoil everything. I look around and try to find its source. Tap, tap. The window.

'Ah, let him in, Dilys. I think our dear Sir Jack wants to meet our guest.' I open the latch and in he hops; with a single flap of his wings he is perched on the arm of Octavia's chair. Grace does well to disguise her amazement.

'Now, Jack, you are just in time to enjoy the crumbs,' Octavia says. 'May I introduce you to Miss Hardwick?' He tilts his head as if considering her question. There is something almost human about his eyes, rimmed by a mottled flash of silver blue, the dark pools of his pupils spilling wider in the low light of the room. She begins to apologise for his shyness; since he arrived a week ago he has been terrified of all except Octavia Herself. 'He is a most sensitive soul . . .' She says, but even as She starts to speak he jumps down and settles under the table by Grace's feet. We peek under in time to see him take what appears to be a low bow. Then he sets to work trying to unpick the laces on the top of her black shoes with his beak.

'Dilys, did you hear me?' I'm suddenly aware Octavia is talking, with a tone that tells me I have done something wrong. I sit up too quickly and hit the top of my head under the table.

'Yes, Octavia?'

Her eyes are trained on me but Her words are directed to Grace. 'You must excuse her, Miss Hardwick, she is rather too often in a world of her own. Dilys, leave us please. I wish to speak to Miss Hardwick alone.'

A look from Grace reassures me she will be fine, and I pull the door shut behind me, slowly. I want to catch a little of what Octavia wants to keep private.

'When Dilys told me she had met you I wasn't sure,' She says. 'But Sir Jack . . . You have made quite an impression. It's extraordinary . . . already one of his favourites!'

In the dining room a pair of wooden doors is all that separates me from their conversation. I could put my ear to the gap but it would not do for Octavia to find me eavesdropping, so instead I sit by the window. I open a Bible and let my eyes skitter across the page, but I am not reading, not really. I am thinking about my brother Adrian and what he would say to all this, if he knew. He won't get to hear about it; I stopped replying to his correspondence weeks ago because it was doing me no good. His letters from India are always the same: he tells me why he left the society, why he couldn't stay, why *I* shouldn't stay. At first I would write back and beg him to return to ask Octavia for forgiveness, but he has made up his mind. I have never told him there's a part of me that envies his certainty. He is convinced all this is wrong, but all I have ever had are half-formed fears. They barge into my head and take a seat, and I'm left wondering whether I invited them in or not. But all that is going to change. Grace has come. Today I felt the Holy Spirit move in me. It is the start of something. For once I have no doubt.

Octavia shouts from the hallway. 'Miss Hardwick is leaving now,' She says. 'Dilys?'

I pop my head out of the dining room. 'I'm here.'

'Miss Hardwick is going. She will join us for chapel next Sunday.'

'Then I shall see her then,' I say, trying to keep my voice steady, trying not to show my delight. But I was right. This is the start of something. I can feel God's hand at work.

Grace turns to look at me as Octavia opens the front door. 'I look forward to it,' she says. 'Goodbye, Miss Barltrop. And thank you, again.'

As I pass the door to the sitting room I see Emily at the table, pouring herself a cup of tea. She must have gone in after I left them. She has to involve herself in everything.

'Don't you have things to be getting on with, Dilys?' she says.

She doesn't look up. She doesn't invite me to sit down. She doesn't offer me tea.

'Run along,' she says. Octavia and I have matters to discuss.'

The Yellow Wallpaper

In light of the fact we have been expecting Christ to return for eight years you would imagine I would be used to waiting, but Sunday feels a long way off. Every time I look out of my window the hands of the chapel clock barely seem to have moved, and the interval between each hourly chime takes longer. Inside the clock tower, Octavia's bell, Little Ben, is inscribed with the prayer: *Holiness unto the Lord. Thy Kingdom come on Earth. Amen.* It rings out a reminder to overcome our sins before it's too late. It is counting down to the time that He will come; I'm counting down to the time Grace will.

Every day Octavia takes a broom and sweeps the demons out of the dining room, scooping them up with the crumbs and dead flies, and depositing them on the back step. The wind stirs up the dust and dances it away but the demons stay and watch through the glass. They must wait for their moment and steal back in, because every morning She is there again with Her brush. I have been busy tidying and polishing my little room to wipe away the thoughts that linger in the corners: visions that rise in my breath while I sleep, then settle on the surfaces, dreams trapped in the fringing on the pink lampshade or clinging to the mirror like a smear of grease.

My room is right at the back of the house, at the end of a landing which is painted green, sage green apparently and, according to Octavia, a completely different shade to the colour in the sitting room, though I have never been able to discern a difference. If I listen carefully I can hear when someone is coming; hear when they reach the top of the stairs. The creaks of the doors tell me whether they are going into Octavia's room, or Emily's, or the box room where Betty sleeps. If I hear shoes on the bare wood of a ladder I know it is Peter, climbing up to his windowless room in the attic. Jingling crockery always signals Betty's approach with some refreshment on a tray. I hear her pass the water closet and the bathroom in which the coffin-shaped tub sits, on past the doorway next to mine where Octavia's Chosen are invited to meet after chapel. And by the time she knocks I am always ready. Ready with a smile and a thank you. Ready to behave just as I am expected to.

It is exactly thirteen steps from the top of the stairs to my bedroom. Though when I walk along the landing myself I stride out to make it twelve. Sometimes for a change I'll squeeze in fourteen smaller steps. But not thirteen. Never thirteen.

Then there are the stairs, eleven of those, each covered in a deep red runner. The best I can do is touch my right foot on the top step twice. I know that doesn't make it even. Not really.

But wanting to believe can be enough. Sometimes it has to be.

Here at the back of the house the ceilings are low and the busy pattern on the wallpaper makes it feel as if the walls themselves are closing in. I have grown to hate the print: watercolour flowers bleeding into a yellow background like ink on blotting paper. It was Octavia's choice. She thought it would make me feel bright and cheerful but it has precisely the opposite effect. A corner has lifted next to the fireplace. I have the urge to peel it back a little more but I daren't touch it; if I started I might not be able to stop until I'd clawed the whole lot off the wall. The furniture was Her choice too: a wardrobe with cut-out patterns of flowerheads and an oak dressing table where I keep a photograph of Adrian in his army uniform. There's a chair in my favourite colour, purple, and a washstand set to match, with waterlilies painted around the rims. In some cultures, Octavia says, they are a symbol of growth, or rebirth. The bud emerges from the murky water and blooms towards the sky. I pray that I may do the same.

———

Work has ceased and the typesetters have put down their blocks, leaving sentences unfinished and rules unwritten. I have come to the Printing Room at the back of The Haven, to deliver an article, but all six workers are standing completely still, gathered around Octavia who is giving instructions. I hover in the doorway and decide to wait. It would not do to interrupt Her.

She is standing in front of the press: an ingenious device that looks for all the world as though it was made for our cause. It does not require brute force to operate so we ladies can turn the mechanism ourselves, and it is beautifully finished. *Practical and decorative: just as we all must be.* Dragons twist their way around the frame, and on the very top sits an eagle – a gold eagle – just like the lectern my father used to stand behind in church. Every time a page is printed the arm of the press lifts and the bird jumps up as though it is taking flight. Octavia says it symbolises the Truth being carried out into the world. And now that we have a Printing Room the little eagle is hardly ever still. We feed the machine blank sheets of paper and they emerge transformed. Well, the others feed it, I don't. Octavia doesn't trust me to concentrate. She thinks I will daydream. And She is probably right.

It's a task that requires you to be constantly alert or the Devil will twist Octavia's words, move the blocks or change the sense of the sentences, so that he can publish his lies. *But we all have our part to play, however small.* So I type up the articles Octavia writes, from scribbled notes, and I bring them to the Printing Room where they can be checked by someone that She trusts.

Muriel Gillett was an obvious choice to operate it; she worked in a printing shop before she retired and still wears the uniform of her employment – a heavy tawny workcoat that protects her dresses from the wet ink. She is assisted in the Printing Room by Elizabeth Broadbent, whom Octavia describes as sensible in all but her choice of hairstyle, which she wears coiled most unflatteringly in two buns behind her rather large ears. Both women wear their sleeves rolled up on their stout arms. Working the press is hard work, and not suited to someone of a delicate disposition.

Octavia is bending over the metal plate, squinting down at the rows of tiny letters that have been slotted into place.

'It won't do,' She says. 'I can't make it out. Have you no bigger font?'

'But this is the standard size,' says Muriel, apologetically.

'And just because the wider world decrees it satisfactory, must we concur?' She hits Her hand on the tabletop, causing the blocks to jump out of place. 'No. It won't do.'

Not everyone has been blessed with the opportunity to live here with Octavia, or hear Her Revelations in person, so we provide them with the next best thing: a monthly subscription of divine insight. She has called it *The Panacea*, and filled it with interesting articles: *How to Prepare for Jesus*, *How to Administer the Healing Water*, *Why Confession is Vital* and *How to Fight Demons*. But for Octavia the Devil is also in the detail.

Never allow the arm to rest on the table . . . In using pepper do not scatter it so it affects your neighbour . . . An 'excuse me' should always follow a sneeze . . . Creaking shoes should be apologised for and corrected as soon as possible . . .

No doubt I will inspire Her to write more rules before the next edition. I was certainly responsible for number nine:

Do not make sandwiches of your bread and butter.

And number fourteen:

There is no occasion on which it is correct to spread a handkerchief on the lap at tea.

This month She is preoccupied with a piece about Sir Jack, which I typed up this morning. That's what I have come to deliver. She wants the non-residents to know that he really is becoming rather clever. He has opened the front of the clock and turned the hands forward by ten minutes, or else he is enjoying a game of hide and seek under the rug. She is certain that he listens attentively to the wireless and is convinced that he will stand and read the *Radio Times*, though as far as I can see he is only interested in two articles: the two little wires that hold the pages together. He picked them out with his beak and caused the whole lot to fall apart, but Octavia just laughed. She hardly seems to care that he has ruined three pairs of my stockings, or knocked down the Staffordshire shepherdess on the sideboard. *He is God's messenger, so we can't begrudge him a bit of mischief.*

Octavia is standing watching Muriel who has cleared the metal plate and has begun again. I decide to bring the article back when She has gone. I could step in just a little and leave the papers on the side, but they may not find them, and besides, I need to tell them that Octavia wants a drawing of a little black bird above each title. She has trusted me to arrange this so I must not forget. I turn slowly back into the corridor and find myself face to face with Emily.

'Dilys. It is just as well that I have found you. You are obviously short of something useful to do – and we know what the Devil does with idle hands, don't we?'

I answer only with silence.

'I need you to type these notes without delay. Octavia asked me to draw up a list for those who seem to be struggling with Overcoming.'

We both know who she is talking about.

'We stayed up after you had gone to bed last night. This is a gentle reminder of what God expects and we want every member to have a copy.'

'Very well, I'll do it now.'

She nods with a smug look that makes me want to take out my pocketbook and make a note against her: *Emily, 2.05 p.m., self-satisfied*.

'Thank you, Dilys,' she says. 'Octavia and I decided you would be the best person to do it.' She means they think I need to be re-minded. When I glance down I see a list of failings, many of them my own.

'There's no place for personality in the Kingdom of God,' she says. 'We must all rid ourselves of the traits that cause discord in the community, or there will be consequences . . . whoever we are.'

ON OVERCOMING

Upon each & all Octavia lays the onus of helping with this great and grave work, by quickly remonstrating with offenders and pointing out their faults at once, instead of allowing the matter room to grow and develop.

Faults which members should confess in the process of Overcoming include:

Nervousness,	Any kind of Temper,
Sensitiveness,	Sulkiness,
Shyness,	Moroseness,
Fear,	Procrastination,
Selfishness,	Discontent,
Self-opinion,	Love of money,
Doubt,	Fear about money,
Jealousy,	Meanness,
Pride,	Extravagance,
Untruthfulness,	Untidiness,
Exaggeration,	Carelessness,
Criticism,	&c, &c.

The Box

It is Sunday at last. Grace will come. She'll be here any minute. I am waiting for her in chapel, turning in my seat to watch the door. Emily has offered to stay behind. 'The young lady, Miss Hardwick,' she said to Octavia at lunchtime, 'she will be joining us this evening. Would You like me to greet her? I'll bring her to the chapel while she still has her coat on. It will be cold out there tonight, I think.'

'Or I could . . .' I began to speak but a glance from Octavia told me there was no point.

'Yes, thank you, Emily,' She said.

Perhaps She didn't trust me to meet her at the door. Perhaps She thought I would get distracted. My mind has been so full of what this means, of what God's plans are for me, that I'm certain She was right.

The chapel door opens but it is not Grace. It is Edgar with his young protégé Donald Ricketts. I have seen them sometimes, taking a stroll around the Garden, but I have never seen Donald in chapel before. He is tall, his fair hair parted with immaculate care down the centre, and he wears a small moustache just like Adrian grew before he went to fight. As he steps into the room, he ushers in a sudden silence; all heads turn to look, all conversations halt.

'Good evening, ladies,' says Edgar brightly, lifting his cane in greeting.

'Miss Barltrop,' he says, walking across to my chair. 'I don't think you and Mr Ricketts have been formally introduced. He has come to stay for reading week. I shall need to be in my usual spot at the front this evening. But may Donald sit himself here beside you?'

'Of course,' I say, wishing I could think of a good reason why he shouldn't. But it is too late. He is already taking a seat.

'Marvellous,' says Edgar. 'Then I'll leave you to it.'

Mr Ricketts sits and pats his knees as though anxious for the service to start. The murmur of chatter begins to rise again but he is still the subject of appraising looks from every direction. It is unusual to see a visitor in chapel; rare to see a man in the Garden at all; unheard of to see one younger than fifty years old. I suppose he could be considered handsome too.

'It is an honour to meet you, Miss Barltrop,' he says, in a voice that's almost a whisper, 'to meet someone so close to Octavia.'

He leans in conspiratorially and suddenly I can think of a very good reason why he shouldn't be sitting beside me. I know what the others are thinking. Their appraising looks have turned to knowing glances. *He made a beeline for the youngest woman in the room.* The fact that he sat here on Edgar's suggestion will be brushed aside. They'll say I was an obvious target. Different. Very few of the ladies here have brown hair any more, and none wear it in a bob. It caused quite a stir when I first cut it short: *a style fit only for radicals and women with loose morals.* But when I told Octavia it came from Paris and was inspired by Joan of Arc, She came round to the idea. Then the others could no longer say what they thought. Not out loud anyway. Funny how you can take the same truth but dress it up differently. Besides, I'd already cut it off by then, and even Octavia can't make hair grow back overnight. It takes time and a good glassful of the Water twice a day. Emily, on the other hand, has never liked it. According to her I already stuck out like a sore thumb. I am tall and gangly. I take up too much space.

'I believe you work as a typist in the society,' Donald says, 'copying Octavia's notes.'

'Yes, that's right.' I look back at the door, willing him not to ask any more questions. I wouldn't want to give the impression that I was showing an interest in him. Octavia says men take very little encouragement. *Treat them with anything more than polite disdain and they can quite easily become inflamed with desire.* No woman is safe. Not even a woman like me.

'I hope to move here permanently when my course ends in the summer,' says Mr Ricketts. 'Though, of course, that decision doesn't rest with me.'

I do not answer, but he carries on regardless. 'There's a lot of debate about your society back in Cambridge. I wanted to make up my own mind, come and see for myself. And Edgar has explained so many things to me. So much that I could not make sense of . . .'

I risk another glance over my shoulder. 'Miss Barltrop, are you . . .'

Listening?

'. . . waiting for someone?' he says. 'A friend of yours?'

'Yes.' I speak without thinking whether that is the right answer. A friend. I hope she is. At least, I hope she will be. But she hasn't come. She should be here by now. 'Perhaps she isn't coming.'

It is not until he answers that I realise that I have spoken the words out loud.

Sitting so close to him I can see his hair has been styled with rather too much pomade. If I could, I would slip out of the chapel and go back to my room, but I can't. Everyone would notice. Everyone would talk.

'Let us sing while we wait for Octavia,' says a voice from the back. Emily walks down the aisle between the chairs. 'A rousing chorus or two should keep us all warm.' I swing round in my chair. And Grace is there. In the back row.

She has come. Just as she said she would. And she is smiling at me: that smile that makes me feel that God Himself has finally noticed I am here.

We stand. There is no organ or piano in our little chapel, so we wait for Emily to set the pitch, and as usual it is too high for most of us to reach.

And did those feet in ancient time . . .

Our voices join hers. Half of the congregation strains to reach the top notes; the others, like me, opt to dip a full octave below it, conflicting tones clamouring to find their place.

. . .Walk upon England's mountains green?

I can tell that Mr Ricketts is holding back. He sings quietly, almost apologetically, keen perhaps to avoid the attention that the full force of a baritone would attract. But as the hymn continues, his voice seems to grow out of him with a warmth that radiates into the thickening air. And our voices, which were reedy and uncertain, are bolstered by the power in his. I can feel the music in my body, vibrations filling up my chest. The same feeling I had when Grace came to visit. In the fleeting spaces between our words I hear the voice of God. And for the first time I feel like I am truly part of this. Like the congregation at the Bunyan Meeting Church, we need no hymn sheet, this is *our* battle cry. 'William Blake must have known the Truth,' Octavia always says. 'The Garden of Eden here in Bedford all along.'

> I will not cease from mental fight,
> Nor shall my sword sleep in my hand,
> Till we have built Jerusalem,
> In England's green and pleasant land.

As we sing the final line, Octavia arrives. She nods at Donald and perhaps I imagine it but I think She glances at me too. She looks tired tonight. And old. She has been in bed for much of the afternoon, one of Her headaches again. The role of saviour is not an easy cross to bear.

'Panaceans, I am being tested,' She says, taking Her place in front of the altar. 'Though I am ashamed to admit it, I have questioned my Father's love for me. Like Jesus in the wilderness, I have feared that I have been forsaken. I have railed against Him and begged Him to ease my suffering.'

I glance at Donald, who looks completely transfixed by Her. Sometimes I forget how impressive Octavia is. She has grown middle-aged and dumpy. Her face, which one might expect to have softened with the passing of time, has become more severe. But divine confidence and authority shine out of Her. Some would call it charisma I suppose. She wears self-belief like a priest's robe, and sometimes I almost think I can see it, gently swaying, diaphanous. God has clothed Her in His Holy Spirit and She enthrals us; we are in thrall.

'You know, dear children, that when you sin I am the one to suffer. When you put your own desires before the needs of the community, when you bicker and backbite, when you are loud and untidy and inconsiderate and common . . .' She puts a hand on the altar to steady Herself. 'Yet still . . . I must bear it. Tonight when I sat down to receive the Lord's Word He shared His plan with me. Through my pen He spelt it out.'

She looks to Emily who nods for Her to continue.

'We know His son was crucified in body, but in His Daughter's case . . . in *my* case . . .' She pauses and smooths Her skirt, '. . . it is my *soul* that is being crucified.' I wonder if this speaks of the difference between the sexes: She always says men are predisposed to be much more concerned with the flesh.

'Stigmata scar my thoughts. And I wear a crown of thorns not on my head but in my heart.' I imagine Octavia is enjoying the poetry of this analogy. 'And so I ask you again to work harder to rid yourselves of the faults that torture me. I say again: God needs you to be colourless, faultless, zero.'

There is muttering in the chapel as members start to voice their support. Promises of 'I will, Octavia' and 'if only the Lord would let us share Your burden'. The guilt is palpable and suddenly Octavia doesn't look so tired. She is fortified by our shame and guilt.

'You must all commit again to the Overcoming. And I am trusting every one of you to help our visitors do the same.' Her eyes find Donald in the congregation. 'Mr Ricketts has been writing to me for some time now. Some of you may have met him already. He has been a regular visitor to Bedford during the last few months. Tonight he is joining us for the first time in chapel.'

From the front row Edgar gives Donald a smile of encouragement, but Peter doesn't take his eyes from Octavia.

'And Miss Hardwick,' She says, directing Her attention to the back of the room. I join the rest of the congregation in turning to follow Her gaze, grateful for the opportunity to look around at Grace again. 'Would you be kind enough to stand so we can see you? Grace has come to learn more about our society. Dilys brought her to our door. I know you will all make her welcome.'

I can feel the room's attention turn to me and I can already tell that I have gone up in their estimation. Kate mouths the words 'well done' from the other side of the room. And from the row behind I hear Rachel Fox whispering to her neighbour: 'Octavia does not usually let visitors come to chapel, not since that newspaper reporter came up from London and misquoted Her so shamelessly.'

Octavia gestures for Grace to sit down again. 'Miss Hardwick, your presence provides an opportunity to remind our members what God expects of them.'

Taking her cue, Emily steps forward. 'Miss Hardwick, have you heard of Joanna Southcott?' Grace shakes her head. 'But you know, of course, that Octavia is the eighth in a line of English prophets the Lord has sent to guide us?' This time she doesn't wait for an answer. 'Joanna Southcott was the seventh. She died a hundred years ago, but before God took her to be with Him in Heaven, he told her she was with child just as Mary had been. Certainly a miracle because she was sixty-four years old!' I look across at Ellen Oliver: this is her story, she is the one who pieced it together. She should be the one telling it, not Emily.

'She was mocked by those who failed to see the truth, but as her stomach swelled her followers gathered and her doctors prepared for the birth – the birth of Shiloh, the birth of a messiah.' Emily sweeps her eyes across the chapel to make sure everybody is listening. Of course they are. She is getting to the best bit.

'When Joanna died they tried to get the baby out. A surgeon cut open her womb . . .' The gasp from the congregation is of pleasure, not shock. 'But inside they found her empty. A ghost baby: the Holy Ghost. The world would have to wait still longer for Shiloh to come.' Emily is pacing now, along the aisle between the chairs, towards Grace. 'Then, one hundred years later—'

'*Exactly* one hundred years,' Octavia interrupts. 'One hundred years to the day, Ellen Oliver came to realise that Shiloh had come. That *I* was Shiloh. The world had been waiting for a man to do the job, when all this time what it needed was a woman!' She laughs because the answer was obvious all along. 'Now it is up to us, ladies!' She raises Her hand, rousing the congregation into a small cheer. Then just as quickly there is silence and when Octavia starts to speak again we all strain forward to hear. It's almost a whisper. 'We are custodians of the Truth and, Miss Hardwick, guardians of a box, in which Joanna sealed the answer to healing the world. Prophecies that will set us free from suffering. Writings that will unlock secrets of the Lord Himself. Joanna knew that the time would come . . . that we would need to fight back against the Devil. And we are the army that God has chosen.' I always enjoy this idea: a line of hats, handbags swinging, infantry armed with white gloves and tortoiseshell haircombs going into battle.

'We are up against the arrogance of men. Miss Hardwick, God has given us the difficult task of persuading the bishops of the English Church to come here to Bedford. To convince them to open their minds and open the box.'

'In accordance with Joanna's instructions,' says Emily.

Octavia ignores her attempts to cut back in. 'And we shall do it. Soon they will come and we shall be ready to receive them. God has shown us that the time is drawing closer.'

We had thought the war would be an end to it, but Octavia says it was just the beginning. *Moral degeneration, turmoil, natural order being turned upon its head.* These are the signs that the millennium will begin.

'God decreed that we must prepare a house big enough for twenty-four bishops to stay in, when they come here to Bedford to open the box,' Octavia says. 'As you all know, we were able to buy Castleside, and I am very pleased to report that the renovations are almost complete. We thank Kate for her tireless efforts overseeing the building work and the purchase of furniture for the bishops' arrival. In the next few months I will be asking you to give all you can to make sure their stay with us is as comfortable as possible. Please start to give some thought to household goods – practical and ornamental – that you can donate.'

Edgar raises his hand. 'Octavia, I would be only too happy to co-ordinate the——'

'That will not be necessary.'

'I have lots of ideas——'

'I'm sure. But when it comes to decoration I think we need a woman's touch, and an English eye. Your nation is famous the world over for many things, Edgar, but good taste is not one of them.'

He goes to say more but thinks better of it.

'Besides,' She says, 'I have already decided that Dilys will oversee the finishing touches.'

It takes a moment for me to realise whose name She has said. I hear it whispered as a question from the rows behind. *Dilys? Surely She has made a mistake.* Edgar turns as if to look at me but it is Donald's eyes he finds. I know what they are thinking and they are probably right. I have never been in charge of anything before. I am not being-in-charge material. Octavia cannot see that, behind Her, Emily is greeting the announcement with a disapproving shake of her head.

'Dilys . . . Did you hear me?' Octavia asks, as though She is saying it for the umpteenth time. 'You have a lot of work to do.'

I nod quickly before She changes Her mind.

———

For those who have not yet seen the Truth, the details can be a little difficult to digest. Octavia knows that. She has read the letters from the ignorant and angry who have seen Her in the papers; though Emily says enough is enough and has taken to hiding them before She can see the words. *Blasphemer, harridan, deluded harpy*. Perhaps Octavia was testing Grace, to see whether she would run at the first opportunity. But here she is. She came and sat in the seat beside me. Donald wasted no time in vacating it straight after the service. Edgar appeared and said something about rushing off for their Bible study, but I think his haste had more to do with hurt pride. After all the hints he has been dropping to Octavia about Castleside, I think he felt sure that he would be chosen to finish furnishing it. But when he made that comment last week about 'dowdy English décor' I could tell Her mind was made up against him.

'Octavia is . . .' Grace makes a noise while she finds the words: not quite a sigh, not quite a laugh, ' . . . a woman standing and preaching like that – I've never seen anything like it. It's quite shocking – and marvellous!' Her wonder makes me feel ashamed. I've taken all this for granted. I didn't choose this life. It chose me. Perhaps that's the reason God has sent Grace: so I can see through her eyes, so I can see how lucky I am.

'When Octavia talked about being the Daughter of God, did She mean that we are all His children?' she says. 'It sounded more than that. Like She thinks . . .' She pauses. 'Dilys, do you believe She is His daughter just as Jesus is His son?'

This is where it could all unravel. This is where Grace might turn and run. The Truth can be difficult to swallow.

'The church of men believes in the Holy Trinity but we believe that God is fourfold,' I say. 'Father, Son, Holy Ghost and *Daughter*.'

'So is Octavia . . . Do you believe this is the Second Coming?'

'No. The Lord has sent Her to prepare the world for Christ's return. Only then will evil be defeated.'

'I see . . .' she says, looking down at her hands. But I'm not sure that she does.

'There is a lot to understand,' I say. 'It takes time.'

I wish she would say something, tell me what she is thinking.

'It is quite an honour for you to be here,' I say. 'Octavia doesn't usually . . .' I look up and see Ellen making her way across to us. I can't help feeling angry. The others crowded around Grace straight after the service with words of welcome and promises to share their favourite scone recipes. If Octavia has singled her out, then it's best they make a good impression, but their good impressions took a full half an hour to make.

'Welcome, Miss Hardwick.' Ellen offers her hand to Grace who shakes it with the tenderness of an old friend.

'Thank you. It's an honour to meet you.'

Ellen is not a vicar's wife or curate's daughter; in a past life she was a suffragette, sent to Holloway Prison for her crimes against femininity. When she became weary of the fight to infiltrate the world of men, she set her sights much higher: on the Kingdom of God Himself. But she still wears the starched strapped-neck collars, puffed sleeves and men's neckties of her youth. And she is still slim enough to fit them.

'Octavia said you were the one who realised,' Grace says, 'that She was . . .'

'Yes, it was quite a time,' Ellen replies. 'When we knew God's will was being done. And in Bedford! I am pleased that you are here. Welcome to the Garden. You have been given a chance to be part of the answer. Isn't it exciting?'

'It is,' Grace says, as if she is answering her own question. 'It really is.' And then she looks at me, her eyes searching mine for something. Is it confirmation?

Ellen lays her hand on my shoulder. 'I'll leave you young ladies to your conversation. I'm afraid it is time for me to head back home for an early night.'

'Goodnight, Ellen. Sleep well.' As she opens the door I see that night has closed in.

'It is getting late,' I say to Grace.

'Do you have to go too? It's just, there's so much I want to know. About what Octavia said. About the box. Have you ever seen it?'

'Me? No! I'm not sure that even Octavia has been told exactly where it is, but when the times comes She knows who to contact; the Southcottians have been keeping it safe since Joanna died.'

'And why do the bishops have to be the ones to open it? I'm sorry, do you mind all these questions?'

I should say, 'Ask away while you can, before Octavia comes to think you have heard all the answers you need, because after that asking questions will be forbidden.' Instead I say, 'I don't mind at all. They represent the twenty-four elders sitting around God's throne. Chapter Four, Book of Revelation. When they come we will know the time is right.'

'And in the meantime . . .?'

'We wait. We prepare for His arrival. We write to the bishops and we try to make them see the Truth. But that's not going to happen without pressure from the masses. Octavia and Emily are designing posters which we're going to put on billboards and buses all across London. They can't ignore us forever.'

'But if there's even a chance it really does contain the answer . . .' she says, her excitement obvious now.

'Then why wouldn't they open it?' I shrug. 'Stubbornness. Octavia says they do not appreciate being dictated to by a woman.'

A noise escapes from her throat: amusement, recognition.

'But what do you think is inside it?'

'All we know is that Joanna wrote instructions and sealed them in a chest. I don't know what they say. It is not our place to know, or to imagine. Only to trust. The box holds the answer that will free us from all this mess. No more pain, no more suffering.'

No more loneliness.

'But don't you wonder?' She falls silent for a moment. 'I suppose that's what faith is. Being part of all this. It must be like being wrapped up. In something warm and wonderful.' She turns to look at me but I keep staring forward. I don't know what to say; so I say what I am supposed to feel; what I have felt since I began to see the society through her eyes.

'It is.'

'I think it's something I'd like to be part of . . . If Octavia would allow it. She has been so welcoming. You all have.'

I turn to her and she is looking straight into my eyes. 'Do you think She would let me join?' she says.

'It usually takes time. She has to trust you. Some members have had revelations, knocked on the door and never left . . . Is that what this is? A revelation?'

'I don't know. I feel . . . something. I'm drawn to this place. I'm drawn to Octavia. When She spoke tonight it felt right. And sitting here with you . . .' Is that a blush? Warm and wonderful, just like she said – suddenly that's how it feels.

'She might. Sometimes Octavia just decides on a person and nothing can sway Her. Like Emily: she came to us as staff.'

'Emily – Mrs Goodwin – was a servant?'

'Of sorts. She didn't have the means to rent a room so she worked for us around the house.' Before she became too important to sully her hands with such things.

'So you think Octavia might consider it?'

'Perhaps.' I look towards the door. 'But are you sure? Leaving all that—'

'Out there?' She looks out across the Garden as if she can see straight through the wall and out to the street on the other side. 'There's nothing I'd miss. I have no family left. My job . . . well, it pays for my lodgings, but my manager, Mr Marshall, expects more from me. Because he pays my wages, he seems to think he owns me.'

'This is not a place to run away to.'

She swallows hard. 'I'm not running . . .'

'I know . . . But . . .Why don't we pray about it?'

We bow our heads and silently I plead with God to let her join us. Not for Him, or for Octavia, not even for Grace. I pray that He will let her join us for my sake.

TO THOSE DESIRING TO JOIN THE COMMUNITY:

You have expressed a wish to come and live with us in the Panacea Society, in Bedford. You must weigh carefully whether this is a divine drawing, or merely the result of your wanting to leave duties which you do not care about, or relatives with which you are not in sympathy, or to love of adventure or desire for change.

You are advised therefore to take seven days' consideration, asking to be shown clearly whether any of the above reasons are urging you, or whether it is a divine leading which justifies you in overcoming all obstacles in pursuance of your desire.

If a person has their own dress-money and is willing to do domestic work which will save us a servant's wages and relieve us of the need to have an outsider, they would have board-lodging free. No wages would be paid in this case.

THREE DIVINE COMMANDS

1. All living in Community must report faithfully anything in their own conduct which they judge to be provocative of discord among others.
2. They must be willing to be reported by others and to have no malice against them, nor to misjudge them in the performance of this duty.

3. Also, they must report others who fall short of the standard which they know will be required of them as citizens of the New Jerusalem.

Let it be clearly understood that none of the Rules and Regulations operating here are matters for you to have any opinions on. On our part, we shall understand that, by deciding to come here, you agree to all the forgoing and that you will submit completely.

SPRING

The simple facts are that God requires a few sensible, matter-of-fact women to take on the housekeeping on Earth, and to begin to give their orders, by word of mouth and on his behalf, until the defeat of Satan and the Divine Jurisdiction begins.

Octavia

Wash Day

Grace wakes me with a knock on my bedroom door. She has brought a bowl of hot water, as usual, but I ask her to leave it outside the door. I don't want to see her, or rather I do not want her to see me. Not until I am presentable; able to be present. Not until I have pieced myself together, washed away the dreams of the night before, brushed my hair, dressed my body to give myself the appearance of being in control. We spend so much time trying to tame our bodies, we make them look neat and obedient, but beneath our disguises they are still wild. They still bleed. And so I wash away the smells of earth and brine, the cloying sweetness of rotting fruit: Eve's apple.

Grace is our servant now. She joined us every Sunday in chapel and after six weeks Octavia asked her to stay. I didn't interfere or make her case, I only hinted that it might be time for us to find some help for Ellen. But Octavia had a better idea. 'Ellen won't have the energy to train her,' She said. 'Better that Betty goes to Ellen and Grace moves in here.' I knew, without a doubt, that the Lord's hand was at work again. Octavia said it was surely part of a divine plan. It was only later that it occurred to me that with a follower in post, She will also be saving eight shillings and tuppence a week on wages.

That was a week ago. It feels like longer. When Grace first moved in, I worried that some of our familiarity had gone. It bolted away like a dog into the woods and, though I tried to call it back, I feared it was lost. For days I'd hardly see her at all; when I poked my head into the kitchen I'd usually find her with Emily, being instructed on *the way Octavia likes things done*. At mealtimes when she carried in the plates I would ask Grace whether she was well, whether she had settled into her bedroom, whether it was starting to feel like home. With the others present all she could say was, 'Yes, thank you, miss,' before rushing out to start her next chore. But she would always pause, just long enough, to find my eyes and give a look that only I could see.

I don't have long before she will knock again. In the mirror above my washstand I style my hair. I like unravelling the strips of cloth I tie each night; ribbons of brown spring out and bounce, jostling for space in line beneath my jaw. But I'm careful never to glance at my face. It reminds me who I am. I see the ghost of my father's eyes: sensitive, too sensitive. They are not quite hazel, not quite green, not quite sure what they want to be. If I looked at my reflection I would see the same nose that grew out of my brother Eric's face when he changed from a boy into a man, before he went to war and never came back. It would remind me that I am here and they are not. And of course whenever I look I see my mother staring back at me.

Another knock.

'I have your breakfast tray.'

Grace again. Half an hour has passed.

'May I come in, miss?'

Sometimes when we are alone she calls me Dilys. It is our secret: an invisible thread that runs along the landing between our bedrooms. Past Octavia's door, past Emily's. I enjoy the thought of dear Emily tripping on it and falling down the stairs, hair streaming down behind her, the sharp knocks of bone against the walls, the stairs, the bannister.

But that's the Devil, he whispers still. I must not give him a foot-hold, or I shall be the one falling. Down to Hell.

'Did you sleep?' I ask. It has become a ritual. I greet her with the same question every morning, and she always gives the same answer in return.

'Like a top!'

It's a saying that always seemed wrong to me. Spinning tops are frantic, they twirl, they turn. But Grace told me that's the joke of it: look at them from above and they seem to be completely still. The faster they spin the more firmly they are pinned to the spot. It is when they lose momentum that they falter.

'And how did *you* sleep, Dilys?' she says.

'Like the dead.' I always say this too, though it is very rarely true. I try to sleep but thoughts knock me in too many directions, dreams veer too violently from one story to the next, until I topple back into consciousness.

'Is Octavia unwell?' I ask her. 'One of Her headaches?' I know there's something wrong or She would be insisting that we gather at the dining table this morning as usual.

'She couldn't face breakfast,' she says. 'Emily came down early and asked to take hers in Her room so Peter is down there by himself.' She places a tray onto my bedside table then looks up at me, mischievously. 'Would you rather join him? I assumed you would prefer it up here but I can—'

'No, no. I wouldn't want to trouble you!' I interrupt her with a grin. 'Up here is fine. It looks delicious. Thank you.'

Breakfast this morning is eggs. Octavia says there are fifty-two ways to prepare them – one of Her sermons in chapel, perhaps. Devilled eggs are one of Her favourites, despite their name, but this morning they are poached, sprouting pale roots where they swirled in the boiling water. I'll cut them up and move them around my plate, I'll eat the toast, but that's the best I can do. When Betty was here I wouldn't even bother to pretend, but when Grace prepares breakfast it feels like a gift and I don't want to seem ungrateful; throw the present aside without even taking the paper off.

I sit down on the bed and pat the space beside me.

'I don't have long,' she says, taking a seat. 'Before I forget, I found this. It's for you.' She reaches into the pocket of her apron, pulling out a letter, bringing it close to her chest to hide the writing from me. 'Wait until you see the postmark. You'll never guess . . .'

I don't need to guess. I know precisely where it has come from. And who.

Grace holds the envelope in both hands, turning it as though she can see through the paper to what is written inside. I want to snatch it from her and hide it away in the box inside my wardrobe. Where I don't have to think about it. Where I don't have to think about *him*.

'It's from India,' she says, as though she is sharing a joke. I can tell she is expecting surprise or delight, but I offer neither, extending only an open hand as a silent command: it is mine, give it to me.

She obeys.

'Dilys, what's the matter?'

As if I could tell her that. As if I could begin to explain.

She stands, walks to the window and busies herself opening the curtains. 'I wasn't prying. I really did find it. At the foot of the stairs.' She pauses but I say nothing to fill the silence. 'Emily must have dropped it. She carried up the usual bundle of letters to go through while she took breakfast. Octavia receives an awful lot of mail, doesn't She?'

Octavia does. But there is only one person who writes to me.

Grace is still talking; still arranging the folds of the drapes; still trying to get me to speak. 'I suppose with two thousand followers she would . . .'

I must say something in reply. Pretend that I am all right.

'Not all of Octavia's letters are sent by followers,' I explain. 'Half are from non-believers. They write to tell Her She is a wicked blasphemer, an affront to the Church. Octavia says they are crackpots. And as the Bible says: *Blessed are ye, when men shall revile you.*'

We mustn't listen to those who refuse to see the Truth. Even those we love.

They have made their choice.

'Grace,' I whisper.

I want to tell her she has done nothing wrong. It is not her I am upset with. It is the letter.

'Grace.' For a moment she does not move, her fingers falling still on the pleats of the fabric, her eyes darting to the envelope, now curled and crushed inside my hand.

'Thank you for finding it,' I say, opening the drawer of my bedside cabinet and slipping it inside. 'It is much appreciated. I'll read it later.' The drawer sticks as I push it shut, then suddenly slams, causing the cabinet to wobble, and a little water to splash out of a glass on top.

'Careful, Dilys,' says Grace, stepping forward with a cloth she conjures from another pocket in her apron.

'I'm sorry . . .'

'I should think so. I've got enough to do today without you making extra work!'

I think I hear a smile on her lips and when I look up I see it there, broadening into a grin. I let out a breath, realising I have been holding it. 'What can I say? I don't know my own strength,' I shrug. 'You're right, though – you'll be quite behind at the rate you're going. Those curtains . . .' I nod towards the window. 'I've never known you to be so thorough! Has Emily been giving you instructions on the correct way to open them? Another of her tutorials perhaps?'

'Now, Dilys,' she says, with affected solemnity, 'you know as well as I do that I have to learn the proper ways, and Emily is happy to teach me.'

'All right, all right,' I say, lifting my hands in surrender.

'Yesterday I nearly served the baked potatoes cut in half instead of scoring them with crosses on the top. Goodness knows what Octavia would have said if Emily hadn't stopped me in time.' The frown she has been wearing to entertain me softens. She drops her gaze, her expression suddenly earnest. 'I want to stay,' she says softly. 'There's so much to do. It is exhausting.'

'I know, I'm sorry.' Now I am the solemn one. 'Forgive me?'

Meeting my eyes again she starts to laugh. 'Goodness, what has become of me, Dilys? I never used to worry about baked potatoes! I just want to get everything right, that's all. Emily *is* helping.'

Emily has what most people would call a kindly face, one might even imagine she was pretty once, in her youth, but not me. I can see through her act of cheerful concern. I am not fooled. Everything she does is for show; every word, every act, an attempt to win Octavia's favour. I was here at the beginning, when Octavia was still called Mabel. Emily came later. She came with nothing and persuaded Her to take her in: into Her home and into Her confidence. And now, every time I walk into a room, she is there, whispering to Octavia, pouring spirits in Her ear like Lady Macbeth or poison like Claudius.

'Well,' Grace says, 'I suppose I had better get on. Emily will have finished her breakfast by now. And poor old Peter is all by himself. I will go and ask him about his plans for the day. I keep trying but I get the impression he doesn't like me.'

'Surely that could never be. He's rather suspicious of newcomers, that's all. Protective of Octavia.'

'You're probably right,' she says. 'And now I shall be protective of you. Eat up. That's an order. Your breakfast will be stone cold if you leave it much longer.'

It is stone cold already. Once she has gone I take a few bites of toast but it's all I can manage. All I really need is spiritual sustenance. I take a square of linen from my bedside drawer and put it into a glass to soak. It takes a few minutes for the healing to infuse the water. I think of it like tea-leaves releasing clouds of amber into the pot, tendrils growing out towards the edges of the glass, but there's nothing to see. Nothing but breath. At first Octavia had to work on each pint of water to transfer Her divinity, but now She's found an ingenious method of storage and supply. She breathes on fabric so that the healing can be dispensed whenever and wherever it's required: God's grace in a glass. She's nothing if not practical.

That's why it's up to women to save mankind; men just can't get themselves organised. *Too busy waging war or trying to beat each other at cricket.* I drink the Water twice a day, more if Octavia thinks I need it. It helps me to think less and believe more; it helps me to drown out the Devil when he whispers in my ear. And to drown out the words I know I will find in Adrian's letter: *This religion is all wrong. It will make you ill if you stay. Write back and let me know that you are safe.*

But I won't.

I will sit and drink the Water instead.

I can hear Grace back in the kitchen below me. Today is Monday: washday. It means she'll be gathering the soap and soda, scrubbing my sheets against the ridges of the washboard. Sometimes I stand and watch her from the kitchen doorway, sleeves pushed up her arms, muscle and sinew moving beneath her skin. She shows me how she prepares the starch for the tablecloths. The recipe has to be followed exactly, grains added first to cold water then to hot. She must stir thoroughly and keep constant watch, otherwise it will thicken and go lumpy. But I won't visit her in the kitchen this morning. I have work to do, Octavia's words to type. So I will sit here at my little desk by the window and watch the sheets blowing on the washing line: puppets with invisible strings. *Leaping and dancing before the Lord* (2 Samuel 6:16). If only our souls could be cleansed so easily.

The Lord will not come to us until we are pure. That is why Grace is here. That is why God sent her to me. To keep constant watch on my soul.

Later, when I return from chapel, I will find a clean nightdress under my pillow. I will take off these clothes, savour a moment of anticipation, before I slip it on and feel it brush against my skin: a shroud of purity, spotless and clean. And by then I will have left a gift under her pillow in return. The Lord's words:

Wash me, and I shall be whiter than snow.

(Psalm 51:7)

Castleside

Grace hands me an apple for my first morning at Castleside as I pass the kitchen door. When she calls me Miss it is no longer a sign of distance, it feels like she is drawing me closer, like she is whispering a joke. I know my lines and the part I must play.

'Now, Grace. What did I tell you? You needn't call me Miss. After all, we are friends, aren't we?'

'We are, *Miss* Dilys.' And I realise this is what friendship feels like: knowing what to say, or being happy to say nothing at all.

Her eyes dart to something behind me. 'Good morning, Mrs Goodwin.'

I turn to see Emily approaching. 'What are you two whispering about?' she says. 'Dilys, I hope you are not distracting Grace. So much to do. And shouldn't you be at Castleside by now?'

I choose not to answer. I carry on speaking as if she is not there. 'Thank you for my apple, Grace. I'll enjoy that.' Emily gives a strange little laugh, which ends abruptly: snatched by the silence that sweeps the room. It makes me feel exposed. No one speaks, but in the blazing silence I can hear their thoughts about me. They know the apple won't get eaten.

'I had better be getting on,' I say, stepping past Emily into the corridor. Emily always says it will do me good to keep busy, that it will take my mind off things. It might be better if I could take my mind away completely, separate brain from body. *Dawdling Dilys, you'd forget your own head if it wasn't screwed on.* But I'm not as useless as they thought. I've brought Grace to the society, and Octavia has put Her trust in me. She really does want me to prepare Castleside for the bishops.

'Just the finishing touches now,' Emily says. 'Remember, the hard work has already been done.' Kate Firth has seen to that. Twenty-eight rooms, cleaned and decorated; floors varnished, walls painted, furniture moved in. She was given two tasks: to co-ordinate the renovation, and to sign all the cheques to pay for the work.

But as Octavia said, she could afford it.

And as Emily said, she couldn't afford not to.

The Lord won't look kindly on those who are not willing to share their blessings, and when it came to raising the funds to buy the property, every member played their part and paid their dues. All were compelled to donate a proportion of their savings. And God was grateful for it. He told Octavia so Himself. 'Finally we'll have a place to accommodate the bishops in comfort,' She said. 'They can have no excuse to stay away now.'

The Garden was ours at last. For years Castleside cast a hulking shadow over the society. Octavia told us its bricks and mortar were imbued with a malevolent spirit, a devil blighting God's Paradise. She would hear its voice tormenting Her over the wall, but all I heard was joy, and freedom: schoolboys studying the skills that are required of them as men, swearing and wicket-keeping, fist-fights and cruelty. I doubt that any consideration was given to matters of religion at all. We had ceased to be a source of curiosity. There was a time when they would dare each other to jump the wall that lay between the back of the school and our Garden, pretending they sought to retrieve a ball that had strayed over, but Octavia put a stop to that. A note sent to the master of the boarders nipped it in the bud. The cane makes a persuasive case and, when it comes to it, a good thrashing is too high a price to pay for a glimpse of most of us. Too old. Too plain. Except Grace. They'd probably have risked it for Grace.

The day came when we gathered to knock down the wall. Peter lifted the bricks out one by one; he'd given up with the sledgehammer. Despite the considerable effort it took him to swing it, he achieved little more than a glancing blow; enough to knock him backwards but insufficient to loosen even the smallest piece of mortar. Octavia dressed up for the occasion in Her veiled hat and fox stole. Since She has been confined to the Garden, She has few opportunities to dust off Her finest clothes. Quoting from Ephesians: '*For he is our peace, who hath made both one, and hath broken down the middle wall of partition between us,*' I think she envisioned the whole lot would come tumbling down like the walls of Jericho. Perhaps if Peter had been given a trumpet, we could have charged through like the Israelites. As it was, he was chipping away with a chisel, refusing Edgar's offers to help. It was Emily who rescued him from the embarrassment of an audience. 'Thank you, Peter,' she said, stepping forward after several minutes had passed. 'You have removed that first brick with such great care. It will be wrapped and kept in the archive as an artefact of this great day. Now, you'll excuse us if we head inside and leave you to your work. I'll send out some refreshments presently.'

He ended up taking lunch and dinner outside. It took all day but the wall came down and the Garden was doubled in size. Octavia insisted, before the workmen were sent into Castleside, that Peter should fence off the very back of the building with a hoarding of high wooden sheets. She said it was necessary to protect our modesty: She didn't want them to be able to see us, or perhaps She didn't want *us* to see *them*. Temptation would come once more to the Garden of Eden and lead to a surge of sinful thoughts. They might unbutton the tops of their shirts, cotton clinging to the sweat on their chests and backs. They would dig the earth and carry piles of bricks as if they weighed nothing at all. Men can do that. They could carry any one of us away to a secluded spot, and we'd be powerless to resist. Besides, the language of men like that would be coarser than the schoolboys'. Coarse like their skin; fingertips rough and unyielding.

All these are thoughts that I can talk about in my next confession.

—

The hallway of Number 12 is dark. Two shafts of sunlight skulk through glass panels in the front door, but seem to lose their nerve in the gloom, disappearing into the folds of coats that hang on hooks behind the door. Even when I open the door, the light trespasses no further than the doormat, but I feel its warmth on my face as I take a breath. The air tastes golden.

At the bottom of the path I turn left past Rachel Fox's front door, then left again into Castle Road, tracing the boundary of the Garden in the streets that surround it. On this side there are very few windows. Walking tucked in beside the wall, I am hidden from their prying eyes and pocketbooks. I count my steps as I always do. When I get to seventy-seven I know I am beyond Octavia's reach. It's eighty-one to the driveway of Castleside but once the renovations are finished She'll be able to come and go as She pleases through the Garden. It's just as well because when the time comes, She'll have to be here to direct the bishops. She's already picked out a hat and which Bible She will read from, and She's got a beautiful shawl that Ellen made for Her with lilies and a cross on the back. She has rehearsed every detail in Her head:

who will stand where, what She will say, exactly where the box will be positioned. She speaks about little else these days.

I turn left again into Newnham Road and immediately through the gate of The Haven to knock for Kate Firth. She said she would show me around Castleside herself. I like the way she says it: castle with a 'ca' not a 'car'. But Octavia thinks a northern accent sounds common, no matter how wealthy the speaker is.

'Kate, are you sure you've got time?' I ask her as she opens her front door.

'Absolutely,' she says. 'It's a pleasure to get out for a while, just let me get my coat.'

Last year Octavia decided The Haven was far too big for a widow to be rattling around in by herself. *Far better that Kate has some company.* So She asked her to take in new members while they sought more permanent lodgings in Bedford.

'How many are staying at the moment?' I say, when Kate returns wearing a black velvet cape with a dusting of tiny glass beads on the collar.

'Eight. It's a pity we can't move a few into Castleside.' But we both know Octavia would never allow it. We may need to receive the bishops at a minute's notice; it would be no good if they arrived to find they were sharing with a houseful of women.

I look past her, down the hallway towards the source of muddled sounds I can't quite decipher. 'They are busy rehearsing,' she says. 'The Blue Room has been taken over for practice. Octavia has asked them to put on a musical evening and they are keen to make sure they are pitch perfect. Mrs Ashcroft is a rather talented pianist so my services won't be required.' She turns to the mirror in the hallway, using her fingertips to comb the wave of greying hair that sweeps up into a soft pile on top. 'Do you play, Dilys? I can't re-member ever seeing you perform.'

That is because I am never asked to.

'I play a little,' I say. 'Very poorly.'

'Well, we can't all be good at everything,' she says kindly. 'Here, you'll need these.' She takes a large bunch of keys from the console table below the mirror and places them in my hand, paus-ing before her fingers part with them.

'They are yours now,' she says. We walk down the path from The Haven and up the next to Castleside, which looms ahead of us. It looks like it has grown up from the ground in red brick. A jumble of different styles of windows on three storeys: some are bay, some hooded; some clustered in pairs or threes; large rectangular panes and small square grids of glass. The lack of symmetry only serves to emphasise the building's size, dwarfing a small white wooden porch which sits atop the front door.

'The big one – that's the front key,' Kate says. 'But you'll be able to come through the back now the hoarding's coming down. Peter's been asked to do it tomorrow.'

'That's good,' I say. But I'm disappointed that I'll no longer have an excuse to walk the streets outside the Garden.

Castleside is even bigger than it looks from the outside, a hallway twice as wide as that of Number 12, with large rooms leading off both sides. 'Let's start in here,' Kate says. 'The dining room. We decided it best to serve meals in two sittings. Twenty-four would be too crowded, even in a room this size.' A large mahogany table runs down the centre of the room, surrounded by twelve chairs. There's an assortment of crockery on the top.

'Members have started to bring donations already,' Kate says.

'But odds and ends are no good. You'll need matching sets. Octavia was very firm on that point.'

I walk across and pick up a side plate which is stacked on top of a dozen or so more. Garlands of green leaves and white flowers decorate the edges.

'Don't look so worried, Dilys. There's a full inventory of what we'll need in there,' Kate says, pointing at a desk in the bay window at the front of the room. 'Oh, and while I think of it, the keys are in the top drawer. The only other set, so keep them safe.'

Back out in the hallway she points out the encaustic floor tiles, matched with such precision that it is impossible to tell which are new and which were there all along. She explains how the plasterer made a mould of the egg and dart cornice to repair the damage in the corner. 'The wallpaper here was unsalvageable, I'm afraid. A pity – it was a beautiful print. Exotic birds. Reminded me of a paper we had back in York, before the war.'

She points to a door on the other side of the hallway.

'That will be a sitting room,' she says, 'same size as the dining room. And if you follow me I'll show you the scullery and kitchen.' I'm starting to panic now, there's an awful lot of space to fill. Why has Octavia trusted me with this? It all looks so empty. No pots or pans. No lingering smell of warm bread or old grease.

We pass a door to the garden and carry on to a room at the very back of the house.

'And this is it!' she says. 'The Opening Room where the bishops will gather to open the box. May I?'

Taking back the bunch of keys, she finds the right one instantly: a single flash of golden brass among the tarnished iron. Behind the door is a small room, no bigger than Grace's bedroom at Number 12.

'What do you think?' she says, evidently enjoying my bewilder-ment.

'It's smaller than I imagined.'

'Yes, this is the ante-chamber,' she says, amused by her own joke. 'The box room if you like! The opening will take place in here . . .'

She opens another door. The sight of the second room is made even more dramatic by its contrast with the first. It must be four times the size of our dining room at Number 1 2, with a high ceiling and oak panels lining every wall.

'I'm rather proud of it,' Kate says. And she is right to be; it creates a sense of occasion. Important things happen in oak-panelled rooms: the Houses of Parliament, church vestries, gentlemen's clubs. Places where promises are made and deals struck. Places for men.

'So here is where it will happen,' I say, more to myself than to Kate. When the lid is lifted, will light pour out and fill the room or music fill our ears like a heavenly choir? Will the earth shake or the heavens tear apart? None of us knows, not even Octavia. But in that moment everything will change. All suffering will end.

'I'm told the box is the size of a large boarder's trunk,' Kate says, 'which is rather apt considering that it will be opened here.' Here where the schoolboys ate and slept, studied and played. We make our way upstairs and, buried beneath the scent of fresh paint, lies the faint memory of another: a mixture of unwashed laundry and expectation.

'After you,' Kate says. 'There are twenty bedrooms, so the majority of the bishops will have their own. Eight of them will have to double up, but we shan't risk them fighting it out among themselves. Octavia will draw up a list of who goes where. And there's a bathroom and lavatory on every floor.'

'I see,' I say. But I don't see. Not really. I don't see how I am going to fill all these rooms with ornaments and furnishings.

'It's all been planned out,' Kate says kindly. 'It's just a question of adding the finishing touches, making it look homely – just like you would a home of your own.' But as soon as the words leave her lips she regrets them. We both know I'll never have my own home to decorate.

Kate turns towards the door. 'I'll leave you now to get your bearings,' she says.

I wait until I hear the front door behind her, then I move across the room, walking slowly at first, then stretching my legs to a stride. With each step, I place my foot down harder, louder, enjoying the click of my heels against floorboards. I clap my hands together, I whistle, I feel myself growing into this space, echoes filling every corner. There is nobody watching me here.

How did this room look when it was a dormitory? Full of books, blazers hanging on the hooks behind the doors. I open the cupboards, hoping to find an artefact left behind but all that remains is a crude picture scratched into the wood: a body part, a male organ. Detached, dismembered. It looks so small and so childish; a schoolboy's defiance; a risk taken; a rule broken. I shut the door again, and hide it away. I shall leave it in the dark. I like the thought of it, the thought that only I will know it's there.

Exploring each room in turn, I find every one identical: bare walls and floorboards, curtainless windows and undressed beds. And a thought scuttles across my skin: they look like cells for lunatics, the whole place a madhouse from which the patients have fled. There's a heaviness in the air. At the very top of the house I step into a room with the feeling that someone else has just left it. Unlike the rest, its door has been left ajar. And it looks as though the mattress has been slept on: it is dipping in the middle, holding the imprint of a body that it has cradled. I touch it, half expecting to find it still warm, but it isn't. Of course it isn't.

Pull yourself together, Dilys.

My mind is running wild with childish stories. As if I am Goldilocks and will be faced, at any moment, with a family of angry bears. But the only thing to fear is Octavia's poor opinion. I really need to concentrate on the job at hand, but starting back down the stairs, I pick up my pace to a run. I can feel my fears lingering in the room behind me. I trip on my own feet. I must take care. Slow down. At the sight of the red carpet on the treads I picture myself lying at the bottom.

Just as I have imagined Emily.

Relief comes swiftly when my feet reach the tiles of the hallway. Back on solid ground. The same giddy joy I used to feel when I played chase with my brothers in Bedford Park. *Tiggy tiggy touch wood!* I squeeze the bannister beneath my hand and remember the terror and the thrill, the dash across the open grass, the exhilaration when I made it to a fence post or a bench and I was safe. Untouchable.

Touch wood, Dilys. Touch wood and hope for the best.

There is still the sitting room to see. I push the door gently and peek inside. There is nothing more than an empty sideboard, dark wood against walls freshly painted in a deep maroon. This is where the bishops will sit after their evening meal. We'll need chairs. Lots of them. Twelve at least so they can use the room in turns. I'll arrange them in small groups around the fire and in the corners. I'll find side-tables and place piles of books on top; perhaps a vase or two, though I'm not sure men care for cut flowers. With a roaring fire it will be quite cosy.

Off the hallway, past the kitchen, I find another door, which Kate did not pause to show me before. When I open it I'm greeted with a cold blast of air and a darkness that my eyes were not prepared for. It's a pantry, long and thin; the light from a single window like the mouth of a tunnel. I walk along the empty shelves on either side, listing in my head the foods we'll need to store: tinned meats and peaches, canisters of flour and sugar; enough to feed the bishops for as long as they decide to stay.

There's a crunch beneath my shoes. Flashes of brilliant light dancing at my feet. I reach down to catch them and something bites me. There's blood on my hand. Glass. Shattered glass. Wide blades and needle-thin shards glinting up from the floor. That's why it is so cold: a small pane in the window has been smashed. And the catch is open. Someone could have reached in and opened it, climbed through.

Too many thoughts crowd at once: the whens and wheres and whos. Why would they break in? There's nothing to steal here, nothing to take; except what they could take from me. Octavia has told me what men can do, what the wall protects me from. She has never shied away from the facts of life or the Sex Question and why the answer must always be 'no'. Someone could have broken in; someone could be here still. Hiding behind a door or beneath a bed.

Pull yourself together, Dilys.

Those childish thoughts again. The window may have been broken weeks ago. Yes, there's no one here but me. Just me. And nothing will hurt me. Octavia blessed this house Herself, before the hoarding went up. She crossed the lawn and sprinkled the Water on the boundary of every room; breathed Her divine protection into every corner.

Nothing can hurt me here.

I've done all I can today. Seen all I came to see. I run for the front door and lock it behind me, my right hand still bleeding, my left pitted with marks where I've been gripping the keys too tightly.

Healing by Post

I want to head straight up to my bedroom, but as soon as I step into Number 12 Grace appears in the hallway. 'You're bleeding,' she says, rushing forward to inspect my fingers.

'It's nothing really. I cut it on some glass.'

Despite my protests, she insists that I take a seat in the kitchen. 'What happened?' she says, placing a bowl of warm water on the table beside me.

'There was a smashed window at Castleside, in the pantry.'

'Dilys, your hands are shaking—'

'It gave me quite a fright,' I say, more defensively than I mean to.

'I'll bet. Perhaps one of the workmen knocked the glass.'

'Perhaps.'

She frowns as she leans in to inspect the cut more closely. 'You don't sound convinced.'

'I did wonder if someone had broken in.'

'A burglar?'

'I suppose so. But there's nothing to steal. Not yet.'

'I wonder what Octavia will make of it . . .'

There's a moment of silence and then I say it: 'I don't plan to mention it to Her.'

I don't want to go running for help on my first day at Castleside. I can already hear Emily: *I knew she wasn't up to it. Would you like me to take over, Octavia?* No, I won't give her the satisfaction. Octavia put me in charge, I won't let Her down.

'But aren't we supposed to tell everything?' Grace asks.

'I'll mention it to Kate. I'm sure it was an accident. She can ask the workmen to pop back and replace the pane.'

'You're probably right,' she says, but now she's the one that doesn't sound convinced. She has wrapped her fingers around mine, cradling them, and I am watching the bowl of water turn pink, clouds of blood spiralling like paint from an artist's brush. I always think of Grace in colours: the purest white to paint her skin, fine brushes dipped into every shade of gold, brown and red for every strand of hair. I imagine God squeezing a line of emerald paste onto His palette, then changing His mind. Green eyes would be too obvious, and so He chooses chestnut brown instead, dark enough to make her skin look even paler and ignite her hair to flames.

'It's for the best,' I say. 'Octavia doesn't need to be bothered with every detail.' She looks up and smiles at me. It's a smile that says, I won't tell, a smile that shows me we have crossed a line, made a pact.

'So, what shall I do with this?' she says, holding out a square of the healing linen, which Octavia has breathed Her blessing on. She insisted on going to fetch it from my bedroom.

'Don't worry, I'll be fine. The bleeding's nearly stopped.'

'Dilys – for goodness' sake!' she says, rolling her eyes playfully. 'You are not very good at letting people look after you.'

I could tell her it is because I haven't had much practice. But I don't.

'Soak the linen first and you can apply it directly to the cut,' I say. She hasn't received her daily ration of the healing water yet. Octavia will present her with a square of linen and a wax seal of protection when she takes her vows to Christ. She likes to keep something back: a wedding present I suppose.

Grace fills a second bowl of water and dips the linen in. 'Like this?'

'Leave it a little longer. It takes time.'

'It's just it looks so . . . ordinary.' For a fleeting moment I see her eyes widen, as though surprised that she has said the words out loud. 'Does it really work?' she says, lowering her voice. We both know that it is blasphemous to question it. And saying something in a whisper does not make it any less dangerous; if anything it's more, because the other person has to lean in close to hear it.

'Dilys . . .?'

I realise I haven't answered her. I cannot tell her that the Water is my salvation, that it is the only thing that keeps me sane; allows me to think straight; quietens the Devil's words. So instead I say, 'I find it calms my spirits. We know it is a cure-all, a panacea.'

'The Panacea Society!' she says. 'To cure all ills.'

'Have you only just realised?' I say, with a laugh.

She stands up and takes the bowl of ruddy water to the sink. Just when I feel close to Grace I spoil it. I say the wrong thing or in the wrong way.

'I thought the name came from the box – the prophecies to heal all suffering . . .' she says. 'I know I have a lot to learn.'

I can feel distance opening up between us.

'Then that's my fault,' I say. 'I should be teaching you about the ministry. How about tomorrow morning? Octavia has asked me to cut the linen. You could bring me some lunch in the Cutting Room . . . If that's all right. If you want to . . . If you are not too busy.'

She holds my gaze and I know she has come back to me.

'I'll have to get permission from Octavia,' I say.

'Of course.' And then she takes my hand and pats it dry again.

Spring is on its way. The Garden is full of new life and optimism, nature nourished by the decay of last year's blooms and rising again, reborn; a botanical interpretation of the Bible. How different it must look since God first created it; since Adam stood and named all the living creatures. I imagine the verdant ferns, the scent of warm rain and teeming life, vines twisting beneath a canopy of leaves in every shade of green, animals with sharp teeth and poisoned fangs. Paradise was dangerous: a place with too many dark corners for the guilty to hide. But it's much more practical as it is today, with open lawns and manicured flowerbeds. Here we shall walk alongside Christ when He returns to us. Though I'm not sure what I'll say to Him. I expect Octavia will do the talking.

It feels good to be outside. Emily is always telling me what will do me good: a good walk, a good meal. She never says a good hiding but I expect that's what she is thinking. *Pain is a good teacher.* That's why God punished us with the horrors of childbirth, though old maids are spared that torture. Or is it joy?

Yggdrasil wears the delicate lace of new leaves; narcissi and crocus crowd into the empty spaces between box hedges. I almost imagine I hear the green shoots tearing up through the soil by my feet, but it is Peter: he is using a clawhammer to tease out nails from the wooden hoarding at the back of Castleside. Edgar and Donald are standing, watching him work.

'Well, the offer stands,' I hear Edgar say as I approach. 'Many hands make light work and all that.'

'I am quite capable of doing it myself,' Peter says, with obvious irritation. 'It was a task Octavia gave specifically to me.'

'As you wish.'

They turn from Peter as I pass: Edgar touching his top hat, Donald his trilby. 'Good day to you, Miss Barltrop,' Edgar says, stepping forward. 'Not at Castleside today?'

Now I'll have to stop and talk. If not, he'll think me rude and will no doubt take out his pocketbook to make a note against me.

'No, not today. It's Wednesday – my turn to prepare the linen.'

Besides, I want to stay away until the window has been mended. Kate knew nothing of the broken pane but promised to let me know as soon as it was done. Until then I can't risk being alone in the house with workmen around.

'Miss Barltrop, what have you done to your hand?' It is Donald who speaks now, in a tone that suggests genuine concern. I look down at the bandage that Grace used to bind the tips of two of my fingers.

'Oh, it's nothing,' I say, putting it into my pocket, 'just a cut. Some broken glass in Castleside.'

'I hope you have bathed it in the Water,' he says, glancing at Edgar who is studying the gold handle of his cane.

'Yes. It will be healed in no time, I'm sure. Now, I really must get on.'

'Of course. Good day, Miss Barltrop,' he says. And as I walk away I hear him say something to Edgar about the need to be careful. They think of me as a child, unable to look after myself. But Octavia has put me in charge at Castleside. Me. Not Edgar.

———

I manage to haul the fabric onto the dressmaker's table in the Cutting Room. There's a metal measuring tape fixed along its edge. It makes it easier for me to cut the pieces. One inch square: that's the standard size for a miracle.

Octavia appears in the doorway.

'You look flustered,' She says. 'Our outward appearance must reflect our soul within.' Perhaps that's why my hair will never lie still. It always looks frazzled. I take my cue, and take my leave. She has come to administer the healing, so I leave Her to communicate with God. Alone.

None of the members has ever seen Her perform this miracle, She cannot summon Her powers before an audience, only behind closed doors, attended by mystery and ritual. I imagine Her, eyes closed, arms raised: an antenna for God's power. *I am receiving You loud and clear.* I wonder if it is like tuning in the wireless; crackling and whirring until she can lock on to His frequency. Her body stiffens and She rocks backwards and forwards, Her breathing quickening, Her pulse racing. Faster and faster. She gasps and then falls slackly against the table. A long exhalation. The linen is imbued, impregnated with the divine, which is trapped in the spaces between the fibres of the fabric.

Well, that's how I imagine it works.

I am not allowed to find out. I wait instead in the windowless room next door where we keep the archives, shelves piled high with records of our lives. One day we will be recognised as discoverers of the Truth; one day scholars will study us, so anything that is written down is catalogued and kept. When Octavia sits down to receive the Lord's instructions at 5.30 every evening, Her scripts are brought here to be filed. And sealed inside these brown-paper packages are our confessions. Twice a month resident members are required to commit their sins to paper and present them to Octavia in person, but hundreds more send them by post. Every transgression is stored, along with every bill from the greengrocer and baker, every leaflet we print, every rule. Our shopping habits alongside our darkest fantasies: a pound of sugar, a dozen rashers of bacon, greed, envy, vanity. All human life is here.

I hear the door of the Cutting Room and return to find Octavia gone, the air heavy with Her influence.

The linen can be spread out on the table now. It is off-white like bandages; it makes me think of hospitals, and Christ's shroud and the jackets that bind your arms across your chest to stop you hurting yourself. Those who write to us for healing receive one small square, cut with pinking shears which gives each edge the appearance of teeth. I like the way the scissors chew their way across the fabric. I stroke it flat to take out the creases where it has been wrapped around the bolt. It rises up behind my touch, and I roll back another layer to reveal a little more. Soon Grace will come to bring me lunch. Octavia relented: She usually insists that we gather at the dining table, but it is easier if She doesn't have to see me eat or, rather, see that I do not eat. So I will take my lunch in here, being careful not to get crumbs on the linen.

'Delivery!' Grace says, as the door swings open violently. 'Sorry! I had to kick it, my hands are full.'

'You certainly know how to make an entrance. Here, let me.' I take a tray from her hands, on it two bowls of soup and two slices of bread.

'It was heavier than I thought,' she says. 'I have brought mine . . . Unless I'm disturbing you?'

'You are a welcome distraction.'

I arrange two chairs to overlook the Garden. Outside, Peter has made progress with the hoarding, one panel already lying by his feet. He turns to speak to a figure who is bending down to tend the flowerbed nearby. It is Emily, using small shears to trim the box hedges back into shape. Last year she had a go at chess pieces but

Octavia said the rooks and pawns looked more like chimneypots, and that the queen was so unkempt that she ought to be beheaded. Since then Emily has limited all topiary to cubes and spheres.

'Did she see you?' I ask Grace. 'Emily – did you mention you were coming to me?'

'They were deep in conversation.'

'So she didn't ask?' I don't know why it should bother me. We're not doing anything wrong. But Emily has been making comments lately. Making a note of how much time we are spending together. I don't think she likes the thought of me having someone to talk to.

'Eat up before it goes cold,' Grace says, handing me my bowl as we sit. I take a spoonful and bring it to my mouth, embarrassed at how loudly I draw it off the spoon. I glance up, expecting to find her looking at me in disgust, but she doesn't seem to have noticed. Either that or she is being polite.

'So this is it?' she says, looking across at the cutting table, with a look of fascination. 'The linen for the Water . . .' She speaks quietly, as if cowed by the presence Octavia has left behind.

Relieved to have an excuse to put my soup down, I reach for a pile of letters on the desk behind her. 'Yes, we send it to anyone who requests it and all we ask in return is that they report faithfully on the results. You can help if you like.' I begin to read from the one on the top. '81 Woodstock Road, Oxford. Dear Madam, my sister has become most dangerously ill with heart trouble and a gangrenous foot. She has been miraculously brought back to life but suffers so much from nerves that mental trouble is feared. Any help would be gratefully received. Yours faithfully, Miss Helen Barr.'

I pass her the ledger.

'So I make a note of her name and address?' she asks.

'Exactly. And a brief description . . . Heart, gangrenous foot . . . Something like that. And we give each one a GP number. That stands for General Protection.'

She starts to make a note. 'This says you are up to 1532 so far.'

'So Miss Barr is 1533. Look at this one: 4 Church Avenue, Bristol. "Will you kindly send me a linen section for divine healing as sent to my sister? My complaint is chilblains, nerves and also my ears discharge. Thank you in anticipation, Yours faithfully, Miss M. Saunders."'

We both burst out laughing. 'Don't be wicked,' she says, trying to make her face wear a sterner expression. 'Poor Miss Saunders. Chilblains are no laughing matter.'

We carry on together, Grace recording the letters while I go back to cutting the linen.

'What about the method?' she asks. 'Are there different doses for different complaints? Surely chilblains would need a different preparation from, say, rheumatism?'

I walk to the cupboard to get a leaflet. I feel her watching me. 'We send out instructions,' I say. 'Here . . .'

DIVINE DELIVERANCE (SLOW BUT SURE) AND HUMAN OBEDIENCE

Instructions to prepare the Water for all internal complaints. Hold the linen section – which will never lose its virtue – in a wine-glass of water while you count to 12.

'But you must say the words *I ask for Divine Healing by Water and the Spirit*,' I explain. 'It can be drunk, or sponged onto injuries. We've found it works best for people with coughs or breathing problems if they inhale it as steam. Or you can bathe in it – for spinal cases or rickets . . .'

She takes the leaflet from my hand and studies it. 'And people write for help from all over the world?'

'Yes.'

'From India?'

I know what she is getting at. She is talking about my letter. From Adrian. But this time I am ready. I have had a chance to prepare exactly what I will tell her. And what I will not.

'We do send the healing to India, yes. Why do you ask?'

'That letter I found at the foot of the stairs—'

'It was from my brother.'

She looks up from the leaflet. 'Your brother?'

'Adrian, yes.'

'I see,' she says. 'It's just you seemed—'

'He used to be part of the society. Like me. But he left. He renounced his faith.'

'Oh.' Grace moves to touch my arm, but changes her mind. 'I'm sorry. I understand now why you seemed upset. It must be heartbreaking to see him turn away from the Truth.'

'It is.'

I wonder now if he was ever a true believer. After the war he said it all made sense – that Octavia would make sure that all that suffering would never happen again. But as time went on he started to question it. To question Her. Why was there still so much pain, so much damage? When he was offered a posting to India he took it. He chose to move far away from all this. Far away from me.

'Do you think he'll change his mind?'

'Not now. I have stopped writing back to him. There's nothing more I can do.'

'But Octavia says those who turn away from Her are the worst of sinners . . .'

'Because they have a choice,' I say. 'There are those who have not yet heard the Truth. But on the Day of Judgement, Adrian can't pretend he didn't know.'

He can't say She didn't warn him. None of us can say that.

'Perhaps God will show him, help him overcome his doubts.'

I say nothing, moving back to the table and picking up the shears to cut another strip of linen.

'Because I've been thinking about that first day I came to visit. In the chapel. Do you remember?'

I smile. I can't help it.

'Sometimes I get the same feeling . . .' she says, tidying the crockery onto the tray. 'As if all this . . . As if this place has chosen *me*. I feel I have started down a road and I don't know where it will take me.'

Taking up the long strip of linen I have cut, I begin to trim it into smaller pieces. 'Healing is a power Octavia discovered quite by accident. She was taking a pill for one of Her headaches. It was resting in Her palm and as She said Her usual prayer the tablet was flicked out of Her hand. She knew God meant Her just to drink the water. And She was cured.' I cut the last square of fabric and lift it to my lips, with barely a touch. 'Faith is enough,' I say. That's what I want to believe. Because it's all I have. *Faith is the substance of things hoped for, the evidence of things not seen* (Hebrews 11:1).

Grace leaves the room with two soup bowls: hers empty, mine full.

And a square of linen in the pocket of her apron.

A gift I had no right to give.

I wait for Octavia to appear in the doorway and tell me I am no good. I wait for the familiar feeling of guilt and shame to creep across my skin. But it doesn't come and nor does She. I should be sorry, but I am not. We are sharing something, something the others do not know. We are planting a seed of friendship in the dark soil of a secret, where no eyes can spy, where everyone is blind.

The Wireless Room

I shall join the others tonight, out in the Wireless Room where Octavia invites members to sit with Her after supper. Designing it was one of Her projects. She decided we should have a place to meet and mingle in the evenings, a communal sitting room of sorts.

From the outside it resembles a large storage shed, but She has furnished the inside with every comfort befitting ladies of our station: wicker chairs, pot plants and an air of middle-class judgement. And this evening She is holding court Herself, sitting forward on Her chair while Peter rearranges the cushion at Her back. Rachel Fox is beside Her: an unusually tall woman with an unusually high opinion of herself. Her hair is completely colourless, the bright white of someone who looks as though she must have suffered a shock. One of the newer members, Miss Tweedie, a portly woman with an unfortunate nose, is tuning in the wireless. And tucked into a corner Ellen Oliver sits with a blanket across her knees.

The group is silent when I step in and Octavia greets me with a look that means She expects the same from me. An irritated wave of Her hand instructs me to hurry up and sit down. Quietly. A wave of the other bids Miss Tweedie to turn up the volume dial on the wireless. At times Octavia resembles a side-show illusionist: She can make objects (in Her case, people) move at will.

Even the announcer's voice appears to jump to attention as She leans in towards the lacquered oak cabinet. The BBC News: 'Negotiations between the mine owners and the Miners' Federation of

Great Britain have failed to reach an agreement about working hours and wages.'

It is what She has been waiting for.

'Just as I foretold,' She says. 'The poison of Bolshevism is seeping into our great land.' She speaks into the wireless as if it were a microphone; as though She is addressing the nation Herself. 'At present the mailed fist still wears the soft glove of humanity, hiding behind the pretence of fairness and justice to miners, but do not be fooled. This is Satan's fight.' She prepares profound statements to use at times like these.

It is just as well that Octavia is so engrossed. Perhaps She will not hear Miss Tweedie, slack-jawed and breathing noisily through her mouth, a habit she will have to change, and quickly, if she intends to stay in the society.

'I had thought of sending word to the Prime Minister,' Octavia goes on, 'to warn him this would happen. But as Emily says, I am at the helm of my own vessel, not the ship of state . . .' I wonder if Her maritime analogy was inspired by the outfit She is wearing this evening: a navy dress with a white-lace sailor collar and knot. '. . . Peter – that cushion is still not right.' She casts a brief glance over Her shoulder then continues Her address. 'Alas, I cannot help these men. They have to help themselves. Though they choose not to.' She is talking about the bishops. She wrote again to insist that they come and open the box, but the majority didn't bother to reply, and those who did answered only with a request that She cease all further communication.

'Well, they had their chance.' She sits back suddenly. Peter, too slow to withdraw his hands from the cushion, finds them momentarily trapped against the chair. Octavia's irritated tut brings colour to his cheeks.

'The downfall of men's rule has begun,' She continues. 'There is no way, except by letting loose the hordes, that the devils may be seen for what they are. *Now* the bishops will begin to fear, won't they?'

I assume this is a rhetorical question, as Octavia's so often are, but Emily doesn't miss the opportunity to agree. 'It is just a question of time, Octavia. Peter and I were saying as much this morning, weren't we?' I see her give him an encouraging nod and mouth the words 'go on'.

'Indeed we were,' he says. 'And when I think of the way the bishops dismiss You, Octavia. Their arrogance—'

'Do not fear they will come round soon enough. I only wish they were all as sensible as you, Peter. If they had a grain of your wisdom they would accept the Truth. But the male of the species is predisposed to arrogance. You are the exception rather than the rule.'

A smile spreads across Peter's face, which blushes an even deeper shade. I see him glance at Emily, than all eyes are drawn to the sound of the door opening. Grace steps through it carrying a cup, which she sets down next to Octavia.

'Thank you,' Octavia says, without taking Her eyes from the radio set. 'You should stay and listen to this. It is a lesson to us all.' Grace knows by now that this is an instruction, not a suggestion, so she stands beside Her, hands locked politely behind her back, head tilted towards the wireless, but like the rest of us she can't hear the voice on the radio. Octavia is not giving her a chance.

'Look at Bournville . . . Port Sunlight,' Octavia says. 'So much has been done for the bettering of the conditions of the employees, they should work all the harder to recompense employers. Some must rule and some *be* ruled . . . and they should be perfectly happy with that. She lifts Her hand to silence us, though She is the only one who's talking, and the voice confirms that She was right all along.

'The TUC is threatening to hold a general strike,' the radio announcer says.

'Inevitable,' Octavia shrugs. 'Just as God told me.' She looks around the room. 'I shall take my cocoa to bed.' With that She attempts a dramatic exit but it takes Her several pushes to lift Herself from the Lloyd Loom chair. And by the time She makes it onto Her feet, the effect is rather lost.

'Goodnight all,' She says. 'And don't stay up too late. Several of you are looking rather tired and drawn. Jesus could be back at any moment and He will be gazing upon these faces.' She waves Her hand to include us all. 'You may not be able to greet Him with a clear conscience but a clear complexion is certainly achievable.'

She stands and lifts Her cup, Peter hurrying to the door to open it for Her. 'I'll see You back across the Garden, Octavia,' he says. There's silence as they step out into the darkness. Miss Tweedie turns off the wireless. Rachel Fox brings a hand up to her face and I see her dab the head of a particularly angry pimple on her cheek.

'I don't believe we have been introduced . . .' she says, surveying Grace.

'Grace Hardwick. Pleased to meet you. And you must be . . .?' She knows very well who Rachel is. I pointed her out from the window soon after Grace arrived, and drew a caricature with words. I've always thought Rachel's eyes are rather too small for her face. Octavia says she is prone to wearing ugly hats, and of course She has told her so. Grace smiled when I told her that. Which is what I was hoping for all along.

'Me? Oh, I am Rachel Fox, *Miss* Rachel Fox. Rather old to be a

Miss, I know, but that is what I am.' She arches an eyebrow. Just one. 'Ah yes, now I think of it, Octavia introduced you in chapel, didn't she? I had no idea you had become a member of our little society. Which street have you bought in?'

She knows Grace has not bought a house. She knows she could not afford to. But Grace greets her contempt with a warmth that almost fools me.

'I'm afraid you are mistaken, Miss Fox,' she says, her confidence unfaltering. 'Octavia has kindly given me lodging and I am helping in Her household.'

Rachel looks at her in amusement: a tom cat toying with a mouse. 'You could come and work for me,' she says. 'I am always looking out for pious young ladies to help me around the house . . . But no, what am I saying? You wouldn't want to stoop so low. You are handmaid to the Daughter of God.' She puts her hand on my arm. 'And to *Her* daughter too. Dilys, I've always meant to ask – does that make you the Granddaughter of God? I suppose it must . . .'

I step back to avoid her touch and feel colour staining my cheeks. I want to slap Rachel across her face and call her a liar. I want to twist her arm until she tells Grace it was a joke, until she says that I'm not really Octavia's daughter. But it is not a joke, and now Grace knows the truth.

I should have told her. I should have told her myself.

'Well, an honour to meet you, Miss Hardwick,' says Rachel. 'I do hope I'll have the pleasure again soon.' She leaves the room, victorious. Satisfied that she has succeeded in embarrassing Grace, unaware that I am the one she has shamed.

'Grace . . .' I say, standing up beside her near the open door-way, but she doesn't turn to look at me. We stand in silence and watch Rachel disappear into the darkness. 'Grace,' I whisper, but she doesn't acknowledge that she has heard, stepping out into the Garden without bidding me goodnight.

'Wait. Can we . . .'

She doesn't stop.

'Dilys, are you quite all right?' says a voice behind me. Ellen's voice. I had forgotten there was anyone else here. 'You look rather flushed,' she says. 'Perhaps you should get a breath of fresh air. Miss Tweedie will keep me company.'

'I'm fine, Ellen.'

'You go.'

Perhaps she is right. If I am quick I can catch up with Grace be-fore she gets back to the house. But after I shut the door behind me I can't see her. I can't see much of anything at all. The moon and the stars have fled.

'Grace,' I whisper. 'Grace?' But I hear nothing in reply. I feel my way along the wall, testing the ground with each foot before I step forward.

'Grace. Are you there?'

There's movement in the clouds: the sweep of a sable cloak re-vealing a moonlight lining. And I see her, stepping out from around the corner of the chapel.

'Why didn't you tell me?' She is looking straight at me, but I can't bring myself to meet her eyes. I focus instead on her mouth. Her lips are slightly open, her breathing quick. 'Why didn't you tell me, Dilys?'

'I don't know . . .'

'Octavia's daughter? That is something to be proud of, isn't it?'

'Yes. Of course.'

'Then why?'

Right now I can't think of a good reason, a good excuse. So I tell her the truth.

'Because that's *all* I am,' I say. 'To the others. I'm Octavia's daughter . . . When you met me I was just Dilys.'

'Did you think I wouldn't find out?'

'I don't know. I hoped we would become friends. We did . . . didn't we? Time went on and it was too late.'

I am not going to cry. I stopped doing that long ago. It doesn't do any good and Octavia can't bear it. The sound of snivelling drives Her to distraction.

'It didn't feel like a lie, Grace. She is not my mother, not any more. My mother was called Mabel. She went away when I was a child. And then again when I was seventeen. She went away. And Octavia came back in her place.'

'What do you mean? You aren't making any sense.'

'My mother wasn't well,' I say. 'She was in hospital.'

'The headaches?'

'Yes . . . partly.' I still can't bring myself to look straight at her. 'She was away a while. It changed Her, changed things between us.'

She sighs. 'I just feel you've been conspiring somehow.'

'Conspiring?'

'Not one of you said – not Octavia, not Emily. We're all told we must confess, tell the truth about ourselves, about other people. What else haven't you told me?'

Only the things that are forbidden. The past that Octavia says is best forgotten.

'Dilys?' She dips down, finding my eyes with hers. 'What else?'

'Nothing,' I say. But that is not true. 'There's nothing else.' I concentrate on believing it so I don't give myself away.

'Finding out like that, it made me look foolish,' she says. 'I thought we were close—'

'We are—'

'But all this time I would never have guessed. She doesn't acknowledge you're—You never call Her mother.'

'No. I call Her Octavia. The Eighth Prophet. Just like everyone else. Because to Her I am just like everyone else. Or perhaps She wishes I was. But I'm a disappointment.'

I have to turn away now. I look across the Garden towards Yggdrasil but its branches have been swallowed up by the night.

'A disappointment?' she whispers in the darkness. 'Is that what you . . .? You are not a disappointment, Dilys, you could never be.'

I want to believe her. Perhaps she believes it herself, but she doesn't know the truth about me. I have never had the gifts the others do. Or the faith. I try, every day I try to be better. But I always fail.

'You don't understand,' I say.

'No, not if you don't let me. You should have told me the truth.' It is no longer anger I hear in her voice. The moon has disappeared again, the chimneypots of Castleside barely visible against the great wave of cloud that looms above it.

'Grace, did you see that?'

'What?'

'Up in the window.' I reach out for her arm. 'In Castleside.' I see a flash of light blink from the room at the very top. But just as quickly it goes dark again, as if the house has drawn its eyelids tightly shut.

'You're changing the subject,' she says.

'I'm not. I saw something.' I think I did but now I am not so sure. 'I saw a light.'

She looks across to Castleside and shakes her head. 'Dilys, there's nothing there. I'm sorry but I can't . . . Finding out like this. There's so much to take in. I need to get to bed.' She lifts my hand from her arm and walks away. 'I'll see you tomorrow. Goodnight.'

I should go after her but I am too much of a coward. I don't want to talk about the past. She might start to wonder if I am like Octavia. And I am not. She hears the voice of God but only the Devil takes the time to whisper in my ear.

Instead I stand and watch the top window of Castleside. Perhaps she was right. Perhaps I was just trying to change the subject. Perhaps I didn't see a flash of light at all.

'Pull up a chair beside me,' Ellen says when I return to the Wireless Room. 'You look like you need to sit down.' With the rest I can pretend, but not with her. 'You really don't look well,' she says, and I wonder whether she has seen herself in a mirror lately, whether she can see what the rest of us can: the pale skin, the thinning hair. The blanket has been tucked so tightly around her knees that I doubt she'd have the strength to free herself from it.

'Thank you for looking after me but Dilys will take over now,' she says, smiling kindly at Miss Tweedie who puts down the copy of the *Radio Times* she is reading and bids us goodnight.

Ellen waits a moment after she leaves, busying herself by tucking the blanket even more tightly around her legs. 'Now, just the two of us,' she says, looking appraisingly at the furniture around us as if it is her first visit to the room. 'Tell me, how is Miss Hardwick settling in?'

I do not answer.

'It must be quite a tonic for you to have someone your own age to speak to,' she says. 'Us old-timers can't be much company.'

I should speak. My silence is giving me away, but I don't want to share Grace with anyone. Not even Ellen.

'It's only natural you want to protect her,' she says.

The truth is I want *her* to protect *me* but I don't say that. 'It was wrong of Rachel to embarrass her like that,' I say instead. 'It was on my invitation that she came to join us. I feel responsible for her.'

Now Ellen is silent. Waiting for me to reveal more.

'I can't explain exactly, but I think it is important that she stays,' I say. 'Important to the society, I mean. I believe she has a part to play.'

'Then you must keep her close. If it is God's will.'

I reach for something in my pocket: the button Grace dropped outside the Bunyan Meeting Church. I have started carrying it like a talisman, squeezing it in my hand.

'God has never singled me out before. I am not . . .'

'You are not Octavia. None of us are.' Ellen speaks to the empty room rather than to me. 'It is not easy to live in Her shadow. But we are all part of God's plan and perhaps, as you believe, Grace is too.'

I nod.

'I think it is time for me to retire,' she says, taking the blanket from her knees with some difficulty. I stand up and help her, offering my arm to pull her gently from the seat. She is made only of air, so frail, so fragile. She walks as if there is ice underfoot, one slip and she would shatter into a thousand pieces. But at least we can see our way across the lawn. The moon has emerged again from behind the clouds, painting our path silver. I look across to Castleside again, and the cold air of the Garden rouses the nerves on my skin, sensitive enough to feel the gentlest squeeze of Ellen's thin fingers on my arm.

'Why don't you stand up to them, Ellen? It should be your feet that Octavia is washing, not theirs.' It is what I have been wondering for a long time.

'I am tired, Dilys. Let Emily and the others have their day. I have but one battle – to fight the good fight of faith. Octavia is right, it is nearly time for the Lord to return, that's what matters. It is the only thing that matters. We just have to bide our time a little longer.'

We reach her back door and she stops to look at me.

'We are the spinsters, the old maids. We are despised by the world but not by the Lord. In Him we have been glorified, He has promised that we shall not die, we shall live here in the Garden until He returns to us here.' I can see her eyes shining, light catching on a film of tears.

'It won't be long now, will it, Dilys? It can't be long now.'

'No, of course not, Ellen. It is nearly time.'

'We must keep faith,' she says, 'and have the courage of our conviction.'

The word makes me think of criminals and cells. I look towards the high wall of the Garden. Are we imprisoned by our own beliefs? We are convinced. We are convicted.

There is a figure in silhouette in the doorway. I unhook Ellen's arm from mine and hand it to Betty, like the father of the bride passing a daughter to her new master.

'Goodnight, Ellen.'

She puts her arms around me and kisses my cheek softly, an embrace from a ghost.

'Goodnight, Dilys. Soon He will come and these old bones shall be revived. Sleep well, my dear.'

By the time I get back to Number 12, Octavia's empty cup has been washed and is standing on its rim, by the kitchen sink. Grace has gone to bed. I pause on the landing, hoping she will hear the floorboard creak, and that I'll hear her footsteps behind the door. It has become a signal between us, the way we say goodnight. The house is our messenger, whispering things we dare not say out loud, but tonight she does not hear it speak, or she has chosen to ignore it. There is no chink of light seeping out from beneath her door and I imagine her lying in her bed in the dark. Should I turn the handle and let myself in? Sit at the foot of her bed and explain why I didn't tell her?

No, I mustn't do that.

I creep into my own room instead and climb under the blanket. I concentrate on the cold of the pillow against my cheek and reach my hand beneath it. There's a note:

Can a mother forget the baby at her breast and have no compassion for the child she has borne? Though she may forget, I will not forget thee.

(Isaiah 49:15)

Talking Pictures

I have left Number 1 2 for the evening; left Octavia, and Emily, and the letter that arrived from my brother in the morning post. I left them behind the walls of the Garden.

The sky is perfectly clear tonight, a legion of stars shining unchallenged on a cloudless sky. A breeze has shattered the black glass of the river, and where the moonlight touches the surface it looks like a host of flapping wings, like flocks of doves. Grace is beside me. We are walking in the warm glare of the streetlights and the dark silences between.

'I thought Octavia was going to say I couldn't come,' she says.

'Only if you hadn't got all your work done. All members are allowed to go, as long as She has approved the film in advance.'

There are a dozen of us heading out to the Regal tonight. We still have to be careful, we are still being watched, but only by each other. Without Octavia or Emily everyone feels more relaxed, almost giddy. We can pretend we are just an ordinary group of respectable ladies. Octavia thinks it important that we are spotted around town, at least once a week, browsing the shops on the High Street, or buying flowers on the market. Sometimes groups of followers will meet at a café for tea, or take a picnic to the riverbank. That is when we might engage a passer-by in conversation, mention the society, give them a pamphlet. *We need to be seen to be approachable and acceptable.*

Though of course, in reality, we are neither.

'I love the talking pictures,' Grace says, squeezing the top of my arm. Does she feel me twitch when she moves her hand away?

'So does Octavia. Well, She used to. She hasn't seen a talkie, She hasn't been to the cinema since . . . it's too far. She can't risk it, not now She knows Apollyon is waiting. But She used to love to go.'

I told Grace, soon after she came to live with us, why Octavia mustn't stray from the Garden. That's when I should have told her that She is my mother. Or used to be. It has been two weeks since she found out, but she has never mentioned it, and nor have I. It is another of our unspoken pacts.

Tonight we'll be in a theatre full of people, but we will be together, sharing the story, taken off into another world; where we've never heard the name Octavia; where we can live in ignorance of the Truth. The thought of it makes me feel calm and anxious at the same time. There are butterflies in my stomach, a fluttering of vivid colours. And amongst them, the dull wings of moths beating a rhythm of dread.

'Gertrude, do keep up,' Kate Firth calls back to one of our number who has fallen behind to adjust the ankle-strap on her shoe. Her instruction causes a moment of confusion, since there are two Gertrudes with us tonight. Gertrude Hill is a thin-lipped woman who carries her shoulders so high that her neck quite disappears inside her collars. She is the only Non-Resident Apostle, given special dispensation to live outside the Garden because she has a husband who is still alive. She's fond of telling us how busy she is kept as a vicar's wife, though Octavia has hinted that it is her duties after dark that are proving exhausting. *He expects her to perform them nightly, and with vigour.*

The other Gertrude – Searson – needs no excuse to avoid conjugal chores: she is estranged from her husband, and answers to no one now. Except Octavia, of course. She is wearing a large feather on her silk hat tonight, black like Sir Jack's plumage. And added to the effect of her large teeth it makes her look a little like a funeral horse.

'It's good to get out, isn't it?' Grace says, as we reach the Swan Hotel lit up on the corner. It is. I think of Adrian's latest letter, folded neatly with the rest, each of them the same: accusations against Octavia, pleas for me to leave. This time he wrote about the months we spent together when Mother was away in hospital, and the day that She came home again. He said that was the moment everything changed and that he could see now how wrong it all was.

It was bad enough when it was just the Devil whispering in my ear, at least I could drown him out with hymns and prayers and sermons, but doubts are more difficult to ignore when they are written down in black and white. Best that I hide his letter away in the box at the back of my wardrobe. Best that I get out of the house.

We turn right into the High Street. It looks so different at night; the shops are sleeping, shutters pulled down over empty shelves. A group of men look as though they are on their way to a public house; a lone figure appears to be on his way back from one. A car horn makes him jump back onto the pavement as he staggers into the path of two headlights.

'You must have taken all this for granted before,' I say. 'You could come and go as you wished.'

'Yes, I suppose I could, but I rarely did. I didn't have the money really. Or the company.' She squeezes my arm again.

'Do you miss it, though?'

'No. It wasn't easy. I was alone.'

'And lonely . . .?'

I turn to her and she answers, but only with her eyes.

———

I follow the disc of light thrown from the usher's torch and squeeze past strangers, feeling exposed and clumsy. It's not until I'm safely in my seat that my eyes adjust. I see a couple stealing a kiss in the corner, and a lady in an elegant cloche wiping her nose on the back of her sleeve. People get a false sense of security in the dark; they think they are invisible so they forget to hide. A young man stumbles on a stair as he tries to find his seat and Grace and I stifle a giggle at his expense.

The seats are crimson velvet and there are drapes either side of the screen. It makes me think of music hall and dancing girls and the backstreet theatres that Octavia reads about in the newspapers. *Boltholes of debauchery. Beautiful on the surface but rotten to the core.* I love the extravagance, the red, the gold, the darkness.

But I must remember that Octavia has sent us here for moral instruction.

The Scarlet Letter, that's what we've come to see. It's about the Puritans, and the scandal of an illegitimate child. Octavia liked the sound of that, a good moral tale about the wages of sin. When we mentioned it after lunch She became quite animated, talking about the Puritans' attitude to sexual relations and the fact they used to have intercourse through a hole in a sheet. I couldn't work out whether she found the idea disdainful or impressive. But She liked the sound of the film all the same. She is surprisingly open-minded when it comes to Her choices; She'll even sign off on a love story to remind us that we are better off without the complications of men. Celibacy is not just a requirement, it is a liberation. Watching a woman mooning over her sweetheart looks so ridiculous when you are a bride of Christ Himself. She likes us to tell Her all about it when we get home, so She can tut and roll Her eyes with the moral superiority She would have enjoyed from a cinema seat.

Grace's face is glowing, reflecting the flickering light of the screen. If I turn my head a little I can watch her. When you are in the dark your eyes work better that way; astronomers searching for a faint object in the sky will always look slightly to the side. And right now, I dare not look directly at Grace. It would be like staring straight at the sun.

I move my eyes down to her fingers which are knotted together in her lap; I look at the fabric of her skirt which sits on the top of her legs and falls over the edge of her knees. I don't often get to study her as closely as this.

I grip onto the corners of my chair. On the screen the heroine is being led onto a wooden platform, and is refusing to tell the baying crowd who the father of her baby is. They force her to wear her shame, a scarlet letter, on the front of her dress: 'A' for Adultery. Grace shuffles in her chair and moves her hand down beside her leg. It is touching mine. I don't move away. I'm not sure I could, even if I wanted to.

So there it stays.

Our hands are still touching when we learn that it is the preacher who has fathered the child. And while we watch him, tormented by his cowardice and hypocrisy, I press the side of my hand against hers.

Ever so gently.

By the time he stands and confesses his sin to the congregation our little fingers are intertwined. It's as if I have no feeling in any other part of my body: every nerve and every sensation alive only in the skin that's touching hers. I am Michelangelo's Adam being brought to life with a fingertip: God reaching down from the ceiling of the Sistine Chapel and jolting me into consciousness.

Caught up together . . . in the clouds, to meet the Lord in the air.
(1 Thessalonians 4:17)

Will this be how it feels when Jesus returns to us? The rapture of salvation? I have seen the others performing the laying on of hands in chapel and now I understand. I can feel the spirit flowing through Grace. I am drowning. Drowning in the light.

As the film comes to an end she squeezes my hand then moves it away, and immediately the heat in my fingers is gone. And all I can think of is Elisha and how he brought a child back to life.

And he put his mouth upon his mouth, and his eyes upon his eyes, and his hands upon his hands . . . and the flesh of the child waxed warm.
(2 Kings 4:34)

Woken from death.

Voices

Octavia always says the Devil is jealous, he wants to tarnish anything that reflects the glory of God, blacken anything that shines with love. And since Grace came, that's me. That's why he is watching me; that's why he is trying to twist and turn my thoughts.

I know what I saw: a face, looking in through the window at Castleside. Not one of the others, not a lady with a pocketbook and pen, not Peter or Edgar. This was a face I didn't recognise. But I knew right away what it meant.

I don't know how long it had been spying, or whether it had a body attached. I was working much later than usual, drawing up the latest list for Octavia to read out in chapel, a request for linen for the bishops: more pillowcases, napkins and towels. When I looked up from my desk, night was pulling a curtain of darkness across the bare windows; the panes fading to black mirrors, reflecting my own image within their frames. And when I snuffed out the desk lamp I saw it: another face merged with my own, a face pressed to the window, a hand held above the eyebrows. It looked just like the face of a man, it had no horns or scales or claws. But I was not fooled. I know it was the Devil that I saw. I know it was the Devil who called my name through the glass. I cried out for God's protection and the face turned away and disappeared.

In the cinema I was filled with God's light. I thought it had driven the Devil from the dark corners of my mind, but now he is not just whispering from the shadows of my thoughts. I have seen him with my own eyes. And I know he is watching me. Just as he told me. Just as he told me in chapel last night.

'The Lord wishes to protect us from temptation,' Octavia said, when we gathered to hear the words She had received through Her pen. 'Before the Fall we were like children, with lives uncomplicated by the desires of the flesh. When Jesus comes we shall return to that blissful state of innocence. But until He does we must be vigilant.'

It's you, the Devil whispered. *She is talking about you and Grace.*

'Members must not embrace, whether in greeting or in consolation,' Octavia said. 'Hands will not be held or shaken. Even those who are in the habit of meeting or parting company with a kiss on the cheek must do so no more. Even the slightest touch could lead to sin.'

Even the slightest touch, he said, *just think where it could lead.*

And I did. I started to imagine.

As I sat there in chapel he whispered all the ways I might be tempted, all the things we would be forbidden to do. And though I tried to drown him out, though I raised my voice to sing Jerusalem, I couldn't help but listen. The thought of her made me thirsty. Made me ache. A heavy weight pulling down inside me, like the pain that comes with menses. As though the butterflies had fluttered further down, or the moths were gnawing at the empty place inside me. Dark and destructive and eating away at the deepest parts like cashmere in a wardrobe. I felt ragged, held together by fraying threads.

I saw you in the dark, he said. *I know the secrets of your heart.*

And something woke in me. A rush of beating wings and pulsing blood.

Anchoress

It is too late. I will never see Adrian again. Not in this life, and according to Octavia, not in the next either. He must have written to Her too, because She knows about his engagement. 'He is choosing to marry,' She told Emily and Peter over dinner. 'He is refusing to follow God's call to remain celibate. He has banished himself from the Garden for eternity.'

The Lord will forgive him, though Octavia cannot. Not now. I will continue to pray for him, though I won't write back to tell him so. Best to cut all ties. Octavia says we must withdraw from him: doubt is infectious, it can spread from one person to another like disease. And even now he tries to persuade me to leave, to move out to India. He says there will always be a place for me with him and his fiancée. Her name is Marjorie and she is from a good family who are mentioned in *Debrett's*. I imagine he hasn't told them about Octavia's calling. I imagine he hasn't told them about me either. And though he promises he'll continue to write, I know this is the end for us.

Last night when I fell asleep I heard him call my name from the Garden. I dreamt that I got up to look out of my window, but when I opened my curtains I found a wall of bricks. And instead of terror I felt relief, that I hadn't found the Devil looking in again. I was safe. And holy. A medieval anchoress being sealed into a crypt at the side of a church. My bed was a funeral bier, and standing over me Octavia read my last rites, Her tears hidden behind a black veil, as a choir sang my requiem. I felt pious and beautiful; a shaft of light fell on my face in the darkness and Octavia whispered that She loved me, then She turned away and left. All I could hear was the scraping of mortar onto bricks as they were piled up one by one behind my door, and I was dead to the world, released from its expectations; alone in silent prayer and mortification.

I've thought about that dream all day, about the women who chose to live their lives among the dead, about all the ways they starved and scarred their bodies, and whether that was what God wanted. In my cell of stone I imagine a peephole for myself. Anchoresses were granted the luxury of spying on the congregation during mass and tonight I'll do the same. It is only 8 p.m. but I have come to bed so I can listen in. I can hear them coming along the landing now. Octavia and the Four meet every night in the Upper Room, next door to mine. It used to be Adrian's bedroom but after he left Octavia put it to good use. She held the first services there, when the faithful numbered only a few. She brought up a hall table to serve as an altar, adorning it with Her best lace doilies, and a coral floor lamp to help Her banish the darkness that has stalked Her for as long as I can remember. But now that we have dozens of members and a chapel in the Garden, it is open only to the Chosen. Peter, Edgar, Kate Firth and Emily: the four living creatures of Ezekiel's vision, the four creatures around the throne of God in the Book of Revelation. They never speak about it to the rest of us, but Octavia has told us it is a laboratory, for the practice of theosophy. And when they welcome angels from the other side it's important that they make the right impression: hand-sewn tapestries on the wall and a vase of daffodils which Octavia cuts from the Garden Herself. She even serves tea and biscuits; the spirits are of radiant form but those with mortal bodies still need sustenance.

It was Edgar who persuaded Her to use Her powers. Receiving

the Lord's Word at Her writing table is a lonely business, but together they can share the burden. And the joy. Edgar reassured Her he could keep them safe, he knew the rules: how to welcome the angels of light, how to banish the angels of darkness, and how to spot the difference. Their confidence is growing. I hear them praying, laughing, crying; cursing the Devil and praising the Lord. They bang on the walls and stamp their feet and raise merry Hell, daring demons to rise up so that Octavia can subdue them. But it is Emily who seems to excel when it comes to spirits. I know this because it is Peter's job to take notes of these experiments, and my job to type them up; lines scribbled in the lulls between miracles.

Emily Goodwin started to play just like one that has had too much to drink. Laughing and laughing like a little child. Kept beating time as if conducting an orchestra. She jumped up and down and stretched her arms out, rocked herself from side to side and spread out her arms and gradually slid down to the floor. It was evident to those present that she saw some beautiful vision, for she smiled all over her face . . . She then stood up and seemed to embrace all present with outstretched arms.

I am never present. I am never invited. I am next door, listening with a glass pressed against the wall. But not tonight; tonight I'm going to take a peek. I open my door very slowly, the hinge creaks and so does the floorboard outside their door, but they do not hear, they are too busy chanting. I bend down and look through the keyhole. Dark green, that's all I can make out. The dark green jacket that Emily was wearing at supper. She must be sitting in front of the door. Suddenly my eye is flooded with light. It takes a moment or two for me to focus. I can see Octavia, just a chink of Her through the narrow keyhole, a slice of eyes and mouth and blouse and skirt, a face without ears, a body without shoulders. From here that is all there is of Her.

It looks as though Emily has stepped behind Octavia, helping Her to take off Her cardigan. And then her hands come to Her neck. Octavia's eyes are wide open, Her face resolute, Her body still. Emily's hands are moving but Octavia does not struggle. Why is no one stopping her? Why is no one prising Emily's fingers from around Her throat?

I am blind again. Another figure has moved in front of the door. Dark blue this time. I reach for the handle but the figure moves and I see Octavia. Emily's hands are no longer around Her neck, they are moving lower. The ribbon on the top of Her blouse is hanging loose. Emily is untying Her. Unbuttoning Her. Undressing Her. Revealing the lines of braiding on the neck of Her petticoat.

Octavia doesn't flinch or blink when the pale skin beneath Her throat is exposed. A figure steps in front of the door, blocking my view, and when it moves I see it is Peter, carrying a chair in each hand. I hear them being put down on the floor and then I see him lying down on them, and the back of his head appears in Octavia's lap.

What are they doing? I don't want to see this but I can't look away.

Without moving Her gaze, Octavia lifts Peter's head into the crook of Her arm. 'Like newborn infants, you long for the pure spiritual milk,' She says, 'that by it you may grow up into salvation.' Her fingers stroke the nape of his neck, and comb up into his hairline. Is this how She used to caress me? When I was brand new, still wearing the creases of birth on my skin?

She said that touching was forbidden. I hear the voice again, inside my head. *But just look at Her, with Peter at Her breast.*

Through the keyhole it looks like something it can't be. I mustn't listen. I can't trust my thoughts and now my eyes deceive me. For the briefest of moments Octavia's eyes seem to look straight at the keyhole. And I stare back, willing Her to remember the mother She never was to me.

Ellen's Parlour

'The country is going to war with itself,' says Ellen. 'I wish I could come with you. I'm no good to anyone sitting here.' She hasn't felt well enough to attend chapel for nearly a fortnight now, so I have started to visit her in the late afternoons.

'We'll be thinking of you,' I say. 'Won't we?' I turn to Grace who is sitting in her usual spot, beside me. She joins me on these visits, when she can spare the time. Ellen enjoys the company, and since what happened at Castleside I don't like to walk outside alone. I'm starting to wonder whether there was a face at the window at all. Or whether I'm seeing things, hearing things; things that aren't really there. At breakfast I looked for any sign of strangeness between Peter and Octavia, any recognition of what they may have done in the Upper Room last night, but there was nothing: no glances, no silences. Just Peter being his usual doting self and Octavia chastising him for spilling tea on the tablecloth.

Ellen reaches out and pats us both on our wrists. Her hands are icy, so cold they burn. But perhaps it's not the touch of her skin that jolts me, perhaps it is Grace's spirit I can feel, flowing through Ellen's body and bridging the space between us. The Devil tries to keep us apart, tries to tell me I can't trust myself. *Think of all the ways you could be tempted*, he says.

I hear him when I am alone at Castleside, when I sit and type at my desk. But I won't stay away. I can't. Whenever we are together I know I am where God wants me to be.

'It sounds like quite an adventure,' Ellen says. 'Reminds me of my missions for Mrs Pankhurst . . . Sneaking around in the dead of night!' We laugh but it is bravado, because although we don't say it out loud, we are frightened. Octavia has told us we must go out tomorrow night to bury squares of linen around the town. The trade unions have confirmed there will be a strike to support the miners, and in three days' time they say they'll bring the country to a standstill and plunge it into darkness – no transport, no gas or electricity.

'Do not be fooled,' Octavia told us in chapel. 'That is just the beginning of their plans. The working man means to stage a revolution and he will lead his armies into battle on the streets, looting, plundering . . .' She pauses, '. . . ravishing. He will not rest until he spoils that which he covets.'

Though we will be safe here in the Garden, we must do all we can to protect important landmarks: the churches, the town hall, the railway station and the bridges. She has breathed on an extra roll of linen and tomorrow we shall bury squares of Her blessing around Bedford. We don't want to wake up and find it has been razed to the ground.

'Mrs Goodwin is drawing up the plans for who will go where,' Grace tells Ellen. 'And Dilys has been put in charge of preparing the linen squares.' She suddenly sits upright. 'Oh, I've just had a thought. If we're going to bury them, won't we all need trowels?'

'Good point, Miss Hardwick,' I say, with an affected solemnity. 'I shall mention it to Octavia. Perhaps She should have put *you* in charge.' I nudge her shoulder with my free arm and salute. And she pulls a face at me, wrinkling her nose.

We can be easy here with Ellen. She is not like the others: she doesn't make comments about Grace's station, or how busy she must be, or express surprise that she can spare so much time to spend with me. Of course it is *my* behaviour they are addressing. They don't think that I should lower myself to a friendship with a servant. We may all be equal in God's eyes but not in Octavia's, so I don't linger too long to talk with Grace in the hallway, and we are careful not to sit together in chapel.

Here in Ellen's parlour it doesn't matter, sitting on the wicker chairs in her drawing room with her knick-knacks all around. You couldn't call it untidy. Octavia would never allow it to be that. But the Bible sampler on the wall is hanging slightly askew, the china dog on the mantelpiece looks like it has just returned from a walk and the cushions are in dire need of plumping, as if a breeze has pushed everything slightly out of its proper place. That could be me of course: I always let out a deep breath when I sit down in this room. My relief could be enough to lift the corner of the rug, or ruffle the blue damask curtains which Octavia picked out. Ellen has always hated those curtains but she would never say so. Not out loud.

'So there is no doubt that the strike will go ahead?' Ellen asks.

'No, the negotiations have failed. The Government is already gathering troops in Hyde Park. We heard it on the wireless after chapel,' I answer. Now that she is not venturing out, she can't even listen to the news. I wonder if Octavia would buy a radio set for her. Ellen can't buy her own: all her savings have been signed over to the society and, by now, I'm guessing the deeds to her house have too. 'The unions have given their word that milk and food supplies will still get through,' I say. 'Though Octavia is not convinced – She says we may have to rely on the Water to sustain us if the strike goes on.'

'If only the bishops would listen,' Ellen says. 'All this could have been avoided. First the war, now this! If only they would agree to come and open the box.' I have never seen Ellen's frustration spill over before, never heard her raise her voice. 'More suffering! Because of them.'

We sit in silence and I rub her hands to warm them; her fingers are as brittle as dry sticks. I must be careful or a spark could catch on her papery skin. There's so little of her now. She'd go up in seconds. Ashes to ashes.

'Will you come?' she says, almost under her breath at first, and then again. 'Will you come here when the strike is called? Will you come and sit with me?'

I laugh. 'But Ellen, you'll be quite safe here. We have God's protection.'

'I know. But . . . all those angry men out on the streets. Octavia says there will be looting. All they'd have to do is break a window. There's nothing I could do. I don't like to ask Betty to sit up with me.'

Tears are pooling in the corners of her eyes. This isn't Ellen, she has always been the strong one, but she looks defeated.

'Of course we'll come,' I say.

We can worry about persuading Octavia later.

Grace tries her best to cheer her. 'We'll keep the fire lit. A cup of cocoa and we'll hunker down for the night. Lock the doors. We'll be quite jolly.'

'Anyway, you'll be the one looking after us,' I say, wanting to remind her who she is. Or who she was. 'You can tell Grace about your days in Holloway while we are holed up. More stories about Mrs Pankhurst.'

'I look back on those days with fondness but not with pride,' Ellen says. 'I was fighting for something that wasn't worth having, Grace. None of it matters; whether women have the vote or not is immaterial.'

'But that makes no sense,' Grace says. 'It is our time. Time for women to rise and make the world better. Isn't that why we are here?'

'We are here to do the Lord's will,' Ellen says. 'It doesn't matter who leads the government. We recognise no authority but the rule of God.'

Those were Octavia's words on polling day when She instructed us not to leave the Garden. It made no difference to me: I don't have the years, or the wealth, to qualify. But I waited for Ellen to put on her coat and hat, to pin on her ribbon of purple and green, and to walk out of her front door and straight into the polling station. I wanted something to happen. Something to change. I wanted someone to do what I have never been able to do: I wanted someone to stand up to Octavia.

The Protection

The weather is perfect. A sign, says Octavia, that God is blessing our endeavours. There's barely a cloud in the sky and the moon is full with borrowed light, so we'll be able to see what we are doing. Clear skies mean it is cold, though. Emily has instructed us to wear extra layers underneath our coats. They'll keep us warm and, if it comes to it, will make it more difficult for any men who might try to force themselves on us in the dark. Grace hands me a rolling pin from the drawer in the kitchen. Just in case. And we can always use our knees; Octavia says a knock in the groin is a very effective deterrent against lascivious men. Though I'm not sure She's ever had cause to adminster one.

'Ready?' I ask.

Grace nods and ties my scarf more tightly around my neck. 'Will you be warm enough?' she says. 'There's nothing of you lately.'

'In this? I'll be fine.' I am embraced by fur, the rabbit coat that Octavia bought for me when I turned eighteen. I thought it rather extravagant at the time but I suppose She saved plenty of money that would otherwise have been spent filling my bottom drawer for marriage.

'Yes,' Grace says. 'Even you should be cosy in that.' She brushes the fur on my shoulder. 'Beautiful . . .' She makes that noise again: something between a sigh and a laugh. Is it longing, or contentment?

I want to tell her that she is exceptional, that I've been thinking about how to describe her and I keep coming back to that word.

Instead I lift the collar of her coat. The dark blue one, I suppose it's the only one she has, and for just a second, my finger is inside the fabric, brushing against the skin of her neck.

Even the slightest touch could lead to sin.

'Dilys? Grace? Are you two ready?' Emily is calling us from the hallway, where a small group has gathered.

'Time to go,' I say, 'this is it!' Bravado again. This feels dangerous, perhaps because Octavia has told us that the country will soon be overrun with lawlessness. Or perhaps it's the thought of being alone with Grace.

'Stay close,' Grace says. As if she has to ask. We leave the kitchen and walk past the clock in the hallway. 12.45 a.m. I should be tired, but I'm not.

'Ah, there you are. Dilys, we need the linen,' Emily says. I reach into my pocket and take out the six small bundles I cut this morning. Each contains eight squares to be buried around the perimeter of each civic building, all cut from cloth that Octavia has blessed with Her breath.

'You all know what to do. At this time of night nobody should see you.' Emily pushes open the sitting-room door to reveal Octavia. She is sitting in Her chair, waiting to deliver Her battle-cry: *Henry V* is one of Her favourites.

'God has called upon us to perform this protection,' She says. 'This is a momentous time for one and all. Stand firm and see what the Lord will do to rescue His faithful children from what is coming upon the world.'

We file past Her into the cold air: troops on parade, fanning out in pairs when we reach the pavement. Kate and Rachel go first, both wrapped in fur-trimmed coats. A passer-by might imagine they are strolling back from a concert or some other entertainment, the satin of Kate's cloche and matching gloves shining in the glow of the streetlamp. The men wear an air of intrigue: Edgar dressed entirely in black, Donald's face barely visible behind the college scarf which he has pulled up around his cheeks. They fall into perfect step with each other, glancing furtively along the empty street, evidently enjoying the cloak-and-dagger of the mission.

Emily sends Grace and me on our way with a silent nod of her head. She and Peter have volunteered to stay behind with Octavia. Plenty of the members are turning out tonight, their departure staggered at different times from various houses. We mustn't draw too much attention to ourselves. Even at this hour there's a chance we could be spotted, and people would think we were up to no good.

They always assume the worst.

'Can we just check all is well at Castleside?' I whisper to Grace as we turn into Newnham Road.

'Of course.' Grace has no idea that I want to check whether there's anyone lurking in the front garden. Half of me is hoping there is, at least then I'd have an explanation for the face I saw at the window.

'It all looks fine,' she whispers as we walk up to the front door. I shake the handle just to check it is locked. There is no one here. No man. No devil. There's no one in the street at all except Grace and me. Alone.

'Yes, all secure.' I turn to retrace our steps and she reaches out for my arm.

'Are you all right?' she says.

How can I tell her I am not? That I am frightened of the dark and the things that could happen in it. Behind the tall trees that shield the house from the road we are completely cut off, and I hear a voice inside my head. It's telling me to do the things I can't stop imagining. Take her hand, it says, draw her close. But those are the Devil's thoughts. Not mine. I would never have thoughts like that.

'Dilys?'

'I'm fine,' I say. My voice sounds strange; my breathing too loud. 'Just cold.'

She puts her arm around me and rubs my side to warm me up. I should tell her to stop. Octavia told us it is forbidden.

But that didn't stop Her and Peter . . .

'Come on then,' Grace says. 'We'd better get on. The mound or the flour mill?' There are two ways to get to St Peter's Church. I don't fancy the castle mound; the ground is uneven and Octavia says it's where the undesirables gather on benches to drink alcohol. Vagrants, that's what She calls them. There are those who came back from the war in limbo, no longer in this world but not quite in the next. Parts of them were sent off to Heaven, an advance party of lost limbs and lost hope. And so they sit and drink and wonder whether they will be made whole again when they make it to God's table. They sit and they stare, grieving for their friends and resenting them for making it out of this life in one piece. A clean break.

'Do you really think it is haunted?' Grace whispers. She is smiling, I can tell.

'Sorry?'

'The castle mound. I thought it was supposed to be haunted.

Wasn't there a siege there? The king's men surrounded it.'

'That's the story. Tried to starve them out, break their spirit, leave them too weak to fight.'

I hear from her breath that she is going to say something. But she stops. She has changed her mind.

'What is it?'

We keep walking.

'You should know about starving,' she says. 'Dilys, I worry about you. Like you said, it leaves you too weak to fight.'

I could tell her the usual things: I have a small appetite or I've been off my food. But what would be the point? She knows something is wrong with me. They all know it. The difference is she has said it out loud.

I'm always fighting, I say. It's all I seem to do. Fighting with myself, with my feelings. And when it comes to eating, I just can't face it. I could do as I'm told and eat it all up nicely like a good girl, but I'm not a girl any more. And I've never been good either. Not good enough. Not for Octavia. Did I say that out loud or in my head? Could she hear my silent words seeping out into the darkness between us?

We walk back onto Castle Street, around the back of the Bunyan Meeting Church, and as we pass it she touches my arm, and turns to me and smiles, just like she did when she sat beside me on the pew.

'Are you glad I invited you that day?' I ask her.

'Of course. Are you?'

'Yes,' I say. But I don't say how much. How I've never been more glad of anything.

There is no one in the street, just the occasional light shining from an upstairs window. It's all quiet at the Higgins Brewery, no gangs of workers in the yard, no foremen shouting instructions or drivers to wolf-whistle as we pass. And it's all dark in the lane which leads through to the High Street; no streetlights back here, just cramped little doorways that lead into pubs. Octavia says working men disappear inside with their pay-packets on a Friday and aren't seen again until Monday morning. Sometimes their wives wait outside, hoping that the hungry cries of their children will persuade them to come out, or at least send out a coin or two. But the women make the mistake of trying to appeal to their husbands' better judgement. *They should know by now, men have no judgement after five pints of ale, better or otherwise.*

The lane narrows into an alleyway, moonlight shining in the gullies between the cobbles and catching on shards of broken glass in a doorway. It hasn't been raining so I'm guessing the puddles we are stepping over must be man-made. I don't want to touch anything, but I'm forced to feel my way along the walls of the alleyway towards the rectangle of light that marks the other end. Staying close behind me, Grace keeps her hand on my back and we edge along; the blind leading the blind. I stumble and feel myself falling, but the alley is narrow enough to keep me on my feet. Grace steps forward and knocks into me, her cheek pressing against my coat. I feel her moving her face against the fur, breathing in its scent. Her arms are around my waist.

She is holding me. I am being held.

She must have reached out to steady herself. Nothing more than impulse. But now she is completely still. She is not moving. And neither am I.

'All right back there?' I say softly.

'Yes, you? Did you stub your toe?'

'I'll live! There must be a loose cobble.'

I need to concentrate on what we've come to do, but my mind is moving too quickly. Running away with itself. Running away from Grace. But it keeps turning back, looking over its shoulder. Perhaps that's why I feel I'm going round in circles.

'We look like gravediggers,' I say as we walk through the gate into the churchyard of St Peter's.

'Or body-snatchers,' she says. 'Mind you, we've hardly come well prepared for that.' She produces a trowel from her pocket with a flourish.

'We've got a rolling pin,' I say. 'Don't forget the rolling pin.'

We start to laugh and she puts her finger to her lips. 'Shhhhhh. You'll wake the dead.' Now she's said it I can't help thinking of the bodies lying just beneath the grass, of the day my father's coffin was lowered into the ground, when I threw a handful of earth on top. I wonder what is left of him now, whether the skin and flesh has all rotted away, or whether it hangs off his bones like strips of ribbon. The Bible says the dead will rise again, but I hope God restores them first.

I'm still laughing. I don't think I can stop but it is making me feel nauseous. It's getting hot inside this coat, I can feel a prickly heat rising up my body, like fingers walking up my leg.

'You're stepping on their graves,' she says.

'Stop it. You're unnerving me.' I nudge into her and we start to walk again.

'Unnerving *you?*' she says.

'I'm sorry?'

'Now you know how I feel. You could have warned me you were a sleepwalker.'

'I'm not. Well, I was . . . when I was a child. How did you know?'

'Because last week you frightened the life out of me.'

I pause to take this in. If it has started again, what have I been doing? Was I talking about her, walking into her bedroom? I try to remember the dreams I've had, the ones where I untie her hair and brush it down her back. The ones where she lifts my arms above my head and slides off my nightdress. What secrets have I told her in my sleep?

'I heard footsteps on the landing,' she says, 'and when I looked out I saw you standing, quite still, at the top of the stairs. Just looking down to the bottom.'

I feel sick.

'I thought you were awake. I tried to talk to you, your eyes were open but you had no idea I was there.'

Did I speak? That's what I need to know but I daren't ask.

'We took you back to bed and—'

'Who?'

'Emily. She heard us and got up. She was actually very kind about it.'

'I bet she was.'

'She *was*. She said we mustn't wake you in case it gave you a shock. I'd never seen anyone sleepwalking before.'

I wonder why Grace didn't say anything, why she didn't tell me the next day. But I don't ask. I want to know if she tucked me into bed and lifted the sheets back over me. But I don't ask that either.

'We'd better dig this side, near the path,' I say. 'Away from the graves.'

'Near the foundations,' she says. 'Makes sense. Here?'

'Yes.'

She bends down in front of me, one knee on the grass, and starts to dig with the trowel. She's almost invisible in the dark; the white skin on the back of her neck is all I can see of her.

'There. Is that deep enough?'

'I can't see. Let me come down and—'

'No use in getting your clothes dirty. The grass is damp.' She looks up and her pale face emerges from the shadows.

'Don't be silly. Let's have a look.' I bend down beside her, feeling my way across the grass to the hole she has dug. In it I find her hand still gripping the trowel. She doesn't jump when my skin meets hers. Nothing. No movement. No words. I hold my breath.

The slightest touch could lead to sin. Just imagine what it could lead to.

'You are shivering,' she says. 'Are you all right?'

She can't hear the voice I do. Calling from among the graves. Is it just an echo inside my head? *The slightest touch could lead to—*

'Dilys, what's wrong?'

'Let's get on, get this done,' I say, determinedly.

We can't stay here, we have to go. Because the voice is urging me to reach out to her in the dark.

I take the trowel and stab it into the ground, leaning it against the side of the hole to gauge how deeply she has dug. 'A good couple of inches. That should do it.' Then I reach into my pocket and place the first square of linen in the hole. Grace covers it with soil again.

'May the Lord protect this place in the dark days to come,' I say. 'Amen.'

'Amen.'

We carry on. Stumbling. Digging. Burying. Praying. Until all eight of the squares have gone. As Grace puts the earth back onto the last little grave she looks up at me and says, 'Let's not go back. Not yet.'

I follow her into the church porch, where she tuts and mumbles something too softly for me to hear, and it's so dark I can't see either. Then a spark of light. As a flame bursts to life I see her face. She's got a cigarette between her lips. She lights the tip and shakes the flame from the match, leaving only the scarlet heat of the tobacco, which burns brighter as she takes a long breath.

And then she speaks. 'Octavia would say it was not very ladylike, I know.'

I want to tell her she is the most ladylike woman I have ever met. Delicate. Strong. That's what feminine is. God Himself has told Octavia that women are mighty. Grace has the power to save me. Every word, every movement, assures me that she can. And she's beautiful. She is so beautiful. Even in the dark.

She takes another breath from her cigarette. 'I know it's not allowed. But tonight we're not there, we're here. I've been saving this packet, hiding it in my bedroom.'

There's just enough glow from the cigarette to illuminate her lips. It makes them look red. Like the lipstick I have seen on the cosmetic counter, the lipstick we are forbidden to wear. Smoke is gathering around us in the porch, the smell reminds me of my brother Adrian. He always liked to smoke, though I'm not sure if it was the act itself or the fact Octavia hated it so much.

'Can I tempt you?' asks Grace and I see the tip move towards me. I shouldn't but I have already taken the cigarette from her, I'm already bringing it to my mouth, placing my lips where hers have been. It's slightly damp. I try to taste any trace of her but instead I get a mouthful of smoke. I'm coughing. I look a fool.

She laughs. 'Take your time. Don't breathe too deeply. Not at first.'

Leaning forward she takes hold of the cigarette, which is still between my lips. She is so close now I can see her; so close I can feel her breathing.

'We may as well have one each,' she says, lighting a second with the heat from mine. 'It's not like I can smoke them once we get home. So . . .' she says, 'what do you think?'

I daren't tell her half of what I think.

'Do you like the taste of rebellion?' she says, trying to coax some words out of me. But I have none to give. Does she want me to feel something? Guilty? Exhilarated? Because I am neither. Surprised perhaps at how easy it was to break the rules. I know I should confess this next time I am called to list my transgressions. But I haven't decided whether I will. Not yet. This is a moment just for us. For me and Grace. And I don't think I'm prepared to share it. Because if I do it will become something else. Something more. Something wrong. And that's not what I want it to be.

I'm not coughing when I breathe the smoke in now. I feel it slip down my throat and swirl around my chest. Then it rises up in waves and my head feels as though it's expanding. As if I might float away.

Reflections

Grace and I are the last ones home. Octavia has stayed up to check us back into the house, and Emily seems almost disappointed that we haven't been set upon by rogues in the backstreets.

'I must get to bed,' I say, 'I'm exhausted,' and for once I don't have to pretend. I spend my nights chasing sleep around my bedroom, a game of hide and seek in which I'm always the searcher. But as we walked home it came to find me. I felt it creeping into the tip of my long shadow and on the corner of Castle Street it caught up, and took my hand: a feeling of calm and contentment seeping in under my coat. Now my legs feel too heavy to climb the stairs. But up I go, a laboured race to wash and get into bed before sleep stills my body and my thoughts.

The face that greets me in the mirror looks twisted, as though one side has melted. Up close I see the illusion: a smear of mud above one eyebrow that unbalances my features. It must be soil from the churchyard, dried on my skin in cracked patches like the scales of a serpent. The smell of tobacco lingers in my hair, shame clinging to each strand in pathetic rebellion. Against what? Against Octavia? Against God Himself? When I am away from this room, this house, this garden, it feels like there's another truth, but now I am back I know there is only one path. Straying from it will only bring pain.

And so will wanting to.

And I wouldn't want to be found wanting.

I had wanted Adrian to write again, though I told myself I didn't. And now there's been nothing since he told me he was getting married. I suppose I was stupid to think he might keep his promise to write, but I didn't think he'd cut me off so soon. Perhaps his fiancée put her foot down. She won't want to be associated with this. With us. With me. She will be busy picking out fabric for her wedding outfit and flowers for her bouquet. He'll wear his military uniform, of course, but then decisions on what to wear are always easier for men. When they dress they don't slip on the expectations that are sewn into the hem of every skirt and blouse.

As I stretch out and put on my nightdress I see the door reflected in my mirror. I imagine Grace is watching, closing one eye so she can look through the keyhole with the other. Against the glare of my lamp I am in silhouette: a shape, a shadow. And I turn sideways so she can see my outline, a hint of the side of my breast, the arch of my back. I let the dreams come and find me, sending fragments spinning into the air between us and she breathes them in: my nakedness, my truth. Suddenly I am tiny, small enough to fit through a keyhole, invisible like air. She tries to stay silent but the thought of me catches in her throat and I hear her gasp.

These are the thoughts I have. And they hurt. They make me ache: sharp pains as though the Devil is torturing me from the inside and I have to make him stop. Sometimes I succumb and climb into my bed and force him out. I reach beneath my nightclothes and exorcise the thoughts of her that make me shudder as they leave my body. And when they are gone I feel powerful and calm and everything seems clearer. I confess every incidence of self-abuse to Octavia. She insists on making a note of exactly when and where it happens. But when She presses me to tell Her what I think about, I don't tell Her the truth. Vague fantasies about kissing young men seem to satisfy Her. When I go outside I collect snippets of body parts to use on such occasions: deep blue eyes, chiselled jaws, broad shoulders. It is the detail that makes the sin more plausible, because if I told Her the real thoughts the Devil puts inside my head, She might send Grace away.

Sea of Galilee

I peel back each layer of fabric slowly, holding my breath; teasing myself with the anticipation of what I might find; challenging myself to guess. Every morning I step into Castleside to find a bundle of packages, donations left by members, wrapped in old scraps of material or newspaper. A set of crystal glasses, or a dozen egg cups, it doesn't matter what's inside, or that they have been left here for the bishops, in that moment they are mine: the wedding gifts I'll never have.

Members used to bring them to Number 12 in the hope that Octavia might see just how generous they were, but She soon grew irritated by all the callers. After Peter took the hoarding down at Castleside, She said there was nothing to stop donations being left just inside the back door here, and so that's where I find them. This morning's offerings were disappointingly easy to guess: the domed backs of three hot-water bottles, the unmistakable shape of a pair of bellows, wrapped so badly that the nozzle had torn through the paper. There was a picture too, a watercolour of the Sea of Galilee, painted entirely in the oranges and browns of a desert sunset: the rocks burnt umber, the water's edge touched by the blush of fading light. I've carried it up to a bedroom on the first floor, the one I'd choose if I could live in this house myself. It is not the biggest, but it overlooks the street at the front and in it I put all the furnishings I like most: a hand-sewn Bible sampler Ellen inherited from her mother; an ivory clothes brush Donald brought with him from Cambridge; a decanter that became an increasingly close companion to Kate's husband in the weeks before he went to war. I'm keeping an inventory of course. Everyone who gives will get their memories back, but once the bishops come, once the box is opened, it won't matter to them any more. There will be nothing to worry about. Nothing to fear. And we'll be far too busy preparing for Jesus to consider whether the chamber pot with the yellow roses belonged to Gertrude Searson or to Rachel Fox.

Until then, this is my house. I have lit the boiler and drawn water from the rainwater tank beneath the kitchen floor. I have plunged each knife into the Spong's Red Seal Polisher which swallows dull blades then spits them out with a flash of light along their sharpened edge. In my mind I do the jobs that Grace does: I swing the carpet-beater into empty air, and heat the blue tin kettle to a whistle. Then at lunchtime she carries across a tray and we sit together. In the kitchen. Where the window is high and no one can see in.

There's a noise downstairs. It sounds like someone is knocking on the back door. It won't be Grace, not yet. Besides, she knows to come straight in. It must be one of the ladies with a donation.

All she has to do is try the handle. Open the door. Leave her parcel. Go.

If I walk downstairs I will have to speak to her, she might want to stay and chat, ask how I am getting on; so I concentrate on hanging the watercolour from the picture rail, holding it up at different places on the wall to find the right spot.

Another sound. A voice this time. I stand completely still and listen. 'Hello?' it says. 'Are you there?' A low voice. A man's voice.

I think of the smashed window that I found in the pantry; the light I saw in the window from the Garden; and all the things that

Octavia has told us that men will try to do to women, given the chance. I am trapped upstairs alone and they have come back. Whoever it was has come back.

I slip off my shoes so I can move silently across the wooden floor. If I make my way to the landing I can look over the bannister and I may be able to see where they are. Then I can decide whether to get out and run or stay in and hide. And pray, of course, I must do that either way.

I make it as far as the doorway, moving slowly, testing each floorboard as if it might give way and send me falling through it.

'Hello? Miss Barltrop? Are you here?' It's a voice I know. American. It is Edgar. 'See, I told you,' he says. 'It's empty.'

'It is too much of a risk,' says another. 'If anyone found us in here . . .'

'Then we'd tell them we came to see if we could help, Donald, come on.'

From out here on the landing I can hear them clearly now, hear their footsteps on the tiled floor of the hall. 'Hello?' shouts Edgar again.

I could go back into the bedroom. Hide behind the door. But my legs won't move.

'It is Wednesday,' Edgar says. 'She told us herself, she cuts the linen on a Wednesday. And if I have to sit through another interminable game of bridge with *those women*, I don't know what I'll do!'

I hear the creak of the stairs. They are climbing up. And I am just standing here. I should hide.

'But Edgar . . .'

'Isn't it worth the risk to get away from all those prying eyes? There's no way we can talk freely with my landlady hovering, and there's no question of us going to my room, it would get back to Octavia in no time. There have already been questions.'

'What questions?' says Donald and I hear their footsteps halt halfway up the stairs.

'Emily's been asking what we are discussing in our Bible study, reminding me that men must follow the rule of women. And Peter is eager to join our prayer meetings. All these months he could hardly bring himself to be civil to me when Octavia wasn't in ear-shot. Now suddenly he's acting like we might be friends.'

I have no choice now. Another few steps and they'll find me standing here, shoes in hand. They'll know that I have heard them.

'Mr Peissart, Mr Ricketts, can I help you?' I try to strike an imposing figure at the top of the stairs. Both men jump and look up to see where the voice has come from.

'Dilys . . . Miss Barltrop. You *are* here,' says Edgar, bringing his hand to his chest as if to steady his heart.

'I am. And so are you. May I ask why?' I hold onto the bannister tightly, my legs shaking.

'We came to see if we could be of any assistance,' says Donald. He looks around, pretending to appreciate the décor but I know he is avoiding my eyes.

'That won't be necessary. Thank you.'

The colour has drained from Edgar's face. I see his knuckles blanching too, both hands gripping his cane too tightly. He tries to force a laugh, looking to Donald for some reaction, but he gives none; the younger man's cheeks seem to wear the colour that the elder's have lost.

'Castleside is out of bounds until everything is ready,' I say, surprised by the burn of anger in the back of my throat. 'Octavia made that quite clear.'

There are too many thoughts let loose in my head, too many questions: a murmuration of starlings, taking form but refusing to hold their shape. I want to know whether Edgar and Donald have been in here before. Whether they have been lounging in the chairs in the sitting room, reading the books I have arranged on the shelves. This is *my* house, filled with the things I have collected and the thoughts I have had. They have no right to be here.

Edgar shrinks back. 'Of course. I had quite forgotten. My apologies, Miss Barltrop.'

I like this feeling. This power I have. This must be what it is like to be Octavia, to dictate and make decisions. He longs to ask me – *will you tell Her, Dilys, will you tell?* But he won't. Not out loud. And I already know I won't ask him the question still swooping and soaring in my head – *the broken window, Edgar. The broken window, was that you?* If I knew the answer I would be required to tell. Octavia thinks the truth is a straight line but when you follow the strand of a secret you find it knotted up. If you're not careful you get tangled in it.

'We'll say no more about it,' I say. And he looks at me wide-eyed and disbelieving. There is silence between us. Silence that stretches out far too long.

'Very good, Miss Barltrop,' says Donald finally. 'It is much appreciated. We don't want to spoil the surprise of the grand unveiling. We'll be sure to stay away until then, won't we?'

Edgar gives a start as Donald pats him on the shoulder. 'A

misunderstanding, yes. Our apologies for disturbing you. We merely wanted to ask if we could help. But I see you have everything quite under control.' He bows, then turns to Donald. 'After you,' he says, following him back down the stairs. I watch them cross the hallway in silence, Edgar striking the floor with a flourish of his cane, Donald looking up at me, his slicked-down hair starting to lift behind his ears. 'Thank you,' he says, mouthing silent words up to me. I hear the back door close behind them and I realise I've been holding my breath. For a moment I felt powerful, but that wasn't really me. It was Grace. I was pretending to be Grace, and the effort of playing her has left me drained.

The General Strike

It's almost midnight and the music has stopped. On the BBC, an announcer's voice breaks the silence to give the final instructions: 'All loyal citizens should keep calm, and determined to do their best to keep law and order.' The moment has come, the strike is about to begin. 'We commend the country to God's guidance and ask that peace may be restored.' Through the crackle of the signal we can hear his sincerity, and is it fear?

There were too many of us to gather in the Wireless Room tonight, so Octavia commanded that the radio set be brought into the chapel instead. Many of the resident members have come, there must be forty at least. Those who live in houses more than two streets away are under curfew: they were told to stay inside once dusk fell. Ellen is feeling too ill to make it down to chapel in the dark, but Grace will be with her and soon I will be too. Octavia agreed that we could keep her company for the night.

It is so dark out there this evening, the moon looks as though it has been bitten to the quick, the thinnest crescent of fingernail scratching the sky. But inside, the chapel blazes with light. Everyone is holding a lamp, and though each one is turned down, the effect is unforgiving: every wrinkle and pimple seen in sharp relief. Rachel Fox looks like she is wearing a dusting of rouge on her cheeks, which is against the rules. She is clearly relishing the drama of the occasion. The prospect of catastrophe seems to brighten her complexion, her eyes are sparkling, her posture primed, as if she is waiting to take on the rioting mobs single-handedly, and if it came

to it she might have to. At times like this it is men who are expected to spring forward and unleash their instinct to fight, but Edgar
and Peter are the only men here tonight, which doesn't fill me with
confidence. And from the look of Peter, who sits fidgeting in his
chair, it's a burden that doesn't sit comfortably with him either.
It's a pity Donald isn't here, at least he has the vitality of youth and
I have seen some of the ladies admiring the curve of his arms when
they think that no one is looking. He is the nearest thing we'd have
to a protector but I haven't seen him since he came to Castleside.
I'm not sure anybody has. When Octavia enquired after him this
morning, Edgar said he'd been anxious to return to Cambridge
before the strike brings the trains to a halt. He looked at me when
he said it, the briefest glance. And when I walked across the lawn
to Castleside Edgar was sitting on the bench under Yggdrasil.

'Dilys,' he said, standing up as I crossed the lawn nearby. 'I am
glad I have caught you. I hope you don't misunderstand anything
you may have heard me say to Donald. It can be . . . difficult living
among so many women. We rather feel like we're in the minority.
Sometimes we just crave peace and quiet.' I smiled politely and
said that I quite understood.

I didn't say I crave it too.

Octavia stands in front of the altar. 'And so the hour has come,'
She says, in a tone that is statesmanlike yet serene. 'We must remember what the Prime Minister said in his address this evening:
"Keep steady, keep steady. Remember that peace on Earth comes
to men of good will." Alas, he failed to mention that the same goes
for women too.' With a sweep of Her eyes She gathers up everyone in the room. 'But let's not waste our prayers on Mr Baldwin.
He should have crushed this rebellion weeks ago. No, my heart

goes out to the King and Queen. God has promised me they will come to no harm. But I only wish that they were here, protected, in His Garden. We should be pleased to have them as our guests!'

There's a noise outside. It is just a dog barking but we're all on edge, braced for something to happen. The entire congregation jumps as the chapel bell above us strikes the first of twelve chimes, all except Octavia who stays perfectly still, eyes closed and head down, as if She is preparing to receive a vision. God has told Her this is a sign. Tonight marks the beginning of the end for the rule of man. Once the country goes to war with itself, chaos and terror will reign, just as the Bible has foretold. Then the bishops will come begging to open the box, and the way will be clear for Jesus to return to Earth.

'We have God's protection,' She says, without lifting Her head. 'Tonight we may hear the cries of the baying crowds in the streets outside, and from our windows see our town in flames. Out there may be a vision of Hell itself, but we are safe in the Garden. Panaceans, we shall come to no harm, for the Lord has given me His word.'

We shall come to no harm.

There is nothing to fear.

But I am frightened. At any moment the world outside could come spilling over the wall, the anger of the working man thrown as a brick through a window, or a burning rag posted through a letterbox. And we all know that we could be a target. Women of independent means. Surely they'd relish the excuse to show us how vulnerable we really are.

With a nod from Octavia, the ladies at the back start to file out of the chapel. It is late and they want to get home and lock their doors; this of all nights is not one to be wandering in the dark.

They take their place in the queue, pairs of feet in a centipede's hundred, shuffling along towards the door. I should leave with them but I want to stay. Octavia is still sitting motionless, attended by Her inner circle; Kate, Peter, Edgar and Emily are gathering, and I feel the same mixture of fascination and repulsion I had when I spied them through the keyhole of the Upper Room.

Slipping behind the curtain into the room at the back of the chapel, which is used for storage, I turn off my lamp and wait in the dark. I said I would go straight to Ellen's house, I should be there by now, but I want to watch. I want to know if I was wrong before.

If they find me they will know I am spying. There is no purpose I can pretend to have, nothing I would have come to find. Only spare chairs, old copies of *The Panacea* and a dried flower arrangement encased in a thick layer of dust. A ladder leads up to the clock tower, identical to the one Peter built to access his attic room. I could climb it but the trapdoor at the top would be too heavy to lift without making a noise.

Emily is lighting church candles in a circle around them on the floor, the flames sending pulses of light across the walls. 'You stand before me as the Chosen, the four creatures around the throne of God in the Book of Revelation,' Octavia says, gently. 'Tonight, man's rebellion fulfils His word and hastens His return to Earth. But, while the Lord's prophecy is realised *outside* these walls, we must look to our own actions *inside* His Chosen Land.'

There is a hint of anger in Her voice, then silence. She used to do this when we were children. When we were very small it was 'take a moment to think about what you have done', but by the time we were six or seven years old, Her silence was enough to wake the guilt in our stomachs, the first stirrings of the moths that would gnaw away inside. Sometimes a few would fly out of our mouths:

confessions blurted, our bodies expelling the feelings of disgust and shame. 'I didn't say my prayers before bed.' 'I broke Ivan's toy soldier, then hid it under his bed.' Honesty is supposed to make you feel better but it never did. The look of disappointment on Mother's face just made the crime more palpable.

The Chosen want to know which of them has disappointed Her. Because one of them has. Or perhaps all of them. They stand with their heads bowed. Waiting.

'The Lord demands obedience,' She says, 'not vanity.' Edgar moves slightly, shifting his weight from one foot to the other. 'There is no brake upon the vehicle of the soul when it goeth down its own path. The powers of a soul uncontrolled by true religion are the powers of darkness.'

This is leading somewhere. Octavia has prepared this speech for a reason.

Stand there and think about what you have done.

'Powers to tell lies and not to flinch,' She says. 'Powers to appear more self-reliant and composed than others, powers to convince, to scheme, to fly in the face of all the simple Earth-conventions.'

She pauses again and looks up towards the back of the chapel.

'Powers to enjoy, to be merry, to be happy in the midst of sin.'

Nobody moves or makes a sound. Then just like that, She turns to them and smiles, drawing them close with warm inflection: 'And that's why I turn to you, my faithful. God Himself has told me that Christ will not return until you are obedient to Him and to His Daughter. But there are those in the society who struggle, who question. Their doubt is the barrier to God's plan. And it is up to us to help them see their error.'

Emily is the only one brave enough to speak: she is the only one who would get away with it. 'We must have order,' she says.

'Indeed, Emily. For the alternative is chaos. And that is the Devil's realm.'

Octavia brings Her hands together, in prayer, then stretches out Her arms in a pose of crucifixion. 'Let His spirit move us. In Ezekiel's vision the wheels move as if one living being. Let us become one. Devoted to His cause. Obedient to His will.'

Without a word they stand in formation, four corners of a square, dropping their heads and closing their eyes. Then without prompting they start to dance, holding hands and moving in a circle. Emily and Peter step forward and press their palms together, then their heads. As they step back, Kate and Edgar fill the void they have left and do the same. I wonder what silent music they can hear, and whether it is the same tune for each. They all move to the same beat. To my mind it looks like the country dancing we do in the summer on the lawn: Octavia the silent caller.

It is not the first time this ritual has been performed, I have heard their feet moving across the floor in the room next to mine, but it is the first time I have witnessed it. Peter's accounts speak of heavenly music filling their ears and I could never understand why I couldn't hear it through the wall. But now it's obvious: it is inside their heads.

I don't know how long it goes on, perhaps half an hour. All this time Octavia's arms remain outstretched and completely still, no shaking to suggest She is tiring. Then suddenly She jumps and brings Her hands together in applause. She is laughing and twirling, giddy with joy.

'Together we praise the Lord!' She says. 'How blessed we are to serve Him!'

In perfect unison, the Chosen stop dancing and stand around Her. 'How blessed we are!' they say, clapping their hands too. They haven't noticed that Emily has started to sway and stumble. She leans towards Peter and lets out a loud moan as he breaks her fall, slowing her descent just long enough for Edgar to step in and save her from hitting the floor. Kate rushes in to help but Octavia holds up a hand to stop her.

'Place her down gently,' She says. 'And Kate, bring the board. I think the Lord has something He wishes to say.'

The two men link Emily's arms and carry her across to the wall, her feet dragging on the floor. With her knees buckled they can lower her in a controlled slump; Peter struggles with the effort of supporting her. I can see her face from here, head lolling, eyes rolling. Kate brings a tray, white with a red rim, then she lifts Emily's right hand and, uncurling her forefinger from its clenched fist, places it on the surface.

'Lord, we await Your Word,' Octavia says, and Peter, Edgar and Kate step back, leaving Emily propped up against the wall. She looks twisted, like a puppet with broken strings and glass eyes. Staring forward she begins to move her fingertip across the tray, drawing red lines without a nib or brush. Is it her blood? The others stand and watch but no one helps; no one seems alarmed. And then Emily twitches and knocks the tray, a crimson stain seeping across it.

'Try again,' Octavia says excitedly. Kate steps forward, picking up the tray and shaking it until the marks are gone. And suddenly I understand: it is flour. Emily is writing in flour, her fingertip uncovering the red tray underneath. Octavia stands over her. 'A crown,' She says. 'It looks like a crown. The sovereignty of the Lord.'

She smiles at the other three, then lifts Her arms and gestures around the chapel. 'Behold, He is here among us. The King of Kings, my Father. He is speaking to us through Emily tonight. She is blessed indeed.'

She turns back to watch Emily reveal more. 'A cross,' She says. 'Four points of equal measure.' Emily is still staring forward. Her finger begins to rise up from the tray, forcing her arm to follow behind it. And then it stops. Octavia, Kate and Peter turn together to see where she is pointing: directly at Edgar.

'What is it?' Octavia says, excitedly. 'What is she trying to tell us? Something about Edgar. Emily, draw for us. Tell us what you see.' But Emily cries out and slams down her hand, sending a cloud into the air. The shock jolts her awake. She looks around the room, then down to her lap; down to the white dust that has made her black skirt chalky. Tutting, she sets to work to brush it off, but with her hand caked in flour she is only making it worse.

She looks up for an explanation. 'Octavia?'

'You were receiving the Spirit, Emily. It was marvellous to behold. Let's get you inside and tidied up,' She says. 'A good strong cup of tea. That's what you need.'

Emily's eyes are rolling again.

'Kate. The door?' Octavia hands her a lamp and Kate does as she is told, holding the door open while Edgar and Peter heave Emily back up onto her feet and help her out into the Garden. Only Octavia stays behind, walking round to blow out the ring of candles, one by one. She picks up a lantern from the altar and raises it above the tray, leaning over to inspect what's left of the marks in the flour. That look on Her face, is it worry? In the near-darkness it is difficult to tell. But something about the way She's hunched over reminds me of who She used to be, when She was sent away.

When She was still my mother.

Then just as quickly Mabel is gone and Octavia is upright, shoulders back, the usual look of determination firmly reinstated on Her face. She leaves the chapel, and leaves me in my hiding place.

———

I wait a few minutes before I step out into the Garden. After the swell of relief that they are gone comes the familiar prickle of panic: I'm alone in the dark, alone with my thoughts, and the imagined horrors that threaten to swallow me. I have to get to Ellen's house. I promised I'd be with her just after midnight and it must be half past by now.

Nothing looks familiar. The jutting angles of rooflines loom like battlements, dotted with arrowslits where light escapes through the gaps between curtains. I imagine archers on every side, loading bows, taking aim. The others will be sitting up in the rooms behind those windows, too full of delighted dread to think about sleeping yet; creeping back downstairs to double-check they are safely locked inside.

Ellen gave me a spare key. I grasp it in my pocket, the metal jutting out between my knuckles just as Grace showed me. 'You could do a lot of damage with that,' she said. 'Give them a shock. Stop them long enough to run.' Fear stalks women just as surely as our own shadows. Why do we talk about light flooding in when it is darkness that rushes to claim us? It's the dark that can drown you in fear, cold creeping up your body like rising water. You can be plunged into it, swallowed by it. The dark can be so deep that you don't know where it ends, or what monsters might be swimming around you. Light is like a shallow bath in comparison. It's something you bathe in. It makes you feel warm.

I am close to the wall that separates the Garden from Albany Road. A faint glow seeps through the trellis on the top, my thirsty eyes gulping stolen light from the streetlamps on the other side. I want to be at Ellen's house, in front of the fire, with Grace and a cup of cocoa. Out here anything could happen to me and no one would find me until morning. My thoughts start to run and my feet follow, taking me stumbling forward. I feel the air pulse. And that's when I hear it: a voice is calling my name. *Dilys. Dilys Barltrop.* It is low. A man's voice. Urgent, like a prompter in the wings of a dark stage, coaxing me to say my lines, to come closer to the wall and whisper back.

'*Dilys,*' it says, '*I can help you get out of there. Dilys. I can help you escape.*'

But from what? You can't escape the voices in your head. You just have to learn not to listen; to let the Truth drown them out.

'*Dilys?*'

I hear a low rasping cry behind me. There's something in the Garden. I have to get to Ellen's house. I have to run. When I reach the door I use my fingertips to find the keyhole. But my shaking hand won't guide the key to its target; it skitters against the metal of the escutcheon like a frantic creature, a mouse trying to claw its way into a hole. I hear the rasping call repeated and then I feel something brush against the back of my head. I turn and see the frantic flap of a black shadow, then it is gone.

At last the key turns and I hear the click of the lock. As soon as I am through the door I slam it behind me, leaning against it with the full force of my relief. But the world in here is even darker. No lamp burning in the hall; the clouded light of the sickly moon too weak to cross the boundary of glass in the high kitchen window.

They must be upstairs. And so up I climb, stepping very carefully, feeling my way along the wall, counting the squares in the pattern of the wallpaper, like the blinded would read Braille. I must be halfway up now. I can see Ellen's bedroom door, and now I'm so close I want to run to it. Run to Grace. But I have to go slowly, pushing through the thick darkness, the air heavy with my own laboured breath.

I knock too loudly, and am admonished by the creak of a chair and footsteps. Grace opens the door and steps out onto the landing, closing the door behind her with a tenderness that tells me Ellen is asleep inside.

'Grace . . .' I bury my head in her shoulder and cling to her. Now I am safe I can't hold back the tide of panic. It crashes over me and I surrender: holding onto Grace, urging her to chase the fear away. I pull her tighter but still it is not enough. Could never be enough. If I could climb inside her I would, passing into her like a ghost through a wall.

'Are you all right? What's happened?' Our bodies are so close that I can feel my heart knocking against her chest. Hammering to get in.

'I thought there was someone following me.'

'My goodness, Dilys. Who? Did they hurt you?' She tries to step back to look at me but I pull her closer, refuse to let go. 'Dilys. Tell me, what happened?'

'Nothing,' I say. 'Nothing happened. It was just my imagination running wild. All this talk about the strike. And it's so dark out there. I let myself get carried away.' I start to laugh and I can feel the panic lurching out of my body.

'Dilys, calm down. You're not making any sense.'

'It was Sir Jack!' I say, and I realise it's true. 'It was only Sir Jack! On patrol in the Garden!'

I felt him fly past my head. I saw him in the shadows. And perhaps the voice I heard was just his call.

'So there was no one there?'

'No,' I laugh.

'Thank God.'

I won't tell her what I heard because now I'm safe indoors, I can't be sure there was a voice at all. As soon as you admit you are hearing things, people start to wonder, don't they? And I've been wondering myself. How can I be sure that it's the Devil who is speaking and not just the whispers of my own desires, the thoughts I dare not say out loud? It's the not-knowing that sends you mad. I should know. I've seen it happen.

'I thought . . .' Grace says. 'You frightened me.' She is angry, I can tell. 'We've been worried. You're so late. Where have you been?'

'I'm sorry,' I say. 'I got held up in chapel.'

'I'm just glad you're safe.' The anger is gone, her whisper now a mother soothing a child. Her voice makes me sleepy, like my legs might give way, and I might give in.

'You're really shaken.'

My heart is still running, still tripping over itself. I let my head fall onto her shoulder again and breathe her in. Now I'm not trying to flee the darkness, I'm asking it to come and take us, envelop us. So we're invisible; so this is not really happening; so my lips aren't really brushing the skin on her neck.

Right now all I can hear is a voice telling me to lift my mouth to hers.

'Dilys?' she whispers. It sounds like a question.

'Dilys . . .' Something catches in her voice. She sounds frightened. But is it fear of me or of herself? Does she want me to do the things I am imagining?

'We mustn't,' she murmurs to herself. She turns her face from mine, exposing her neck to my lips. 'We shouldn't.' But she doesn't move, she doesn't walk away. Her body is rigid. I can feel her chest rising and falling, feel the tension in every breath.

'Grace!' The voice is not a whisper, it's a shout. It is coming from behind the door. Ellen has woken up. 'Are you there?' she says. 'Please! Where are you?' We rush into her bedroom and I sit on the edge of her bed.

'We're here,' I say. 'Don't worry.'

Ellen looks at me and then at Grace. We are not invisible any more. I wonder whether she can read the look on my face, feel the heat from my body.

'You get some rest,' I say. 'We'll be right here.'

Ellen closes her eyes. In this light she looks younger, her cheeks not quite so sunken, her skin not quite so pale.

'We decided she'd be more comfortable up here,' Grace says softly, busying herself at the fireplace behind me. 'And it's just as well. She could hardly stay awake.' Her voice sounds thin and timid. She is avoiding my eyes. 'Cocoa?' she says, with a forced brightness.

'Yes please.' I sit on one of the two chairs she has pulled up to the fire, and look across at Ellen. 'How did she seem, before she dropped off?'

'Oh, a little anxious at first. I was here at about eleven o'clock and I could tell she was starting to worry when it got to midnight,' she says, rubbing her knuckles with the tip of her thumb. 'But in the end it was a bit like seeing in the New Year – all a bit of an anti-climax.'

'All quiet so far?' I ask. 'No noise out on the street?'

'Nothing. But it's only just gone one o'clock now. There's still time.'

I watch her pour cocoa from a pot that's warming by the fire and when I take it our hands touch.

'Dilys,' she says, looking down. 'Out there, on the landing . . . when you didn't arrive I was worried . . . And then when I saw you in such a state . . . I was . . .'

'It's understandable on a night like this.'

With our words we pretend that nothing happened but something has passed between us. She knows. Perhaps she has known all along. Since that first day in the Garden. Since before I knew it myself.

When she looks up at me again, I tell her silently; I tell her everything. That when I am with her I am in the wilderness, tested like Jesus, hungry and desperate. Tempted by the Devil.

I stretch forth my hands unto thee: my soul thirsteth after thee, as a thirsty land.

(Psalm 143:6)

I feed her my thoughts, sending them across the space between us, letting them linger just before her lips. I look at her and in my mind I kiss her, and with her eyes she finds my mouth. She is the first to look away, shuffling in her chair, smoothing down her skirt and making that noise she makes. But this time I think I know what it means: it is longing, not contentment.

'Dilys,' she says. 'We can't . . .'

'I know. Don't worry,' I whisper. And for the first time in my life I feel that I am in control. To crave each other is not a sin, as long as we don't give in. Just knowing is enough. Just knowing that she is tempted by the Devil as I am. It is another pact that we make then and there, without saying a word.

'It's cold,' I say.

She looks up.

'The cocoa, Grace. I'm afraid it's cold.'

I smile and she laughs with such relief, as though I have saved her from falling, pulled her back from the edge of a cliff.

'Well, I'm sorry, *Miss* Dilys, but at midnight, when you were supposed to be here, it was piping hot. I can assure you.' She pauses. 'I'm glad we're friends, Dilys.'

'The best of friends.'

SUMMER

The matter of sex-relations or what is called
the Purity Question must be dealt with. Write
down in actual words any sins of impurity . . .
Do not be afraid to use the words 'adultery',
'self-abuse', 'unholy thoughts'. It will comfort
you to know that no one is entirely free from
sex-difficulties.

Octavia, *A Reply to Those Sealed People Who Are
Enquiring About Confession*

The Vow

She is lying face down. Her arms are by her sides, her legs slightly apart, a halo of red hair fanning out around her head. Grace is not moving, except for a momentary twitch of her hand. She will soon be dead: her old life will be over.

'May Almighty God grant you His grace to fulfil your resolutions,' Octavia says, standing over her in front of the altar. Grace is a body wrapped in the shroud of her Sunday best, the white cotton of her blouse falling against the skin at the small of her back. Her navy skirt is trimmed with military braiding, small brass buttons marking each corner by the hem. It makes her look like she is back-to-front, a casualty of war who twisted as she fell.

'In this you symbolise the death of all that is past and a commitment to serving Jesus as your husband,' Octavia says.

Today is Grace's wedding day. I am one of the guests. Once the ceremony is over I'll join the long line of well-wishers and congratulate her. I'll take a piece of the cake she baked this morning. There will be no groom to hold the knife with, no bouquet to throw, no going-away outfit. And no need to bid an embarrassed farewell: there will be no marital bed to rush to. Or recoil from.

Grace kneels at Octavia's feet and speaks: 'I make to God, in Your hands, the simple vows of chastity and obedience.' Octavia dispensed with the bit about poverty. She has always been drawn to the pomp and ceremony of the Catholic Church but when dogma compromises comfort, something's got to give. She places Her hand on Grace's head, touching her hair: 'You are a bride of Christ,

and soon you will look upon His face and call Him husband. Soon
He will return.' She signals to Emily, who steps forward with a
glass of water on a tray. 'And now you are reborn in Him, your
new life will be eternal. Now I share with you the gift He hath
bestowed on me.'

She takes a pair of tweezers, and fishes out a piece of linen that has
sunk to the bottom of the glass. Just as my father used to administer
the Eucharist, She holds the glass to Grace's lips and lets her sip.
'You are blessed,' She says. And after she has swallowed, Grace
replies as she has been instructed: 'Blessed indeed.' Only the two of
us know that I gave her a square of linen all those weeks ago.

One of many secrets that bind us together.

Octavia will bestow one more gift on her this evening. Now that
she has walked down the aisle and made her vows to Jesus, Grace
is one of us. Octavia reaches into Her pocket and pulls out a small
scarlet case. I know that it is held together with tiny stitches, each
carefully sewn by hand. I know that a small bone button holds the
flap down at the front, and inside is a disc of red wax and a hand-
written card. I know it is identical to the one I carry with me always; the one I was given when I took the vow.

**Within the wax enclosed is sealed up the LIVING
BREATH. The seal of protection in the Coming
Dangers is to be kept in a safe place easily got at and
is to be worn on the person when travelling or when
dangers begin to threaten. If opened or tampered with
it will lose its virtue.**

I know all this because Octavia asked me to sew it for Grace. 'How
neat your stitches are,' She said when it was done. But She did not

know the reason I had taken so much care. She didn't know the thoughts I'd had when I sat with my needle and thread, stitching on the safety pin that will attach it to the inside of her camisole.

Grace stands and takes it from Her hand, bows her head and sits in the seat beside me. Today I am at the front. Today it is my day too. Octavia said it was only right that I should do it, since I am the one who brought Grace to the society.

'On this joyous occasion we have another reason to celebrate,' She says. 'Good sense has prevailed. *God's* sense has prevailed. He answered our prayers to protect England from the forces of darkness and after nine days the newspapers have reported that the strike has been brought to a peaceful conclusion.' Emily starts to clap and, taking her lead, the congregation welcomes the news with applause. But the mood is subdued. Octavia's prophecies of death and destruction have not been fulfilled. As though answering the question none of us is brave enough to ask, She says: 'Are those looks of disappointment on your faces? It is true, we had hoped that this would be the beginning of the End. But have faith. The Bible speaks of the terror of men and perhaps the fear of what might have been will be enough to persuade the bishops to come. Take heart—'

She is interrupted by one of the ladies blowing their nose into a handkerchief. Noisily. Octavia's eyes respond immediately, darting to find the perpetrator. 'Thank you, Miss Tweedie,' She says, 'for choosing this moment to unblock your nasal passages so freely. I hope it has brought you some relief. But I must insist that you do not join us in chapel when you have a cold. The rest of us should not be subjected to the risk of infection, or forced to endure the sounds of the symptoms it induces.'

Miss Tweedie stands and leaves the room with a mumbled apology.

'Now where was I?' Octavia says, clasping Her hands together.

'The time is near . . .' Emily prompts Her.

'Yes, yes. The time is near. In fact we have some news. I was *horrified* at first,' Octavia says with exaggerated amusement. 'But Emily saw it right away – a blessing in the most unlikely disguise!'

'It has been reported in the press,' says Emily, rising from her chair to stand beside Her, 'that a Mr Harry Price believes he has something of ours in his possession. He has written to inform us that he intends to open Joanna Southcott's box.'

A murmur ripples through the congregation. The air hums with energy. Emily pauses to enjoy the shocked glances; the unspoken questions that are filling the room. She has a new dress for the occasion: Eton blue with a Peter Pan collar. Perhaps she thought it would make her look younger, but it has precisely the opposite effect. 'For those of you who are not familiar with his name, I should explain that he is a psychical researcher, a ghost-hunter—'

'A charlatan!' Octavia cuts in.

'Indeed. A man who, unfortunately, has been able to charm the ignorant public with his parlour-tricks. You may remember he came to prominence during his investigation into the hauntings at Borley Rectory in Essex, for which he was given far too much attention in the newspapers, in my opinion.' Emily is allowed an opinion now; it's a luxury not afforded to the rest of us. Peter sits forward in his chair as though willing her to go on.

'He has told members of the press that he has been given Joanna's box,' she says, 'and that he intends to open it in front of an audience—'

'Without the bishops,' Octavia states. 'Disregarding any of the instructions Joanna left.'

Emily nods sagely; it's one of the faces she's been perfecting recently: wise but suitably deferential. 'But of course this box he has is not Joanna Southcott's at all,' she says. 'Octavia knows the true prophecies are still safe, still sealed, still secret. Quite simply, the whole thing is a scam.'

'Mr Price has ambitions to discredit us,' Octavia says, 'but as the Bible tells us: In the last days mockers will come—'

She is interrupted by another voice from the back of the room. 'Then what do you intend we do to stop him?' Edgar leaps up from his seat, fists clenched by his sides. 'What I mean is that we cannot stand idly by. Someone needs to act.'

'And we shall,' says Emily firmly, taking a very small step in front of Octavia to shield Her from his interruption. 'You would be wise to have a little more trust, and practise a little more patience, Edgar. If Mr Price intends to court publicity then we shall take the opportunity to exploit it. We shall spread the Truth.'

Edgar stands for another moment, then sits back down, cowed into silence by the many rows of faces that have turned to look at him. Peter rolls his eyes before swinging back to face the front.

'Do not forget,' says Emily, stepping aside to reveal Octavia. 'We have God on our side.'

———

'Did I look nervous?' Grace asks me.

'No, not at all. You were marvellous.' I have stayed behind in chapel to help her tidy away the last of the cake and the napkins. She called them serviettes but Octavia didn't hear her, so no harm done.

'I remembered all my lines. That's something, I suppose.'

She kneels down to sweep up the crumbs that have fallen to the floor. I want to touch the top of her head like Octavia did. 'I'm afraid your moment was rather overshadowed by Her news,' I say.

'Yes, the famous ghost-hunter. I'd never heard of him. Had you?'

'Yes. Years ago Octavia began to take a keen interest in the paranormal. She was quite a fan of his for a time. He exposed a few spiritualists who were conning the vulnerable. One medium swore she was spouting ectoplasm. Turns out she had filled her mouth with bandages soaked in egg white.' I look at her and shrug. 'Gives the same effect apparently.'

She sweeps the last of the crumbs and gets back to her feet. 'But Octavia believes in ghosts, doesn't She?'

'In the spirits of Heaven and Hell,' I say. 'Because *they* are real. But there are plenty of crooks who will prey on grief with lies. And plenty of widows and mothers only too ready to believe them.'

'The war has provided a plentiful supply,' she says.

'Precisely. But Octavia admired the fact that Harry Price seemed to know the difference.'

She steps out of the chapel door and shakes the crumbs away into the breeze.

'So,' I say, when she returns, 'you are officially a Panacean now. How do you intend to spend your wedding night?'

She looks up and meets my eyes. I think I have made her blush. 'I have no plans. Why?'

'Well, I think that we should mark the occasion. How about a cigarette?' I can tell she wasn't expecting that. It's what I wanted. To surprise her. To have the power to do it. To have the strength. 'Consider these a wedding gift,' I say, peeking a pack out of the pocket in my skirt. Before Grace came, everything was black and white, there was only what Octavia approved of, and what She didn't. But now the boundary has been blurred, smudged like red lipstick. As soon as you cross the line you've got your back to it and you cannot see how far you've gone.

'Dilys!' She tries to purse her lips in affected disapproval, but her impersonation of Emily is sabotaged by a broad smile.

'Octavia asked me to post out the letters for the healing so I ran a little errand of my own.' I have been hiding the packet in the box at the back of my wardrobe, taking it out, slipping a single cigarette from the rest, holding it between my fingers, bringing it to my lips.

'Come on.' I take her hand and lead her to the room at the back of the chapel, and as I hold back the curtain I think of the night of the strike. I still wonder if Octavia knew that I was there.

'How are you with heights, Grace?'

'I'll be brave,' she says. It's no more than ten steps up the ladder to the clock tower, but when I get to the top I have to push the trapdoor open with my head. I'm aware that she is standing underneath me, underneath my skirts. I feel exposed. I don't seem to mind.

'Pass me that dust sheet,' I say and she takes a cover off a row of chairs and throws it to me in a bundle. I have to lean away from the ladder to catch it one-handed and I'm close to falling. It's dusty up here and there's barely room for two of us. 'Are you coming?'

She passes a lamp, then climbs up. At the top we have to hold each other and balance on the ledge to lower the trapdoor. And when we sit, our knees touch, our legs are tucked to opposite sides: a mirror image.

'Well, this is cosy,' she says. 'As long as you don't mind spiders.'

I do. I do mind spiders. But right now I couldn't care that there are cobwebs crowding the dark corners. I take the cigarettes and matches out of my pocket and hand them to her.

'Thank you,' she says. 'Shall I do the honours?'

'I think you'd better. I'm still a novice.'

A match bursts into life and the smell takes me back to the churchyard and her lips glowing red in the darkness. This time I'm closer, close enough that I can breathe the smoke when she exhales; close enough to taste the tobacco and feel my head start to swim. She takes the cigarette, swaps it to her left hand, then brings it to my mouth. Her fingers are almost touching my lips. The air is getting thicker, smoke gathering in the dim glow of the lamp.

'Thank you, Dilys,' she says. 'It was very kind of you to buy these. And brave. Are you sure that no one saw you?'

'I was careful.' I saw Ethel and Mildred on my way into town but they were heading home.

'That's good,' she says, but there's something in her voice that leaves me unconvinced.

'Are you all right?' I say. 'You seem quiet.'

'This is my wedding day, I am deliriously happy,' she says, flatly.

'But you're not.'

'I'm fine. Just ignore me.'

'You know that's the one thing I could never do.' As I say it I hear a smile on her breath, then just as quickly it is gone.

'It's just, I was so desperate to be a part of this. I thought any doubts I had would get swept away, but now I'm more confused than ever. There is so much that I don't understand, that doesn't make sense . . . Last week we thought the world was coming to an end, everyone was so frightened. But nothing happened.'

'We live in fear. That's what we do. It's how the Lord keeps us on a righteous path.' I say it with a smile, to try to rally her mood, but she is not laughing. This is not a joke. The air is so murky with swirling smoke that I can't see the edges of the room. She puts the cigarette to her lips, then passes it back to me, our hands touching as I take it from her fingers.

'I have been called for my first confession,' she says. 'Now that I am sealed, Octavia says I must begin Overcoming. I keep thinking about it, wondering what I should say and . . .' She stops and looks down at her lap.

'And what you shouldn't?'

'Yes.'

Octavia says a guilty conscience is a blessing. It reminds us to repent and ask forgiveness. But I've grown so used to feeling shame that I don't know which thoughts I should be feeling guilty for.

'You'll be fine,' I reassure her.

'I have seen ladies coming out of their confession looking terrified,' she says. 'Last week Elizabeth Broadbent emerged in floods of tears.'

'Octavia approves of tears in confession,' I say. 'They show true commitment.'

She smiles. She thinks I am joking.

'You'll be fine, Grace. She'll call you in, ask you to sit opposite Her at the table. You will report on any questionable behaviour you have witnessed in others, then She'll ask you to admit your own transgressions.'

'What should I say?'

'It's best to be prepared — times you have been envious or greedy, things you have said about people behind their backs, that sort of thing. She'll write them all down and then She will ask questions.'

'What kind?'

I turn away. I mustn't say, because they are the questions I've been desperate to ask her myself. The secrets that I shouldn't long to know.

'Dilys?'

'She'll want to know what thoughts you have,' I say, hoping that she won't see the colour rising to my cheeks. 'What you think about, when you are alone . . . in bed. When you are bathing.' When you are sitting in chapel trying to quieten the Devil's voice that whispers in your ear.

I daren't look at her but I can hear her breathing; shallow gasps snatched through open lips. Does she know that I ache to hear her confession? To know whether she touches her body in all the ways my hands could never find her.

'Have you told her what *you* think about?' she says.

'No. Not the truth.'

'Why not?'

I feel a rush of something. Heat between my legs. The thrill of shame, and I can't answer. She turns to face me.

I mustn't do the things I long to, the things I think about as I'm falling asleep.

But is it really a sin to kiss her on the cheek, as friends do?

To bring my mouth to the very edge of hers?

Run the tip of my finger just inside where I can feel the damp heat of her breath, my hand making a barrier we cannot cross, so we can share only sighs and unspoken fantasies?

Pinch her bottom lip. Gently. Slowly. And tug it towards mine?

'Dilys, stop,' she whispers, pulling away from me. 'What was that?' I hear a door closing: someone has come into the chapel. Without saying a word I stub out the cigarette and she turns off the lamp. The sudden darkness is a shock. I can hear Grace's breath again: the fear and exhilaration.

Shafts of light slice through the swirl of smoke around the edge of our dust sheet, piercing the gaps between the wooden floorboards and reaching up like the bars of a cage. Someone has turned on a light downstairs. Footsteps in the chapel, the scrape of curtain rings being pulled across the pole. Then nothing until a slight tremor moves through the trapdoor beneath us. Someone has put their foot on the bottom rung of the ladder. I can't breathe. I'm going to give us away. I'm going to cough and this rising panic in my stomach will surge out. I am not going to be able to hold it in. I reach down and pinch the back of my wrist, twisting the skin until I feel a sting.

Everything is silent and still. We sit and wait, but there's nothing until we hear the footsteps again, moving away this time. And we fall back into the darkness.

'I think that was Emily,' I whisper. Perhaps I imagine it but I can smell lavender water: the perfume she applies so liberally every morning. When I walk into a room I can tell if Emily has been there before me; she leaves a sickly scent behind her. I used to like lavender. It made me think of summers in the Garden. But now it makes me think of bees. Swarming. Stinging.

'What would happen if they found us?' Grace whispers.

'We'd be in trouble, they'd smell the smoke . . .'

'No, if they found *us*, up here, together?'

'I don't know,' I say, because that's the truth.

Would they guess what we have been doing?

In my head.

'They wouldn't understand.'

I don't understand it myself.

'You're Octavia's daughter,' she says. 'But I'm just a servant. She could turn me out onto the street.'

What makes her think She wouldn't do the same to me?

We fall silent again, the dark wrapping around us like a shared blanket. 'Everything will be all right,' I whisper. It won't be long now, then the bishops will come. And whatever is inside the box, I have faith it is the answer: an end to suffering and earthly desires, no more hunger, no more craving. It will take away the agony of this longing we feel.

And all we will have is love: pure, uncomplicated, divine.

A Calling

See no evil. Hear no evil. Speak no evil. The three wise monkeys sit and watch me from the shelf above my desk. Well, two of them do, one is covering his eyes of course. I was thirteen when Octavia bought that ornament for me and I immediately had the feeling they were spies. Before I did anything I shouldn't, I would turn it to the wall to hide their faces; but now I know that it would make no difference. Only God can see our secrets; He could whisper mine to Octavia anytime He wanted. But He hasn't.

Besides, She has more pressing concerns than me. Her nightly audience with Him is taking longer than before. We sit in the chapel and wait for Her to arrive and share His lessons, but sometimes the words have flowed so quickly She cannot decipher Her own writing. And since She can't remember anything more than sitting down and lifting Her pen, it can take a while to piece together. Lately She has delegated the task to Peter, who often sits up late into the night poring over Her scripts. He says he is an interpreter, a translator of the Word of God. 'I've got it!' he'll exclaim over breakfast the next morning, as if he's cracked a cryptic crossword clue. 'The phrase was "Bride of the Lamb".'

This week there has been only one subject: Harry Price and his plans to open the box. The Lord has assured us that the true prophecies are safely hidden but that we must use this opportunity to spread His Word. Octavia says that, first, She has a duty to try to save Mr Price from himself. She has written to warn him that She cannot guarantee that the opening of this bogus box will not unleash the wrath of the Almighty. 'Think very carefully, Mr Price, for your eternal soul is in peril.' I know that's what She said because I typed it up from Her notes first thing this morning.

At eleven, Emily knocked with another two sheets for my attention 'about the unpleasantness at dinner last night'. It really was a most awkward scene. We arrived at the table to find five places set. When Octavia announced that She had invited Edgar to join us, Peter was quite suddenly taken ill and, after making a long apology to Octavia, retreated to his bedroom. It hardly got the evening off to the best start. From the moment Edgar arrived, Octavia could barely contain Her irritation: the way he talks, the way he eats, the way he coughs. Especially the way he coughs. He really is sure of himself, but last night it was clear that Octavia is starting to have doubts.

'But what of the role of man, of Adam?' he asked Her, stabbing a curl of butter with his fork, as his butter knife lay idly on the side of his plate.

'The Lord has been clear,' said Octavia. 'Salvation is born from the Mother, from the Daughter, from the female—'

'But man was made in *His* image,' he said. And here he made two mistakes: interrupting Octavia was bad enough but he did so before he'd swallowed his mouthful of mashed potato. 'Do You not see, Octavia? It is men who hold the power in the end. It is the bishops who must open Joanna Southcott's box. Without the bishops You have no power to fulfil her prophecies.' He sat up higher in his chair. 'The Lord Himself sent me from America to bring His Word to You. He speaks to me. He tells me that I have a part to play. Do You refuse to see it? Do You refuse to recognise my place at His table?'

A knife flew across the room and struck the wall. Octavia looked as shocked as the rest of us at the realisation that She had been the one to throw it. Sir Jack, who had been sleeping with his head under his wing, leapt off his perch on top of the sideboard and hopped down to inspect a smear of gravy on the floor. Octavia, meanwhile, looked down at Her empty right hand, then at Her left, which was still holding a fork.

Emily stood up. 'Edgar, you have gone too far,' she said. 'Octavia will not recognise your calling because it does not come from God.' Taking his time to wipe his mouth on his napkin, he left the table and bowed before he left the room. 'Excuse me, ladies.'

Seconds later, we heard the front door shut behind him, and I saw a fleeting smile dance across Emily's lips as she walked to Octavia and took the fork from Her hand. 'I wish You could have been spared that, Octavia,' she said. 'Why don't You have a lie-down?'

Still staring at Her hands, now empty of both knife and fork, Octavia seemed to wake from Her thoughts. 'Yes, thank you, Emily. I feel a headache coming on.'

'You rest,' Emily said. 'With Your permission, I shall make a few additions to the rules. It's only right that all should have the chance to learn from Edgar's mistakes.'

INSTRUCTIONS FOR HOUSEHOLDERS (APPENDIX 14):

(a) Men, foreign or English, must not shake hands with gloves on. They should wear dark suits in the evening or apologise for 'not changing' or having 'sports things' on.

(b) Some apology for the noises incident upon a cold should be made. (It should be remembered that very much coughing is merely habit.) An apology or remark of some kind disarms criticism and prevents the nerves being fretted by annoyance.

(c) Cackling laughs, mirthless laughs, merely habitual laughs are to be avoided.

(d) Never put your knife and fork at right angles to the plate. It is done abroad but not in England.

Emily made no mention of not interrupting, speaking with your mouth full or raising your voice. These were all outlined in the original draft of *Instructions to Householders* and were rules that Mr Peissart should have known.

She also neglected to add anything about throwing knives across the room.

———

I can hear a man calling my name downstairs. It's a voice I don't recognise. It must be my mind playing tricks again, no man would be calling for me. But as soon as I step onto the landing I know there's something wrong. Grace is halfway up the stairs, running up towards me and I can hear shouting. A woman's voice now too. I try to get past Grace to see what is happening.

'It's all right, Dilys,' she says.

'What is happening?'

'I don't know. There's someone at the door, someone trying to get in. Emily is dealing with it.'

I can hear Emily now. Telling them to leave, to go away. Telling them they are not welcome. 'We should help her,' I say, setting off down the stairs again, but Grace continues to climb, blocking my way.

'She told me to come up here out of the way,' she says. 'She wants me to stay up here, Dilys. You too. We'll only make matters worse.'

I'm too high on the stairs to see the door from this angle but I hear the man's voice. 'Is she in there?' he is shouting. 'Why won't you let me speak to her? What have you got to hide?'

Grace reaches the step below me, turns me back around, and with her hand on the small of my back we climb up to my bedroom. 'Who was it?' I ask her as we sit together on the bed. She looks shaken. So am I. The only people who come knocking are believers. Or occasionally the postman.

'I don't know,' she says. 'I didn't recognise him.'

Downstairs, I think I hear him shout my name again. I wonder if Grace heard it too. I want to ask her but I'm frightened that the answer might be no; that I might be imagining it.

'Grace, what was he saying when Emily asked you to come up?'

'I didn't hear. The bell rang, Emily answered it and then I heard a commotion and when I ran out into the hallway she told me to come up here with you.' She puts her arm around my waist. I want to go and listen at the top of the stairs but when I start to move she squeezes me more tightly.

'Stay,' she says. 'Emily wants us to stay up here. And we always do what Emily tells us. Don't we, Dilys?' She arches a single eyebrow.

The front door slams and there's silence for a minute or two. Then I hear Emily's footsteps on the stairs. Grace takes her arm away and stands up. 'I'll go and find out what's been going on,' she says. I follow her out of my bedroom, and find Emily on the landing.

'Who was that?' I ask her, but she doesn't reply, she doesn't even meet my eyes. Grace leads her into my bedroom where she sits down on my bed.

'Would you like some water?' I say.

'There's no need to fuss,' she says, curtly. 'I'm fine.'

'Who was that?' I ask again.

'Nothing for you to worry about, Dilys.'

'Well, it sounded pretty worrying to me. I should go and fetch Octavia.'

'No, no,' she says, firmly. 'She is out in the Wireless Room. And I'm sure you wouldn't want to cause Her distress.'

'Why, what is going on?'

She looks across to my bedroom door and studies it for a moment, then with a sigh she drops her head. 'I'm afraid that man was a newspaper reporter, prowling around for a story. He wanted to interview Octavia about Joanna Southcott's box and Harry Price's little stunt. But we all know what happened last time She gave an interview.'

She was pilloried. Mocked. Her words twisted.

'He wouldn't take no for an answer,' she says. 'He put his foot in the door and when I wouldn't let him in he turned nasty. He said things . . .'

'What things?'

'All lies.' She looks up at me and I feel like I am being observed. 'He is trying to slander Her, Dilys. He said Her ideas are madness. It is nothing that we haven't heard before. But he has obviously done his research.' Perhaps I imagine it but the corners of her mouth seem to twitch a little as she says it.

Madness. He has obviously done his research.

'Are you all right, Dilys?' Emily says. 'You are very pale.'

'Yes. You did well to see him off.'

'Anything to protect Octavia.'

'Did he ask about me?' I say. I have to know whether I really did hear him shout my name. Or whether it was all in my mind.

'You, Dilys?' She shakes her head and wrinkles her forehead as though struggling to understand. 'Why would he be interested in *you*?' And suddenly she seems amused by the suggestion, glancing at Grace, a smile on her lips. 'No, Dilys, he didn't ask about you. But perhaps . . .' Her expression is suddenly pensive; she stares at the door again and sits in silence, scratching the back of one hand with the fingers of the other. 'Now that you mention it, I think we should take this as a warning.'

'A warning?'

'Yes. I don't want you walking around outside, Dilys. Those vermin will stop at nothing to get to Her, to discredit us. They could try to get to you, and I hate the thought of it making you anxious; wondering if they'll be waiting down the street when you walk out. It doesn't bear thinking about—'

'But, that's not what I meant—'

'We must all do whatever we can to protect Octavia. From now on you should stay within the Garden.'

'I don't think that is necessary.'

'You may not. But Octavia will be the judge of that. And when I tell Her what that man had to say, I'm sure She will agree with me.'

Sleepwalking

I can't move. Hands are holding me, fingers pressing into my arms.
I try to struggle free. I fight. Get off me. I have to get away.

Dilys, stop. Calm down.

I have to get away before I'm trapped.

They are bricking up the wall. They are going to shut me in.
Bury me alive. I can hear them singing the requiem. I need to get
away but someone has caught me. Dragging me back.

'Dilys, stop. It's all right. Dilys, please . . . It's me.'

Grace.

It's Grace.

Her face comes into focus now. She is still holding my arms.
Too tightly. She is hurting me.

I'm in the hallway with Grace.

I turn to the front door but I can't find the latch. Someone has
moved it. Someone has taken the handle away. And there's no way
out.

'Get off me. Let me go.'

'I'm sorry. Dilys, you were dreaming. You were shouting,
clawing at the door.'

I can see the handle now. It must have been there all along, half way down the door, just where it always was. I look down and I see grazes on my fingers. She puts her arms around me.

'It's all right,' she whispers. 'It was just a dream.'

'But I could hear them. They were . . .'

'Don't worry. Let's get you back to bed. Your heart is pounding.' So is hers, I can feel it. Her arms are around me, pinning my arms to my sides.

'I woke you up. I'm so sorry.'

'It's all right.'

'What was I doing . . .?' My knees start to buckle, she is the only thing that's stopping me from falling. '. . . Tell me.'

'You were shouting. Trying to get out. Let's get you back to bed.' But neither of us moves. There's the taste of salt on my lips. My face is wet. I'm crying. I bury my head into her neck, just below her ear, and let my tears soak into her skin.

I'm so sorry, Grace. I haven't had a dream this vivid since I was a child.

'You're all right,' she says. But I know I am not. Our nightdresses are all that separate us. Two layers of cotton keeping my skin from touching hers.

'Come on.' She puts her arm around my waist and takes my weight, lifting my hand and placing it on the bannister. There's a lamp at the top of the stairs but I can't see who is holding it.

'Grace?' a voice calls down.

'She was sleepwalking again.'

'You'll see her back to—'

'Yes. I'll look after her. Goodnight.'

The light floats in mid-air across the landing, then disappears.

I'm not sure I can make it to the top. Sleep clutches at me. I want to lie here on the stairs. I want her to lie down beside me. I can hear my voice but it can't be mine. It is too far away.

'I know. Nearly there now. Then you can sleep.'

———

I am back on my bed and Grace is standing over me. She has taken a handkerchief from my drawer and is wiping my face, smoothing back the strands of hair that are stuck to my skin. In the lamplight I can see something on her face. I reach up to touch it but she steps back. Grace, what is that? There's an angry red mark splashed across her cheek.

'You were fighting in your dream. I got in the way,' she says, holding my hand in her own. 'You were asleep. You didn't know . . .' But now I do. And the truth makes her cheek burn redder in accusation. It tells me I am no good. That I don't deserve her. I am whispering I'm sorry. Praying to her that she will forgive me. I try to stand up. I want to stay and tell her but sleep is dragging me away: back into oblivion.

———

I am dreaming that I am kissing her cheek, tracing the edge of the mark with my lips. I am dreaming that I'm lifting her arms above her head, that I'm reaching down and catching the hem of her nightdress between my fingers. I want to take it off her. I want to see her. All of her. But I can't. My arms won't move. They won't do what I tell them to do.

I am back in my bed and she is beside me, wiping the tears of longing from my face.

'It is all right, Dilys. Everything is all right.'

And as long as it is just a dream it can be.

My bottom lip catches on the crest of her collarbone as if it wants to stay behind and kiss her there. But I can't let it. And so I will it to move on, barely brushing her skin as it passes. It won't linger until it gets to her nightdress; it is craving the taste of cotton and the safety of separation.

Through the fabric we are Puritans. Not touching. Not really. It's all right. As long as it is just a dream.

She arches her back and my hands move underneath her. Now I am the one holding her; telling her that it is not a sin; telling her to be quiet. I can feel every nerve in my body, feel the tide of blood inside me. I feel wide awake. I am in control. Of everything. We don't undress. I kiss her through her nightdress. Tender ferocity. My body shivering at the thought of what I know I will do: delicious anticipation of my transgression. My mouth climbs the inside of her thighs until I find the heat between them. The fabric is rough against me, against my lips. Through the scent of soap and starch I taste her skin.

And the butterflies dance beneath my touch: a rush of beating wings.

Awakening

The chapel bell wakes me, the chimes sounding distant at first, but becoming louder, each strike awakening a memory from the night before; stretching out, yawning and uncurling itself from the pit of my stomach. My body is still asleep, still languishing in the thrill of last night's imaginings. But my mind is waking. Nausea creeping its way under the twisted bedclothes.

In my dream she begged me to kiss her.
In my dream she begged me to stop.
We can't. We mustn't. We are just friends, Dilys. The very best.

A knock at my door. It will be Grace. I don't want to see her, not after what I did; not after the thoughts I had. She will see it on my face, she'll know what I have been dreaming. But she's already turning the handle. She's already opening the door.

'Breakfast. I'm sorry it's late. I overslept.' Her voice is quiet. She doesn't meet my eyes. She doesn't look at me at all.

'That's all right. I've only just woken up myself.' I pull the bedclothes up around me, feeling suddenly exposed, grotesque. My body feels lumpy and misshapen. I imagine my skin, blotchy beneath the white of my crumpled nightdress. I feel magnified. I can smell my own body, my own shame.

'You had a restless night,' she says, laying the tray on my bedside table, then sitting on the edge of my bed. 'You were up half the night . . .' I can feel her eyes on me now: willing me to say more; to admit what I did; what we did. But I can't.

'I'm sorry,' I say. 'Was I sleepwalking again?'

She stands up and steps away from the bed. Away from me.

'You woke up, Dilys. You were awake.' She brings her hand to her cheek and finds a memory there. The memory of a slap. Or of a kiss. In my mind I see both: a blur of bodies pressed together. Pushing each other away, grasping each other too tight. I couldn't breathe. I couldn't stop. Fury and desperation; escape and surrender.

'I'm sorry,' I say, 'I can't remember.'

What happened. What I did. And whether she wanted me to.

But perhaps I do. Perhaps I just don't want to say it out loud. Give something a name and that's what it becomes; words bestow truth upon it; make it real.

Grace walks back to the tray, dropping a square of linen into a glass of water. 'Your daily dose,' she says. 'That will make everything better, wash everything away. That's the way with you, with this place. Stay silent. Say nothing. Just pretend it didn't happen.' Her voice is cold, weary. I want the other Grace, the one who was in my bed last night, the one who pulled at her nightdress to try to free herself. In my dream she whispered, 'Please,' she said my name and made that noise she always does. Somewhere between a laugh and a sigh. She wanted my mouth on her. On every part of her.

She walks to the door, then stops, standing with her back to me. 'You can lie to them, Dilys, you can even lie to yourself, but you can't lie to me. I know. After last night we can't pretend any more. I know how you feel.'

'Do you feel the same?' I whisper. But only after she has closed the door behind her and I hear her steps reach the top of the stairs.

The water is cold by the time I get out of bed but I enjoy its sting. I can't think of anything but its burn on my skin. I fish the linen square out of my glass and drop it into my washbowl, stirring the water to make it spin around and release its power. Then I take a brush and scrub myself: the Water cleansing the stains that soap could not, pain sterilising me like fire.

As I start to dress, the thoughts creep in again. Sharp stabs in the pit of my stomach, heat between my legs. As I slip on my stockings I imagine her hands running up them. I lift my nightdress over my head and breathe in the smell of the cotton, taking the fabric between my lips. And I can taste last night. Under here I'm lost. I'm caught. A butterfly in a net. And I want to stay here, inhaling memories of her.

If she walked in now she would see me: exposed and ridiculous. I need to get dressed. I need to be contained. I choose a coat dress with a Medici collar that stands up like wings. Octavia calls it taupe; Emily insisted it was camel, but she soon gave in to Octavia's better judgement. But why am I thinking of them now? I can't let them into my mind when Grace is in there. They might eavesdrop on the things I'm trying not to say out loud. They might find out. No, I need to get to work.

I walk downstairs quickly, ready to turn the corner and rush out past the kitchen. But I needn't have worried, Grace is not waiting in the doorway. The kitchen door is pushed shut, a margin of light marking the edge of the frame, and through the gap I hear raised voices. 'No,' I hear her say, 'there's nothing to tell.'

I try to nudge the door open a little more, but the creak of its hinges gives me away. 'Good morning,' says Emily, turning abruptly towards me. 'Did you sleep well?'

'Yes, thank you.' Stepping into the room I try to look as though I had intended to enter all along.

'I'm afraid I can't say the same myself. You were up again, Dilys.'

I remember the light of a lamp at the top of the stairs. It must have been Emily out of bed. I must have woken her. But she doesn't know what happened when Grace took me back to my room. She couldn't.

Even I don't know that.

The thought grabs me like a hand closing around my throat. And I can feel my body betray me: traitorous marks rising up on my skin, blotches the size of fingertips branded onto my neck. When I was a child, Mother used to say that she could tell when I was up to something because I'd break out in a rash.

'Poor Dilys . . .' Emily looks me over like a surveyor might appraise a derelict building. Damaged, defective. Unsound. Her head is tilted slightly, anyone who didn't know her might almost believe she was concerned. But she is startled into a straighter posture by something in the hallway: the sound of post being pushed through the letterbox. I hear the thud of paper falling onto tiles. And so does Emily. Her eyes go first, darting to the doorway, then her head jerks in the same direction, rousing her body to lurch after it. She is rushing past me, which is not like her: she's been working hard to perfect a glide, because Octavia can't bear the sound of heavy footsteps. The letterbox snaps shut and she bends down, with some difficulty, behind the front door, one hand picking up the letters, the other pressing against her lower back.

'Let me help you, Emily,' I say, but she has managed to straighten up. She is already shuffling through the envelopes.

'No need,' she insists, tucking them into the front of her cardigan. 'There's nothing for you, Dilys.'

—

It must be later than I thought. The sun has already woken the Garden. Every flower is wide-eyed and watchful; Yggdrasil's leaves emerald against a cloudless sky. It's in summer that this place looks most like Eden; like the picture in the Bible Octavia gave me when I turned eight; the Eden from long ago and far away. It's in summer that the dahlias arrive for their annual holiday, unpacking their garish wardrobe, shouting from the flowerbeds in exotic tongues. Octavia planted the first of them when we were children: orchid dahlias with petals that curled into points. They looked like the paper windmills we played with on the beach in Norfolk. Now they stand among a clash of other varieties: heads striped red and white like sticks of rock; orange-petalled faces that look as though their tips have been dusted with sugar. I wonder if they remind Octavia of the seaside, of the day we flew a kite and my brothers buried me in the sand. Of the times before She was taken ill.

Someone asked Her once why She was so fond of dahlias but She said only that they were a lesson from God about dignity. They stand up straight and tall, never buckling beneath the weight of their beautiful burden.

The thought makes me feel stronger. I must get to work.

—

As soon as I step through the back door of Castleside I hear someone at the front. The doorbell is ringing. I move slowly into the hallway. Through the stained glass panel in the door I see a figure bend down. Fingers poke through the letterbox.

I don't want to see anyone. Not today.

'Dilys, are you there? It's Edgar. May I please come in?' His voice is thin and frayed. 'Dilys, please, would you open the door?'

I walk away, intending to ignore him, but he calls again. He is not going to leave me alone until I talk to him, so I unlock the front door, just enough to show my reluctance without being rude.

'Edgar,' I say. 'Why didn't you come to the back?'

'After last time, I thought it best—'

'I'm afraid I am rather busy.'

'I was hoping to have a talk with you. To ask your advice,' he says.

I open the door slightly wider, which he takes as a cue to step inside. His grey suit is as pale as his eyes, which, added to his white hair, gives the impression that he is covered in dust. Or flour. The thought brings back a memory of the rituals I watched from behind the chapel curtain.

'I'm told that you have everything ready,' he says, looking around the hallway.

'Almost.'

'Well, you have done a marvellous job. I just hope Octavia appreciates it. She doesn't find it easy to let others share Her triumphs.'

The silence that follows is full of expectation. I can feel he is waiting for me to say more. He wants to know how far he can go, how much he can say.

'I do not seek praise, Edgar. I merely do my duty in the Lord's name.'

'Of course, of course. As we all do. But you must be proud of what you have achieved.'

I am. If he opened the door behind me he would see the clusters of chairs arranged around the room, the dark green sofa donated by Kate, the wicker chair from Ellen's parlour, the Persian rug from Rachel Fox's bedroom. If he stepped into the dining room he'd see the table set for twelve; the kitchen fully stocked with utensils, a row of enamel pans decorated with a flash of green around each rim.

'Edgar, you wanted my advice about something.'

'Yes. It's . . . well, it's rather a delicate matter. But I thought if anyone would understand, Dilys, it would be you. We have known each other a long time.'

It is strange that he should say that, that he should think it. I don't feel that I know him at all. And I'm certain he knows nothing about me. At least I hope he doesn't.

'Dilys, it's about Octavia. I am concerned for Her.'

Again he pauses as though he has uttered a codeword to which I will respond. I half expect him to wink or give me some other sign. The situation is starting to feel absurd, but I know that every word could be dangerous. I won't speak. He could use it against me.

'You know yourself that Emily appears to have increasing influence,' he says, 'and, as Octavia's favourite, she seems to be enjoying certain privileges and powers that the rest of us do not.' He has a sheen of perspiration on his face now, his eyes seem to move of their own volition, darting around the hallway as though following the path of an invisible fly.

'We are Her followers but you are Her daughter. You must be concerned.'

I'm trapped now. If I let him go on, I will be complicit in my silence.

'I trust Octavia to know what is right,' I say.

'Of course, of course. And that's why those of us who love Her and want the best for Her must stay close, and look after each other. We mustn't be divided.' He has come this far. Too late to turn back now. He will say what he has come to say. 'There will always be those who spread lies, and falsehoods; those who choose to live in suspicion. But I came to ask you, Dilys, to remember that I want the best for your mother.'

'We all do.'

Edgar pauses to consider how to phrase what he is going to say next. But he is interrupted by the sound of the back door opening. With a panicked look he darts into the dining room.

'Hello?' I call.

Grace steps into the hallway.

'I brought your lunch,' she says, handing me a brown paper bag of what feels like sandwiches. 'I thought it would give us a chance to talk. But I don't have long.'

I want to ask her what she and Emily were talking about this morning but I can't. Edgar is listening. Edgar will hear.

'I'm sorry,' I say, trying to keep my voice level. 'Not now. It is not a good time.'

I turn my eyes towards the dining room so that she will understand, but the gesture is lost on her; she is already walking away.

'Of course,' she says flatly. 'Not a good time. It never is.'

She walks out of the hallway and I hear her shout: 'Octavia wants you back by three o'clock. She is holding a meeting at Number 12.'

Then I hear the back door slam.

Webs for Destruction

'Thank you all for coming.' Octavia speaks as though we had a choice. 'It is under grave circumstances that I summoned you here.' She says 'summoned' but I am starting to think She means 'summonsed'. Octavia is holding court, standing at the head of the dining table, staring at us one by one. She is deciding who the guilty party is. I can already hear a whisper inside my head.

Someone has done something wrong. Someone will have to be punished. She knows. About last night. I feel like I am falling.

'To talk bravely behind people's backs of what one will not say to their face is cowardly, unworthy of a true believer,' She says. 'To talk. But also to listen.' She rests Her hands on the table and leans forward. 'Both are sins in my eyes.'

To talk, but also to listen.
She means Edgar. The things he said at Castleside this morning.

Octavia digs Her fingertips into the tablecloth, the one embroidered with posies of forget-me-nots, the one with an orange juice stain which, try as she might, Grace just couldn't get out. Emily sits on Her right-hand side, Peter beside her. I am alone on the opposite side, Sir Jack patrolling the tabletop between us.

'This morning there was a sign.' Octavia walks to the sideboard and takes a glass from the nearest drawer. No, a jar: it has a lid on, but it appears to contain nothing more than a tangle of dark brown wool. 'A sign of evil in our midst,' She says, holding it up in front of Her face, and giving it a little shake.

The wool begins to unknot itself, stretch out a mass of spindly legs. In the jar She has a spider. A big one. Bigger than those I have tried to ignore in the rafters of the clock tower. Sir Jack begins to hop and call out with an abrupt 'chyak chyak' of excitement. But he is promptly shooed off the table by Octavia and registers his disappointment with a disgruntled shake of his wings.

'This morning I found him crawling on my Bible,' she says, watching the spider's desperate attempts to climb out. 'And I knew that it was time to act.' She walks to my side of the table and brings the jar to my face. I can see the creature magnified through the thick glass, and behind it Her eye looking through for my reaction. I watch the spider's pathetic scramblings and try not to betray my disgust.

'Spiders are thought to be innocuous and harmless,' She says, walking back around the table and lifting the jar over Peter's head so that it appears quite suddenly not an inch from the tip of his nose. 'But they are very subtle over their prey and they weave webs for destruction. Just as your enemies try to weave a web about you.' She tips the jar upside down to agitate it again, then places it on the table. 'As we are told in the Book of Job . . .' She says, looking around for one of us to recite the verse.

'*The paths of all that forget God and the hope of the hypocrite shall perish*,' Emily says. '*For it is but a spider's house; he shall lean upon it, but it shall not stand; he shall hold it fast, but it shall not endure.*' She shudders, imagining perhaps the footsteps of a spider on her skin.

'An enemy is among us who is weaving his web,' says Octavia. 'But we shall destroy it. We shall take a duster and knock it down.

Take a brush and sweep it away.' She takes her seat. 'I am sorry to have to share with you the news that the Devil is among us. As soon as I showed the spider to Emily she knew at once. Edgar has been sent by Satan himself to infiltrate us. He has been questioning the Truth and trying to persuade others to join his rebellion.'

To talk, but also to listen.

'Emily was trying to keep the painful truth from me until she had proved her case against him. But the time has come. I command you all now, in the Lord's name, to share what you know of his treason.' She nods at Emily who produces a notebook from under the table and opens a blank page, cracking its spine.

Peter is first to speak, projecting his voice like an actor reciting lines: 'He has talked before of the place of man, that the male carries the seed of life.'

'Thank you, Peter, and tell us, have you ever heard him question Octavia, or Her teachings?' Emily asks gently.

'He thinks he has a calling,' Peter says, adopting the upright posture of a witness in the stand. 'That he has been chosen by God and that Octavia refuses to recognise it.'

'Yes, he said as much one night at supper. Anything else, Peter?'

There's a click when he parts his lips; his mouth sticky with apprehension. He pauses, then his words rush out. 'He has been holding meetings with Donald.'

Emily looks up from her notepad. 'Meetings that they would not permit you to join. Isn't that right, Peter?'

'No. I mean, yes. That is, they wouldn't permit me to join. They know that I am loyal to you, Octavia . . .' He glances up at Her, then looks down at his hands, which sit clasped together on his lap.

'Indeed you are,' nods Emily. 'Go on . . .'

'Edgar believes that the Lord has a role for us too,' continues Peter. 'For men. He believes that he has been chosen.'

'Yes. So he tells me,' Octavia says. 'But Edgar believes himself to have powers he does not possess.'

The nib of Emily's pen scratches across the page of her notebook, interrupted only by the occasional flap from Sir Jack who has taken the opportunity to sneak back up onto the table and creep closer to the jar.

'Peter, have *you* ever met with Edgar in private?' Octavia asks.

'No.'

'Never?'

'No, Octavia.'

'But you tried to?'

Peter swallows slowly as though his throat is inflamed, as though he can taste the rancid smack of infection. 'Only to—'

'We thought it might be useful,' Emily cuts in, 'for Peter to hear what they were saying.'

Octavia steeples Her fingers. 'But they would not let him join. And that deepened your suspicions.'

'Yes,' Emily says, looking at Peter and widening her eyes to prompt him to go on.

'I have seen Edgar and Donald in town together numerous times,' he says. 'And deep in conversation in the Garden. They always fall silent when I approach them. I've written down every occasion . . .' He begins to search his jacket for his pocketbook. 'Every occasion—'

'Well done, Peter,' says Octavia. 'Diligent as always. Why don't you run along and find Donald? So we can ask him ourselves. He has taken up lodgings in the same house as Edgar for the summer.' Peter's body slackens in relief, then he takes his cue, standing and dipping his head in a solemn bow before leaving the room. I stand up to follow him, but Emily makes it clear, with a wave of her hand, that I will be required to give evidence of my own.

'Dilys,' she says. 'Is there anything you can report about Edgar? Anything you have failed to report in the past? Anything you should have told us?' There's an edge to her voice. She wants me to think she knows already. Perhaps she does.

'Possibly,' I say. 'I'm not sure I can prove anything.'

'But you have witnessed suspicious behaviour?'

'I'm not sure about suspicious. He came to Castleside one day while I was working. He was with Donald then.'

'And what were they doing?'

'They offered to help. It seemed like something and nothing.'

'But it can't have been both, Dilys. Either something was going on. Or nothing was. Was that the first time they had been in Castleside?'

'I'm not sure.'

'And what about the broken window?'

She does know. She has known all this time.

'In the pantry?'

'Yes,' she says, making a note in her book. I can't bear the noise of that pen. I want to snatch it off her and stab the nib into her eye.

'I found the window like that,' I say. 'It could have been broken for days . . .'

'But it's possible it was Edgar.'

'Well, I suppose so, yes.'

With the satisfaction of a barrister who has forced a confession from the stand, Emily lifts her pen. And her eyes.

'Anything else you think could be relevant?' If she has been watching him she'll know he came to see me today.

'He was at Castleside earlier. He seemed anxious.'

'About what?'

'He said he wanted the best for Octavia and it was up to us to protect Her.'

I watch Emily start to write again. I don't notice Octavia reaching out for the jar and by the time I turn to Her She has unscrewed the lid and tipped its contents onto the table. The spider is still for a moment and then he starts to move, his two front legs tapping the cloth ahead to make sure all is safe for the other six to follow: a blind man with two canes. Perhaps he doesn't see the flash of black. Perhaps he only feels it, as Sir Jack springs forward and catches him in his beak. I see the briefest twitch from the tangle of legs as Sir Jack drops them next to a posy of embroidered forget-me-nots. And with that the bird throws his head back and thanks Octavia with a grateful 'chyak chyak'.

The Opening Room

I close my eyes but I can hear every detail. Sir Jack pins the tangled mess of spider under the claws of his foot, then sets about devouring his meal. He isn't going to rush it, picking each morsel with the tip of his beak and swallowing it with a snap. In my blindness I can still see the twisted angles of broken legs. Sickness rising as though I am being force-fed the brittle pieces of death myself; imagining the crunch between my teeth, a frantic crawling as the creature comes to life again and tries to escape the confines of my stomach. I jerk my chair back, knocking into the table as I rush out of the room, hands covering my mouth.

'Dilys!' Octavia calls after me but I do not stop. By the time I run past the kitchen I am heaving. At the back door, fresh air floods into my chest and sweeps the rising nausea back down into my stomach.

I look up and see Grace rushing out of the kitchen towards me.

'I need a walk. Some air,' I say. I have to get away in case Octavia comes out to find me. I start to move but my legs give way. Grace grabs my arm and I let her take my weight. 'Come on,' she says, leading me down the passageway at the side of the kitchen and out onto the lawn. We stop when the sickness threatens to overwhelm me again. 'Deep breaths, Dilys.' I'm not sure whether it is her voice or mine I hear. But I have to keep walking. They'll be watching from the windows. We reach the back door of Castleside. I grip the door handle but I don't have the strength to push it down.

'Here, let me,' Grace says. As soon as we are through the door

I lean against the wall, pressing my cheek against the cool plaster.

'Dilys, try to breathe,' she says. 'What happened?'

I need to calm my thoughts but I can't catch them. There are too many scuttling inside my head, and when I close my eyes I hear the snap of a beak. The crunch of legs.

'I'm going to be . . .' My body lurches but nothing comes. I can't remember the last time I ate anything.

'There was a spider . . .' I say. 'Octavia had a spider.'

'A spider?' She is looking at me as if I am delirious. 'You aren't making any sense.'

'She found it on Her Bible. She said it was a sign that Edgar is against Her. Emily knew,' I say. 'Emily knew about the broken window. Kate must have told her.'

'Kate? How do you know? What did Emily say?'

'She asked about the broken glass. But I don't understand – if she has known all this time why did she wait until now to ask me about it?'

'Emily likes to keep secrets,' Grace says, her eyes avoiding mine. 'She wants everyone to think she can see into their thoughts. But she can't. You know that, don't you?'

I'm not sure I do know. Sometimes I'm not certain of anything. What if Emily has been watching me? Listening at my door? My body heaves again.

'Dilys,' she says. 'I think you should sit down.' She takes my arm and leads me to the first doorway in the corridor.

'We can't go in there. That's the Opening Room. Octavia doesn't want anyone to see inside until—'

'I know which room it is,' she says. Her voice is harder now, determined. 'We need to talk. No one will think to look for us in there.'

I surrender. I haven't got the energy to fight her.

I don't think I could say no to anything she asked of me.

———

'We shouldn't be doing this,' I say. But *shouldn't* doesn't mean what it used to.

I lock the door behind us as we step into the Opening Room, greeted by the scent of beeswax. Twenty-four wooden chairs, heavy like thrones, line the walls of the room. In front of them stands a table and on it lies one of Octavia's Bibles. Everything is ready.

'So this is it,' Grace says. 'The stage is set.' She runs her hand along the oak panelling, and I stand and watch the way she moves, the way stray strands of hair fall onto the back of her neck. I breathe slowly, deeply. And I have only one thought now: we are locked inside this room together and no one can find us, no one else has got a key. The only other set is hidden in the desk. She reaches the table and places her fingers on the top.

'That's where the box will be opened when the bishops come,' I say.

'On here?' She turns to face me, her back against the table, and then she lifts herself on top of it, legs swinging beneath her like a child.

'What are you doing? That's for the box.'

'But the box isn't here yet. Nor are the bishops. Without them it is just a table,' she says, sliding Octavia's Bible out of the way and then patting the space beside her. 'Come and sit with me.' She falls silent and falls still, her legs no longer swinging. 'Come on.'

Not on there. We mustn't sit on there. But *mustn't* is another word that's lost its meaning lately.

She presses on, agitated by my hesitation. 'For goodness' sake, Dilys. How will the bishops know? And what will they care anyway? That's if they ever come.' As soon as she says the words she looks as though she regrets them. 'I'm sorry, Dilys, it's just—'

'They will come. Octavia has promised.'

'But what if they don't?' she says, gently. 'I've been thinking about it since the night I was sealed. Do you never wonder, Dilys? Harry Price says he has got the box and Octavia can't be sure he hasn't, not when She has never seen it Herself. She never leaves the house. It doesn't make sense.'

'I don't know.'

'But you believe?'

'I have faith.'

'Dilys, I'm not sure I do. If you are so sure, then tell me.'

God brought her here to save me and now she is trying to lead me away from the Truth. She is wrong. The bishops will come, they will open the box, they have to. Because I can't live with the torment of feeling like this much longer.

But what if they don't come? What if they don't?

'Dilys, have you really nothing to say? That's what we do, isn't it? Do not question, do not argue, only obey. Octavia would be proud of you.'

When she looks at me I feel the longing in her: the fury and the fear. I watch her chest rising and falling. She leans back on her arms and lifts her head and I can see her neck, her collarbone.

'What do you want me to do?'

'I want you to come and sit with me. On here. I want us to talk about what's been going on.'

But I don't want to listen to this. I want to drag her off that table, shut that mouth of hers. *Do not argue, do not question, only obey.* I'll wrap my arms around her, make her stop. I need her lips on mine so I don't have to talk. So I don't have to think.

I walk towards her and she leans back on the table.

I shouldn't be doing this. But *shouldn't* doesn't mean what it used to. Not any more.

The Confession

As soon as we step through the back door of Number 12 we hear it: sobbing coming from the sitting room. It sounds like a child, the cry of an abandoned infant, gasping as his body tries to catch its breath.

From the hallway we hear Peter: 'Donald, please—'

'Don't touch me. Get your hands off me!'

There's a scuffle, the muted thud of a body knocked against a wall, then Octavia's voice: 'Peter, I think it is best if you go. Donald is understandably uncomfortable in the presence of a man. And after everything we have discovered—'

'Octavia, I was only trying to help—'

'Of course, Peter, but I think it is time for you to attend to that errand we discussed.'

I hear the scrape of chair-legs on the floor. 'And Peter – do be careful,' She says. 'Don't forget we are dealing with Satan himself.'

I grab Grace's hand and pull her behind the door of the dining room before Peter steps into the hallway and leaves the house.

Through the double doors that separate our room from theirs we hear only snatches of what is being said. Disjointed words: 'Repent' and 'the Devil' and 'sin'.

'What are they doing?' Grace forms the words silently, with exaggerated movements of her lips. I put my eyes to the crack where the two doors meet, but it is too narrow to see, so I put my ear to it instead.

'You have confessed to committing sin, here in the Garden of Eden,' Octavia says, with unnerving calm. What is She talking about? Perhaps Donald has admitted that they broke into Castleside. Perhaps it was them after all. 'Now there is nothing for you to do but repent, Donald. To tell the Lord every detail of your sin. Get onto your knees,' She says.

Donald takes a gulp of air; he is not sobbing now, but crying out in fear. 'Please, Octavia! Don't make me say it.'

'I said *get down* on your knees.' She spits the words at him.

There is another voice, Emily's voice. She must be in there with them. 'Octavia does this for your own good,' she says. 'She is the one who suffers most. She must stand and hear of your betrayal. She asked you to get down on your knees. Do you refuse to obey Her?'

Donald cries out: 'All right. All right!'

There's a brief moment of silence and when Octavia speaks again Her voice has changed: softer in volume and gentler in tone, like a nurse explaining a painful procedure.

'Very good, Donald. Now that you are prostrate before me, you must confess. You were meeting with Edgar, in secret . . .'

'He said he had work to do, that You did not understand. He said that what we did . . . He said it was a covenant for the glory of God—'

She interrupts him with a cruel laugh. 'A covenant? Donald, it was the worst of sins, an abomination in the eyes of the Lord, and in the eyes of the law.'

An abomination. She can't be talking about the broken window.

'I can see nothing else than for you to be handed over to the police to be punished—'

– 214 –

'No, please, Octavia. Please!'

'But it is judgement in the next life you should fear. You have given yourself over to Lucifer, committed this unholy act of Satan—'

She is interrupted by the sound of knocking on the front door. Fists banging as though they mean to smash it down. Keeping my body hidden, I peer into the hallway in time to see Emily rushing out to open it.

'Where is She?' says Edgar, through clenched teeth. 'Where's Octavia? I have just returned to my lodgings to find Peter rummaging in my room—'

'You'll have to come back later, Edgar.' She has her back to me but I can hear the satisfaction on her lips. 'Octavia is busy at the moment. She is busy talking to Donald. He has rather a lot to say.'

'Where are they?' he says, barging his way in. Emily reaches out to try to hold him back, but he shoves her with such force that she falls into the wall.

'Octavia, he is coming!' she shouts. 'Someone help! He means to kill Her!'

Instinctively I step forward into the hallway, to try to block his path, but I am too late, and he pushes past me. 'Octavia,' he says. 'I need to speak with you. I can explain.' As he turns into the sitting room he stops dead. Through the open doorway I can see Donald trembling at Octavia's feet. He lifts his eyes to Edgar with a look that communicates what he has done, what he has said.

An abomination.

Suddenly I understand, they have been sinning together, performing the acts that men will try to force upon us if we are not vigilant. *See*, the Devil says, *even the slightest touch can lead to sin.* I look around to see if they have heard him, but he speaks only to me, only in my head. *Just like you and Grace*, he says. But this is not the same. This is fornication, vile depravity; violent acts where bodies are defiled and innocence stolen. Acts devoid of love and tenderness. That's what the Bible says. This is not the same. It's nothing like the way I feel for Grace.

'Octavia!' Edgar shouts. 'What have you done to him?'

He steps forward and Octavia cries out, lifting Her hands up to protect Her face.

'Get away, Edgar,' She says. 'Get away from me.'

Emily pushes past us into the room, putting herself between them.

'I can explain,' he says. 'Just let me explain.'

'I trusted you,' Octavia says, Her voice breaking. 'The words of the scripture have come to pass: *Beware of false prophets, which come to you in sheep's clothing, but inwardly are ravening wolves.*' She gasps and grabs onto the back of a chair to steady Herself. '*Mine own familiar friend, in whom I trusted, which did eat of my bread, hath lifted up his heel against me.*'

There's the creak of a wooden drawer; Emily has reached out to Octavia's desk and is looking for something inside. 'Get back, Edgar,' she says. 'I will not let you torment Her any more.' She brings her hand out of the drawer and I see it: a blade. It is Octavia's letter-opener. A gift from my father.

'Get out,' she says in a whisper. Over and over again. Get out, get out. And then she shouts, a voice so loud she startles even herself: 'Get out!' She has finally gone too far. Octavia will stop this, She will take the knife away before someone gets hurt. I look to Her but She does not move, She does not speak, She is staring at the knife as if Her eyes are trying to focus on it.

Edgar cries out and something in him is woken, he darts for the door, knocking into me as he turns down the hallway. With the paperknife lifted above her head, Emily chases after him. 'In the Lord's name I command this devil to get out.'

What right has she to speak in the Lord's name? What right to issue commandments?

'Dilys . . .' I hear a crash and turn to see Octavia holding onto the edge of the sideboard. There are pieces of broken vase behind Her. 'Dilys . . . I . . .' Her legs start to fold and I rush to catch Her.

'The knife,' She whispers. 'Do you remember?' She is studying my face as if she hasn't seen me for years. 'It has "Jerusalem" inscribed on the handle. When I saw it I knew. The Lord called Emily to deliver me from evil, to banish Edgar from the Garden.'

JUDICIAL STATEMENT TAKEN DOWN
FROM DONALD RICKETTS

(i)   Donald Ricketts and Edgar Peissart were alone
after lunch. The latter reached out his hand and
caught D by the arm and he pulled him down to
sit on his knee. He took his hand and put it into
his own against his head, then he kissed him.
D sat there some time and thought it was only
demonstration of affection.

(ii)   EP asked D to go to his room and he sat on a chair
and EP on another. He made him lie down on
the bed with him and EP laid down on top of him.
Nothing else transpired. EP asked him to come
up again to his room at night and D said 'no, he
didn't think he could'.

(iii) EP asked D to go up to his room with him. He
kissed D incessantly! The same practices on the
bed. D went to his room after supper and stayed
the night with him, they undressed straight away
and went to bed. E told D that the covenant David
and Jonathan made together was the exchange of
'seed'. That night he gave his seed to D and D gave
his to EP. Then he put his seed into D's mouth.
[. . .]

(iv) EP told him that he wasn't to tell 'these women'
and that if he were asked he was to say only that
certain friendly relations had passed between
them.

The Divine Mother

The wind is picking up. As I cross the Garden to visit Ellen, I see a
billowing sail: Grace is struggling to tame a picnic blanket that has
been lifted by a gust. I could walk across and talk to her but I
won't. Not here. Not in full view. Octavia and Emily will be out
here any moment; they plan to take their lunch outside today,
though I think the weather may have other ideas.

They are very rarely seen apart now: Octavia is so grateful that
Emily was there to protect Her from Edgar's fury. 'Thank goodness the Lord guided her hand to the knife,' She said when Peter
returned and asked what had happened. 'She gave no thought to
her own safety.'

'Any one of us would have sacrificed ourselves for the Daughter
of God,' said Emily, with rehearsed humility. Then she looked at
me. She didn't mention the fact that I failed to raise my hand, or
voice, to Edgar.

She didn't have to.

I am not invited to their picnic, which is a relief to me. There will
be only one topic of conversation: the wickedness that Edgar has
brought into the Garden, the acts that he pressed Donald to commit.
They have spoken of little else, poring over the repulsive details of
his perversion, like a scab to be picked. Octavia says you have to call
a sin by its proper name and she does not shy away from the details,
the abhorrent mechanics of their sodomy. 'Like animals,' She says,
'rutting like animals out in the fields. Two men unhindered by the
tenderness of a woman's touch, unfettered in their lust.'

I can't bear to hear it, can't bear to think about the nakedness, the violence. The way Octavia describes their sin makes it sound like an act of war. I imagine the thrust of bayonets, the piercing of flesh; desire consuming them like the red mist of rage. Men are blinded by the urge to overpower and conquer. Perhaps this was violation by mutual consent.

Passing under Yggdrasil's branches I think about the day that Edgar sat waiting for me on the bench. 'I hope you don't misunderstand what you heard us say . . . Sometimes we just crave peace and quiet.' He must have thought me such a fool. Since I heard Donald's confessions I have not been able to bring myself to visit Castleside. It feels like occupied territory, tainted by the fantasies of victory and surrender played out within. Did they climb the stairs to my favourite bedroom, committing their sins beneath the painting of the Sea of Galilee? Perhaps they laughed at me as they undressed and threw their clothes on the fuchsia armchair in the corner, laid their bodies on the bedspread embroidered with blue-green ivy. *Poor Dilys. She has no idea.* I can't bear the thought that they met in the rooms where Grace and I have sat together. Castleside was our place. It was mine. But they have taken it from me. Tainted it. Tangled up their story with ours. And now the way I feel for Grace is stained, sullied by their sin.

When they broke the pantry window they let the Devil in and he has tormented me ever since. Tricked me. He has made me dream things I shouldn't dream. And do things I shouldn't do.

Ellen's door is unlocked, and I find her sleeping, her tiny frame bolstered by a pile of pillows. I sit at the foot of the bed and study her: eyes sunken, cheeks severe. Perhaps Death cannot accept that the Lord will not let him take her. He lingers in this bedroom, gnawing at her a little every day, snatching away a piece at a time. Is this what eternal life will mean: kept alive but still ravaged by time? Soon enough there will be nothing left of Ellen but her bones.

'Dilys, is that you?' Her eyes are slow to open. It takes her longer to wake these days. 'How lovely,' she says. 'How are you?' We have an unspoken rule that I don't ask her the same question in return. Because neither of us will like the answer.

'I'm all right. I think. Soldiering on.' She motions for me to pass her the glass on her bedside table.

'Still incarcerated?' she says. Her smile is just as it always was, but now the rest of her has shrunk it looks oversized, too big for her face.

'Yes, I'm afraid so. Still confined to the Garden.' I long to get out and take a walk by the river, but we both know I wouldn't get away with it. Emily will have told the others to be vigilant. I wouldn't get further than the street corner before one of them raised the alarm.

'It's for your own good,' she says.

'Perhaps.'

'You seem a little downcast today . . .' She pauses as if deciding whether to say more.

'Oh no, I'm fine. I just need to get out and stretch my legs, that's all.' I stand up and walk to the window. 'It was such a beautiful morning. Though it looks like it has turned.' The wind that snatched Grace's picnic blanket has been busy sweeping the dark clouds towards us. 'It's starting to rain.'

I watch the drops hit the window, each trying desperately to cling on before taking the inevitable slide. Some weaving a weary path, others speeding to their fate: a few heady moments of free-dom before they are lost in the puddle that is forming on the windowsill. The rain is really coming down now. The heavens have opened: that's what my father used to say. I used to run outside in the hope I'd meet a falling angel. But my mother warned I should be careful what I wished for: there are angels of darkness as well as of light.

'Quite a storm,' I say.

'So it's just as well that we are both confined,' says Ellen. 'Come. Sit. Tell me what I have missed. There must be some intrigue.'

'I'm afraid it is rather more serious than that. Has anyone been to see you?' I perch beside her.

'About what?'

'Edgar.'

'Well, I know Octavia was starting to have doubts about him. He was insisting the Lord had singled him out for a special role.' She shuffles on her pillows. 'Help me sit up, would you?' I give her my arm, and she pulls herself forward while I rearrange them.

'Better?'

She nods and I lower her down, gently.

'Octavia was not convinced, but he had rather more luck persuading others. He recruited one of the young men, Donald.'

'Really?'

'He was holding meetings in secret, meetings where they performed . . .' I'm blushing. Octavia would never blush to say it. 'They performed certain unnatural practices.'

Ellen is not easily shocked, but I can tell this was the last thing she expected to hear. She brings her hand to her mouth as though the thought of it has made her nauseous.

'Men, laying with men,' she gasps, 'here, in the society? That is . . . oh, poor Octavia!'

'I'm afraid there is no doubt,' I say. 'Donald Ricketts gave a full confession. Edgar stormed into the house and I thought he meant to attack Octavia. Emily chased him out with a paperknife.'

'A paperknife? Dilys, slow down. I'm having trouble taking all this in.'

'Emily was . . . I've never seen her like that before. If he hadn't run I really think she might have stabbed him.'

'I'm sure you are mistaken, Dilys,' she says kindly, putting her hand on top of mine. 'Emily would never do such a thing. She was probably terrified!'

'Typical Ellen,' I say with a smile. 'Always seeing the best in everyone.'

'What do you mean?'

'You weren't there. You didn't see. Emily wasn't terrified, she was enjoying every second of it.'

Ellen squeezes my hand, then moves it back to be beside her other, on top of the covers. 'So what is being done about it?' she asks. '*Something* will have to be done.'

'Donald Ricketts has gone back to Cambridge to finish his final year. Octavia told him She quite understands that he won't be back – that it would be too distressing for him to return to the place where it all happened.'

'And Edgar?'

'There's to be a hearing. He sent a note begging for Her forgiveness, said he could explain. She is going to call for him when She is ready. Until then he is forbidden from contacting any of us. And we are forbidden from speaking to him.'

'But he is living in a Panacea house . . .'

'Yes, he lodges with Mrs Jenson. She has been instructed to leave his meals outside his bedroom door. Though she hasn't been told why.'

'I suppose it's not as if he'll be going anywhere,' Ellen says, looking to the window. 'How fortunate that he donated his savings to the society when he joined. Just imagine if he had the means to run before he had repented.' She pauses and holds her head completely still. 'Can you hear something?'

I can. Footsteps, and voices. She reaches down and smooths her covers.

'You are not expecting anyone, Ellen?'

'No.'

I open the door to find Octavia on the landing. 'Dilys,' She says. 'We are quite giddy. We had intended to take our lunch on the lawn but the rain – it came upon us so quickly!' She is out of breath; Her voice loud and Her cheeks flushed. 'We thought we'd come and see Ellen instead. Is she awake?'

Before I get a chance to answer, She leads the charge into the bedroom. 'Ellen, dear, please excuse our interruption. We seek shelter from the storm. Surely Noah himself did not see rain as heavy as this.'

'Come in, Octavia,' says Ellen. 'You are very welcome. Dilys, can you call Betty to bring tea?'

Octavia takes a seat without waiting to be asked. Emily does the same: she likes to emulate Octavia in all things.

'Ellen,' Octavia says. 'I have decided you need to get well again. I need you, the society needs you. There is so much to do and I simply can't spare you to lie around in this gloomy room any longer.' Ellen tries to force a laugh but the result is a prolonged bout of coughing.

'This illness can be nothing serious. The Lord has made us all a promise: eternal life for those who dwell here in the Garden of Eden. I have been praying, Ellen, and the Lord and I both agree that the time has come for you to recover.'

Ellen turns to me. 'Dilys?'

'Yes?'

'That tea.'

'Yes of course.'

I am reluctant to leave her, but I make my way to give Betty the instructions. On the bottom stair I hear the back door open. Grace is struggling in, arms full of plates and packages. She is soaked to the skin, strands of hair stuck to her face, rain dripping from the tip of her nose. She is grumbling under her breath: too much to hold, not enough arms.

At the sight of her, I laugh. I can't help it. For a second she glares at me but then she surrenders with a smile.

'Wet out there?' I say. 'That pork pie is sodden.'

'The pork pie?' she says. 'Is that all you can worry about?'

'Yes. Unless . . . oh no . . . please don't say the Victoria sandwich has perished in the flood.' With her arms full she uses her elbow to nudge me, and almost drops a plate of sandwiches.

'I was just setting everything out when the rain began,' she says. 'Octavia and Emily just upped sticks and ran. And I was left picking up the pieces . . .'

'Of pie.'

She rolls her eyes. 'Yes, very good. What are you doing here?'

'I came to see Ellen,' I say, nodding towards the stairs. 'Do you mind if I leave you to sort this out with Betty? Ellen sent me down to ask for tea but I don't want to leave her too long.'

'I understand,' she says.

By the time I get back to Ellen's bedroom, the door is opening and Octavia's head appears. 'Dilys, just in time,' She says, pushing back a stray hair from Her forehead. 'Help us to get Ellen downstairs.'

'Downstairs? Do you think that's a good idea?'

She answers with a look intended to silence me. But it doesn't.

'She is still very weak,' I say.

'Dilys, it is settled. It will be a very relaxed affair. We haven't insisted she change for lunch.'

We help her out of bed, pulling back the covers to reveal a frail body in a floral nightdress. It pains me to see how thin she has become, and I realise I haven't seen her legs these past few weeks. I've not seen her out of bed at all; she's been tucked up and slowly disappearing. I lift her feet down to the floor and Emily and I take an arm each, expecting her to take her own weight when she stands. But she is too weak and we end up near-enough carrying her. When we turn the tight corner from the landing to the top of the stairs I feel her body stiffen in pain.

'Are you all right?' I whisper.

'Yes, yes,' she says, brightly. 'Octavia is right. It's time I got up and stopped feeling sorry for myself.'

Grace serves the picnic on Ellen's dining table and, bolstered by the fruit cake Betty conjures from the pantry, it stretches out to feed four of us. I manage a cucumber sandwich, but Ellen doesn't take a single bite. She looks like she is struggling just to sit up straight.

'Has Dilys told you about Edgar?' Octavia asks her.

'Yes, she started to—'

'A wicked business,' She says. 'He burst in like a man possessed.'

'He *is* a man possessed,' Emily corrects Her. 'There can be no doubt of that after the evidence brought before us.'

'If it wasn't for Emily, I could have been murdered in my own sitting room,' Octavia says. 'The Lord would not let the Devil prevail. Emily was His instrument. She was my protector.'

'It sounds terrifying,' Ellen says. 'Dilys tells me Emily had a knife.'

'She did,' Octavia says. 'My paper knife. Inscribed with the word "Jerusalem". It was God's hand that led her.'

Ellen is expected to react with excitement, but I can tell she is struggling to muster the energy. Under the table I can see her hands screwed into fists; pain gripping her like the jaws of a dog, then tossing her aside. She snatches a breath before it comes to bite again. But Octavia seems unaware that Ellen's gasps might be prompted by anything other than shock and concern.

'I'm afraid it doesn't end there,' She says. 'Peter went to Edgar's lodgings and found documents in his room, letters that incriminate him. It's beyond any doubt . . . Satan led this man to us. He is the serpent in our Garden, sent to tempt and to corrupt. He always was rather reptilian in manner.'

'How you must suffer,' Ellen says. She always finds exactly the right words, but then she has had a lot of practice.

'She does,' Emily cuts in. 'But we are quite delighted to find out the enemies. At the present moment we are like Red Indians collecting scalps.'

Ellen has started to sway in her chair.

'It has been a shock,' says Octavia, looking down at Her plate. 'The great strife between woman and the powers of evil are coming to a head. I must be the one to face it.'

'How?' Ellen manages to ask.

'That is the question. Edgar is too wicked to keep but too wicked to keep out – if he leaves the society goodness knows how he may slander us.'

Ellen pauses, pretending to give the matter some thought, but I see her push back, tensed against the pain that looks like it is trying to drag her off her seat.

'Emily, would you be kind enough to pass a boiled egg?' Octavia says. 'Emily . . .'

There's a crash: the sound of a fork dropping down onto china. Emily's plate has cracked in two. She is sitting perfectly still, eyes rolled back into their sockets, one hand motionless in front of her, the other still gripping her knife.

'Emily . . .' Octavia says, in a whisper now. 'Emily, can you hear me?'

She says nothing, does not blink, does not give the slightest twitch.

'Who are you?' Octavia says. 'In the name of the Lord I command you to reveal yourself.'

'I am the Divine Mother,' a voice says, a deep voice that is not Emily's own. 'My Daughter . . . I have come to Your help . . . You shall not suffer this alone. I have come to establish the kingdom of My Son. Send the man to New York. He will die.'

'The Divine Mother,' Octavia says. 'The Holy Spirit sent to me in female form.' She brings Her head onto Her hands as though She is fainting. I jump up and rush to revive Her, but Her hunched body starts to shake and gasp. I can't remember the last time I saw Octavia cry but I realise that's what She is doing. I hear Her sobs. Great gulping sobs.

'Octavia, are you all right?' I say and She lifts her head to meet my eyes.

'He has heard me, Dilys. God has heard me and answered my prayer. He has sent help. Don't you see?' But all I see is the twitch of a smile on the very corner of Emily's lips.

'The Lord has heard me,' Octavia says to Herself. 'I am not alone any more.'

But She was never alone. I was here.

Eve's Shame

There's a question lodged in my throat. Words scratching like fish bones: Why. Why now. Why Emily. I sink down beneath the bathwater and hold my breath. It struggles inside me, kicking against my ribs, fighting to be free. It scolds like steam. Then up it rises, surging into my cheeks and out into the water. Doubt rushing up and breaking as bubbles on the surface.

Why would the Spirit come to Emily after all these years?

I take another lungful of air. Hold my breath. Repeat. With my head in the water I can hardly hear them: Octavia, Emily and Peter in the dining room below me. Their joyful sobs and praise-be-to-Gods sound very far away, as though their awe and exhilaration have been subdued. That's how I feel: muffled, distant, hollow. I should be downstairs celebrating with them. I should be elated. The Lord has sent the Holy Spirit to us; He has sent the Divine Mother, that's what Octavia believes. She heard the prophecy from Emily's lips. *Send the man to New York. He will die.* And in Her mind it's as good as happened. Right now they are planning Edgar's banishment. Imagining his death. Breathing a sigh of relief that he will no longer be their problem.

They barely noticed when I made my excuses and slipped away for my bath. Fridays are always my turn. Every week I come up and fill the enamel tub before supper, while Grace feeds the boiler in the kitchen. Missing it would have meant waiting for another week; missing it would have meant sitting in the dining room and pretending. So instead I scrub my body clean, use a brush to slough off the dry skin, lather up my hair with olive oil shampoo. I will have to be quick. My arms are turning to gooseflesh. The bath is getting cold but I can't top it up. I'll need to use the last of the hot water to wash my napkins in the sink. I thought my bleeds had stopped, that perhaps I really had reached middle-age prematurely; or that my body had realised the futility of its monthly chore. I thought that irregularity had finally given way to complete absence. But yesterday I felt the familiar stab of Eve's shame.

I had a show of old blood, brown like rusted iron, a slurry of mud. It made me think of the neatly tended beds in the Garden. It made me wonder if that's what women are. Whether that's the ache they feel each month: the space inside them heavy with the weight of soil and possibility. Octavia talks about girls being deflowered. Girls Out There. Like roses being dead-headed or daisies being wrenched from the ground. It always seemed so violent, but perhaps that's the way it has to be: a new generation fed by the decay of the one that came before. The sacrifice of nature.

But not in here. Not for me.

I hear a shriek downstairs. I'm not sure whether it is an exclamation of ecstasy or alarm. When I left them Emily was still insisting she couldn't remember a thing about what she said at Ellen's dining table. 'Tell me the words again, Octavia,' she said, bringing her hands up to the back of her own neck, perhaps to calm the hairs that might be standing on their ends. 'I said that Edgar will die – is that right?'

Octavia had not realised She was expected to answer. Her eyes moved slowly around the room, Her body swaying slightly in Her chair. She looked as though She'd had rather too much to drink but I know She had not. It was Emily who'd had a small glass of sherry pressed into her hand once she 'came round'.

'Yes, Octavia, tell us again,' said Peter, rushing to the sideboard to get a pencil and sheet of paper. 'I shall write this down. We need to make a record of everything that passed.'

'The wages of sin is death,' Octavia whispered to Herself, but Peter didn't hear. He had already turned his attention back to Emily, staring at her wide-eyed and alert as if he was seeing her for the first time. 'I am only sorry I wasn't there to witness this miracle for myself,' he said, touching the pencil to his tongue and starting to write. Betty had been sent to fetch him straight away, but by the time he arrived at Ellen's back door, Emily was wearing a self-satisfied grin that told me she was feeling quite 'herself' again and was no longer imbued with the divine.

'Dear Lord,' he said, kneeling beside her as he rushed into the room. 'Well I never. It has happened. It has really happened!' He kissed the hem of her dress, then sat cross-legged at her feet, his hair seeming to spring up off his head in excitement. 'Our Heavenly Father has sent the spirit of the Mother to protect us all. Isn't it wonderful?'

'It is,' I said. 'It is.' But the words made no impression on me, gave me no joy, left me no feeling.

I stand and step out of the bath, drops of cold water running down my neck. I reach out for the towel that is hanging on the stand beside the door, and wrap it around my shoulders but it does nothing to warm me. When I take out the plug they'll hear the water gurgling through the pipes above their heads: the thoughts I whispered silently beneath the surface.

Why Emily? Why now?

The Trial

Edgar's time has come; he has been called to trial. Emily said it was best to keep the matter private; Octavia will tell the congregation once he has been dealt with. But Peter and I have been called as witnesses to his wickedness.

Octavia is standing at the chapel altar. 'He has revealed His Daughter to the World, through me, and now He has sent the Holy Spirit in the form of the Mother. He is sending reinforcements for the battle that is about to play out in this room.' She laughs at how wrong the church of men has been. How blind to the Truth. 'Look upon Emily's window,' She says, 'a prophecy in stained glass. *Jerusalem which is above is free, which is the mother of us all.* And now the Mother is among us.'

Everything is just as Emily wants it, and everyone just where she wants them to be. Edgar had no choice. He had to come if he didn't want to be turned out onto the streets: the society has all his money. He is sitting alone next to a small table; a black box, a Bible and the Jerusalem knife arranged neatly on top. His pocket watch and cane have been taken from him. And all that remains are rounded shoulders in a faded suit. He is already defeated. Peter and I are standing level with him, our backs against the chapel wall.

'This is the Divine Court of Jerusalem,' Emily says. 'Here we shall bring Satan to trial.' She is filling time, keeping him guessing, keeping him here. He has no idea that at this very moment Grace is at his lodgings, packing up his things. Octavia has bought his ticket for the *Aquitania*, which leaves for New York in ten days' time. There was no question that She would let him stay in a society house until then, so Emily has organised a room for him near the station. Grace will go ahead to arrange his books and hang his clothes in the wardrobe. It will be as though he has been living there all along; as though none of this ever happened.

'You must give evidence against Satan,' Octavia says. 'You are his accuser. Every sin you have committed must be laid at his feet, for you are under his control. What was the nature of your relationship with Donald Ricketts?'

'I can explain,' he says. 'If I may be permitted to speak. I can explain it all.' He keeps his eyes fixed on Octavia, but I can see from the slight tilt of his head that he senses Emily's presence behind him; that he is wondering what she might be doing, might be planning.

'The Bible speaks of the secret male combination,' Octavia says. 'The combination that Cain tried to force on Abel—'

'But this is all a misunderstanding,' he says. 'Really there is no need for—' He flinches as Emily puts her hands on his shoulders.

'You will get your chance, Edgar,' she says, leaning down to speak into his ear. 'But this is a trial, we need to present our evidence first. Donald Ricketts gave a full account of what passed between you.'

'He was a sensitive young man,' he says, turning round to face her now. 'Perhaps he mistook my kindness for something else . . .'

'But do you expect us to believe that he misunderstood the sentiments you *wrote* to him?' says Octavia. He swings back round to Her as She takes the lid off the box beside him. 'I have read your correspondence with Donald,' She says, lifting out a bundle of papers. 'You look surprised to see them, Edgar.'

He stares at the letters, which She holds in front of his face, and starts to pray in a whisper. 'Oh God,' he says. 'Oh God. Oh God.'

'I should think you are surprised,' She says. 'You tore them up. But Peter found the pieces in your waste paper bin and put the jigsaw back together with parcel tape.'

Edgar is moving now, twitching as though he is struggling to sit still in his seat. Octavia steps back and begins to walk around the room, quite casually.

'Love letters,' She says. 'This is the most deceptive point in the whole thing: you thought that what you felt was so extraordinary that it must be of God!'

Love. Is that what Edgar thought it was? How could it be? Octavia says men do not have the capacity to love as women do.

Edgar drops his head, squeezing his eyes tightly shut, trying to stop the tears from spilling out between his lashes, but he can't stem the silent tide. Is it the memory of what has passed that he cries for, or the fear of what is to come?

Still walking, Octavia holds out a letter at arm's length and narrows Her eyes to read from it. 'Here you write: "My dear Donald, a feeling ran all over my interior as though you were alive within me!"' I can feel heat rise to my face. My thoughts turn to buttons being undone, fingers intertwining, lips brushing skin. Then all I can think of is the taste of cotton nightdress on my lips. His words describe the way I feel when Grace's skin touches mine.

And suddenly I pity him. Has he suffered as I do, torn between torment and rapture?

For love is of God; and every one that loveth is born of God, and knoweth God.

(1 John 4:7)

Octavia brings the back of Her other hand up to Her mouth, to contain an affected laugh. '"How greatly our souls or seed are knitted as one man!" you write here. "There exists in us one life that can never be broken again!" Oh Edgar, how you were both deceived!'

He jumps to his feet, snatching the letters from Her hand. 'There was no deception. As it is written in the Bible, Octavia, *the soul of Jonathan was knit with the soul of David, and Jonathan loved him as his own soul.*' He takes another step. 'And David said: *Thy love to me was wonderful, passing the love of women.*'

'Homosexuality is the gravest of sins because it denies woman: the saviour,' Octavia says. 'In exchanging seed with man you deny the need for womanhood.' She looks past him, and nods to Emily. By the time he turns to the table the knife is gone, and Emily is behind him pushing him down onto his seat.

'What are you going to do?' he cries out. 'Octavia, what are you going to let her do?'

'Sit quietly,' Emily says slowly, savouring every syllable. 'Sit still and you shall be delivered from your sin. Remember Lot's wife and do not turn back.'

Without warning she falls down onto the floor, her body folding then stretching out, every limb rigid, every muscle taut. She is shaking violently, her head thrashing from side to side, fighting an attacker only she can see.

Does she actually believe it? She has lost herself in her own pretence, so determined to be like Octavia that she'll do anything to prove it. She brings her hands to her throat, gripping tightly until she can hardly snatch a rasping breath.

'Oh God,' Edgar says, keeping his eyes fixed forward. 'What is it? What is she going to do?' I hear a low grunt and Emily stops suddenly, lying absolutely still and looking at the ceiling.

'Who are you?' Octavia shouts to her.

'I am the Divine Mother. I command that this son be delivered from the control of Satan.'

She pushes herself onto her knees and brings her hands together, the palm of one curled round the other which is grasping the knife. 'I answer only to the Lord,' she says, in a jagged whisper. 'The Lord alone.'

Emily tries to stand but falls back, scrabbling to her feet then staggering forward to his chair. Still he does not turn to face her. So when the knife appears at his throat he jumps. 'Sit still,' she shouts. And then she whips the knife away, walking round to face him and slashing at the air between them.

Nobody steps forward.
Nobody tries to stop her.
Not even me.

Octavia is standing completely still in the corner, one hand on the altar, the other on Her forehead. There is no life in Her eyes, no colour in Her face. How far will She let this go? 'Get out of him!' Emily shouts. 'Demons be gone! Repent, Edgar, denounce your feelings – unnatural, abhorrent – they have no place in the Lord's Garden.'

A feeling ran all over my interior as though you were alive within me.

Give something a name and that is what it becomes. But unnatural, abhorrent: that's not what this is. Because that would make what I feel for Grace wrong. And it isn't. It can't be.

I have to get out. If she turns to me she'll see, she'll know. With every heartbeat my chest tightens its grip and leaves me gasping. My stomach heaves, the tang of sickness burns my throat and my body lurches towards the door.

'All who sin must repent!' Emily shouts into the air as I stumble into the Garden.

But what if I don't want to be forgiven? What if I'm not sorry for what I feel? And for the things we have done, in my dreams, in the dark? How will I be saved?

———

No one came after me. All eyes were on Emily. Except Edgar's: by then he had covered his face with his hands. I wanted to run away but I could hear it all, the sound of splintering wood and the cries of an animal: snarling, wild. I couldn't help myself, I had to look. Through the prism of the stained glass all I could make out were shapes; a figure twirling and whirling as if she was dancing. Then everything was still. Everything fell silent and I hid behind the Wireless Room and watched them come out. Emily and Peter linking Edgar's arms and marching him back to Number 12. Octavia walking behind.

The door of the chapel had been left ajar, and as I entered, the last of the daylight seemed to hurry out behind me, shafts of gold stepping aside for dusk's shadows to take their place. Edgar's chair was lying on its side by the wall; a mess of scattered papers on the floor. In the struggle Peter's packing tape had not held up and the sheets were a series of torn pieces once more. But the table was still standing, and the Bible was on the floor beside it, the corners of the leather cover dented, the gold stripe of the fore-edge looking cracked and torn. Perhaps Emily threw it down to hit a spirit only she could see. I imagine she rubbed her hands together with the satisfaction of someone who'd just swatted a fly.

I climbed up here into the clock tower and shut the hatch behind me. It's a place where only Grace will think to look. I didn't want to go home, I didn't want to face them. But they'll wonder why I wasn't at dinner. I'll have to stay up here all night with the spiders and their webs. It is too dark to make my way down the ladder now, I could fall and break my neck. I wouldn't want Grace to find me like that.

'Dilys?' It's just a whisper but I can hear her voice, coming to me in the spokes of light that are seeping between the floorboards. 'Are you up there?'

I feel my way across the floor and find the ring on top of the hatch.

'Yes. Can you help me down?'

She climbs, wrapping one arm around the rung at the top and using her other to reach out for my ankle. When my foot finds the ladder I feel like jumping. I can't wait to get out of the darkness, as if there is something up here, as if there was something waiting all along.

'I've been looking for you everywhere,' she says. 'What are you doing? Octavia said you were taken ill.'

'At the trial. Edgar was . . . Emily had the knife.'

'Oh God,' she says. 'What did she do? By the time I had un-packed his things and walked back, they said Peter had taken him in a taxi. I must have passed them on the way. Did she hurt him?'

I shake my head. 'I don't know. I had to get out.'

'When I got back,' she says, 'Emily was standing in front of the sitting room mirror, just staring at her neck. There were scratches of dried blood and her blouse was torn around her throat. Octavia said she had done it to herself . . . Emily said she couldn't remember.'

'I didn't go back in,' I say, starting to panic again. 'I've missed dinner. They will wonder where I am.'

'It's all right,' she says, reaching out for my arm. 'They thought you were unwell. I told them I had checked and you were asleep in bed.' She looks past me, to the room behind, and sees Edgar's chair, still lying on its side. One of the legs is broken. 'What did she do?' Her voice is slow and deliberate now. 'Dilys. Tell me.'

'She said Edgar was under the control of Satan. She said he had to be freed.'

Grace's attention turns to the scraps of paper on the floor. She bends slowly, and nudges the pieces with her fingertips.

'Letters,' I say. 'Between Edgar and Donald.'

'Screwed up, torn to pieces . . .' Her hand recoils; she takes a sharp breath and she looks at me. She wants me to mirror her shock, she wants to see it on my face, reflecting back at her, but I don't feel anything. When I think of what I saw it's as if I am watching a silent film, black and white memories sandwiched between crimson curtains. I can't hear Edgar sobbing or Emily crying out, not if I concentrate and chew the side of my mouth to stop the tears from spilling over.

Looking down, I see my hands are in hers now, they are shaking, she is trying to hold them still. But I don't deserve her tenderness.

'I didn't stop her,' I say, jerking them away. 'I didn't tell her to stop. She said he was unnatural, abhorrent . . .'

'Try to breathe,' she says. 'Dilys, please, try to calm down.'

'Edgar said it was love. He thought it was from God.'

She takes my chin in her hand, tilts my head up towards her own, and with her eyes she holds me still until I find my breath.

'And what do you think?' she says.

'Perhaps it was. Isn't love the Lord's gift to us all? *Beloved, let us love one another; for love is of God; and every one that loveth is born of God, and knoweth God.*'

'Oh Dilys,' she says, closing her eyes and falling silent for a moment. 'If they even heard you speak like that. Think about what they have done to Edgar . . .'

'I know.' They would never understand. They couldn't.

She takes my hands again. 'If this is how it is going to be I just . . . I don't think I can stay here . . .'

I can't move. I can't breathe.

It is all my fault. I should never have invited her to visit that first day. She could have lived a life of ignorance, a life outside the Garden. And the Lord would have forgiven her. She couldn't have been damned for denying the Truth, if she had never heard it. But I am selfish. I wanted us to be trapped in this together.

I still do.

'We can't go on like this,' she says. 'Broken chairs and knives. What if they found out . . . what if they knew we'd been meeting like this?'

'It is all Emily's doing. She's taking over.'

'But Octavia is letting her.'

'Octavia struggles,' I say. 'All this . . . She has a heavy burden. When I was growing up . . . I remember . . . I saw the torment that She suffered.'

'And what about you, Dilys? What about *your* torment? All this is making you ill.'

She talks as though I have a choice. 'We have to stay,' I say. 'It's too late. You have made your vow to follow Octavia. If you turn your back on Her, you turn your back on God.' And on me, Grace. You turn your back on me. 'You can't leave. Promise me you won't.'

'Dilys. Calm down. You're hurting my hand. Your nails are digging—'

'Promise me you'll never mention it again.'

AUTUMN

The Voice of Jerusalem the Divine Mother . . . set the
seal upon Octavia's faith and works in a wonderful way.
We were shown that the more we could lay our worst
sins on Satan the better, for by our endeavour against
him he was about to be cast out . . . Emily Goodwin,
never knowing what we said, voiced the Mother's
answers and judgement, condemned us for what we had
no idea was so rooted in us . . . [and] exorcised them
from us – à haute voix. The victim generally collapsed
in a flood of truly penitent tears which 'The great
Mother' literally wiped away

      Rachel Fox, *The Sufferings and Acts of Shiloh Jerusalem*

THE TEN COMMANDMENTS IN THE
SPIRITUAL COURT

(1) *Thou shalt have no other Gods than Me.*
Idolatry will include devotion to one's idea of how to do
a thing, or to one's own tastes or opinion.

(2) *Thou shalt not make unto thee any Graven Image.*
This will be taken to mean the imagination in regard
to illness, fear, private interpretation in regard to the
Divine Mother's admonitions etc. must be overcome
viz.: 'I thought you meant so and so.'

(3) *Thou shalt not take the Name of the Lord Thy God in vain.*
By resenting reproof . . . or by bringing up trivial things.

(4) *Remember the Sabbath day, to keep it holy.*
To cause discomfort owing to lack of tact. Under
this heading come unpleasing manners, unnecessary
noises, high voices, humming, singing, ugly table
manners, lack of courtesy and politeness etc.

(5) *Honour Thy Father and Thy Mother.*
Obeying behests of this mission and all Divine
Commands in connection with it.

(6) *Thou shalt do no murder.*
Be a kill-joy: show temper – or pour forth complaints
from a crooked or cantankerous disposition,
moodiness, depression etc.

(7) *Thou shalt not commit adultery.*
You have definitely endeavoured to marry yourself
to Holiness and Goodness, do not create grounds by
which you may be divorced. Why pray 'Deliver us from
evil' if you insist on trying to bring your own evil into
the Kingdom?

(8) *Thou shalt not steal.*
To give way to jealousy and try to win praise which
belongs to another, or to secure work for yourself
which they should be allowed to do, will be counted as
stealing or fraud.

(9) *Thou shalt not bear false witness against thy neighbour.*
Care must be taken by the Plaintiff to state their case
fairly in the Divine Mother's Court.

(10) *Thou shalt not covet, etc.*
It is useless to covet what has been a predestined
position.

There is no forgiveness in the new kingdom – *all must be
altered*, not forgiven.

The New World

Octavia says we have entered a new era. Emily told Her so, or the Divine Mother did; sometimes even She finds it difficult to know which of them is speaking. But either way She is convinced the Lord has sent His Holy Spirit to wield the rod of correction. Emily has issued new rules and made it clear there will be consequences if we don't follow them. She does not say what the punishments will be and no one dares to ask. Questions of any kind are no longer permitted. Edgar's treachery has proved that those who doubt are led from the righteous path. That's what Octavia told the congregation the day after his trial.

'I hear there have been whisperings,' She said, 'from those who heard a commotion in the chapel or saw him leaving here in a taxi. I ask you to ignore rumours and listen to the truth – sordid though it is to hear.'

Her candour about how and where the two men had 'shared seed' was rewarded with gasps of shock and modesty. 'Edgar came bursting in . . . and the Divine Mother saved me,' She said, smiling down at Emily who was sitting on the front row. 'She took up the knife . . .'

More gasps.

'. . . God revealed that she would be an instrument for the Holy Spirit . . . She said "send the man to New York, there he shall die."'

At this the room fell silent, the only sound a frantic tapping: the heels of Emily's shoes kicking against the floor as she jerked in her chair.

'Have you come?' Octavia said. 'Have you come with a message for your children?'

'I am the Divine Mother,' a voice said when her body had stilled. 'I say again. Do not question. The serpentine line with its dot below is a devilish sign implying doubts on fundamental matters. There must be no "buts" or "if nots".'

And Octavia said, 'Amen.'

Afterwards, at supper, Peter told Emily her voice had been so strange it sounded like she was speaking from her eyes. She shook her head and said she couldn't remember a thing about it.

———

We have gathered on the lawn, this evening. Though the Garden's leaves have started to rust, summer's heat still lingers in the airless chapel, and there were too many of us to sit in there tonight, so we carried chairs outside. All of the resident members are here, except Ellen of course; even Grace was told to prepare a cold supper so she could be spared from her duties in the kitchen. She is not sitting beside me. We are very careful to keep our distance when we are with the others now. Emily has been watching us and always seems to be nearby; quick to interrupt if I step into the kitchen with a question; ready to hurry Grace along if she lingers with my tray. *We have to be careful*, Grace said.

Careful is what we are being.

'There are those of you who seem to have forgotten what is expected,' Emily says. 'But in the new world it will become criminal to annoy, to distress, to depress or to irritate.' A single burnished leaf lands by her feet, one of the first to drop. Soon the Garden will be stripped of its colour. And its dignity. Yggdrasil, already blushing at the thought, will watch its threadbare gown slide to the floor. And then no one will stop to sit on the bench around its trunk: it is too dangerous. The winds come and tear away loose twigs and branches.

When Adrian was a boy his head was split open by a falling bough; Octavia said it was God's punishment and insisted he confess his crimes. He always had a scar after that.

I suppose he still does.

Kate Firth hands a stack of papers to Rachel Fox on the end of the front row; she takes a copy and passes it on.

'Be warned,' says Emily. 'I shall not stand by and watch the Daughter suffer for your thoughtless behaviour. These are the new commandments. Failure to follow them will not be forgiven.'

'She is right,' Octavia tells the gathered congregation. 'I have been too gentle, indulged you, but the time has come to mete out retribution. As Jesus said: *Those whom I love, I rebuke and chasten: be zealous therefore and repent.*'

Just like Edgar must do.

This evening Octavia shares the news that the Divine Mother's instructions for him have been followed. His ship has set sail. 'Gone,' She says. 'As we speak he is crossing the Atlantic. He will trespass in this country no longer.' She does not mention that Emily had to put him on the train to Southampton herself. He'd been terrified to leave the house alone since she'd told him about the 'pleasant chat' she'd had with the Chief Constable of the police. 'I told Edgar the matter was settled,' she said when she returned from his lodgings, 'but that if any constable saw him out on the streets, he would be asked to accompany them to the station.'

She checked on him every morning after that, and brought him a daily dose of the Water. That's something else Octavia doesn't mention to the congregation; I only know because I heard them speaking on the landing. 'Do you need more squares?' Octavia said. 'I'll call Dilys. She can get some from the linen room.'

'No, no need to trouble her. I have a bundle in my desk,' I heard Emily say.

'I suppose it is only right that we make sure he is well enough to travel to Southampton.' It sounded almost like a question.

'We must prepare him body *and* soul, Octavia. You told me Yourself the words the Lord's Spirit spoke through me. We must send him back to America.' Emily paused, then said: 'He will get what he deserves. I will make sure of that.'

I wonder if she gave him a supply of blessed squares for his suitcase; I wonder if he is drinking the Water right now; whether he has a porthole in his cabin and whether he sits and thinks of Donald still.

———

After the meeting, we return to Number 12 for supper.

'We are delivered from him at last,' Octavia says, as Grace carries in a platter of cold meats. 'But no sooner is one enemy vanquished than we must turn to fight another. So long have men ruled the Earth that they think they have sovereignty over us. But they shall be defeated . . .'

Peter looks down and adjusts the napkin on his lap.

'Except you, Peter,' She says, pouring a little milk into Her teacup. 'You are hardly like a man at all. If only others could share your piety.' She pauses to pick up the teapot. 'In fact, I think Peter should be part of the squadron you are assembling, Emily.'

'What squadron?' he says, reaching for a slice of cured ham.

'To take on Harry Price. Though I hoped the sorry saga would pass over without attention, it seems that the newspapers have fallen for his trickery. He has announced to the nation that he will open the box this Friday evening in Westminster.'

'How can he open it if he doesn't have it?' Peter says. But as soon as he asks the question he dips his head again: bracing himself for censure.

'He can't,' Octavia says. 'He is just as I said – a fake, a charlatan—'

'A mountebank!' says Emily, looking proud of the fact that she has managed to slip in another Shakespearean reference.

'Indeed, Emily,' says Octavia with a smile. 'I shouldn't wonder that he has bought himself an old travelling trunk and painted "Property of Joanna Southcott" on the top. But no one will be fooled when the time comes.'

Grace glances at me and leaves the room to refill the teapot with hot water.

'He will be shown to be a fraud. And when he is, we shall give our testimony,' Octavia says. 'We shall tell the assembled audience about the true box. When the news spreads, then the bishops will surely agree to come. They will have to.' She adds a single spoonful of sugar to Her tea and stirs it. 'So what say you, Peter?' She says, pausing to take a sip. 'Will you be part of the battalion?'

'I will,' says Peter. 'Of course I will.'

'Excuse me,' says Grace, who returns with a fresh pot, 'but if you are asking for volunteers may I put my name forward? I should like the chance to spread the Truth.'

Octavia looks up at her. 'You would have to make sure all your work was done.'

'I would, Octavia.'

'Then I can't see why not,' She says. 'It would be good to have someone younger present.'

Grace walks behind me and leans across to clear an empty plate from the table.

'What about you, Dilys?' she says. 'I'm sure you must have your name down already?'

'It is out of the question,' Emily says. 'We agreed that Dilys must stay in.' She turns to Octavia. 'That newspaper man that came to the door was determined to get his story. And it is only going to get worse now Mr Price is going ahead. We agreed – Dilys could be a target for the press who are so desperate to—'

'I can't see how I'll come to any harm,' I interrupt. 'I won't be alone, I'll be with you.'

'I'm not sure you are up to it,' Emily says, 'you haven't been yourself lately. At Edgar's trial you seemed quite unwell.'

'Just a bout of sickness,' I say. 'I want to stand alongside you, Emily. I am one of the few who was present throughout this . . . unpleasantness with Edgar. I have seen the works the Lord called you to perform. The others haven't been as blessed as I.' I look straight into her eyes, and she knows what I am saying: there are those who are finding it difficult to believe that God has chosen her as His divine instrument. When I delivered an article to the Printing Room this morning, the room fell silent. Miss Broadbent jumped and busied herself with the typesetting, but Mrs Gillett tried to draw me in, asking for the details of Emily's trance: whether her eyes rolled, whether her voice changed accent or pitch, whether I thought she really couldn't remember.

'I am one of the few who can give testimony to the miracles I have witnessed in you,' I say to Emily, gesturing for her to pass the cheese board.

'Very well,' says Octavia, without looking up from Her plate. 'It is settled. Ask Kate and Rachel, and the Keeley sisters. That makes eight – a good omen.'

I have won.

Westminster

We are huddled together, eyes down, collars up; our umbrellas jostle for space, sending trickles of water down the backs of our necks. We stepped out of the tube station at Embankment, and straight into the storm. Dark clouds have robbed London of its light, and turned the afternoon to early dusk, but there are no streetlamps to guide us as we walk. They won't be lit until eight o'clock when the exhausted sun finally gives up trying and turns in for the night.

'Black over Westminster,' Emily says, leading the way along Victoria Embankment to Great George Street, 'completely black.' She doesn't say it is a sign. She doesn't need to. It's what we are all supposed to think. Tonight Harry Price will try to fool the world but he shall be exposed, and we shall speak the words of Truth. All eight of us have come. Kate and Rachel jumped at the chance. And Mildred and Ethel Keeley were delighted to accept the invitation. The two sisters walk together with linked arms. Their similarity is so striking they are commonly mistaken for twins, attention they encourage by wearing matching clothes. Today they arrived at Number 12 in square-necked skirt suits: Mildred in claret with a coral hat, Ethel wearing the same shades in reverse. Octavia invited them to join us in the sitting room, then sent us on our way with a sip of the Water and a stack of leaflets to hand out after 'Mr Price's sideshow'.

CRIME AND BANDITRY, DISTRESS AND PERPLEXITY WILL INCREASE UNTIL THE BISHOPS OPEN JOANNA SOUTHCOTT'S BOX.

'This is an adventure!' Grace whispers beside me. 'It is a long time since I have been to London.'

'Me too.' Several times a year Father was called to meetings at St Paul's, and sometimes he would take us with him. If there was time, we'd end the day with a rock bun or Shrewsbury biscuit; but for him the real treat was always riding on the train. We would stand on the platform and watch the engine race in, a shock of white hair streaming behind it in the wind. 'Here she comes,' he used to say. He always knew the right spot to stand, so that when the driver pulled the whistle we would be swallowed in a screeching cloud of steam.

Today it was Emily who sat beside me in the carriage. Grace took the seat opposite and I spent the journey trying not to stare at her. When the train went through a tunnel, my eyes reached out to her in secret, and I could almost taste her on my lips, an imagined kiss stolen in the safety of the dark. She smiled at me but Emily didn't notice: she was busy with her copy of the *Telegraph*. 'Have you seen this?' she said, in a voice that told us we were all expected to listen. 'Mr Price has written to the bishops himself,' she said. 'Though I doubt he'll have any more luck than we have. Here . . . *My Lord Bishop*, et cetera, et cetera, *the public opening of Joanna Southcott's box . . .*' She paused to put on her reading glasses. '*As your Lordship knows, a considerable amount of superstitious tradition has grown up around this box, supposed to contain a divine revelation. The box could, of course, be opened without any formality* – Oh could it indeed? – *One feels, however, a natural reluctance to violate the definite wishes of a dying woman no matter how misguided.*'

With this she rolled her eyes. 'He says he should like to open the box in circumstances in accordance with her dying injunctions. But what does it matter? He doesn't have Joanna's box. Why won't they be told?'

Nobody answered her, except the rain which was drumming an accompaniment to the train's rhythmic song. *But what if he does*, it said. *What if he does, what if he does?*

———

We shelter under the arch of the Dean's Yard at Westminster, unsure whether to make a run across the quadrant, or wait. There's no rain now, but the air is still heavy with the threat of it. Racing clouds have stalled and come to rest on the roof of the abbey, no longer able to bear their own weight. The wind has dropped and the storm that railed in the distance fallen silent; but I can feel it is coming, creeping across the river, biding its time. There's a whisper in the air, a crackle of electricity like the fizz of an electric bulb, and as London holds its breath to hear it, the sky explodes: a flash of white lightning, a clap of thunder so close that I shut my eyes and wait for the bricks above me to fall. Then all I hear is the sudden pounding of rain where the shock has cracked the clouds apart.

A thinning of the space between our world and the next. That's what Grace said when she came to visit that first day, when we felt joy, when we felt the touch of the Lord. But tonight the sky is being shattered; tonight the God of the Old Testament is tearing through it, the God of punishment and vengeance. I know what Octavia would say, that the Lord is raining down His judgement on Harry Price's blasphemy.

'I think we'll just have to make a dash for it,' Emily says, checking her watch. 'It is five to seven.' We lift our umbrellas and start to run, shrieking as we jump over puddles, laughing as the muddy water splashes our stockings. All of us. Even Emily. We hear a cheer coming from the entrance of the building, and as we climb the steps towards it we are greeted with smiles from a small crowd of people. They have evidently been watching our sprint across the lawn with some amusement, and shuffle up to make room beneath the arched balcony offering shelter from the rain.

We are swept along into the foyer, sharing a brief moment of camaraderie: survivors of the storm, weak with laughter as we shake off our umbrellas and fix our hair. Nobody knows us here. Nobody knows who we are or why we have come.

But Emily won't let us forget. 'Are we all together?' she says, her manner suddenly brusque. 'Let's go upstairs. We'll be able to look down on everything from up there.'

She means look down on every*one*.

The Opening

'It reminds me of our Bunyan Meeting Church,' Grace whispers as she takes a seat beside me on the balcony. She is right: high windows, pale cream on the walls, there's even an altar of sorts (a table set out with three chairs behind it), and a full congregation. Every seat below has been filled, there must be three hundred people here tonight.

'I think that's him,' she says, and it's as if the whole room has heard her. Chatter fades to a low murmur as a man in a black dinner suit steps out from a doorway set into the oak-panelled wall. It is the man whose photograph we have seen in the newspapers. From this vantage point my view of him is distorted. He looks shorter than I expected, his oversized eyebrows trying a little too hard to compensate for a lack of hair on the top of his head. By the time he walks the few small steps to the table the room has fallen silent.

'Good evening, ladies and gentlemen, and members of the press,' he says, holding out his arms then nodding to the cluster of men with cameras set up on stands. 'Please allow me to introduce myself. I am Mr Harry Price of the National Laboratory of Psychical Research. Tonight I can promise that you will witness the opening of the box sealed up by Joanna Southcott. What I cannot promise is that its contents will save the world!'

There is laughter from the crowd below. Mr Price raises his hand to call for quiet. 'First I should explain the provenance of what we are about to see. Joanna's box arrived at my offices with a letter written by a man who has asked to remain anonymous. The

paper bore the embossed heading of the Carlton Hotel and a tele-
phone call to the manager confirmed that a man of the same name
had recently been a guest. If you will bear with me I shall read an
extract from it.' He takes a letter from his chest pocket, unfolds it,
clears his throat and starts to read.

SIR,
It is with some diffidence that I venture to send you
the box herewith as I am not sure you will welcome it.
For very many years my family had in our employment
a seamstress and gardener – a sister and brother
named Ann and John Morgan. These Morgans were
the surviving children of a Mrs Rebecca Morgan (née
Pegarth) who, as a young girl between the years 1798
and 1814, was the sole companion of Joanna Southcott.
The box was entrusted to Rebecca by Joanna on her
deathbed with the dying injunction that it was to be
opened only in the time of dire national need and in
the presence of a number of bishops.

'Morgan,' Grace whispers under her breath. 'Dilys, is that the
name? Is that the family who have the box?' I don't answer; I don't
know the answer. Octavia never told us who they were.

'Dire national need!' says Mr Price, looking up again with a grin.
'It was easy for us to make the excuse that the country wanted saving,' he laughs. 'We had a wide choice of evils – from politicians to
jazz – that we wanted to be rid of!' He is enjoying this, enjoying the
cheers from the crowd who have come to laugh at our beliefs. 'This
letter,' he says, holding it up above his head, 'states that Rebecca
left the box to her son John, and before *he* died John asked our

gentleman – the man who wrote this letter – to take charge of it.'

At the end of our row, Emily is getting to her feet. 'Mr Price,' she shouts in a voice strained by the effort of making itself heard. 'You should be ashamed of yourself. You would have these people believe that you have Joanna's box in your possession, but you know very well that it is a lie.' Chatter breaks out across the room and members of the audience turn around in their seats. Mr Price shields his eyes from the lights to locate the source of the interruption, making a small bow in our direction.

'Madam, I am confident that I can prove its pedigree. I have made a number of checks on the facts outlined in this letter which I will be happy to share in more detail with the gentlemen of the press. But for now, if I may be permitted to continue—'

'You shall not continue,' she shouts. 'I have come to give testimony of the true box and the power that it has to save this great nation.' In the rows around us people start to jeer: *Religious zealot*, they say. *Shut up. Let him speak.*

'Madam,' says Mr Price, 'if you wish to stay, then please sit down, otherwise I shall have to ask you to leave.' She does as she is told, muttering to the rest of us: 'These heathens shall see the Truth soon enough.'

Mr Price turns his attention back to the letter. 'Now,' he says, 'where were we? The gentleman writes that as a lad he was allowed to look at the box as a reward for good behaviour. He says: *It was always the Morgans' most cherished possession and it is quite certain that the box as now forwarded is exactly as it was sealed by Joanna South-cott in 1814.*'

Emily stands again. 'Lies!' she says. 'All lies!' but the audience shouts her down. Mr Price holds up his hand to silence them. 'Madam,' he says, looking up to the balcony once more, 'can I assume that you are a member of the Panacea Society which sends out healing? If so, then I must inform you that our gentleman was well aware of your claim upon this box, but concluded . . .' He pauses to quote the letter again. '. . . *that it were much better that a corporate body should arrange for the opening.*'

I should stand up and tell them that this is not how it is supposed to be. Octavia has promised the bishops will come. It won't be long now. And then everything will be set for Jesus to return to us. None of us will have to suffer; no one will be hungry, or thirsty; we won't want for anything any more. I should tell them about the fires already built in the grates, the bar of soap on every washstand, the polished silver on the sideboard. I should tell them that the Opening Room has been clad in oak, that Octavia has found the perfect spot on the perfect table.

The table where Grace sat.

What if they never come? she said. *How can Octavia know the box is safe if She has never seen it? When She never leaves the house?*

Emily shouts down again: 'It is a different box. The true box is being kept safe until the bishops agree to open it.'

'An interesting hypothesis,' says Mr Price, 'but your leader, Octavia, has declined my request to provide a photograph of it. Do you really expect twenty-four bishops to give up their time to come to Bedford for this "other box" when you can provide no proof?'

Grace reaches out beneath her coat which is lying across her knees. She finds my hand. *You were right*, I tell her in my head, *the bishops aren't coming, they'll never come. Not after tonight.* The sudden knowledge of it makes me dizzy.

'Having heard its story, I think it is time to bring in the box itself,' Mr Price announces, and on his signal a man carries it along the aisle between the seated spectators. I look down the row and see that Emily has sat back down. 'Twelve and a half inches long by nine and a half inches wide,' Mr Price tells the audience as it passes, 'and weighing eleven pounds. It is strongly made, of walnut, much aged, held shut with two steel bands. And strong silk tapes with large black seals bearing the handsome head of a young George the Third.'

It is placed on the table in front of him and he steps back to inspect it like a surgeon might study a patient before lifting his scalpel. 'The wood is inset with the initials J.S. in mother-of-pearl.'

'J.S.!' Grace whispers, placing her hands on the balcony and leaning forward to get a better view. 'Joanna Southcott.'

What if this is the box?
What if it is? What if it is?
I whisper it under my breath like a prayer.

'Dilys,' Grace says, gently. 'Calm down. Deep breaths. You're all right.'

But I am not all right. The bishops aren't coming. They are not coming because the box is here. Now. Harry Price is going to open it without them and what will happen when he does? Will God send His judgement upon all those present?

'Deep breaths,' Grace whispers.

All I can think of is the newspaper cuttings Octavia pastes inside Her book: floods and earthquakes, death and destruction, signs that we are in the End Times. What if the ceiling caves in under the heavy clouds that hang above the abbey? What if I die tonight?

How can God forgive me when I am not sorry for what I have done? For what I feel?

'I invited ten mediums to put their so-called skills to the test – to do their best, or worst,' says Harry Price. 'Nearly every one said they believed this box contains manuscripts or books, which would be a pretty safe guess considering its provenance.' A man steps forward and hands him a pair of heavy shears with which he cuts the first of the steel bands.

What if it is? What if it is?

I can't keep up with what Mr Price is saying: something about the weapons of secular science and X-ray machines. 'I am sure that Joanna's prophetic soul never visualised the fact that – bishops or no bishops – the contents of her box could be examined without open- ing it,' he says. 'But after taking negatives through the box in various directions I was able to see the mysteries locked inside. Ladies and gentlemen, Joanna Southcott secured a number of her valuables – coins and jewellery – and put them in this box. No great surprise that a dying woman would do such a thing. But the photographs show an item that I certainly was not expecting . . .' he says, pausing to tease the audience with a lengthy silence. 'I can reveal to you now that inside this box Joanna Southcott sealed . . . a pistol!'

The crowd is brought to life; several people stand up in their seats; voices swell with excitement and is it fear? 'Ladies and gentlemen, if I may . . .' Raising his hand, he calls for order. 'I admit I was con- cerned that the pistol had been wired in such a way as to discharge and kill a bishop or two. But I can assure you we have taken every precaution – the only person at risk of harm tonight is myself!'

The man with the shears steps forward again, cutting the second band and the silk tapes too. Mr Price takes up a crowbar in his right hand. 'May I have absolute quiet, please?'

The room is silent, muscles are tensed, eyes straining.

'I have to get out,' I say. I stand and start to move down the row, stepping on Peter's feet, pushing past Kate. I stumble over Emily's legs and fall down into the aisle.

'Dilys!' she says, and I hear a shot, and I see a flash of light. Oh God, what has he done? What was waiting inside the box to punish him? I can smell something acrid and sour: the scent of freshly dug earth and burning metal. Climbing onto my knees I look down and see smoke. The box is lit up again; searing flashes of lightning; claps of thunder.

'Dilys, it's all right,' Grace says. I turn and see her moving down the row towards me. 'It's all right.'

'Get her out,' Emily says, and I see them staring; strangers turning to watch as Grace leads me up the stairs to the door at the back of the balcony. I turn round and see Mr Price lift a pistol out of the box. 'No need to fear,' he says, holding it above his head. 'It is completely rusted!'

'Mr Price. Hold it still, one more for the camera,' a man shouts. He reaches up and brings a flame to the top of the T-shaped frame he is holding and there is another flash, another bang.

Oh God!

'It's just the camera,' Grace says. 'Look, nothing happened.'

But that's why every breath I take feels like a bitter frost, that's why my blood is freezing and my body won't stop shaking.

The box is open and nothing has happened. Nothing has changed.

The Answer

'Listen to me, Dilys, you've got to calm down.' Grace looks through the glass of the door and into the foyer. 'They are starting to come out.'

'I thought – when he took the lid off – I thought something terrible—'

'I know, try not to think about that now.'

'It made me think of my brothers on the battlefield. What they must have gone through, what they must have seen.'

She is holding her umbrella over both of us, rubbing my back with her other hand. 'You've had a shock,' she says gently, 'we both have, but now we know . . .'

But I don't know. I can't make sense of it. There are too many thoughts, too many, all running in different directions, too quick for me to catch them. All trapped inside my head like spiders in a jar.

Octavia said the box was safe. She said he couldn't have it.

'They are coming out,' Grace says, leading me down the stone steps away from the door. 'Emily and the others won't be long.' She turns to face me. 'Dilys, listen, we have to leave the society. You can't go on pretending. Not now.' For a moment there is nothing but silence, broken by the sound of the door swinging open and the chattering crowd spilling out onto the stairs.

'We can't leave. We can't turn our back on the Truth.' I can hear myself saying it but the words don't belong to me. Not any more. Perhaps they never did. *You can't go on pretending. Not now.*

I open my mouth to speak but Grace has turned away. 'You want to hear the *truth*, Dilys?' She hands the umbrella to me and steps out into the rain, walking up to a young woman who is one of the first to come down the steps towards us.

'What was inside?' Grace asks her. 'What was inside the box? We left when he picked up the pistol.'

'Oh, you didn't miss much after that,' the woman says with a grin. 'The rest was a load of ol' nonsense. A few books – romances mainly – and a few bits and bobs, a dice-cup and some money-weights. Rather a worldly collection for a religious fanatic.' She looks up to the sky and shudders. 'This weather's not easing off, is it?' she says, and then she dashes off across the quadrant, looking as though she is trying to outrun the rain. Grace comes back to share the umbrella with me. She takes the handle again without a word.

She is waiting for me to admit it. *A load of old nonsense.* That's what it amounts to. That's all my life has been.

'All this time,' I whisper. 'I've been waiting for an answer that was never going to come.' She brings her free hand up to my back again, but as soon as I feel her touch she snatches it away.

'Emily . . .' she says in a voice loud enough to stop me from saying more.

'There you are,' Emily says, walking towards us with the others following behind. 'I knew this would be too much for you, Dilys. I tried to tell Octavia.'

Is she going to say anything about what just happened in there? Are any of them going to say it out loud? She opens her handbag, her cheeks reddening as her fingers fumble with the catch. 'For goodness' sake,' she says under her breath, taking out a bundle of leaflets and turning back to the other five. 'We'd better give these out quickly, people won't hang around in this rain for long.' She turns and starts to walk away. 'Grace, you keep an eye on Dilys. Keep her out of the way before she makes even more of a spectacle of herself.'

I move to follow her. To tell her it is wrong. All of this is wrong. But Grace holds my arm. 'Just go along with it,' she whispers. 'We need to sort out what we're going to do.' We stand and watch the five of them thrusting leaflets into reluctant hands. Some in the crowd slow down long enough to snatch a page as they pass by, but most don't see them at all, their heads dipped to shield their faces, hat brims pulled down, hands too busy lifting collars to reach out to receive a piece of paper. One man stops to take a leaflet from Emily, damp and distorted where the falling rain has swollen the print.

'You were that crackpot shouting out in there,' he says, with evident amusement. 'When I read about this box in the papers I was hoping you lot would turn up tonight – add to the entertainment.'

'We *turned up*, sir,' Emily says, 'to tell the Truth, to call on the bishops to open Joanna Southcott's box. The real box. The one in which she sealed the miracle that will save this great nation.' She'll be enjoying this, she can go home and tell Octavia she was abused and pilloried, and by a man who is obviously working class.

'Good God,' he says, shaking his head with a smile. 'You really do believe it, don't you? Even after all that in there.' He looks down at the leaflet. '*Crime and banditry, distress and perplexity will increase until the bishops open Joanna Southcott's box.* Well, it's a bit late for that, isn't it? The cat is out of the bag so to speak.'

'That wasn't the box.'

'Oh come off it,' he says. 'Four sides and a lid? Looked like a box to me!'

'Joanna may well have sealed up several boxes before she died . . . But the true box — that contains the prophecies — has yet to be opened.'

Grace leans to me and whispers: 'So suddenly there's more than one?'

I should have known; I should have known that Emily would have an answer. She has an answer for everything. *Do not question, do not argue, but only obey.*

The man shrugs and walks away, calling back over his shoulder: 'You old maids need a man to take your mind off this nonsense. I'd like to give you all something to think about.' He stops to wink at us as he passes. 'Madness,' he says, with a cheerful satisfaction. 'A bunch of lunatics the lot of you.'

I hear the words and suddenly I'm running, eyes stinging with cold rain and hot tears. *Madness.* That's the truth. It's a secret I can't keep any more. I push my way into the crowd and allow myself to be swept along. I don't care where this tide of people is taking me. I can't go back to Bedford. Not now.

I feel a hand grab my arm and I push it away. 'Dilys,' Grace says, 'it's me. Come on.' She pulls me behind her, through a doorway into the side of Westminster Abbey.

'You can't just run off like that,' she says. 'Emily will get suspicious.'

We're standing in the cloisters. Moonlight falls as fretwork on the stone floor, blue against the warm glow that spills from lamps strung at intervals from the vaulted ceiling. It is dark, and silent. It is beautiful. I just want to stay here for a moment, in silence, but Grace won't be quiet. 'Dilys, please, talk to me.' Her whisper sounds so loud in here, so exposed, as if she is delivering a line on stage; as if the wall will slide back and reveal an audience. I'll see the row of stone arches is just a painting on a gauzy curtain. And all this is just a show.

'Dilys, what is it? Why did you—?'

'Madness. Lunacy. That's what he said—'

'Men like that are not worth listening to.'

'Is that what I am, Grace, is that what you think I am? Mad?'

'We *both* believed in the society,' she says. 'I wanted to believe it. I wanted to believe we were the answer, that we could solve the world's problems, end all the suffering. But I can't – not now. I'm going to leave Bedford. You should come with me. You'll never get better until you do.'

Better? I turn away towards a tomb that is set against the wall, a stone coffin with clawed feet like Apollyon. Like the window in the Bunyan Meeting Church. I can feel Grace close behind me, her hand on my shoulder.

'I've been worried about you, Dilys – not eating, walking around in the middle of the night. And sometimes when we're together, I don't know what you're thinking – what you want from me.' She stops and steps closer. 'And now all this with the Divine Mother? Trials and exorcisms? It's getting dangerous, Dilys. We have to get out.'

'But what about Octavia?' I say.

'You mean your mother?' she says angrily. 'For goodness' sake, Dilys, why don't you say it? Your mother.'

'All right. My mother. I can't just leave her.'

'Why not?'

Now *my* breath is snatched away. It feels as though my throat is being crushed, a hand around my neck, squeezing so the words can't come out. *Why can't you leave her, Dilys? She is no mother to you. She doesn't care. She never did.* I try to say it out loud but all I hear is a low moan that leaks out of my mouth before I can stop it. I'm not sure if it is sorrow or relief.

Grace wraps her arms around me and my body is no longer my own, no longer under my control; it is shaken by the sobs that stumble out of the deepest parts of me. She is right. Octavia doesn't care. She has watched me suffer. She made me believe in her wretched religion and it has made me as mad as her.

'I've been hearing voices.' I breathe my secret into Grace's neck.

'What?' she says, pulling back to see my face. 'Voices? What kind of voices? What do they say?'

'I thought it was the Devil come to tempt me.'

'Is that what you think?'

'No, I think it was my own thoughts all along. I think *I* wanted to do the things he whispered. It was always me . . .' I feel her body tense against mine. 'I can't trust myself any more, to know what's real and what is in my head.'

I want her to tell me that I haven't imagined how she feels. Or what we did. But I still can't bring myself to ask her.

'There were things I should have told you,' I say, 'about the others.'

'What things?'

'Rituals. I saw Octavia and the Four in the Upper Room – I saw her undressing. She was . . . Peter was lying at her breast.'

'What?' she says, stepping back from me. Now her body is shaking, I can feel it through the air between us. 'Everything they did to Edgar – and all along . . . Why didn't you tell me?'

'I didn't want you to think that I was going mad.' There is silence between us and I cannot bear it. I ache for her to speak but she says nothing. 'Grace, that's what they said about my mother when they took her away. They said she was mad. They didn't understand that she was hearing the voice of God. But then Ellen sent her the pamphlet in the hospital, the one about Joanna Southcott. And it all made sense.'

'So when you said she went away, she was in a *madhouse*? She was——'

'She tried to take her own life.'

Grace starts to pace, looking down at her own restless feet. 'And thanks to Ellen it all made sense,' she says, shaking her head.

'It meant the voices were from God.'

Her hands are clasped tightly together as if it is a strain to keep them still.

'Who else knows about this?'

'No one.'

'A secret even Emily doesn't know,' she laughs bitterly. 'Well, I suppose that's something.'

She walks away from me and sits on a stone seat between the pillars; she runs her hands through her hair, scratching her fingers across her scalp, closing her eyes. 'We've got to leave, Dilys. I can get a job somewhere else but I've got no money, nowhere else to stay. Is there anyone you know? Anyone who would help us?'

'There's no one.'

'There must be. What about your brother – Adrian?'

'It's too late. He wants nothing more to do with me.'

'Is that what he said?'

'He said I could go and stay with him in India, but since he wrote to tell me he was getting married I haven't heard from him.' I had my chance and I didn't take it. 'It's too late.'

Something seems to awaken in her. 'Dilys, are you sure he——' But she is interrupted by a noise in the dark and we both stop and stay absolutely still.

'Dilys, what if it isn't too late?' she whispers. 'What if there was a way, would you take it?' It's a question that's too big, too deep; a question that could swallow me up like the sea. Like the dark.

'*Dilys*, do you trust me?'

We hear another noise, footsteps this time. 'Ah, there you are,' says Kate. 'I thought I saw you two ducking in here. Dilys, are you quite well?'

'She wanted to get away from that dreadful man,' says Grace, 'the one who was so rude to Emily.'

'Well, if you are all right, I think we'd better go,' she says. 'It's been quite a night. The arrogance of Mr Price. And those people who came to watch tonight. Not one of them would listen. They refused to hear the Truth.' She turns and walks to the door. 'I hardly dare imagine what Octavia will say when we tell Her.'

Grace stands up and finds my hand.

'Well . . .?' she whispers. 'Do you?'

'Yes,' I say.

Yes, Grace, I trust you.

Branches

As we turn into Albany Road it hits me again. I want to run. I can't go back into Number 12, I can't pretend that nothing has happened, that everything is just as it was. If I go back into that house I may never come out again; if I step back into the garden I might be trapped once more, blinded, like I have been all these years. All the way home my body has been aching. I can feel the secret burning beneath the surface of my skin. We could leave, I tell myself silently. Over and over again, in case I lose my grasp on the truth of it.

In case I lose my nerve.

'You are very quiet, Dilys,' Emily says as we walk alongside the fence that marks the edge of the garden on Albany Road. I am quiet. I haven't had the chance to say anything at all, not to Grace. Emily has made sure of that, she has not left my side. I haven't been able to ask her what she meant, how we would go. And where. She seemed so certain. *What if there was a way?* But as we turn into the front path of Number 12 it no longer seems possible. We've got no money. Nowhere to go.

'Dilys.' I am startled by the sudden volume of Emily's voice. 'Dilys . . . did you hear me? I said it is best if I am the one to tell Octavia.'

'Tell her what?'

'For goodness' sake . . . About Mr Price. I think you had better get straight up to bed.'

It looks like Octavia has gone up already, as there are no lamps burning in the hallway. At least I won't have to face her, that's something, I suppose, because I'm not sure I could hide this secret;

the very idea of it is too big, it is crammed into my chest, crushing my heart. At any moment it could come spilling out; words from my mouth or tears from my eyes. And then they would know what we are planning.

Although I don't yet know myself.

I sit on the edge of my bed and listen. Two sets of footsteps on the stairs, then voices on the landing, before I hear the creak of Emily's door and the sound of Peter climbing the ladder to his attic. Perhaps I should get into bed myself but I need to be ready to leave, ready in case Grace plans to run away tonight. Perhaps I should pack a suit-case. But what if someone found it? *Think, Dilys. What would Grace do?*

I need her here. I need her to explain.

She hasn't come up yet. Now the others are in bed I will creep down and find her and then I'll know. I'll know she really said the things I heard her say. That I didn't imagine them. I take a lamp from beside my bed and make my way along the landing and down the stairs. Everything is black, no light from the sitting room or dining room. The kitchen is dark too.

And empty.

'Grace?' I whisper, stepping out of the backyard into the court-yard. 'Are you out here?' but I receive no answer.

I walk on, turning out into the garden. 'Grace?'

She can't have gone. She wouldn't.
Not without me.

She must be waiting for me in the clock tower. We'll be able to talk there. She'll be able to explain.

Stepping into the chapel I call her name again, louder this time. I shake the bottom of the ladder. 'Grace, are you up there?' But she is not.

Oh God. Oh, dear God.
I shouldn't have told her about the voices.
About Octavia.

I think of the letter hidden beneath the others in my wardrobe, the one Mother wrote to us after she was sent away. I wanted to believe her. I wanted to believe she hadn't left by choice or weakness. So I watched her build this chapel; watched the followers come and take their seats on either side of this aisle. I listened to her stand and preach at this altar. Folded on top is the priest's stole that she wears, the one that was my father's. Her beliefs have grown so very far from his. Like the branches of a tree. In the beginning you couldn't see the split, but as time went on Octavia bent further and further from the truth we had been taught. And then she broke away. Broke down.

I think of Yggdrasil. I think of the bough that fell on Adrian's head when we were children. I think of the blood that trickled into his eye.

I pick up the stole and bury my face into the fabric.

I kneel and pray to the God of my childhood. The God of my father. The God who sent Grace to me. I pray for Him to show me which branch to follow.

I pray for strength.

Mabel Barltrop
St Andrew's Hospital
Northampton

11th August 1915

My Dear Children,

Try, my dearest ones, to stand up for Mother through
thick and thin & know that God has been leading her
Himself to do a difficult bit of work which needed
doing and needed more courage than to face a
cannon! Great joys are coming to us all I know.

I want to be very open with you. I had been shown
that I have – (and I hardly like to write it, but I
think I must) – _great_ mental activity & that my quick
perceptions are of use to God in some way.

God mercifully took from me conceit, in as far as
it might lead me to desire to be known in the world
& all I do will be anonymous as Pride has spoilt so
many.

To make a long story short, as I don't wish to bore
you, – my sufferings have been most dreadful,
for when God gives Spiritual Vision, unless it be
sanctified by suffering it would be dangerous. Little
by little he is healing me, no one else, no doctor, no
nurse, could heal me.

The Devil has tried to destroy me several times,
to drive me out of my mind, so I could not do
what I had to, and of course the absolute dearth of
sympathy and understanding on the part of everyone
at home has made it very serious. I suppose it was
'in the plan' that I should be 'alone' & have none to
help.

Dear children, do try and rise to all the teachings,
& comfort your Mother who has suffered agonies
untold and has only done her duty to you all & to her
country in following God's leadings. You see, dears,
God is drawing very near to the Earth, at least Christ
is, & we are all going to be spiritualised and made
perfectly happy and lovely things will happen. Kneel
down at night and thank God for helping Mother
to do this work and for helping her get happy again
and also ask Him to guide you to get ready in simple
ways. Ask Him to give you the gift of Faith, also I
beg and entreat you to write to me, just a few words,
saying 'Mother, we trust you & we will do as you say'.

Your loving Mother

The End

There is pain in my knees and when I try to stand my legs won't hold my weight.

'Dilys, how long have you been in here? I've been looking every-where.' Grace helps me to my feet. 'It was lucky I saw your lamp. When you weren't in your room I . . . You have to come with me.'

But I still don't know where we will go. She hasn't explained.

'*Now*, Dilys.'

Has the time come so soon? So quickly that I don't have time to change my mind.

She leads me out of the door and across the lawn away from Number 12.

'I thought you had gone,' I whisper. 'Without me . . .'

'Octavia left a note asking us to come to Ellen's as soon as we got home. I didn't see it until everyone had gone to bed.'

It's Ellen's house we are crossing to now; there's light shining from every window, a figure in silhouette in the back doorway. Now the storm has passed, the night has grown heavy, sodden with gloom.

'Thank goodness you're here,' says Betty, holding the door wide and waving us to go in.

'Dear Ellen is going to help us,' I say. She is going to help us leave.

'No,' Grace says, squeezing my arm too tightly. 'Ellen is—'

'Is Dilys here?' shouts a voice from the top of the stairs. 'Has she come?'

It is Octavia. I don't understand.

Betty nods to me, her eyes wide.

'Come up,' Octavia calls. 'I've been waiting. Where have you been?' Her tone has a forced calm but the words are coming out too fast, there's something wrong. I start to climb, unsteady on my feet. The bannister underneath my hand is shaking, it feels as though the world is trembling, but as I reach the top I see that it is Octavia, knocking her knuckles against the wood. She doesn't appear to realise she is doing it.

'Ellen has been asking for you,' she says.

'Ellen. Why?'

She reaches up and rubs her temples. 'She has been rather poorly and anxious.'

She is looking down, she won't meet my eyes.

'What's *wrong*, Octavia?'

'I'm afraid she has got it in her head that . . . that she is going to die.'

'And is she?' The words choke me as I speak them.

Not Ellen.

She can't be.

There's too much happening at once, the world is spinning too fast and I can't keep up.

Octavia looks up, her voice suddenly irritable, angry. 'Of course she is not *dying*, Dilys. The Lord has promised us eternal life. You know that. And so should she. But I can't make her see sense. I've told her over and over again – she just won't listen!'

She means she won't agree, won't do as she is told, won't sit up, won't get better. I used to believe that none of us would die, not while we lived here in the garden, not when we had so much to prepare for Christ's return. But that was before.

Nothing is certain any more.

'All Ellen needs is the Water,' Octavia says, 'then she will be well again. Perhaps if you have a word with her, Dilys . . . Reason with her . . . Do you think you could try?' It is the first time I can remember her asking me to do something rather than telling me to.

'All right.'

Octavia nods and moves as though she intends to pat my arm, but she changes her mind and turns to walk downstairs, already saying something about seeing whether Betty has made another pot of tea, already pretending that it's all a lot of fuss about nothing. She has taken her leave and taken her lamp so I am left to feel my way along the landing to Ellen's bedroom. I knock gently on her door but there is no answer.

'Ellen, it's Dilys,' I whisper as I step into the room. I can smell the stale darkness that has gathered in every corner; it is creeping forward and suffocating her, making her breath heavy and laboured. Her face is illuminated by a single lamp that is standing on her bedside table; her eyes are closed, her arms are folded over her chest, too tidy, too perfect, too symmetrical somehow. She looks as though she has already been laid out.

'Ellen, I'm here.'

'Dilys . . .' It is an effort for her even to open her eyes. 'I'm so glad to see you. I'm so sorry.' Her voice is quiet but unmistakably Ellen's. Even now she has a tone of polite apology, as though she is merely leaving luncheon before the petits fours are served.

'Ellen, what's all this Octavia is telling me? That you think . . .' I can't say it. 'Ellen, you are strong.' My attempts to rally her sound pathetic.

'No, Dilys, I am dying. The Lord has a new plan for me, a new calling. I have accepted it.'

But I can't, I say silently. I won't.

'I'm not afraid,' she says, 'and you shouldn't be – not any more. You've spent your life in fear. It's time to be brave.' She looks at me and gives me as much of a smile as she can muster. 'What do you always say to me, Dilys? Think of Mrs Pankhurst.'

I laugh and the shock of it spills tears onto my cheeks.

'Tell me about the box,' she whispers, closing her eyes again. 'I want to hear all about it. Was Mr Price humiliated?'

'Yes, it was just as Octavia said it would be.' I speak the words before I have had a chance to think them. But how could I tell her the truth?

'So it won't be long now, before the bishops come?' she says.

'Any day now. Ellen, you must get better so you can be there to see it.'

But I am not sure she is listening. Her eyes are closed, the only sound is the rattle of her breath.

Now she is sleeping I can pull myself together. I should be an expert by now, but I'm not quite the same as I was before, nothing seems to fit back quite as it did, and it's getting harder to find the scattered pieces of myself.

There's a gentle knock on the door. 'I've brought you some tea,' Grace says. I don't want tea, I don't want anyone to interrupt this time I have with Ellen. Even Grace. But she is coming in anyway, laying the tray on the dressing table.

'How is she?' she says.

'Weak, but she'll come round.'

She'll have to.

I can't bear to lose her.

Grace pours the tea and carries the cup to the bedside table beside me. I feel her hand on my shoulder.

'She won't,' she says. 'Dilys, it's cancer. She's known for some time.'

I don't want to hear this. I don't understand why she is telling me these things. Why she is saying them out loud.

'The night of the strike when you were late,' she says. 'She told me she'd found a lump.'

I turn towards her so suddenly that her hand is knocked off my shoulder. 'She told *you*? But why didn't—'

'She has been concerned about you,' she says. 'We both have. She didn't want to worry you.'

'Then *you* should have told me,' I say. 'I thought we told each other everything.' But we both know that's a lie: it has always been secrets that have bound us together.

'It is too late,' she says. 'She should have seen a doctor. She wanted to but Emily insisted that the Water was all she needed. And of course Octavia agreed. She forbade it, said that medicine was unnecessary when you have the Lord's healing. And you know Ellen – she would sooner die than disobey Octavia.' She looks down at her, still sleeping in her bed, then kneels beside me. 'Dilys, I know this isn't what you want to hear. I'm sorry about Ellen, I'm sorry for all of this. But did you mean what you said tonight? About leaving?'

'I can't talk about this now. I can't think about it. I need to be here for Ellen. She might wake up, she might hear us.'

'It's too late for Ellen,' she says. 'Look at what they have done to her. Look at what their rules have done. The Water won't save her. Nothing can. Not even you.'

'That's enough! You're talking over Ellen's body as if she is already dead.'

Grace gets to her feet and leaves the room without a word. As she pulls the door shut behind her, Ellen whispers: 'Don't be too hard on her, Dilys. She is a good friend to you.'

'She shouldn't have said—'

'That I am dying? Dilys, I am.'

'No, you are not. You just need to get some rest. Octavia has promised we will never die, we are the chosen . . .'

How much I want to believe that now, what I'd give to make it true.

She is looking at something in the corner of the room. Her eyes wide open now. 'I'm ready,' she says, but she is not speaking to me any more, she is talking to herself, smiling at a joke only she understands. 'He will forgive me,' she says. With the lightest squeeze of my hand she closes her eyes again.

'Ellen,' I whisper. 'Ellen. Don't go. I'm frightened. I've been hearing voices. Just like she did. Like Octavia. Ellen . . . please!'

But she isn't listening any more. I shake her hand but it is limp in mine. Her breathing is fast and shallow and then it stops. I am losing her.

'Ellen, wake up!'

'Tell Octavia I am sorry,' she says between snatched breaths. 'It is my fault . . . I should have been better . . . The Lord might have let me stay if I was worthy to serve Her . . . I have let Her down.'

'No, Ellen. You are the best of us.'

'I had doubts,' she whispers, 'about the Divine Mother. My faith was tested and I was found lacking.'

'No, Ellen, wait, there is something I have to tell you . . . about tonight. You can't go now. Not before you know the truth.

Octavia was wrong, all this is wrong, there is no box, there is no answer, there never was.' Her eyes flicker open and find mine. She inhales slowly as if she is savouring a sweet flavour, but her outward breath is a violent splutter: the bitter taste of death. And then nothing. There's no struggle. No gasp. Just silence. And stillness.

She is holding her breath.

———

My tea has gone cold.

When Ellen wakes up we'll have a fresh pot and I'll call down for some biscuits. A little sugar will do her good. And it must be nearly time for breakfast, I can see the dawn starting to creep through the curtains already.

I'm so cold. Though I've still got my coat and hat on. I never did get round to taking them off. I hope she doesn't think me rude. No, Ellen doesn't worry about things like that. She never did. She's wearing only a nightdress, she's got goosebumps on her arms, I will climb into bed beside her, that will keep her warm, I'll pull the blankets up around us, and blow out this lamp, so it doesn't disturb her, and we can lie together in the darkness and talk about her days as a suffragette.

There is light in the doorway, and a voice. It says why are you sitting in the dark, Dilys. It says, where are you. Emily steps forward and holds up her lamp to cast its light around the room. Dear God, she shouts, what are you doing in bed with her?

She thinks she is so clever but she isn't.

Isn't it obvious, I say. I'm keeping her warm. She is freezing. Emily reaches out and touches Ellen's cheek but her hand jumps back. I say, see, I told you she was cold. Ellen is sleeping. She will feel better when she wakes up. And then we're going to have tea and biscuits.

Emily stops the clock above the fireplace and covers the dressing table mirror with a blanket so that Ellen's soul does not get trapped inside it. She opens the window to let her spirit fly out of this room and up to Heaven. *She thinks she is so clever but she isn't.* Ellen isn't dead. She can't be. But I say nothing. There is no point in arguing with that woman. I'll just wait until she is gone and then I'll climb out of bed and shut the window myself. I can't have Ellen sleeping in that draught. It will give her a stiff neck. And she wouldn't like that. Not at all.

I pull back the curtain and see morning flooding the street below. The milkman is making his deliveries and there is a man standing just across the road, wearing a dark coat with the collar pulled up around his neck and a hat, a homburg I think. He is absolutely still. Watching. Waiting. Looking across at Number 12. And he sees me. I know because he looks up, he looks straight at me and I see into his eyes.

They are the eyes of my brother Adrian.

It's the Devil, I whisper, pulling the curtain back across the window and climbing back into Ellen's bed, don't worry, we are safe in here, he cannot reach us in the boundaries of the garden, and death cannot come to snatch us away.

I hear a voice outside the bedroom door. It says, no Emily, she can't be dead, the Lord gave me His promise, eternal life for all who believe in me.

Then there's another voice. It says, Octavia, have faith and re-member that our Lord Jesus was resurrected after three days.

It says, perhaps the Lord is planning another miracle.

It says, we need to keep her body warm so she can rise again.

The Visitor

I am sitting up. The curtains are open. Grace came to me, she helped me out of Ellen's bed, and back into the chair, then she wrapped me in a blanket. She tucked Ellen in with extra layers too and slipped a hot water bottle beneath her covers. There is one by her feet. That was my idea, she hates having cold feet.

I'm still holding Ellen's hand. I squeeze it to tell her everything will be all right, but there's nothing in return. All the tenderness has gone from her fingertips. And all the warmth.

There are purple bruises on her translucent skin. When Octavia came she said it was time for someone else to take a turn to sit by the bed. Emily tried to drag me away, she prised my fingers from Ellen's hand, but when I let go her arm didn't fall back to the bed. It stayed just as it was. It was reaching out to me.

You see? I said. I can't leave her. She wants me to stay.

I'll think I'll brush her hair. Soon the angels will come and she'll want to look her best for that. I see their light flooding in, rays falling across the bed. I told Grace I'd go, I whisper. I said I'd leave. But Ellen, when you come back, when God sends you back, I'll stay in the society. I will believe.

The hands of the clock are stopped at ten past three. Time has stood still. But at intervals Betty appears. She brings tea and toast. They stand on the side untouched. Sandwiches. Soup.

Cake. Ellen opens her eyes and says Dilys you have to eat. Keep your strength up for when I come back. I know she's right but I just can't face it. There are pillows behind me and more blankets. And my clothes are different. Though I can't remember changing them.

I say, Ellen you must be thirsty. I take a square of linen from her bedside table and put it into the glass. Then I put the glass to her lips. They are black now. There, take the Water, it will revive you, I say. But she won't. I tip a little into her mouth but it pools behind her teeth then seeps out down her chin.

———

They are coming for her. The angels are coming. I thought they would fly in through the window but I hear them on the stairs now. An army of angels on the landing. I wonder if they will take me too.

If I ask them. Nicely.

They file into the room in line. No wings. No halos. No white robes. These are angels clothed in black. A heavenly host in mourning weeds. Long skirts, high-necked jackets. There's a flash of white handkerchief as they dab the grief from their faces. But most just look frightened. A look in their downturned eyes that gives them away: She said we wouldn't die, if it could happen to her then it could happen to me. There is an awkward shuffling by the door as those trying to leave the room squeeze past those who have yet to come in.

We have not gathered to mourn, Octavia says, we are here to

give praise. For Ellen shall be resurrected. Soon she shall return from Heaven with news from the Lord.

The angels say Amen.

Then I am alone with Ellen once more.

———

Night comes. Lamps are lit. And I watch the heavenly light creep round the edges of the curtains again. There are roses placed in vases around the room, and someone has put a posy of lavender in my hand. It must have been Grace.

She is standing beside Ellen's bed with a man I have never seen before.

'Have you come to take her to Heaven?' I ask them.

'No, Dilys, this is Dr Williams,' Grace says.

'Miss Barltrop, I haven't seen you for very many years,' the man says. 'Do you know me?'

I don't.

'I used to treat your family when you were a child.'

Perhaps he is right, but I don't remember. He has come to make Ellen better.

'No, Dilys, he needs to sign her death certificate,' Grace says.

But she won't be dead for much longer.

Octavia said so, she said Ellen will rise after three days.

'It has been four days, Dilys.' Grace turns to the man I don't recognise. 'Doctor, she has been sitting here all this time. You understand my concern?'

He nods.

'I will leave you to it,' she says. 'I'll make sure you are not disturbed.'

The man puts on his glasses and uses a handkerchief from his pocket to cover his mouth and nose. He leans in to inspect Ellen's body. I could tell him that she is coming back, I could try to make him understand. But he won't. He is a man of science, so married to the religion of rationality that he cannot see the truth. That's what Octavia would say.

He takes a notebook out of his brown Gladstone bag and starts to make notes. 'Ah, the date . . . It's gone clear out of my mind. Do you happen to know it, Miss Barltrop?'

He lifts his pen and looks to me for an answer. But I have no idea.

'Do you know what day it is?'

I don't.

'Or the time?'

I shake my head. The clock is stopped at ten past three.

He returns to his notebook, glancing at Ellen occasionally while he makes his notes.

'You have been here for four days,' he says gently, screwing the top onto his pen and looking at me. It squeaks as he turns it. 'She is gone, Miss Barltrop. I am a doctor, do you understand? Ellen is dead.'

I can't bear the squeaking sound. Now he is tapping his pen on the edge of his notebook. What has he written in there? Has he made a note of my sins to report them to Octavia?

'Miss Barltrop, do you understand? Ellen is dead. She is not coming back . . . whatever you may have been told. Arrangements are being made for her funeral.'

The truth rips through my body, tearing out the flesh inside my chest and leaving only my heart behind. It knocks against my bare ribs, bruising with every beat. They are going to bury her in the ground. She is gone. She is not coming back.

'She killed her,' I say.
'I beg your pardon, Miss Barltrop?'
'Emily killed her.'
He says, 'I see.' But I can tell he doesn't see it at all. I can tell by the way he is looking at me that he thinks it was me. It was my sin. I was going to run away. I was going to leave. He thinks that's why the Lord took Ellen. He thinks that's why she is never coming back.

But he is wrong. It wasn't my fault.

'Miss Barltrop, when was the last time you ate anything?' he says. 'Have you managed to get any sleep?' I don't know the answers to his questions, but he keeps asking them anyway. 'If you would allow me to give you some medicine,' he says. 'To calm your nerves . . .'
He takes a sachet of powder from his bag and dissolves it in a glass of water. It is the one I put to Ellen's dead mouth. But I don't tell him that. It tastes bitter when I drink.
'That will help you to get some rest,' he says. He is on one side of me, and suddenly Grace is on the other. They are helping me to my feet.
'I will write my recommendations,' he says to her.
'Thank you, doctor,' she says. 'You'll send it to the address I gave you? And as we agreed – no mention of this to Mrs Barltrop or Mrs Goodwin.'

I'm on the landing. Then the stairs. Grace is holding my arm. I am being held. The man is gone now and it is just us. Together. We're in the garden. On the lawn. There's the seat where you and I sat, Grace. When you first came to me.

She says, 'I remember.'

She says, 'We don't have much longer, before the truth comes out. I have found out, Dilys. I have found out what's been going on.'

She says, 'I need you to understand.'

But I don't. I don't understand what she is saying or how I got to be here on the edge of my bed. She is kneeling down and taking off my shoes. She is talking about Emily and a letter, and Adrian. And I want her to slow down and tell me again because I can't make sense of it.

She says, 'I'm sorry. I should have told you.'

But told me what? I am under the covers and my clothes are gone. I am wearing a nightdress. She is stroking my hair.

She says, 'I have hidden it in your Bible, Dilys. Read it when you wake up.'

She says it's not too late.

The Judgement

I see him at the window. Staring in. Those eyes of black glass that never blink. Sometimes he wakes me with a tap of his beak on the pane, because Sir Jack wants me to know he is watching; he wants me to see him shake his feathers and take flight.

He is going to find Emily, and report back.

No one has been to see me, not even Grace. I saw her walking with Emily across the lawn, through the wet leaves that have fallen from Yggdrasil. I knocked on my window but they didn't look up.

No one comes when I shout through my bedroom door either. It is locked, just like it is in my dreams. I don't think they have bricked me in, not yet, I can still see through the keyhole, but perhaps that is next. I have to get out before that happens. I'm not suited to a life of contemplation. There is too much I don't want to think about.

My only escape now is sleep, but it won't take me, won't snatch me away. My body starts to float but my head won't follow, it is tethered to the bed. Dreams come while I am still awake, delights and horrors unfolding here in my room, so even then I can't leave these four walls. I am trapped between wakefulness and slumber.

I can hear a dream approaching. Footsteps along the landing. The sound of a key in the door. Perhaps this time my imagination will take me away. Take me somewhere else.

Perhaps Ellen will come and find me.

'Dilys, it is time to get up and get dressed. This has gone on long enough.'

'Mother?'

'You need to come to chapel.' Octavia is opening my wardrobe and taking out clothes. 'Put these on.' But I can't move. I've forgotten how. My door is open but I don't think I can leave this room.

'Where's Ellen?' I ask, but Octavia says nothing. She lays a dress out at the foot of my bed. It is taupe or camel, I can't remember which.

'Come on, Dilys. You need to get up.'

'Has she woken yet?'

She turns away and opens the drawers where I keep my stockings. 'Dilys, Ellen has gone to be with the Lord. We buried her last week.' She says it as if I should know, as if I have just forgotten, as if it is a minor detail. And suddenly I remember. I was lying beside her, trying to keep her warm. She was as cold and hard as stone. And then a man came. *Ellen's dead, whatever you may have been told, she won't be coming back.*

'Last week?' I say. 'But . . .'

It doesn't make sense. How long have I been in here for?

'I should have been there for her funeral.'

'Don't get agitated,' Octavia says. 'You have had a fever. You were quite delirious. I think you must have caught a chill in all that rain in London. But you must get better. I need you to. It reaches a point where you have to question whether you are being . . . rather self-indulgent.'

'So Ellen didn't . . . she wasn't resurrected?'

You were wrong, Octavia, that is what I want to say. *You were wrong.*

'Dilys, please,' she says, pulling back my covers. 'We need to

– 294 –

get to chapel. The Divine Mother has insisted that *all* resident members must be present.'

'You mean *Emily* has insisted?'

'For goodness' sake!' She raises her hand so suddenly that for a moment I think she means to strike me, but she brings the palm up to her own forehead. 'Only the Lord knows what I would have done without her to guide me this past week, while you have been up here sleeping. It's all been too much . . .' Her voice snags on the sharp edge of an emotion, lying just beneath the surface. 'Emily is the only one who understands my torment, who understands what needs to be done.'

'I'm not coming to chapel,' I say and the thrill of rebellion runs through me.

'You *will* come.' She grabs my arm and pulls me up, jerking my body out of bed before my mind has the chance to follow. I need to lie down again. I start to slump back but she won't let me. She holds onto me, her grip pinning my arms down to my sides, digging her fingers into my flesh. '*I* have to obey the Lord in everything – though I suffer for it,' she shouts. '*I* have to follow his will. And you will follow mine. Stand there.'

Then all I see is white linen. My arms are up and my nightdress is being lifted, exposing my body.

Grace, I whisper. *We mustn't.* But this time I don't mean it.

I feel the tug of my hair as she brings it over my head. Impatient. Rough. A few strands must have caught in one of the buttons on the collar. And I'm tangled up in the fabric.

Yes, Grace, I trust you. Yes, Grace, I will leave.

But when the nightdress is gone it isn't Grace I see, it is Octavia. And she can see my body. All of it. A body she hasn't seen since I was a child, now transformed by curves and hair. Too fluid, too fleshy: unwieldy and greedy and vague. She tries to look away but I see the disgust on her face, and the jealousy. She is looking at the figure she once had.

'I didn't realise . . .' she says, her voice suddenly softer. 'You have got so thin, Dilys.'

I grab the blouse and cover myself, cover my shame. Octavia looks away and turns to face the corner of the room and I slip on the underwear she has laid out, and the dress.

Sitting down I slide the stockings on my feet, up my legs. Where is Grace? I remember walking with her across the lawn. She was trying to tell me something. I'll have to find a way to ask her. Perhaps I'll get a chance in chapel. She will tell me what has been happening. How long I have been lost in here.

'Now, do your hair,' Octavia says, turning back to me. 'I'll return in five minutes to take you down. Five minutes, Dilys.'

I look up but she is already walking out of the door.

'Octavia, I dreamt I was locked in. That I couldn't get out.'

She doesn't stop, or look back. 'We were keeping you safe,' she says. 'You have been sleepwalking again. You could have fallen on the stairs.'

She closes the door behind her. And I hear the key turning in the lock.

———

It is standing room only. It looks as though every one of the resident members has accepted the call. But there is no sign of Grace in the chapel. Not yet. I'd be able to see her auburn hair, but all I see are smudges of brown and grey, indistinct ladies of indeterminate age.

I'll stay here in the back corner, close to the side wall, so I have something solid to lean against. There are too many people crammed in, too much opportunity for accidental contact: the knocking of an elbow or the brush of a hand. I don't want anyone to touch me, or speak to me. I don't want anyone to see me either, but perhaps they can't – voices are distant, faces are blurred. Perhaps I am not really here: trapped between wakefulness and slumber.

The murmur of voices dies down and Octavia and Emily stand at the altar.

'Panaceans, thank you for coming, there is much news to share with you this evening,' Emily says. 'Before we begin I should like us to remember Ellen Oliver, who is continuing her devoted work for the society, in the realms of Heaven.'

'As you all know,' says Octavia, 'we had hoped that she would be resurrected, we prayed for the Lord to perform a miracle . . .' Her voice sounds thin and uncertain. 'But we must *all* understand that our prayers were selfish. We asked the Lord to let her return to us because that is what *we* wanted.' She looks to Emily who immediately steps forward to speak.

'What is important is what *God* wants,' she says. 'He spoke through the Divine Mother to confirm that Ellen has been called ahead to Heaven and when Christ returns to Earth she will be by His side.'

The silence in the chapel is absolute. No one shuffles in their seats; no one scratches their hair or picks their fingernails; no one draws attention to themselves at all. Octavia might take it as a sign that they have something to say.

'When Ellen returns she will be of radiant body,' she says, addressing the question we dare not ask. 'Now she has passed into the realm of Heaven she has no need of flesh and blood.' The air is thick with unspoken doubt, like the heady smoke of incense.

Emily steps forward again. 'And in releasing her from her mortal body, the Lord is making a new covenant with us, another promise that we are His chosen people.' She raises her arms as though she is standing on a soapbox, or at the foot of Mount Sinai. 'Firstly – He took Ellen on the very night that some of us went to witness Mr Price's blasphemy. Though men refuse to see the Truth, the Lord knows that *we* keep faith, He knows that we will see the *real* box opened . . .' She pauses and raises her eyes to Heaven. 'Secondly – He took her on the eighth of the month, after eight weeks of illness, which surely points to the name Octavia. And thirdly . . .' this time she brings her hand to her chest, 'on the very night she left us, a picture of a caged bird at Mrs Whittington's fell off the wall. A clear sign that dear Ellen has been freed from this world of sin.'

'It should be a comfort to us all,' Octavia says. 'Blessed Ellen! She is the first of us to look upon the face of Christ. I imagine she will be telling Him all about us as we speak.' She smiles, her upturned lips twitching with the threat of tears. 'We thank God for Ellen's life of integrity and uprightness which has been equal to that of Job,' she says. 'We recognise her to be a link between us and the Incorruptible Fold. And we bid her adieu, until we see her again.'

There's a stifled sob from somewhere at the back of the chapel and a number of women bow their heads in silent prayer.

'In the meantime,' Octavia says, 'we shall keep everything ready for her return. Ellen's house shall be sealed up, so that when she comes back to us she'll find everything just as she left it: all her clothes in her wardrobe, her favourite chair still sitting by the fire. She'll feel like she has never been away.'

'Her servant Betty will make weekly visits to Ellen's house to keep everything clean,' Emily says, 'but day-to-day she will be looking after Octavia and those of us who live at Number 12.' Emily's eyes scan the faces of the congregation, then stop abruptly when they find mine. 'She is moving back in with us.' She gives me a smile, but I don't know what it means. Betty can't come to live with us, there's no room. Grace lives with us now.

Where is Grace?

I look around the chapel again but I can't see her. Why isn't she here? All resident members have been called to the meeting to-night. I want to shout her name until the congregation parts and I see her standing among them. But she isn't here. Memories come back to me of her arm in mine; we walked across the lawn, she was trying to tell me something, but what did she say?

'The Lord has made a new covenant and we keep our side of the accord,' Octavia says. 'The time has come to cleanse the Garden of all evil, to cleanse ourselves of the spirits that lead us to sin. Day after day I am forced to sit and listen to your confessions – your jealousies and petty quarrels. There are those of you too prone to take offence; those too needy for my attention; those who like to sew the seed of discord. Well, now it stops. I can live like this no more!' Octavia steadies herself on Emily's arm and nods for her to continue.

'We shall begin the Casting of Controls,' says Emily. 'For this act, members shall be required to hand in to me a list of their inhibitions, peculiarities, annoyances and temptations. They shall then be called before Octavia and the Divine Mother who will perform a banishment of the spirits that control them. Those who refuse to cast out the demons will be cast out themselves. Indeed, I must inform you all that, for that very reason, Grace Hardwick, who came to us to help with domestic chores, is no longer a member of our society. She has moved on. I hope you will all join me in praying that she finds her way back to the righteous path.' She looks at me again. 'Though I fear she may have strayed too far.'

Gone. Grace is gone.
She can't be. She wouldn't leave me.

But what if she has?
What if she's gone and it is too late for me? *She may have strayed too far.* Did Emily find out what she was planning, did she find out about us? I need to find her. I need to find Grace and ask her what is happening. I try to move towards the door but there is no room, no one is moving to let me through. I have to get out. I can't breathe. I push my way through the bodies in front of me and fight my way to the door.

'All shall be called to confess their secrets,' Octavia says. 'When she ate of the tree, Eve knew shame and hid herself from the presence of the Lord. But there will be no hiding in the Garden any more.'

The Betrayal

Her door is closed. I knock, hoping Grace will answer, hoping it was all a lie. But when I push it open there is no one inside. Just an empty bed and stripped mattress. There is nothing left of her: the shelves are cleared, even the scent of her has fled, no trace of her on the pillow or the blanket that has been neatly folded on the bed. I lie down on it, in the spot where she lay every night. So many times I thought about climbing in beside her. But now it is just me. She is gone.

I could step out of the front door and start walking, but in which direction would I head? I have nowhere to go, no idea where she is.

'I'm afraid she left no message for you,' Emily says. I look up to see her watching me from the doorway. 'It must be quite a shock. I know how close you two were. She told me all about it before she left.' She sits down beside me on the bed, making herself comfortable. She is not going to rush this opportunity to toy with me. 'Aren't you going to ask what happened?' she says.

I'm not. I won't give her the satisfaction. Though every part of me is desperate to.

'I discovered that she wasn't honest in her commitment to God,' she says. 'She had started to question things, she thought she knew better. And it came to my attention that she had gone behind Octavia's back. She was conspiring, undermining Her.'

'What? How?' I couldn't help myself.

'Oh Dilys, your confusion is wearing a little thin. You are not as fragile as you pretend to be. I have seen you two whispering together, sneaking off into corners, into the clock tower . . .' She raises her eyebrow and laughs.

I can feel the panic rising from my stomach, into my chest, up into my throat. The thought of what she might know. What she might have told Octavia.

'Where is Grace?' I say.

'She has moved on, Dilys. We made sure she will be quite comfortable.'

'Where?'

'Octavia and I decided it was best to keep that information confidential. There is no need for anyone within the society to have anything more to do with her.'

'But you'll be going to visit her like you did with Edgar?'

'No, no. That was a special treat reserved for him. I wanted to make sure he was going to leave for good. We won't have any problems with Grace: she was only too happy to go. The poor thing found your feelings for her rather . . . too much.' She is laughing at me now, disguising her scorn for me as pity. 'From what she told me she had to fight you off. I saw the mark on her cheek. That's right, isn't it, Dilys? You hit her when you were wandering around in your nightclothes?'

'I was sleepwalking.'

'Oh, is *that* what you were doing?' she says. 'I watched you from the top of the stairs. She took you back to bed . . .'

Oh God. What does she know?

'I can't help blaming myself,' she says. 'I encouraged Octavia to let Grace join. I thought it would be a good idea to have someone who could look after you . . . keep an eye on you. I never imagined you'd end up with your eye on *her*. Still,' she says. 'I wouldn't have known about Edgar's break-in at Castleside if it wasn't for Grace.

And she told me a great many things about you, Dilys. I feel I know you much better than I did before.'

This isn't true. None of it is true. Emily is twisting everything.

'Grace wouldn't do that.'

I don't believe it.
I won't.
I have faith in her.
And faith can be enough. Sometimes it has to be.

But what if Grace was telling my secrets? Spying on me all along. I thought that Kate had told Octavia about the window but I never found out, I never asked her. Everything is unravelling: snag one stitch and the whole line is tugged out behind it.

'Poor Dilys,' Emily says. 'She has left you.' She pats my leg and I knock her hand away. It feels good. I have shocked her. I have shocked myself. And I want to do it again. I want to lash out. I want to hurt her. Spill her blood. Grab her hair and smash her face into the wall. But once I start I might not be able to stop.

'It's been a shock,' she says. 'But try to calm down. I have decided not to worry Octavia with the details. But if you leave me no choice . . .'

I'm going to be sick. I run out of Grace's room to the lavatory. There is no food to come up. No, my body is trying to rid itself of Grace, purging the memories that I have collected; the butterflies that have danced inside me since the day she first came. *She has left you.* With every retch I delve deeper, but I can't let go of them. I push my fingers down my throat to try to force them out. I can feel the burn of separation as they shoot into my chest. I taste their bitterness. But I can't let her go.

'I think you'd better lie down,' Emily says, from behind me. 'She was a dangerous influence, Dilys.' She takes my arm and leads me across the landing to my bedroom, and I haven't got the energy to resist. What's the use in fighting now?

'We are better off without her,' she says. 'Settle down now.' She pulls back the covers and I climb in with my clothes and shoes still on. 'I'll get you a drink.' She picks up the glass by my bed and walks back to the bathroom, where I can hear her filling the glass. When she returns there is a square of linen swirling around in the water as though she has stirred it.

'Here, this will make you feel better,' she says.

I want it to wash the taste away but it doesn't; the water itself seems to have taken on a bitter flavour. It feels gritty in my throat as I swallow.

'That's right, drink it all up,' Emily says. When the glass is empty she takes it from my hands and walks to the door. 'A nice long sleep,' she says. 'And when you wake up let's hope you have a little more perspective on what's important.'

I hear the key turn in the lock and I am trapped again. Thoughts crawling inside my head. I can feel them clamouring over each other, a mass of sticky wings and knotted legs. I wish I could open up my skull and let them out. I'd take a knife to it myself if I thought I could make them stop. Was it all a lie? Did she ever care for me at all? Perhaps she stepped into the sitting room to make her confession to Octavia. Perhaps she was whispering my secrets to Emily that day in the kitchen.

I climb out of bed and look out of the window. I watch the washing blowing on the line.

Wash me, and I shall be whiter than snow.

I thought the Lord had sent her to me. It seemed so clear. But now I can't make sense of it. My thoughts won't stay still, they are dancing like my nightdress in the breeze.

I remember that night. Her scent, her heat, her breath. The taste of cotton. She wanted me to find every part of her. But there's another memory. *We can't. We mustn't. We are just friends, Dilys. The best of friends.*

In my dream she begged me to kiss her. In my dream she begged me to stop. And I'm too tired to know what was real and what was not. I climb back into bed and I try to stay awake. I need to think. I need to understand.

Beloved, let us love one another: for love is of God; and every one that loveth is born of God, and knoweth God.

Emily said that it was sinful and unnatural. Is that what Grace thought too? *Dilys*, she said, *if this is how it is going to be I just don't think I can stay here.* And now she is gone. And I can't make sense of it, I can't stay awake. That must be why it's called falling asleep because once it takes hold you are powerless to stop it. It's inevitable. Irresistible. You fall when it comes to sleep. And when it comes to love.

I can't keep my eyes open. When they close, the lids burn red like the tip of a cigarette.

The Truth

I am alone. In bed. I still have my shoes on. I can feel fingers creeping across my skin. Cold like Ellen's. And a hand around my throat again. I can't move. Heavy with grief. Choked with sorrow.

I don't know how long I have been asleep for. Or what time it is. Or what day. How long has she been gone? I manage to climb out of bed, my legs are heavy, they feel as if they don't belong to me. The door is still locked. I can't get out. There's no chance of leaving now. Did Grace tell them that too? Did she tell them that I planned to go with her?

I hear footsteps on the stairs and I stumble back to bed. Whoever is on the other side of the door knocks softly, turns the key in the lock and walks in. 'Miss, are you awake?' Betty whispers. I close my eyes and pretend I am asleep, dead to the world. 'Miss, you are wanted downstairs. There's a telegram arrived. Emily says it's important.'

It might be news of Grace.

'A telegram from who?' I say, startling Betty by sitting up in bed.

'I don't know, but it's caused quite a shock. I think you ought to come.'

At least it will get me out of this room.

'Betty, do you know what happened to Grace? Where she's gone?'

'I'm afraid I don't know, Miss. I haven't seen her. But you know about Ellen's funeral?'

I nod.

'About time,' she says. 'It wasn't natural what they did, trying to keep a body warm like that. But you stayed with her, Miss Barltrop, all them days. You looked after her. I came to see you, do you remember? I brought you food. You wouldn't leave her side.' She uses the corner of her apron to wipe tears from her face. 'I know you took it hard. Are you feeling better?'

'I . . . I'm not sure.'

'It's been a lot to take in,' she says.

'It has.'

'But I shall look after you now. I'm here, I've moved back into my old room, so everything's back to how it used to be.'

How it used to be before Grace came.

'Miss,' she says. 'They are waiting on you downstairs.'

'Yes. The telegram.'

———

I'm only halfway down the stairs when I hear raised voices. Emily, Octavia and Peter are gathered around the table in the sitting room. Octavia has her head in her hands.

'Dilys, we've had word,' she says, looking up as I enter, 'from America.' Her voice is shaking and so are her hands.

'You'd better come and sit down,' Emily says. 'I thought you should hear it before we make the announcement in chapel tonight; after all, you were . . . involved.'

'Octavia?' I say, taking a seat between her and Emily. 'What is it?'

'It has happened,' she says. 'The prophecy has been fulfilled.'

She slides a piece of paper across the table to me, marked 'Western Union'.

EDGAR PEISSART TAKEN ILL ON CROSSING TO NEW YORK. TREATED IN HOSPITAL ON ARRIVAL. DIED TWO DAYS LATER. CAUSE UNKNOWN

'But how did they know where to send it?'

'Octavia paid for his ticket,' Emily says, her voice measured and cold, 'so they traced Her as next of kin.'

'It is just as she said it would be,' Octavia says, 'just as the Divine Mother said: "Send the man to New York. He will die." And now he's . . . oh! We knew to expect it but to receive the news so soon . . .' She puts her head into her hands again, rubs her temples and looks up. 'It's just such a . . .'

'Shock,' I say.

Emily corrects me: 'Relief.'

But when I look in Octavia's face it is something else I see. Is it fear?

'It means there can be no doubt now,' Octavia says, staring past us all to a picture of the crucifixion on the wall. 'No doubt that the Lord has sent the Divine Mother to speak through Emily.'

'It is the strangest feeling,' Emily says, 'when the Spirit comes to me I know nothing of what it says. It is just like falling into a deep sleep. But this is proof.'

'Anyone who questioned it can now have no doubt,' Octavia says, still staring at the painting.

Anyone who questioned it must now be silent. Unless they want to be next.

'You said he'd get what he deserved,' I say. Emily looks up as if she has just woken, and something passes between us, an under-standing, a secret, a truth.

'Yes, the Lord made sure of that,' she says. 'We must give rev-erent thanks that He rid us of the man who sinned so deeply.' She smiles at me. Victorious. But the world is spinning again. Too quickly. Spinning with questions. What she gave him when she went to visit. What she might have put into the Water.

'If you'll excuse me,' I say, rising suddenly from the table. 'I need to lie down.'

Grace said she had found out something. I remember now. She was trying to tell me a secret. Is this why she had to go? *We don't have long*, she said. *Read the letter when you wake up.*

———

I thought she might have left something under my pillow; that used to be our place, the place where we could hide the words we dared not speak out loud. But there is nothing there; nothing in the wooden box where I store the notes and letters that I have kept. I tip them out onto the bed and shuffle through. Perhaps if I read them I will remember, I'll be able to work out what has happened; what I have done; and what I should do next.

Can a mother forget the baby at her breast and have no compassion for the child she has borne? Though she may forget, I will not forget thee.

That was when she found out Octavia was my mother. That was when I told her there were no more secrets. Which was the biggest lie of all.

Among the letters I find her button, the dark blue one, the one that fell off her sleeve that first day when I invited her to visit. I hold it in my hand and squeeze it until tears prick my eyes, but I can't make them fall. I should be sorry that I ever met her but I can't be, even now. I don't want to let go of her, even if all I have to hold is pain.

Pain and a small blue button.

I will not forget you. That's what she said. And I wish I could believe it. But now she is gone, perhaps it is easier for her to forget this place, to forget she ever met me. Just like Adrian has. His letters are here too, but there is nothing new among them, nothing that I haven't read before. Both he and Grace tried to tell me but I wouldn't listen.

I didn't hear until it was too late.

I pull out all the clothes from my drawers, but I don't find anything hidden there; I take my books from the shelf and shake each one by the spine; I stand among the mess strewn around my feet and search my mind but I can't remember what she said. *Read it when you wake up.* Or did I imagine that too? I have to find it. I have to find something. A sign that Emily was lying; that Grace didn't want to leave. A sign that what we shared was not all in my head.

The poor thing found your feelings for her rather too much.

I reach for my Bible and that's where I find it: an envelope addressed to me. It has already been opened. Inside is a letter from my brother, Adrian.

Edward Reeves Esq.,
Jessop and Son,
5c Harper Street,
Bedford

Dear Miss Barltrop,

Please do not be alarmed by the headed notepaper on which this letter is typed. I write on behalf of your brother, Adrian, who is most concerned about your situation and anxious for reassurance that you are well.

He has instructed me in my capacity as his friend rather than his solicitor. We were chums at school and have kept in touch since – Adrian sharing exotic stories of his life in India and I, in return, writing with news from here in Bedford.

I hope you will excuse me for speaking plainly, Miss Barltrop, but he has confided his fear that your mother's so-called religion is not just misguided, but dangerous. Though her notoriety has caused him much personal embarrassment, his only concern is for you, his dear sister, and the effect that confinement among those zealots is having upon your health.

Though he writes to you regularly, he receives no replies, and is becoming increasingly worried about your well-being (for since your mother has cut him off he would not know if some illness or accident befell you). In desperation he asked me to work as a detective on his behalf and keep a watch on your house. I made no sighting of you for several weeks until I made what I believed to be a positive identification through the window of the empty property, Castleside. At Adrian's request I have tried on several occasions to get word to you, by shouting messages over the garden wall. I came to 12 Albany Road and insisted on speaking to you or your mother but was prevented from doing so.

This confirmed Adrian's suspicion that there are those within the Panacea Society who are obstructing his attempts to contact you. It is not clear whether you are receiving his letters (or indeed whether you will be given the opportunity to read this one) but Adrian is quite determined to help you and will not give up until he has done so. Miss Barltrop, he urges you to consider going to live with him and his new wife in India. He is quite convinced that away from Bedford you would see the society's beliefs are false.

If you are reading this, I must impress upon you the importance of getting word to me at the above address. Any correspondence would be in the strictest confidence and you have my word that I will assist you in any way I can.

Yours sincerely,

Edward Reeves Esq.

Thoughts crash over me, crests high enough to knock me off my feet. Between each one I grab a breath and then I am submerged again. The voices, the faces, they were never in my head . . . the man I saw at the window in Castleside . . . the reporter at the door. Was he a reporter at all or did Adrian send him too? . . . I heard him call my name, and then Emily said I should stay inside the garden . . . She said it wasn't safe. But safe for who? She wanted me to think that Adrian had given up on me, but he was trying to get word to me all along.

Tears are falling down my face. The fear that I have carried is flowing out of me, I can feel it leaving my body. I am not mad. I am not mad. I say it over and over and then laughter rises up inside me, just like it did on that first day Grace came to visit the chapel, when I felt God's Spirit.

I cry and I laugh and I cannot stop.

It was Emily all along. It was Emily's scheming that made me think I was hearing voices. It was always Emily. Keeping the truth from me. Is this what Grace found out? Why would she have left me this letter if she didn't want to help me? *Guilt*, says the voice in my head, *because she had been telling your secrets. Revenge, because Emily forced her to leave. Love*, it says, *because she loved you. Perhaps she still does.*

I tuck Adrian's letter back into the envelope and as I lift the flap I see something written there.

Psalms 35:17
Luke 8:17
Matthew 28:20

I reach for my Bible and look them up one by one.

Lord, how long wilt thou look on? Rescue my soul from their destructions, my darling from the lions.
For nothing is secret, that shall not be made manifest; neither any thing hid, that shall not be known and come abroad.
And, lo, I am with you always, even unto the end of the world.

Love, says the voice in my head. *She loved you, she still does.*
I know what I have to do.

The Exorcism

I have to get out. 'Let me out of this room.' I am shouting, banging on the door but no one is coming. I open the window. Octavia! Help me! Betty calls up from the garden. I put my leg over the sill as if I am going to jump, and they come running. Emily unlocks the door and Octavia pulls me back. From the brink.

'Octavia, Emily, help me. There's a devil here. Don't leave me locked in with him. I need to get out.' I struggle against Emily, who is holding my arms behind my back. 'He is there. Do you see him? Octavia, do you see?' I stare at two flowers on the wallpaper and imagine they are eyes. 'He is watching me, Octavia. He has come for me.'

She follows my gaze and looks to the same spot, cowering when she sees the face I have described.

'Dear Lord,' she says. 'Dear Lord, deliver us.'

I catch a glimpse of myself in the mirror; my hair is wild, there's a smile on my face. 'His eyes, Octavia,' I say. 'They are red like the coals of Hell.'

'It is horrible! Too horrible!' she cries out.

Emily lets go of my arms and I see her pull the Jerusalem knife from her sleeve. She must carry it with her all the time now. I suppose she never knows when she might be called to cast out a spirit.

'I am the Divine Mother,' she says, stepping forward. Not even bothering to fall into a trance. 'In the name of our Lord Jesus Christ I banish you. You have no power here. This is the Lord's jurisdiction.'

She cuts the air with the knife, then lifting it with both hands she runs at the wall, using the blade to slash the wallpaper. She is cutting the wrong flowers but I don't point out her mistake.

'Open the window!' she shouts. Octavia is nearest but she struggles to lift the casement. It is stiff, and there is a knack to it.

'I'll do it,' I say.

With growls and bared teeth Emily chases the invisible demon to the open window, then slams the sash shut. Octavia is sobbing, she is swaying on her feet. I take her arm and sit her on the bed. She looks up at me.

'It is over,' Emily says. 'The Lord has protected us.'

But it is not over. Not yet. I stand up again, lift the water jug from my washstand. The one decorated with lilies. And throw it at the wall.

'Dilys . . .!'

'Get them out!' I shout. 'All I can hear is their voices.' I am hitting my head now, pulling at my hair. 'Divine Mother, free me from their control.'

'There are more,' Octavia shouts. 'Help her. Hold her down.'

As they push me onto a chair, I struggle. Just enough. So I can be sure they feel the devil in me. And then I go still. I stare at a knot in the floorboards. Emily stands behind me. I am vacant. Docile. I am ready.

'You must confess everything,' Emily says. 'Lay charges against the Devil. For he is the one that leads you to sin.'

'I am under the control of demons!' I say. 'They are trying to send me mad. I have heard them calling my name over the garden wall and I have seen them waiting outside for me in the street. They take the form of ordinary men. But I know they are demons. They whisper to me about Adrian.'

I look straight up into Octavia's eyes, for any sign that she knew, any hint that might give her away. But there is nothing.

'They tell me that I am mad, that all this is madness.'

Octavia staggers back as if she is wounded. I try to stand up but Emily pushes down on my shoulders. I can feel her fingernails digging through the fabric of my dress.

'Do you wish to be delivered?' she says.

'I do! I want to be free of them.'

Octavia lifts her hand above my head and says: 'Then I condemn these failings as being no good, not of God. What else do you confess?'

'Desires,' I say. 'Feelings of love. Feelings that were consummated. We lay together. I broke my vow to Jesus.'

'Your vow of celibacy? Oh dear Lord, who is he?'

'Grace.'

'Grace?'

'We made love.' As I say it I am smiling at the memory; smiling as I snatch my secret out of Emily's hands. She can't use the truth against me now, she can't expose me if I have nothing to hide.

For nothing is secret, that shall not be made manifest.

'She lies,' Emily shouts. 'Grace would have told me. She confessed everything. I would have known . . .'

No, Emily, only Grace knows the truth. Only Grace knows what happened the night she took me back to bed; the day we were locked inside the Opening Room. She didn't tell anyone what we did. Not even me. But I have dreams, and memories, and lines of scripture written on notes inside my Bible. And I know that she loved me, that is our truth. Whatever I may tell them now.

'It was the Devil's work,' I say. 'He seduced me. With ecstasy. With rapture.' Octavia lurches forward, and I open my eyes. She has grabbed the knife from Emily and is pointing the tip towards my face. Her hand is shaking.

'I touched her,' I whisper, dropping my head and pushing my hands between my knees. 'We lay together in Castleside. On the table where the bishops will gather.'

Octavia steps back suddenly and sits down on the bed. 'My own daughter.'

Emily says: 'That's why Satan has tempted her. To hurt you. Stand up, Octavia. I'll ask again. Dilys, do you wish to be delivered?'

'Yes.'

'Then, Octavia, You must condemn her sin . . . Octavia!'

'I do,' she says softly. 'I condemn it all. No good. Not of God.' She is still sitting on the bed. She looks exhausted. Defeated.

'But there's something else I need to confess,' I say.

Again Emily tells Octavia to stand up and this time she obeys, handing the knife back when she reaches the chair.

'Murderous thoughts,' I say, dropping my voice to a whisper. 'I have thought about hurting Emily. Of pushing her down the stairs.' Now I'm the one taking my time; I'm going to enjoy this. 'The Devil told me I should creep into her room while she slept.' I lift my hand in front of my face and study my fingers. 'Take her neck and squeeze it. Or take a poker from the fire and cave in her head.'

'Oh dear God,' Octavia says. 'He is trying to get you to do his work.'

'He has made me hate her,' I snarl, rolling each delicious word around my mouth before spitting it at her. 'I despise her.'

Octavia brings her hand to her mouth and backs away. 'She is possessed,' she said. 'She is lost. He has got her.'

'Not yet,' Emily says. 'Do you wish to be delivered?'

I turn round to her and smile.

'I do,' I whisper.

Emily calls Octavia forward.

'Then I condemn these failings as being no good,' she says. 'Not of God.'

Emily walks round to face me and rests her Bible on top of my head. 'I command in the name of Jesus that this daughter be delivered from the control of evil spirits.' The knife in her other hand is pressing into the skin of my neck.

My eyes roll back into my head. 'I am free,' I whisper. 'I can feel them leaving my body.' Then I look at her and say: 'They can't hurt me any more.' And my body goes limp in the chair.

The Secret

I am delivered. Healed. Restored.

The fact the Devil chose to infect me with such abominable thoughts and deeds has elevated me in Octavia's estimation. She thought I was beneath his notice. She didn't think I had it in me.

'The Lord forgives you,' she said when it was all over, 'and so do I.' Then she put her arms around me. I think I was expected to hold onto her. Or cry. Or both. But it is too late for that: twenty years too late.

'No one else need ever know what you have confessed,' she said, and then she looked at Emily, who answered with a nod.

'My poor daughter. To think of the torment you have suffered. If only we could cleanse your mind of the memories of all those unnatural acts . . . Well, you mustn't think about it. About *her*.' But of course she is all I want to think about. Grace and where she might be and how I will find her.

And, lo, I am with you always, even unto the end of the world.

Now the demons are gone I am calm. That's what I told Octavia. That I feel lighter, that my mind is quiet, that I can feel God's love once more. I said the whole experience had made me ravenous, which is just what she wanted to hear. And she put forward her theory that with all those spirits inside me, my stomach had been restricted. Apparently evil can suppress even your appetite.

Betty set out a light lunch in the dining room.

'It is such a relief to be out of my bedroom,' I said. 'I feel like I have been freed.'

Emily advised caution, warning that the demons could have left some traces of mischief in me.

'No, I have complete confidence in the power of the Divine Mother,' I said. 'I felt them leave, Emily. It was wonderful.'

Octavia is quite convinced there is no need to keep my bedroom door locked from now on. She can see that I am quite recovered: I ate two egg sandwiches and a small piece of lemon drizzle. But I can't leave the garden, not yet. 'Not while the Devil is still at large.'

Fortified with tea and cake, Octavia and Emily went to the chapel where they have a busy afternoon of exorcism planned. Every member has been given a time to present themselves, and make their confession, and after half an hour each one will emerge a different woman. After such a harrowing morning, Octavia insisted that I must get some rest. I agreed, of course, but I had no intention of going to sleep. From my bedroom window I watched them cross the lawn and disappear into the chapel, and when I was sure they were gone I went back along the landing to Emily's door. To find the letters she has been hiding. The letters from Adrian.

I turned the handle softly but it would not move. I pushed my weight against it. I slammed my fists until the door shook in the frame. But she had locked it.

———

And that is why I have to do this now. That's why I'm standing here, shivering in my nightdress. My hand is on the doorknob again. But this time Emily is behind the door. I can hear her sleeping.

It must be after midnight. Octavia was first to bed, just after the chapel clock chimed nine. Then I heard nothing until Emily climbed the stairs and Peter his ladder to the attic. I sat on my chair and listened to Betty moving in the kitchen below my bedroom, tidying pans, washing teacups, then rattling the front door to check it was locked. She walked across the landing to Grace's room; I suppose it is her room again now. And then I waited, I waited for everything to fall silent, but the restless house would not quieten: floorboards creaked to get comfortable, water murmured in the pipes, walls and windows settled into a fitful sleep.

If anyone finds me now I can still pretend I have got up to use the lavatory, but once I go into Emily's room I will be out of bounds. If I'm discovered they will know I am up to something. The doorknob does its best to betray me with a click of its catch. I stop and wait to check I haven't woken her. I can hear her heavy breaths, louder now the door is ajar. It is the first time I have stepped into this room since it became hers. When I was a child it was my parents' room. Mother would allow us to come in so she could tell us all a story, then nanny would scoop us up and tuck us into our own beds. Emily looks like one of the hags from the fairytales we read, before Octavia decided that Hans Christian Andersen was ungodly and every night was Matthew, Mark, Luke or John.

Emily is lying on her back, eyes closed, mouth slightly open. In the lamplight she looks so small, you could almost imagine she was harmless, powerless.

And right now she is. I could do the things I told them I had been thinking of. I could wrap my fingers around her throat. I could take a pillow and smother her; hold it over her face while she twitched

and twisted; press it down until she lay still. The taste of cotton
would be the last she'd ever know.

Cotton. Grace's nightdress.
But I mustn't think of her. Not now.
I need to find Adrian's letters.

Emily isn't moving. The sight of her makes me think of something else, of Ellen lying still and stiff in her bed. For a moment I
am breathing in her memory: the acetous scent of decaying flowers
and stale silence. But I am not imagining things. I never was. It is
Emily's perfume I can smell. There's a bottle of lavender water on
her bedside table and beside it is the Jerusalem knife and a small
bunch of keys, which I pick up and hold tightly to muffle the jingle
of metal. One of them must fit her bureau.

The first is too big but the second unlocks the top drawer.
There's nothing inside it but writing pads and headed notepaper. I
try the next drawer down. It sticks at first but I open it enough to
slip my fingers inside, pushing down a pile of papers that are
jammed behind the lip. There are newspaper cuttings: headlines
about earthquakes and storms. And among them is a letter in
Adrian's handwriting. I fold it twice and hide it in the palm of my
hand. And just then I hear Emily stir. She rolls over to face me. She
stretches out but her eyes are still closed. There must be more
letters but I don't make a sound now.

'Betty?' she murmurs, rolling onto her other side. She is going
to wake up; she is going to find me here. I stand and wait for her
breathing to sink back into its steady pattern. And when she falls
still, I slide the drawer back, gently, and make my way round to
the door, returning the keys to the bedside table.

The Jerusalem knife is gone.

'Dilys,' she says. 'What are you doing in here?' Her eyes are shining in the darkness, her voice is on the edge of breaking. She is frightened. Of me. And for a moment I cannot help smiling. *You don't need to be frightened, Emily, I am only sleepwalking.* I lift the lamp and she cries out, covering her face with her arm to protect herself. And I stand perfectly still, shining the light on a pair of invisible eyes on the wall. My voice is slow and flat.

'Ellen,' I say. 'Is that you? Have you come back? Do you know where Grace is?'

Without looking at her I turn and walk out of the room. I want to run but I take each step slowly. Back into my bedroom. Back into my bed. And I take Adrian's letter, which is screwed up in my fist, and I hide it under my pillow until I can be sure that she won't follow me. Only then do I open it.

Edward Reeves Esq.,
Jessop and Son,
5c Harper Street,
Bedford

Dear Mrs Barltrop,

I have been instructed by my client, Mr Adrian Barltrop, to record his concerns about the health of his sister, Dilys, who he has come to understand is suffering with 'nerve-problems'. He has written to you on this subject on a number of occasions but, having received no reply, has come to the conclusion that you are either choosing to ignore his letters or have been prevented from reading them by some third party.

He strongly suspects that you are being given false counsel by those closest to you and urges you to put the needs of your daughter ahead of the 'religious mania' which he feels has divided his family and taken over his family home. Furthermore, he has come to understand that a gentleman, Mr Peter Rasmussen, is living with you in 12 Albany Road. It is his belief that this is wholly improper and, in light of stories of immoral practices between you, asks you to put a stop to this arrangement with immediate effect.

A copy of this letter has been kept on file as proof that it was sent. Failure to reply will result in Mr Barltrop taking legal action against those who are obstructing his sister's access to treatment.

Yours sincerely,

Edward Reeves Esq.

Deliverance

I am smiling. It is the thought of Emily's face last night, the image of her cowering in bed. She who is the holder of secrets, the one who calls all others to make their confessions. Now I have the knowledge. I am the one who knows what she has been hiding. I have the truth she has locked away in the drawers of her bureau.

I am going to get away from here. From her. From all of this. *It is not too late.*

I sit at my desk and write to Adrian. I tell him that I'm going to get out. That I will find a way. *Send help at 6.15 p.m. on Saturday, when they are all at chapel. Come and help me.*

Further than seventy-seven steps away. Far enough that Octavia can't follow.

I write all this, take a stamp from the box of letters in my wardrobe, and put the envelope in my pocket. If I can get to Castleside I will be able to sneak out and post it. So I will take breakfast downstairs with them this morning. I will prove that I am well and that they don't need to worry. I will get dressed, and style my hair and present myself at the table. I will eat and smile and chat. I will ask them how they got on with Kate Firth's casting out yesterday, and how many demons they chased out of her body. I will pretend that nothing happened last night. Emily won't say anything. Not in front of Octavia.

But when I take my place at the breakfast table there is hardly a word spoken by anyone. It is toast this morning, so everyone is concentrating on eating quietly. I can tell Octavia is trying to ignore the scraping, the crunching, the swallowing; and by the time we have finished she is struggling to sit still. 'I am going to my room,' she says, flinching at the sound of Betty collecting up the plates.

'Before you do,' I say, 'I can't find my keys for Castleside. Do you have them? I plan to get back to work there today.' I'm trying to sound as if it is an afterthought. Unimportant. Peter stirs his tea and knocks the edge of his saucer with the teaspoon as he lays it back down. Octavia jumps out of her chair.

'You'll have to talk to Emily about it,' she says. 'I really must get to my room.' She is already halfway out of the door. Emily is waiting for me to ask her, but I won't. There is silence between us, a silence uncomfortable enough to make Peter stand up, make his excuses and go.

'I have your keys, Dilys,' Emily says. 'We thought it best that I keep hold of them while you were acting so . . . erratically. For your own safety. I'm not sure where I put them but the back door is unlocked anyway and you have no need to open the front now the work has finished. Unless you were planning to go somewhere.'

'I need access to the Opening Room. There are a number of details I need to see to. Some pictures to hang.'

'Everything has been taken care of,' says Emily. 'Octavia asked me to take over while you were resting. Best that I keep hold of the keys.'

'I'll speak to Octavia about it,' I say. 'When she is feeling better.'

'Yes, do. And so will I. I'm sure Octavia will ask the Divine Mother for guidance on the matter. It is obvious to me that you are still not well, Dilys.' She pauses as if deciding whether to say more. 'After last night . . .'

'Last night?'

'You were out of bed.'

'I think you are mistaken, Emily. I slept very soundly. Perhaps it was you that was dreaming. Perhaps the burden of God's expectation is getting too heavy for you to bear.'

———

She thinks she has won but Kate said there was another set of keys in the drawers of the desk in Castleside. She told me so the day she first showed me around. The back door is open and everything is just as I left it. I'm greeted by the smell of new paint that became so familiar in the weeks I spent here, when Grace used to bring my lunch and sit beside me. This is my place. I am the only one who knows about the scratched drawing in the cupboard, the dents on the doorframe and the damp that is creeping up behind the skirting board in the corner of the front bedroom. I know every imperfection and every scar. I know the frayed cord on the sash window where I used to sit and watch for Grace coming up the path, the loose doorknob I turned to rush out to the front door, the cracked tile in the hallway where I would stand and count to eight, then eight again, before I let her in. We'd sit in the kitchen on two dining-room chairs and talk about the others while we ate lunch. Sometimes I'd bring a stool and insist she put her feet up. She'd close her eyes and I'd roll up her sleeve and stroke her forearm until the tiny hairs on her skin rose up to meet my touch. If I close my eyes I can imagine her scent on my skin; if I bring my fingers to my lips I imagine I can almost taste her. She is written between the lines of my fingerprints, like the powder that's left behind when you touch a butterfly's wings.

When I get away from here, I'll find you, Grace. I'll take your hand. We'll walk beside the river and we'll laugh again. It's not too late, Grace. Not for us.

But my desk is gone. Emily has moved me out. She has found the keys. I run to the front door and try the handle but it's locked. Of course it's locked. I rest my head against the stained glass and think about the letter in my pocket, and then I start to see shapes moving, turning the vivid colours of the glass dull. There are footsteps on the gravel outside and the sound of the letterbox being lifted. An envelope drops through it and lands by my feet.

'Wait,' I say, kneeling down to shout through the letterbox. 'Excuse me. I'm sorry about this.' Half a face appears in the opening, just a pair of eyes.

'I'm afraid I've mislaid my keys,' I say. 'Could I trouble you to put this in the postbox when you pass it, please? It's urgent.'

The eyes smile in at me. 'Of course, miss.'

I need to keep my voice steady; I mustn't give myself away. 'Thank you. Rather strange to be posting a letter out to you. It's usually the other way around! But it really is vital that it is delivered.'

'Do you live here now, then?' he says. 'It used to be the old schoolhouse, didn't it? I've seen you've been busy getting the place sorted out.'

'Yes, we are hoping to open up for some guests very soon. I live at 12 Albany Road. Do you have any post for me: Dilys Barltrop? Or my mother Octavia . . . Mabel? I can take it now if you like.'

He stands up, and I see a pile of letters being shuffled in his hands. 'One for Mrs Barltrop,' he says, and I have to stop myself from snatching it when he pushes it through the door.

'Thank you. You'll definitely post the one I gave you? It's important.'

'I will, Miss. Good luck finding those keys.'

I let the letterbox fall shut and rest my forehead on it, listening to the footsteps moving away across the gravel. Only when I am sure he is gone do I sit back on my heels and tear the letter open.

Edward Reeves Esq.

Jessop and Son,

5c Harper Street,

Bedford

Dear Mrs Barltrop,

I write to you again on behalf of my client Mr Adrian Barltrop on a matter of great urgency. Since we have received no reply from you and no assurances about the well-being of Miss Dilys Barltrop, your son has determined to return to England himself. His ship left India two weeks ago and he is expected in Bedford any day.

He wishes to warn you that, though you appear to show no pity for his sister's suffering, there are those who are prepared to assist him in getting her the treatment she so desperately needs. With the help of a concerned party, Mr Barltrop managed to get a doctor to diagnose Miss Barltrop. His orders were that she must be taken away from Bedford to a specialist hospital immediately and that any delay could have grave consequences. With the opinion of an expert in this field you can no longer afford to ignore Mr Barltrop's fears.

Any refusal on your part to allow access to the patient will be considered a criminal offence and action will be taken accordingly.

Yours sincerely,

Edward Reeves Esq.

All this time I feared I was going mad; I thought my mother's secret had become my own, but it's the very thing that will set me free. *What if there was a way*, Grace said, *would you take it? Do you trust me?*

Adrian sent a doctor to me. *With the help of a concerned party.* Grace was the one who brought him to me on Ellen's deathbed. She is probably sitting with Adrian right now, planning how to get me away from here. This is the only way that he could get to me. To force Octavia to let me go.

Now all I have to do is sit and wait. And behave myself. Bide my time until Saturday; sit quietly in chapel; bow my head in silent contemplation; sit and watch Emily attack demons with the Jerusalem knife; drink the water; praise the Lord; chew quietly. Be invisible: colourless, faultless, zero.

Just as I've been taught.

Seventy-seven Steps

Time has slowed and I wonder if they are coming for me at all. My letter to Adrian might still be in the postman's pocket. I see him standing by the postbox, the wind picking up and snatching it from his hand. Flinging it into the river. I see it lying on the surface, soaking up the water, my blue handwriting starting to bleed into the paper, then disappearing into grey. But I must stop thinking the worst.

I pace around the outside of the garden and listen for Grace, hoping she will call from the other side of the wall. She is with me when I sit on the bench by the tree; when I climb the ladder into the clock tower; when I watch the washing dancing on the line. *Wash me, and I shall be whiter than snow.*

I know they are all watching from their windows. But they can't see Grace. Only I can see her, in my memory. Only I can hear her whisper: *It won't be long now.* But I am frightened I will give myself away, that I won't be able to keep the truth inside. It shouts for me to let it out. When Emily looks at me over breakfast it is all I can do to stop myself from slamming her head into the table, from screaming at Octavia, 'Look at her. Look what she has done. To Grace. To Ellen. To us.' It is all I can do to stop myself telling her about Adrian. But I can't let them know what I am planning. Besides, I know she wouldn't believe me. She listens only to the Divine Mother now. I think it is a relief to pass the burden to someone else; any question, any problem and Emily takes out her Bible and her knife. She closes her eyes and gives Octavia the answer she wants to hear; and sometimes the one she doesn't. Since that telegram arrived from America she doesn't have to worry about saying the wrong thing. It is all the truth.

'You are very quiet, Dilys,' she says.

Yes, Emily, I am choosing not to speak. I might say too much and then Octavia will lock me in my room again. 'Just tired,' I say. Of you.

I sleep as much as I can. When I have typed up the latest directive, or delivered another article to the Printing Room, I lie on my bed and think of Grace. It passes another minute, another hour, another day. Every second spent is a second closer to escape.

In my daydreams she is waiting for me across the street. I walk out of the house and pull the door shut behind me and she smiles. But when I fall into a fitful sleep she always turns away. I step into the road to follow her and I don't see the car coming towards me. I only hear the crack of my bones as I am thrown over the bonnet.

———

'You can walk with me to chapel, Dilys,' Emily says. 'It is six o'clock, we had better go. We mustn't keep Octavia waiting.'

'Go without me,' I say. 'I am not feeling well. I'll follow on.'

'I'm sorry to hear that,' she says, but she is not sorry, not really. 'Octavia was suffering earlier too.'

As she walks out of my bedroom I realise it is the last time I will see her. This is the end for us. But she has no idea.

'Emily—'

'What is it?' She turns back, agitated that I am making her late.

'I'll be down shortly.' I mustn't say all the things I want to. But I stand and think them as I listen to her leaving; thirteen steps along the landing, eleven down the stairs. From my window I watch the others heading into chapel. They look so ordinary. So benign. Up here I will get everything ready. Octavia does not tolerate tardiness, and I'm not sure why it matters to me now, but I want to leave everything just as it should be, the three wise monkeys watching on as I make my bed and arrange my books. I am not taking anything with me, except my fur coat and the Bible she gave me on my eighth birthday. I'm hoping I'll find God in there: the God I knew when I was young. In my pocket I have a blue button, and the notes Grace left under my pillow. I kept them all. I can't bear the thought of Emily finding them after I've gone, but neither can I bear to throw them away.

The chapel clock is chiming six.

I go to Grace's room to look down at the street. I haven't been back in here since the day Emily sat on that bed and told me her lies. I haven't been back in here since then, because it is Betty who sleeps in here now. Because Grace has gone.

And soon I will be too.

There is no sign of Adrian outside, but he will come. I know he will. It is time. Time to walk along the landing. Time to walk past Octavia's bedroom door. Time to whisper goodbye, in my head. There is no point in saying it out loud. She is in the chapel now, healing the sick and delivering the sinful from the Devil. And it wouldn't matter what I said, she wouldn't listen. She never has. If I told her, she would find a way to stop me. Or get Emily to. She gets Emily to do all the difficult jobs now. That way she can concentrate on being worshipped.

At the bottom of the stairs I check the front door, just in case, but of course it is locked. I'll have to climb out of the window in the sitting room, go through the net curtain that separates In Here from Out There. There will be no witnesses to my passing, it is gone six, everyone is at chapel now; even Sir Jack is asleep, perched on the edge of the sideboard, his eyes closed. I pull Octavia's wicker chair to the window and lift the catch that holds the casement down. The frame rumbles in the grooves either side but opens no more than a few inches before it sticks: wood against wood, screeching in pain. I bow my head and I am praying, praying for a miracle, and with my eyes still shut tight I reach up and try to move the window again. Please God, let it open.

Suddenly I feel someone shove me from behind, a knock on the back of the head which sends me falling forward into the glass pane. I turn and see a flash of black; I feel the flick of fingers against my skin. I try to see but my eyes are fighting to stay open, as if the air itself is slapping me across the face. There's someone pulling my hair. I reach forward to fight them but there is only empty space. No chest or arms. No body. I bring my hands up to my face and that's when I feel him: the scratch of claws and feathers. He jerks, kicking back into my head as he propels himself into flight. But he stumbles in the empty air, his talons snagging on the skin above my eye. I feel him tear free. I see the clump of feathers that his tail has left in my clenched fist. I watch him bounce from wall to wall, sending ornaments toppling and a vase crashing to the floor.

He is coming at me again, a spiteful whisper, razor sharp as he cuts through the air with serrated wings. I lash out with my arms to beat him back from my face, but he fights back, cackling like a madwoman. I must cover my eyes. That beak could pierce them, pluck them out, peck away at all the light and leave me lost. I fall back into the window and I hear it creep: a long crack crawling across the glass.

'Dilys . . . what in the Lord's name?' Octavia is in the doorway.

'What are you doing? Sir Jack! Sir Jack, that is quite enough!' He flies another clumsy lap of the room then settles on the table, shaking his feathers with a guilty shrug.

'Dilys?'

I touch my hand to the skin above my eyebrow and realise it is wet.

'Dilys. What is going on?'

'He attacked me,' I say. 'Your bird attacked me. Emily's doing, I suppose. Has she been training him like she has been training you?'

'Dilys, that's enough.'

'This isn't right,' I say. 'You aren't supposed to be here. You're supposed to be in chapel.'

'I had a headache. I was a little late in sitting to receive the Lord's words this evening. What is going on? I heard the commotion from upstairs.' She looks at the chair, and the window, then she looks at me, wearing a fur coat in the sitting room. 'Dilys, what are you doing?'

'I am leaving.'

'You can't leave,' she says, calmly, as if the act of saying it makes it true.

'But I am, Octavia. I need to get away from here, from her . . . from you.'

She steps forward and for a moment I think she is going to reach out and touch me. But she doesn't. She makes her way as far as the table and steadies herself on one of the chairs, arms shaking, eyes cast down.

'Dilys, we are so close now. Once the bishops come—'

'They will never come, Mother. I watched the box being opened myself.'

There is silence, then she stumbles back, knocking against the sideboard. 'Don't you dare,' she whispers, 'you will not speak like that. I forbid it.'

But even as the words leave her lips she already knows: I won't do as I am told. Not any more. I pick up a leather-bound Bible from her desk and hit the window, and from the big crack smaller shoots grow. I hit it again and the shattered pieces fall out onto the path outside.

'Dilys, stop!' she shouts. 'Oh Emily, thank God! Do something!'

She has come. Of course she has. Emily is standing in the doorway now. 'Octavia, are You all right? Has she hurt You? I said she was a danger.'

'No, I'm quite safe. But Dilys is—'

Emily interrupts. 'When You weren't in chapel I came back to check on You. What is she doing?'

'I'm leaving,' I say.

'Have you finally lost your mind?' she says, the hint of a smile in her words. 'Be careful, Dilys, you can get locked away for behaving like this.' She turns to Octavia. 'Isn't that right?'

'Emily . . . please, don't!' Octavia gasps. And I realise. Emily knows her secret.

'She found out,' I say. 'Is that why you let her take over?'

'She is not *taking* over,' Octavia says, her voice rising to a cry. 'I told her myself. She could see how I suffered. We prayed *together* for the Lord to help me . . .'

'And He sent the Divine Mother?'

'Yes, Dilys!'

I start to laugh. 'Perhaps it is time for Emily to make *her* confession. To tell you the things she has been keeping secret. Adrian has come to England. He has been trying to see you but she wouldn't let him. She has been hiding his letters from you.'

Emily shakes her head, but colour is flooding her cheeks. 'This is ridiculous. She really has gone too far this time. Octavia?'

But my mother says nothing. She doesn't make a sound. She is holding her breath, covering her mouth with her hand.

'And what else is she keeping from you?' I ask her. 'I've been wondering about Edgar. About why she went to see him every day. So concerned for the health of a man who had sinned against you. Do you really think it was your *healing* she was putting in his water? Convenient that her prophecy—'

'So now I am a murderess?' Emily shouts before I can say any more. 'This is lunacy. She needs to be locked up.'

'No, Emily. That is not going to happen,' I say. From here in the window, I can see two figures. They have come for me, they are rushing up the path. Octavia and Emily have no idea. They jump when the knocking starts.

It is time.

I step on the wicker chair and make to climb out, but they rush forward. 'Dilly, the glass!' Octavia grabs my coat and pulls me back. And when I look up I see it: a shard sticking out of the frame. It would have cut my throat.

Did she call me Dilly? The name she used when I was small.

'Come with me, Mother,' I say. 'Adrian will look after us. He is taking me to India.'

'You know I can't. Apollyon is waiting. Out there. To devour me.' Her breath is ragged. She is staring at the window as if demons might fly in through the broken pane. 'Oh Lord, protect us!'

Emily rushes to the door. 'Betty, don't let them in!' she shouts into the hallway, but it is too late. I hear footsteps, then two men come in. They are wearing white coats.

'Miss Dilys Barltrop?' the first man asks me. 'You need to come with us. Otherwise we have been instructed to call the police.'

—

At the end of the garden path there is a black van waiting. I want to run to it but I must concentrate on walking, one foot in front of the other, head up, back straight, as if I'm wearing a corset. As if I have the faith and discipline to contain myself. I walk past the broken glass; the net curtains have snagged on the window frame, and the breeze has caught them, sucking them in and out as if the house is gasping for breath. My mother is standing behind them, looking out. Emily is by her side. 'She is leaving God's Chosen Land,' she is saying. 'She is choosing to follow the Devil's way. There is nothing You can do for her now.'

But I know the truth, Emily, and soon Mother will know too.

I left two letters under her pillow after breakfast.

Letters from Adrian.

For nothing is secret, that shall not be made manifest; neither any thing hid that shall not be known and come abroad.

'Are you taking me all the way to India?' I ask the two men, as they open the doors at the back of the van.

'No, Miss!' one of them laughs, putting his hand on the top of my head as I stoop to climb in. 'Slowly now, we don't want you hurting yourself, do we?'

'Dilys!'

From the darkness within I hear his voice and my legs give way.

He has come.

I am safe.

'Adrian?'

'Dilys, I'm so sorry.' He reaches out and helps me onto a wooden bench that runs along the inside of the van. 'I've been trying to get to you for so long.'

The door slams shut and we are locked in together. It is dark, the only light cutting in through two vented windows in the back doors.

'It really is you . . .' I say, bringing my face close to his. 'You have a moustache . . .' I was expecting the little boy I used to play with when we were children, when we used to sit and listen to Father preach.

'Yes, Dilys. I have a moustache.' He smiles gently and takes my hand in his, brings it to his lips; in the gloom it looks so pale, like crisp white linen.

'Listen,' he says, looking up into my face, 'I need to you to understand where we're . . . My God, Dilys, you're bleeding.'

So I am. Just like the day the branch cut his head.

'You still have the scar, Adrian.' I reach out and touch the puckered line above his eye. There are tears on my fingertips; the blood has turned them pink. I remember the day Grace bathed my hand in the healing water. She took the bowl and made me clean.

'*Wash me, and I shall be whiter than snow* . . .' I say.

'Dilys?'

But I don't have time to explain. We need to go.

'Mother will come and get me,' I say. 'She'll try to stop me.'

'No, Dilys. No one's coming. No one will stop us. Not now.' He pulls me down next to him and wraps his arms around me. 'They wouldn't dare.'

'I thought I was hearing voices,' I whisper. 'I thought I was going mad. But all the time it was you. It was you, Adrian. You were trying to send word, weren't you?'

'Hush, dear girl, you're safe now. Everything will be all right. We're going to take you away from here. We'll look after you.'

He means Grace. He means they'll look after me together.

'Where is she?' I try to say it, but the thought of her makes my throat burn, makes my tears fall. Relief flooding out of me. It rises up in waves and my head feels as though it's expanding. As if I might float away. Just like that first breath of Grace's cigarette. Just like that night in the churchyard.

'Where's Grace?' I say, pulling away from him. 'She's the one who helped you, isn't she?'

'Yes. She saw me watching the house and she came out, walked past me on the street, whispered there were things she had to tell me. We arranged to meet by the river. She told me what has been going on in there . . . What Mother did with Peter. It's disgusting.' He turns and looks out of the window. 'She told me *that woman*, Mrs Goodwin, had been hiding my letters. And she managed to get that doctor to see you, which is more than I could do alone. I'm so sorry, Dilys. She has been a better friend to you than I have been a brother. She obviously cares about you very much.'

She loves me. That is our truth. I wonder if she told him that herself. Or whether she chose to keep it secret. I wonder whether Adrian would understand.

'Mother's religion has made you ill. Grace wants you to get better. We both do. Here,' he says, reaching inside his jacket pocket to pull out an envelope, 'she asked me to give you this.' Inside is a note, written in Grace's hand:

Beloved, I wish above all things that thou mayest prosper and be in health, even as thy soul prospereth.

(3 John 1:2)

And suddenly I am starting to unravel; moths gnawing through the threads of hope that have been holding me together.

'Where are we going, Adrian?'

'Far away from all this.'

'But Grace is coming with us, isn't she?'

He looks down at our hands again and squeezes his fingers around mine. 'Dear girl,' he says. 'All in good time.' The slam of the driver's door makes me jump. 'We have to get you away from here first—' Adrian starts to speak but his voice is lost as the engine starts up. It makes the van shake. Or perhaps I am the one shaking. Through the two small windows in the back I watch Albany Road start to move, terraced soldiers on parade, marching into the distance. We drive past the corner, past the streetlamp.

We've come more than seventy-seven steps. Too far for her to get me now.

'Deep breaths,' Adrian says. 'Here, have a good old glug of this, it'll help to calm your nerves. I can't imagine what it must have been like, in that house.' I take a sip and taste the bitter fire of alcohol. 'A nip of brandy,' he says. 'That's it, drink up. It'll do you good. Now rest your head on my shoulder, Dilly, and try and get some rest. We haven't got far to go now.'

But we have. We have a long, long way to go. We're going all the way to India.

I close my eyes and imagine we're already at sea; imagine that every jolt and turn of the van is a wave buffeting a swaying ship. I imagine that it is lulling me to sleep. When I wake up we'll be there. Grace will be waiting.

OCTAVIA'S DIARY: 1915

I followed a nurse through a very handsomely
furnished corridor. I noticed that she locked and
unlocked many doors, but I did not worry about this, as
I thought I was being taken to the house of rest.

I suddenly, however, found myself in a corridor,
where obviously insane persons were wandering
aimlessly about. One came up and made hideous
snatchings at me; others surrounded me with
curiosity. I said to the nurse: 'This is not the place
I want to come to . . . this is a terrible mistake. I
have not been sent here as a lunatic.' She replied:
'Oh I have heard that kind of tale before,' and
remembrance of novels I had read rose up before me.
A hard, cruel look came into her face, which warned
me that it was wiser to conform amiably for the
moment lest I should be subjected to personal force.

The door was open of a padded room in which, as
far as I can remember, I saw a naked lunatic. I was
put into a small bedroom next to it, with a window
which would only open about six inches and had heavy
wooden shutters. There came distressing sounds
from a distance. At the end of the corridor was the
nurses' mess room where, at intervals, noisy meals
were in progress. Just across the garden was the great
kitchen where washing-up for five-hundred patients
was done. Everybody knows the power to irritate of the

sound of washing up! Each door in the building had to be slammed shut to make it lock, and could only be opened by a noisy key.

I ask, is not all this enough to make a perfectly sound person nervous? I ask again, is not all this enough to make a slightly nervous person insane?

The Crossing

I haven't seen the sea, or the sky. There is no window. It must mean I am below the water-level. But I'm safe here. I'm not drowning. Not any more.

The cut on my head is healing, a nurse washed away the blood when I arrived. 'Try not to touch it,' she said, rather officiously. But sometimes I knock the scab, and once I start picking, I can't seem to stop. Perhaps I'll have a scar like Adrian's. I have no mirror to check. The cabin is so sparse. In fact there isn't much of anything; just a metal bed and a scratchy blanket. And I'm finding it hard to sleep at night, there's too much noise: the metal doors slam and locks turn, trolleys rattle by, delivering meals further down the corridor, and sometimes I can hear screams. I imagine they must come from excited children playing hopscotch up on deck.

There is so much humanity packed into a confined space. It makes me think of Edgar who spent his last days at sea, trying to stay standing as the ground was moving beneath his feet. Sometimes the ship lists so violently that I struggle to get out of bed. Everything is always moving. Nothing is still.

We set sail three days ago. I think it's three. I've lost track of the passing hours. I have no watch, no clock, the meals that arrive on trays are the only way to gauge the time of day. A surly woman passes them through a hatch in the door, like letters through a letterbox. I can only see her eyes.

'When will we be there?' I ask.

She doesn't answer.

But I know it won't be long before we begin a new life in India. Adrian told me that, when we arrived on board. I didn't wake until the back doors of the van creaked open, and even then I didn't want to move, I wanted to sleep. He helped me out and walked me up a flight of steps into the ship. Inside it looked just like a grand house, waiters in white suits were waiting to greet me.

'They'll look after you, Dilys,' Adrian said, giving one of them my arm. 'You're safe now. Get better and then we can start a new life together, in India. I promise.'

'You, me and Grace,' I said.

He embraced me and I felt as if he would never let me go. 'All this,' he said, 'it's not forever, and it's for the best – I had to get you away from *her*.' Then he turned away and left. He must have gone to his own cabin to make arrangements.

We'll arrive just in time for the best weather, the monsoon season will have passed and cloudless skies will give the sun free rein to shine. It will take me time to get used to the climate – every day is hotter than a Bedford heatwave, that's what Adrian once said in one of his letters months ago – but I long to see the sun, to feel its warmth on my face, just like I did the day I met her. The day I went to the Bunyan Meeting Church.

'Grace, do you remember?' I whisper, and she makes that noise – somewhere between a laugh and a sigh; somewhere between longing and contentment. She is standing behind me, resting her chin on my shoulder. I knew she would come.

And, lo, I am with you always, even unto the end of the world.
And now she is coming with me to the other side of it. To India.

'I have something of yours,' I say. 'Something you lost.' She can sew it on at last, onto her dark blue coat. I try to reach into my pocket but I can't. And when I look down I am wearing different clothes: clothes without pockets or buttons; clothes with buckles.

'I'm sorry, Grace. I can't find it.'

But she doesn't seem to mind. I feel her breath on my neck. Her hands move up to find me, her fingers trace my collarbone, across my shoulders, down to my fingertips. And then she takes my hands in hers and draws me close, wraps my arms across my body, tightly, too tightly, so I can't move at all.

She is holding me. I am being held.

Appendix

CASE BOOK: FEMALES 19

No. 7586 Name: Barltrop, Mabel
June 24th, 1915 – CAUSE Predisposing: –
                            Exciting: Change of Life
                            Number of attacks: 2nd
                            Duration: 3 months
                            Form of mental disorder:
                            Melancholia

'Mabel Barltrop was in bed, her eyes were suffused and bloodshot: the face bruised. She said that the condition of her eyes was caused in the effort to strangle herself and not by any direct injury. She felt all her nerves were springing. She then said that she had committed the unpardonable sin, which was preaching religion to people and not practising it herself, and had better destroy herself.'

'Is very nervous and somewhat hysterical – says she has lost all control of her nerves.'

'States that she has got hold of an evil spirit. That all the powers of darkness are after her and fill her with terror. Makes constant restless movements, picking at the wall and drawing the bedclothes up and thrusting them down.'

'She tells me that occasionally she is inclined to injure other people, and that she also has suicidal thoughts. A short time ago she did attempt to drown herself, but unfortunately she could swim.'

'She says she feels sure she would kill her son (for whom she has a great affection) should he come to see her. Last night she became violent and attempted to strike the other patients. She requires constant supervision; and has been moved to prevent her doing harm.'

'Patient has been writing letters to the King. She apparently imagines she has had a special Revelation from God telling her how the war was caused and the way to stop it. She is somewhat incoherent and strange in her conversation.'

'She writes a considerable amount of nonsense. Her delusions are of such a nature that they warp her judgement of almost everything. She believes that she has been specially chosen by God to improve mankind etc. She exhibits a most compelling ingenuity for "catching up" people when they converse with her.'

Author's Note

In the dining room of a Victorian house on Albany Road in Bedford I sat and waited for an archivist to return with the first box file. On the walls, framed posters warned of 'Crime and Banditry, Distress and Perplexity'; in a glass cabinet were leather-bound volumes of the nightly messages Octavia believed she had received from God. Inside that first file I found a jumble of sealed envelopes, each marked 'For the Divine Mother: If unopened please burn'. I took Octavia's paperknife and I opened them one by one, reading the confessions of members of the real Panacea Society. Just as their leader had commanded, every detail of life had been preserved – room upon room of brown parcels cataloguing every business and spiritual transaction. With the kind permission of the Panacea Charitable Trust, which maintains the archive, I was able to plunder its secrets over a number of months. The sections of the novel printed in bold are quoted from source material, including letters, society instructions and case notes relating to Mabel's psychiatric treatment.

Among the many diaries and albums was a photograph of the Panacea ladies taking tea on the lawns of 'the Garden of Eden'. While those around her chatted, a young woman was looking up, straight into the lens of the camera. It was a photograph of Dilys Barltrop and – already fascinated by the society – I became intrigued to uncover her story, and *The Rapture* began to take shape.

No offence is intended towards any living relatives of Panacea members. Though this is a work of fiction, the majority of the characters and their experiences are inspired by fact, though dates have been changed to condense the story into a year. In the case of Mabel's medical notes I have combined two reports from two stays in different hospitals. My writing of Dilys, Octavia and Emily was informed by correspondence and diary entries; and details of Edgar and Donald's relationship were taken from confessions and letters. I know much less about the many members who lived in neigh-bouring streets but have borrowed their names and circumstances to imagine the wider cast of characters.

The only wholly invented person in the novel is Grace, who took up one of the positions of unpaid servant offered to those who didn't have the means to buy or rent a place in 'the Garden'. There is no evidence that Dilys had any romantic relationship with anyone in the society, though other members confessed to attractions and intrigues, so here I intertwine their stories with hers, and in fiction give her a love affair that reality may never have afforded her.

The real Adrian Barltrop sent numerous letters to his mother, threatening legal action and accusing Emily Goodwin of keeping his correspondence from her. Research suggests he employed mes-sengers to get help to his sister, who was eventually sent away to recuperate. But despite a period away from the society, the real Dilys chose to return to the society and spent the rest of her life in Bedford.

I owe many of the facts about the structure and theology of the Panacea Society to research carried out by priest and historian Jane Shaw for *Octavia, Daughter of God: The Story of a Female Messiah and Her Followers*, her non-fiction book written at the invitation of the last surviving members. Details of the opening of the 'other' box were drawn from *Exploding the Southcott Myth*, Harry Price's own account in *Leaves from a Psychists's Casebook*.

Parts of this story were written in the homes and gardens in which it is set, where I was able to handle the linen that Octavia had breathed on, climb into the clock tower, and sit and make notes in Dilys's bedroom. As the ageing members of the Panacea Society began to die, their rooms were sealed up and their belongings kept just as they had left them. Everything was made ready for the day they would return with Jesus by their side. Even after Octavia's death in 1934 the Panacea Society continued to attract new members, and by 1943, when Emily Goodwin died, there were eighty living in Bedford and nearly two thousand worldwide. Conservative estimates suggest 130,000 applications were received for the healing water, and linen squares were still being posted to believers around the world until the death of the last member, Ruth Klein, in 2012.

Today Octavia's house and her Garden of Eden are open to the public. The Panacea Museum still keeps the secret of the location of the 'real' box believed to contain Joanna Southcott's prophecies. That box has yet to be opened.

Acknowledgements

So many people are written into the pages of this book – in the fabric of the story and the words that stitch it all together. Perhaps it is only fitting that a novel about a remarkable group of women should be published by a team that's almost exclusively female. *The Rapture* is certainly better for their passion and talent and my experience all the richer for watching them at work.

I must thank staff at the Panacea Museum in Bedford for sharing their knowledge on my very first visit, and for their continuing patience when I kept coming back. Gemma Papineau and Vicki Manners were an invaluable source of information and support. Of course, this novel would not have been possible without the permission of the Panacea Charitable Trust which looks after the society's archives – thank you David McLynn and Sean Gillen for the opportunity to explore them. My gratitude also to Leslie Price of the College of Psychic Studies, and to Joy and Vernon White for a gaslight tour behind the scenes at Westminster Abbey.

To Laura Williams of Greene & Heaton – the first, the best – who believed in this story before I'd even written it. You walked by and wished me luck when I stood up in public and shared my early scribblings. Who knew you'd become my agent? Thank you for being there at every step with calm words and cake. This is *our* book.

My editor, Louisa Joyner – your insight and intelligence mean you saw things in this story that even I didn't know were there. No matter how well I get to know you, I'm still in awe! Thank you, Dr J, for everything.

May I state here on record that Libby Marshall is not only the hardest working person in publishing, she is also the kindest. Katie Hall in marketing is, quite simply, a genius. Lauren Nicoll, my publicist, has championed this book with passion and care. And I'm so grateful to designer Donna Payne and photographer Jeff Cottenden for such a delicately sinister cover. (I'll always cherish the memories of the day we spent at the Panacea Museum with a stuffed jackdaw.)

There are so many other steps in turning words into books and Anne Owen has guided *The Rapture* through this transformation. Copy-editing (Tamsin Shelton), proofreading (Jane Robertson) and typesetting (Dave Wright at Typo•glyphix). Each have left their mark on this story. Thanks to the entire team at Faber. This book could not have been in better hands.

The friends, old and new, who have supported me during the writing of this book are too numerous to mention. Thankfully they know who they are. But how can I not thank Emelie Olsson for her generous and genuine joy in my successes; Poppy Bagley for tea on a Biblical scale; Elodie Harper for blazing the trail; Claire Adam and Bev Thomas for sharing the journey; and Chloe Keedy for reading my pages and (more often) my mind.

Authors Jenny Ashcroft and Louise Jensen were early readers who gave me the confidence to submit, and I thank all those agents who took time to meet and talk about their vision for my debut.

It would have been so much more difficult to write in the first place without the support of my parents, Susan and Andrew, and parents-in-law Jennifer and Chris. Thank you for all you do for our family.

Which brings me last, but certainly not least, to my husband Richard and our children Kitty and Freddie, who could be forgiven for thinking I really had joined a cult. Thank you for understanding my obsession, for giving me the time and space to write and for bearing with me when my mind was with a society of ladies in the 1920s instead of in the moment.

Richard – knowing it was my dream was enough for you; and that means the world to me.